TOWNSHIP OF WASHINGTON PUBLIC

3 9149 09115082 1

W9-AFC-353

TOWNSHIP OF WASHINGTON PUBLIC LIBRARY
144 WOODFIELD ROAD
TOWNSHIP OF WASHINGTON, N.J. 07676

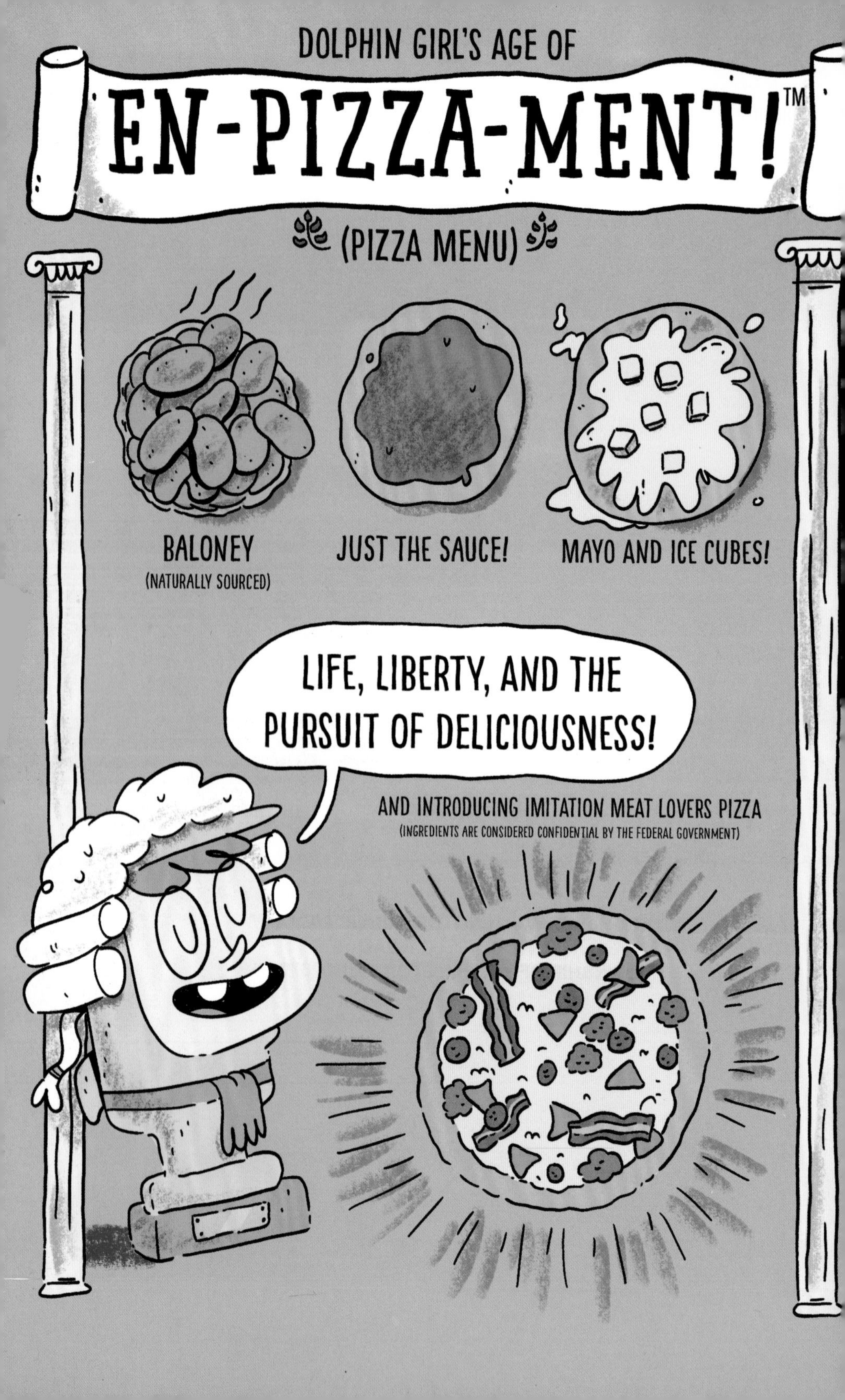
DOLPHIN GIRL'S AGE OF
EN-PIZZA-MENT!™
(PIZZA MENU)
BALONEY
(NATURALLY SOURCED)
JUST THE SAUCE!
MAYO AND ICE CUBES!
LIFE, LIBERTY, AND THE PURSUIT OF DELICIOUSNESS!
AND INTRODUCING IMITATION MEAT LOVERS PIZZA
(INGREDIENTS ARE CONSIDERED CONFIDENTIAL BY THE FEDERAL GOVERNMENT)

THE BURDEN OF CHOICE RESTS IN YOUR HANDS!

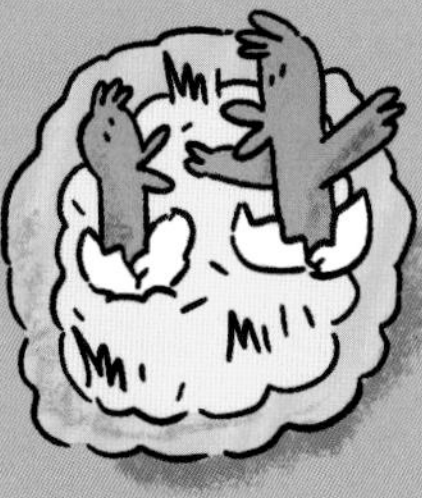

FARM TO TABLE

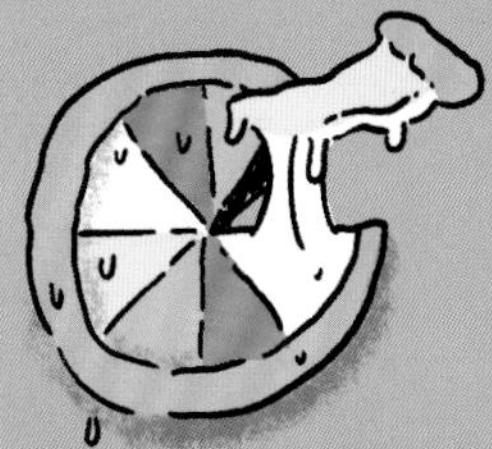

SALT WATER TAFFY

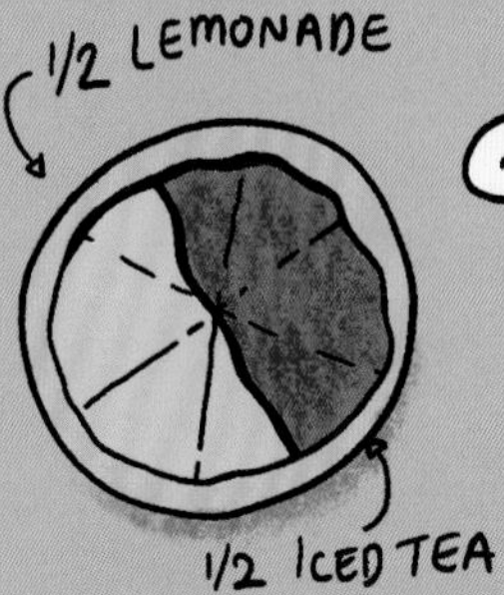
1/2 LEMONADE
1/2 ICED TEA

GOLFER'S DELIGHT

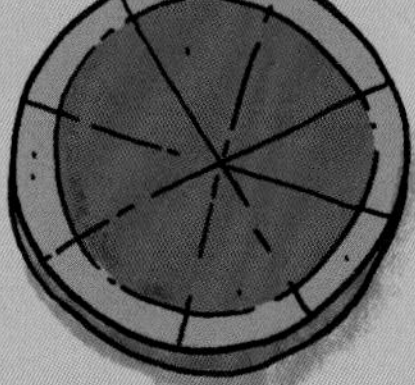

MACKINAC ISLAND FUDGE

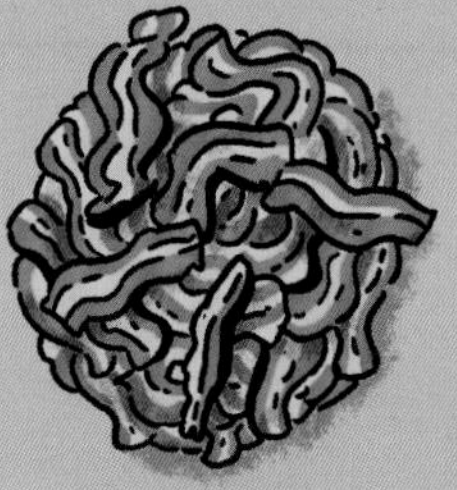

ALL BACON

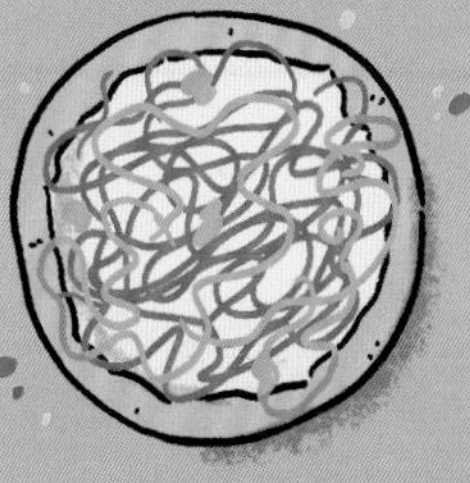

KETCHUP AND MUSTARD

EVERYBODY LOVES BREADSTICKS!

(NO EXCEPTIONS!)

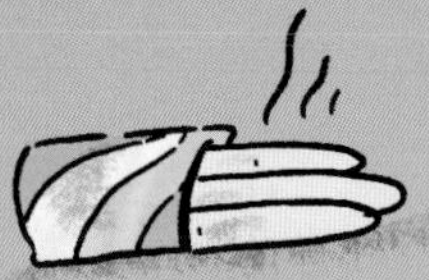

ORIGINAL

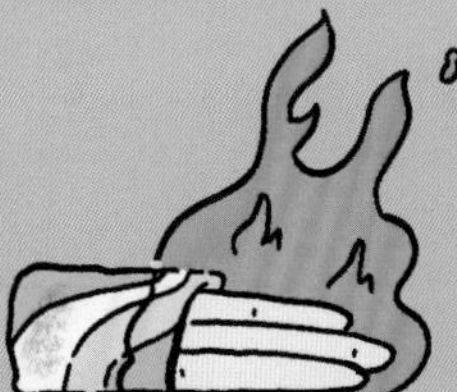

NOW AVAILABLE IN "ON FIRE"

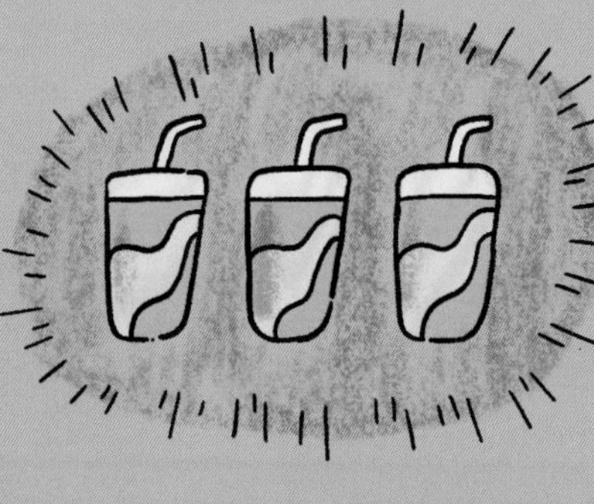

ALSO TRY CAPTAIN DUGONG BRAND 'PIZZA POPS!' IN THREE 'EDIBLE' FLAVORS!

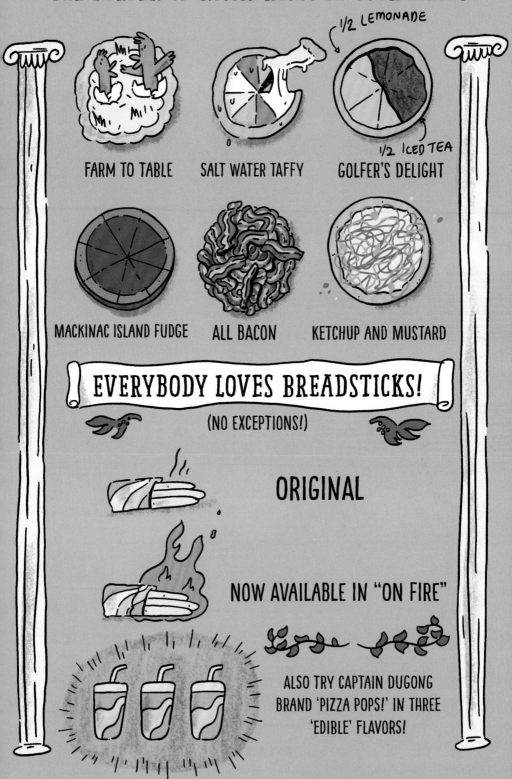

DOLPHIN GIRL

Eye of the
BALONEY STORM!

DOLPHIN GIRL

Eye of the BALONEY STORM!

WRITTEN AND ILLUSTRATED BY
ZACH SMITH

COLOR BY LETICIA LACY

PIXEL+INK

PIXEL✚INK

TEXT AND ILLUSTRATIONS COPYRIGHT
© 2021 BY ZACH SMITH

ALL RIGHTS RESERVED
PIXEL+INK IS A DIVISION OF TGM DEVELOPMENT CORP.
PRINTED AND BOUND IN SEPTEMBER 2021 AT C&C OFFSET, SHENZHEN, CHINA.

IMAGES, CLOCKWISE ON PAGE 35: EARTH — IXPERT/SHUTTERSTOCK.COM
SMILING DOLPHIN — NATASNOW/SHUTTERSTOCK.COM
LEAPING DOLPHIN — NEIRFY/SHUTTERSTOCK.COM
SPACE SHUTTLE — DIMA ZEL/SHUTTERSTOCK.COM
LEAPING DOLPHINS — MURATART/SHUTTERSTOCK.COM
LIGHTNING, PAGE 48: JEEDY_JOY/SHUTTERSTOCK.COM
FIRE, PAGE 116: WEERACHAI KHAMFU/SHUTTERSTOCK.COM
YEARBOOK BACKGROUND, PAGE 207: SECOND BANANA IMAGES/SHUTTERSTOCK.COM

WWW.PIXELANDINKBOOKS.COM

FIRST EDITION
1 3 5 7 9 10 8 6 4 2

LIBRARY OF CONGRESS CATALOGING-IN-PUBLICATION DATA
NAMES: SMITH, ZACH, AUTHOR. | LACY, LETICIA, COLORIST.
TITLE: EYE OF THE BALONEY STORM! / WRITTEN AND ILLUSTRATED BY ZACH SMITH;
COLOR BY LETICIA LACY.
DESCRIPTION: FIRST EDITION. | [NEW YORK] : PIXEL+INK, 2021. |
SERIES: DOLPHIN GIRL; [2] | AUDIENCE: AGES 8-12. | AUDIENCE: GRADES 4-6. |
SUMMARY: "SUPERHERO-IN-TRAINING DOLPHIN GIRL MUST TEAM UP WITH A RIVAL
TO STOP AN ENEMY FROM CREATING A COLD-CUT CATASTROPHE IN DEERBURBIA."
IDENTIFIERS: LCCN 2021014201 (PRINT) | LCCN 2021014202 (EBOOK) |
ISBN 9781645950196 (HARDBACK) | ISBN 9781645950202 (PAPERBACK) |
ISBN 9781645950974 (EBOOK)
SUBJECTS: CYAC: GRAPHIC NOVELS. | SUPERHEROES—FICTION. |
DOLPHINS—FICTION. | LCGFT: GRAPHIC NOVELS.
CLASSIFICATION: LCC PZ7.7.S6427 EY 2021 (PRINT) | LCC PZ7.7.S6427 (EBOOK) |
DDC 741.5/973—DC23
LC RECORD AVAILABLE AT HTTPS://LCCN.LOC.GOV/2021014201
LC EBOOK RECORD AVAILABLE AT HTTPS://LCCN.LOC.GOV/2021014202

DOLPHIN GIRL IS THE SUBJECT OF A COEXISTENCE AGREEMENT BETWEEN
TGM DEVELOPMENT CORP AND ZACH SMITH, ON THE ONE HAND, AND PATRICK MORGAN,
TAESOO KIM AND ED ACOSTA, THE CREATORS OF WHALEBOY, ON THE OTHER, AND APPEARS
IN THIS BOOK SUBJECT TO THE TERMS AND CONDITIONS OF THAT AGREEMENT.

FOR THE TEACHERS IN MY LIFE:
MRS. MONIQUE SMITH OF MOUNTAINVIEW
ELEMENTARY (MY WIFE/SPIRIT GUIDE),
MRS. KRISTIN TURNWALD OF GRAND VIEW
ELEMENTARY (MY EXTREMELY FUNNY SISTER),
MRS. DEBBIE SMITH WHO IS NOW RETIRED FROM
LAKELAND HIGH SCHOOL (MY #1 ALL-TIME
MOM), AND TO ALL THE TEACHERS
WHO HELD THE WORLD TOGETHER
DESPITE BRATTY PARENTS
DURING THE COVID-19 PANDEMIC.

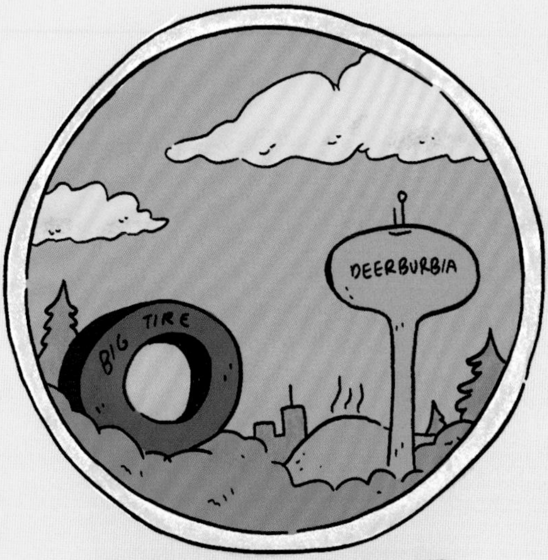
BIG TIRE
DEERBURBIA

PART ONE

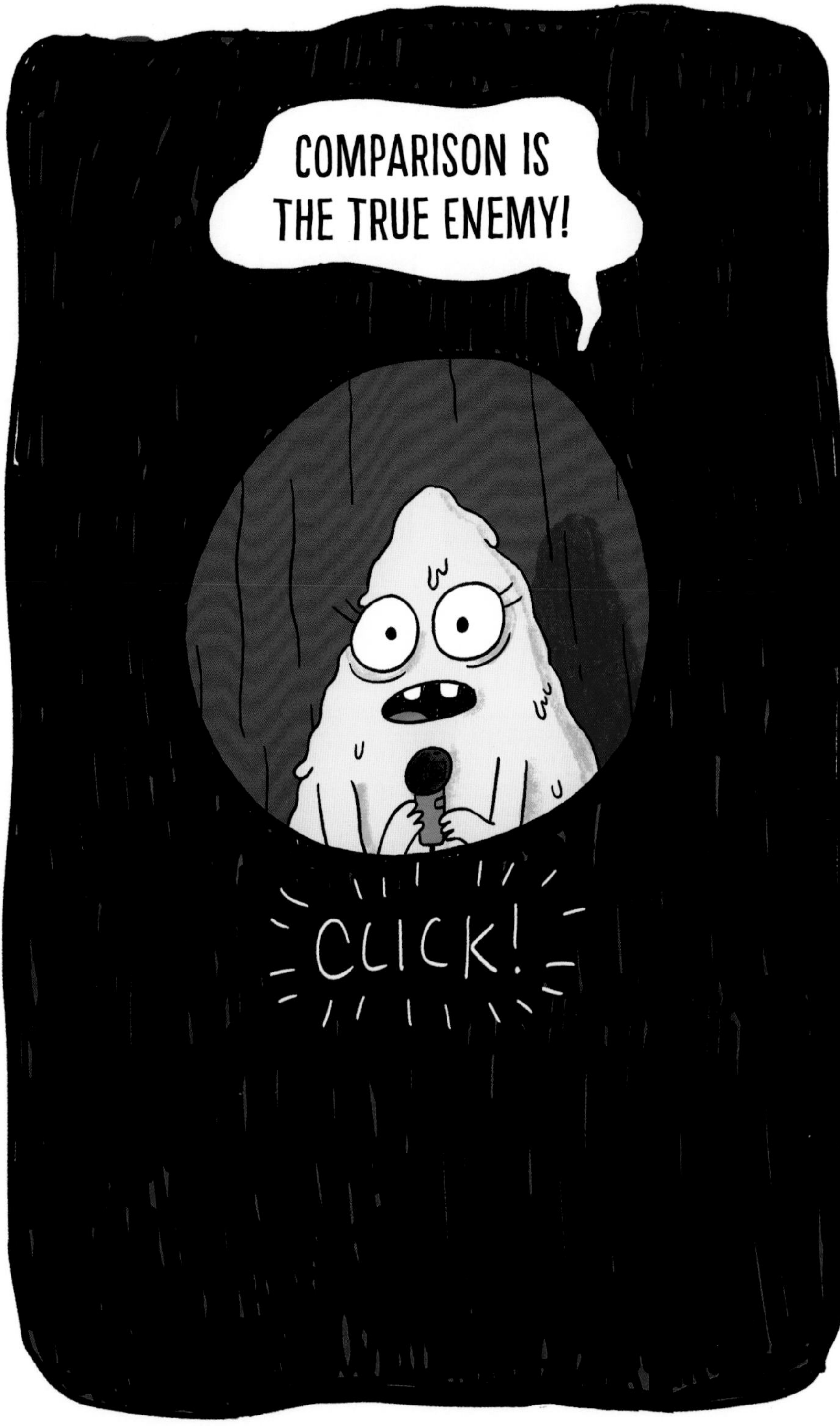
COMPARISON IS THE TRUE ENEMY!
CLICK!

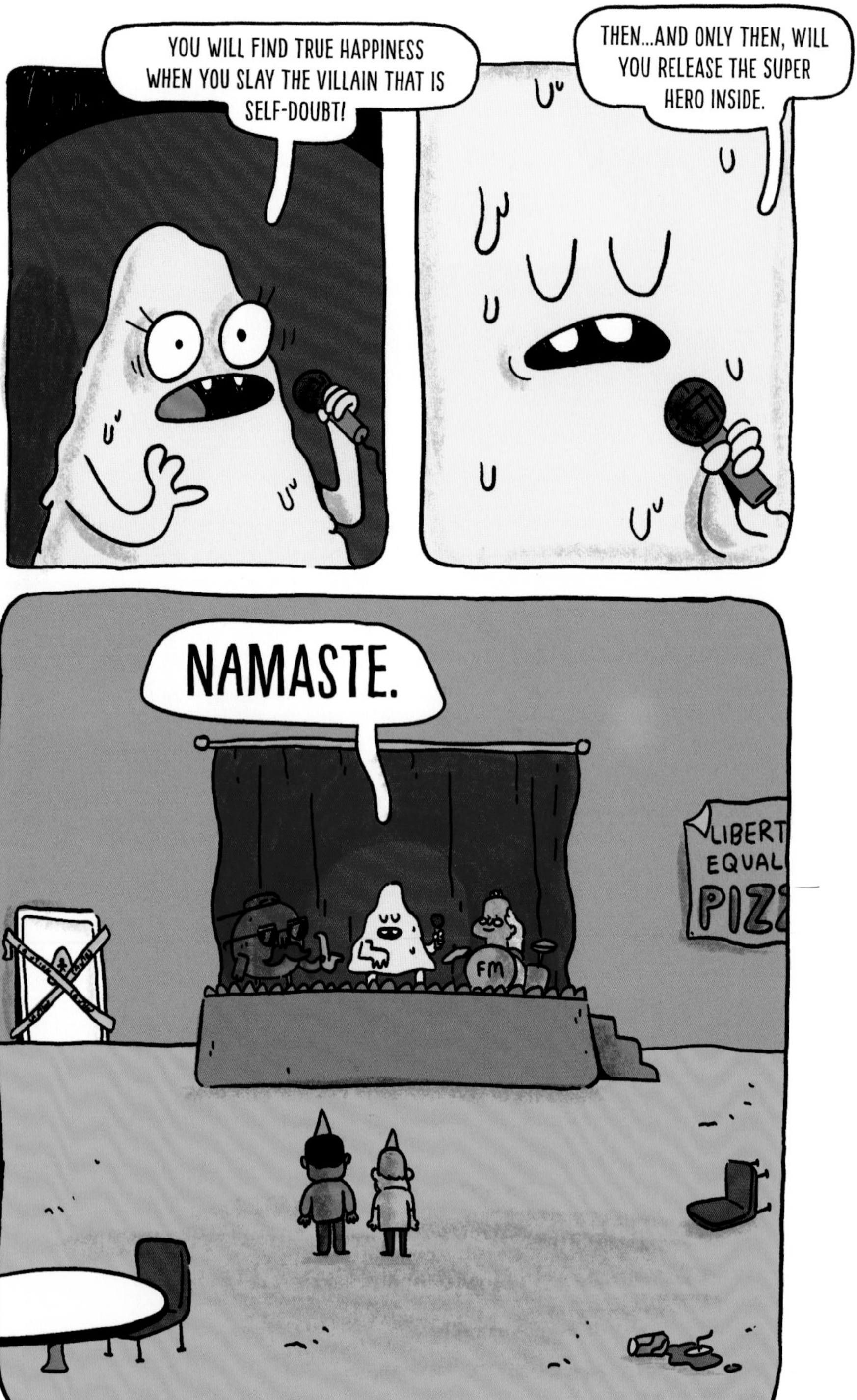
YOU WILL FIND TRUE HAPPINESS WHEN YOU SLAY THE VILLAIN THAT IS SELF-DOUBT!
THEN...AND ONLY THEN, WILL YOU RELEASE THE SUPER HERO INSIDE.
NAMASTE.
FM

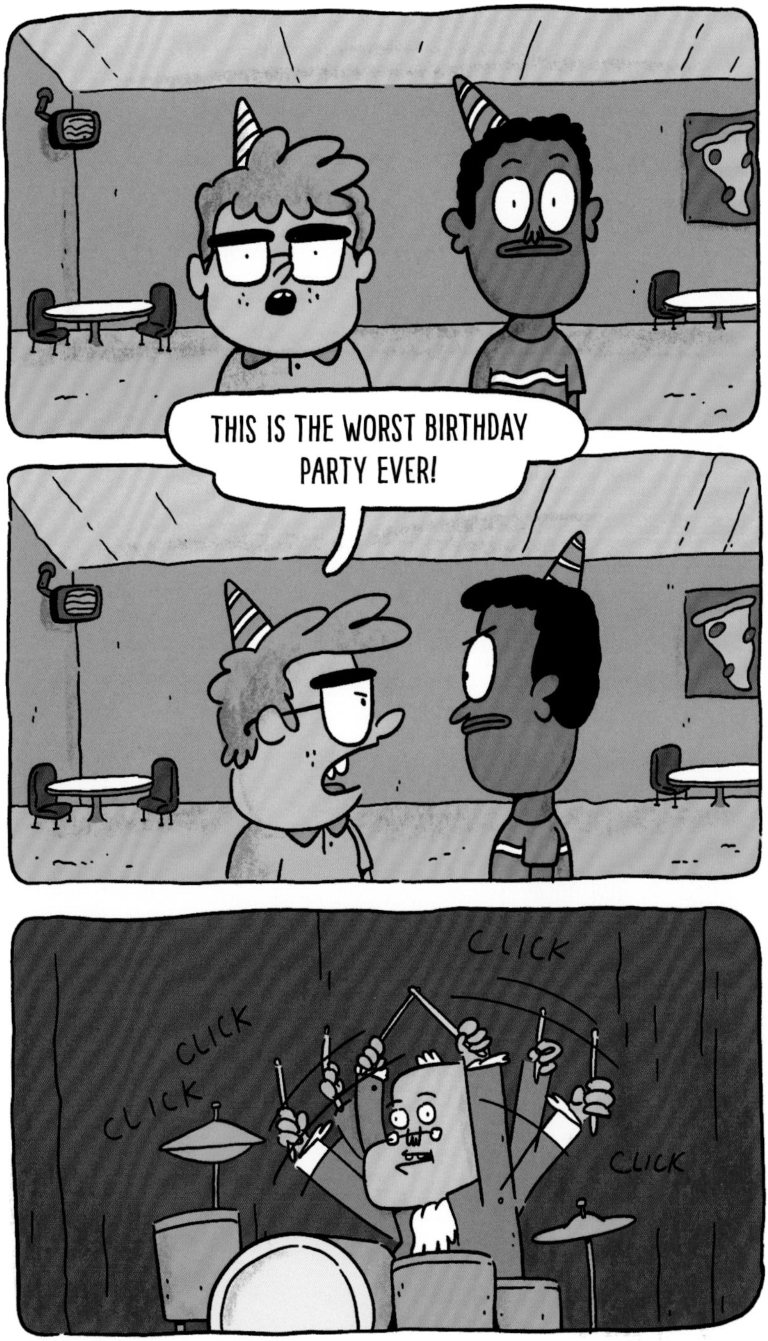
THIS IS THE WORST BIRTHDAY PARTY EVER!
CLICK
CLICK
CLICK
CLICK

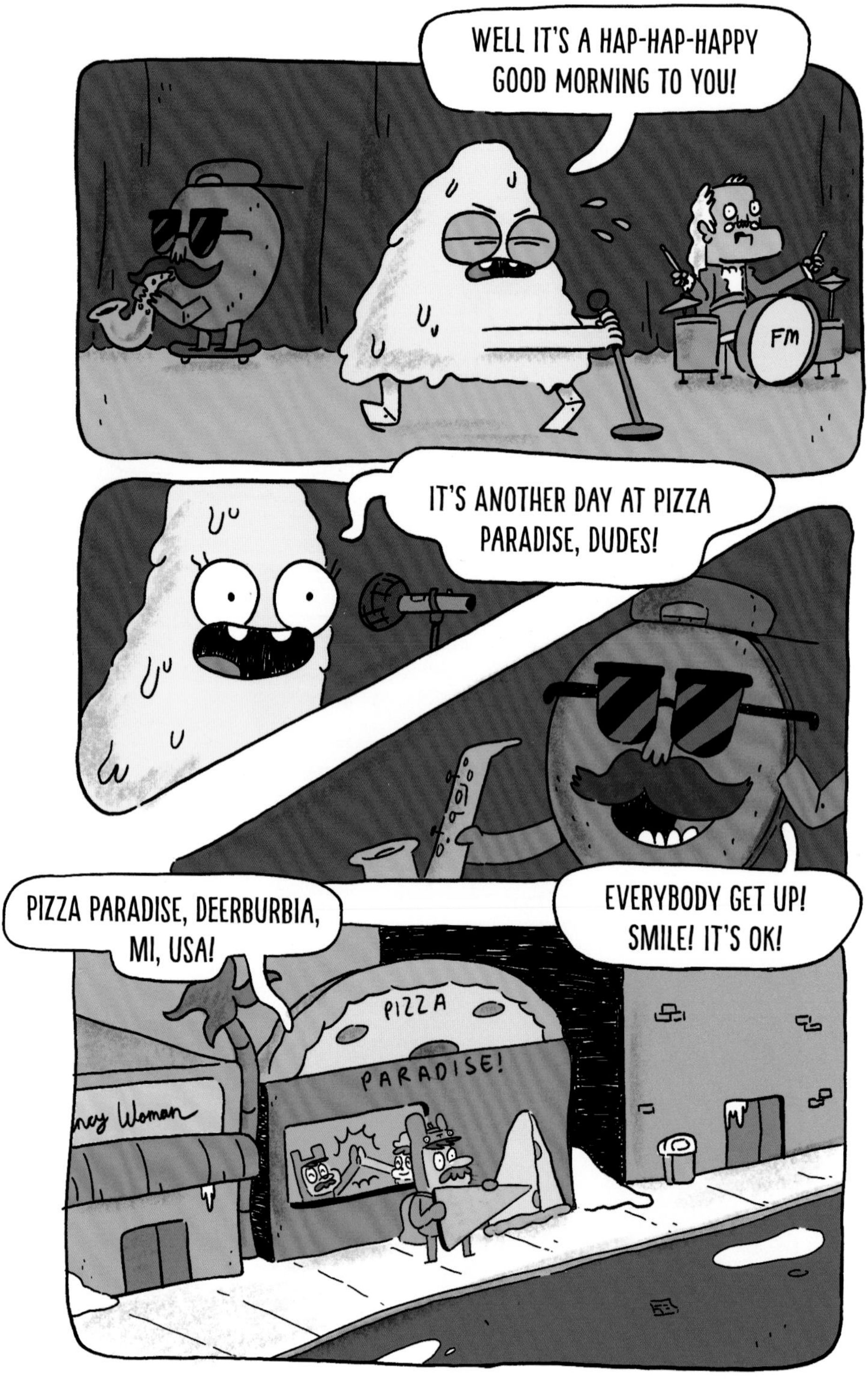
WELL IT'S A HAP-HAP-HAPPY GOOD MORNING TO YOU!
FM
IT'S ANOTHER DAY AT PIZZA PARADISE, DUDES!
PIZZA PARADISE, DEERBURBIA, MI, USA!
EVERYBODY GET UP! SMILE! IT'S OK!
PIZZA
PARADISE!

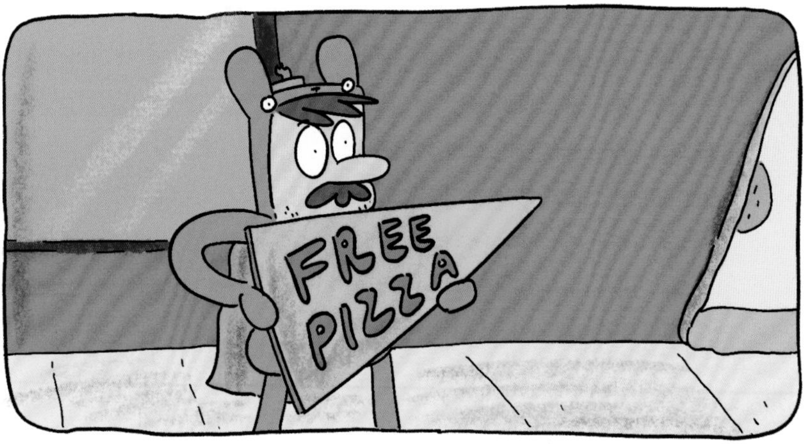
FREE
PIZZA

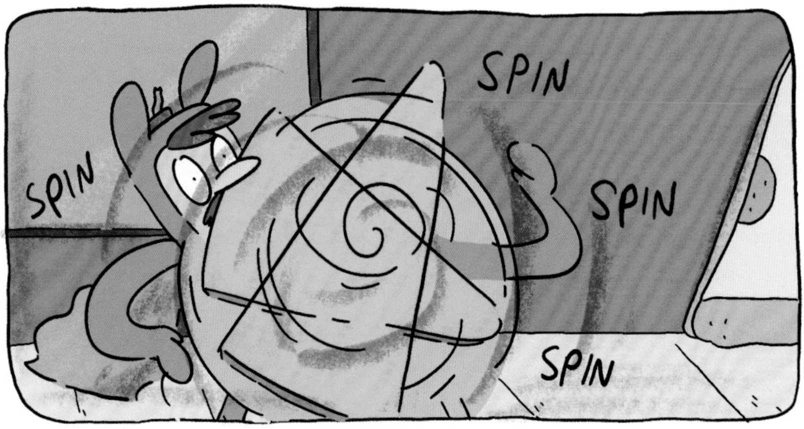
SPIN
SPIN
SPIN
SPIN

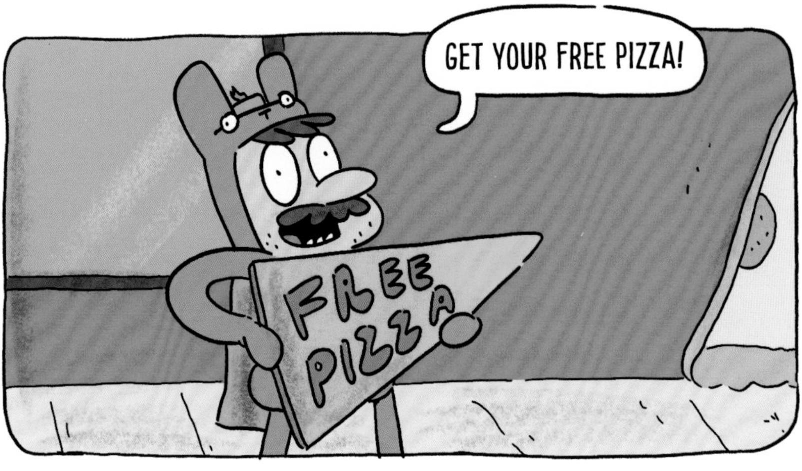
GET YOUR FREE PIZZA!
FREE
PIZZA

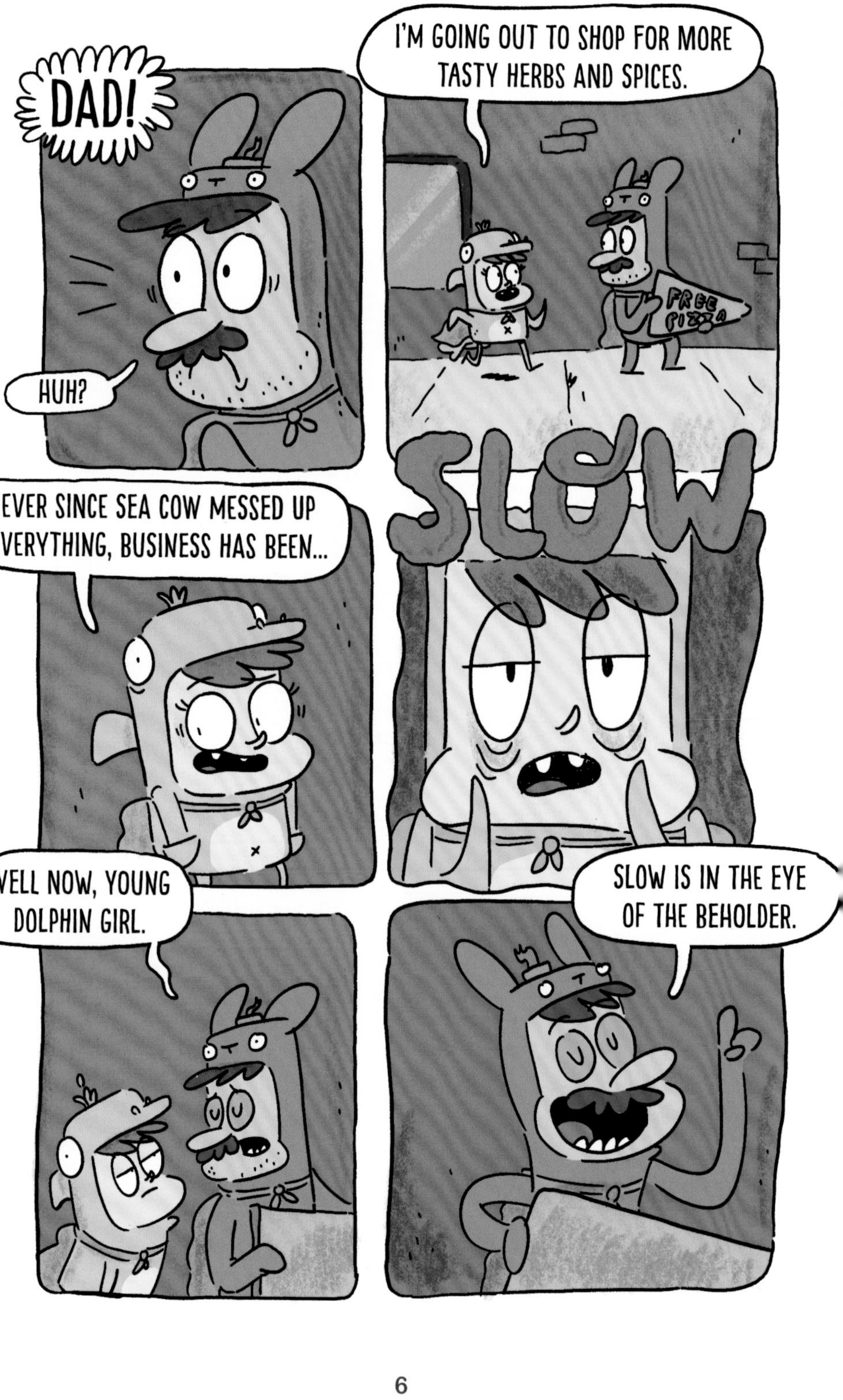
DAD!
HUH?
I'M GOING OUT TO SHOP FOR MORE TASTY HERBS AND SPICES.
FREE PIZZA
EVER SINCE SEA COW MESSED UP EVERYTHING, BUSINESS HAS BEEN...
SLOW
WELL NOW, YOUNG DOLPHIN GIRL.
SLOW IS IN THE EYE OF THE BEHOLDER.

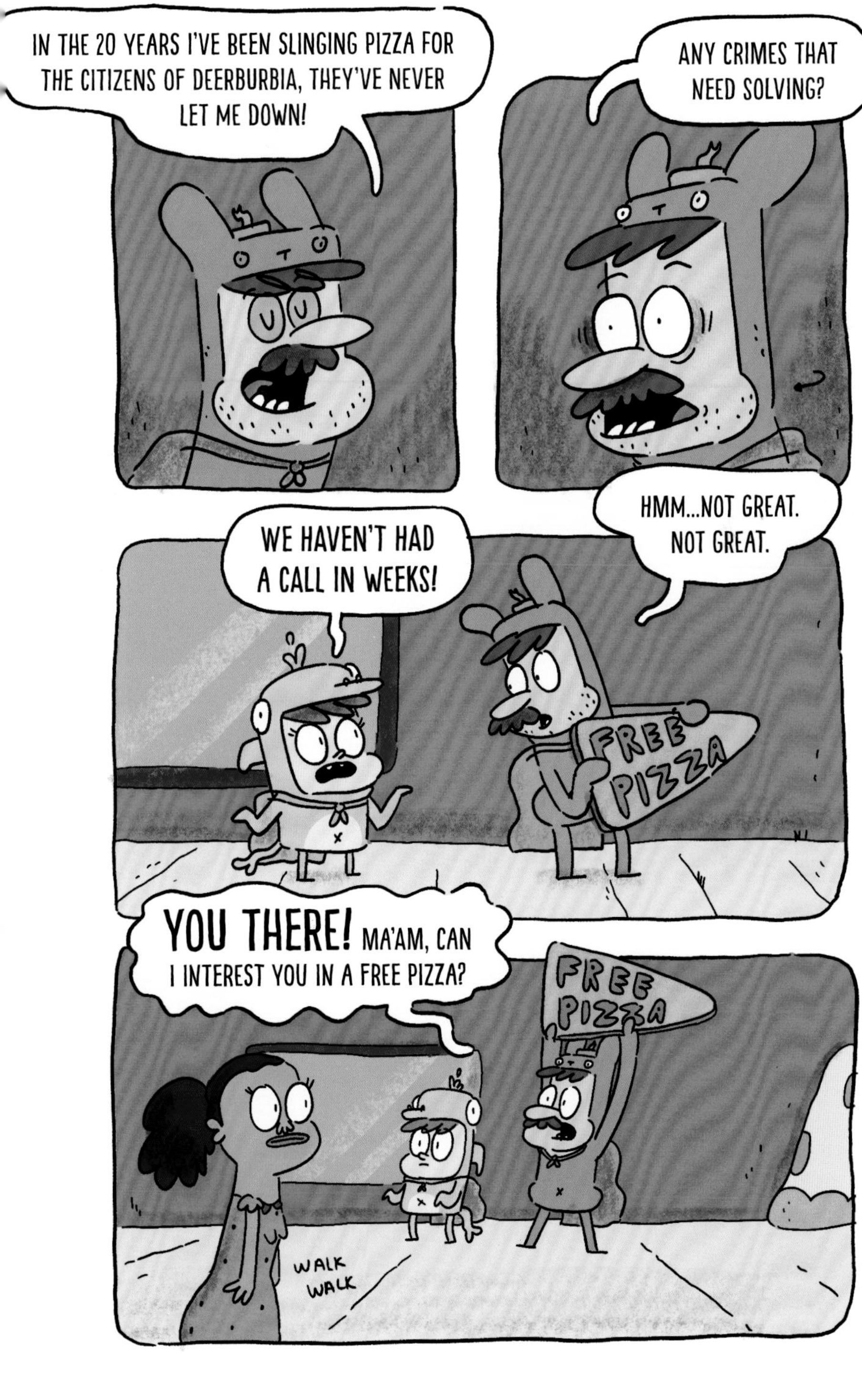
IN THE 20 YEARS I'VE BEEN SLINGING PIZZA FOR THE CITIZENS OF DEERBURBIA, THEY'VE NEVER LET ME DOWN!
ANY CRIMES THAT NEED SOLVING?
WE HAVEN'T HAD A CALL IN WEEKS!
HMM...NOT GREAT. NOT GREAT.
FREE PIZZA
YOU THERE! MA'AM, CAN I INTEREST YOU IN A FREE PIZZA?
FREE PIZZA
WALK WALK

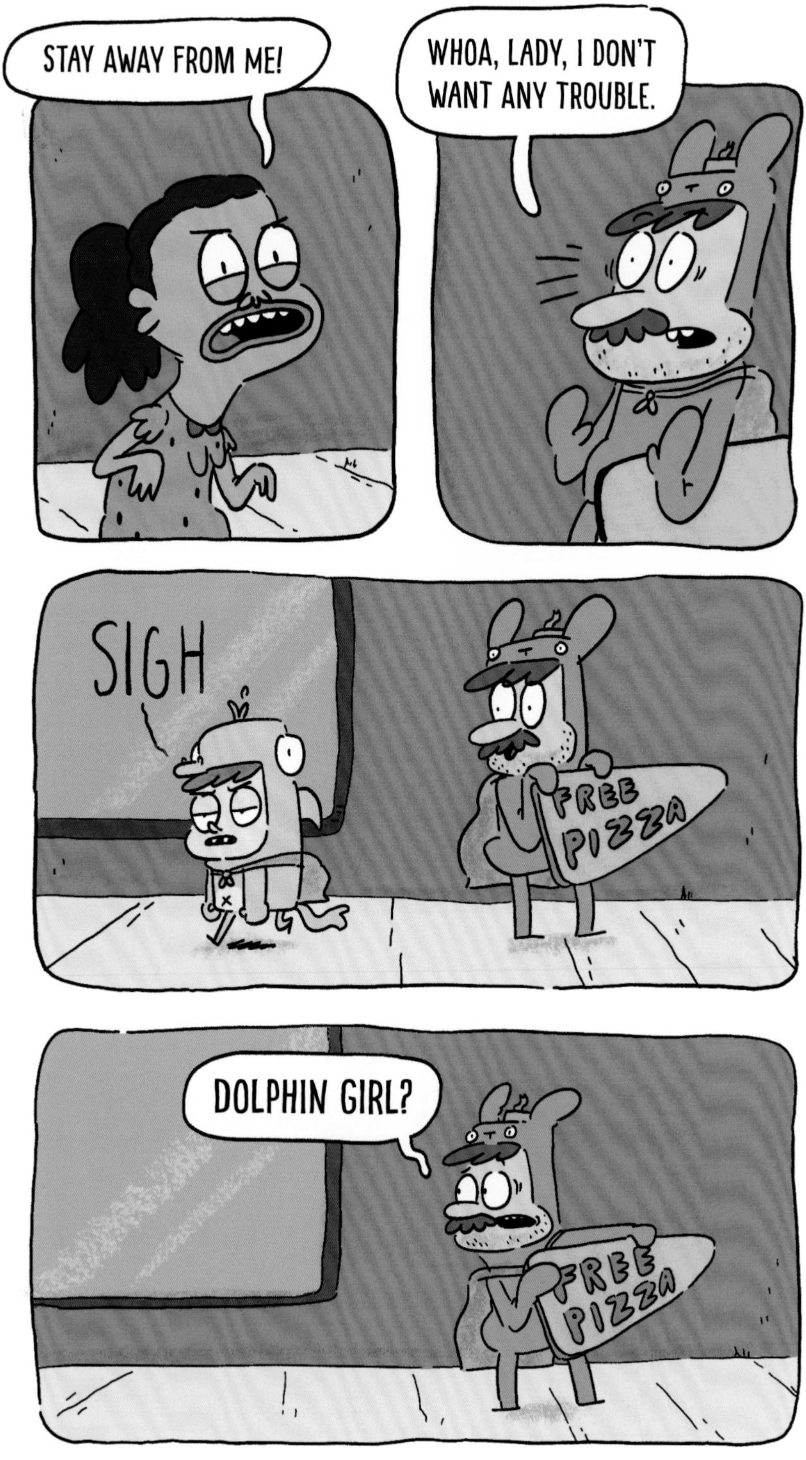
STAY AWAY FROM ME!
WHOA, LADY, I DON'T WANT ANY TROUBLE.
SIGH
FREE PIZZA
DOLPHIN GIRL?
FREE PIZZA

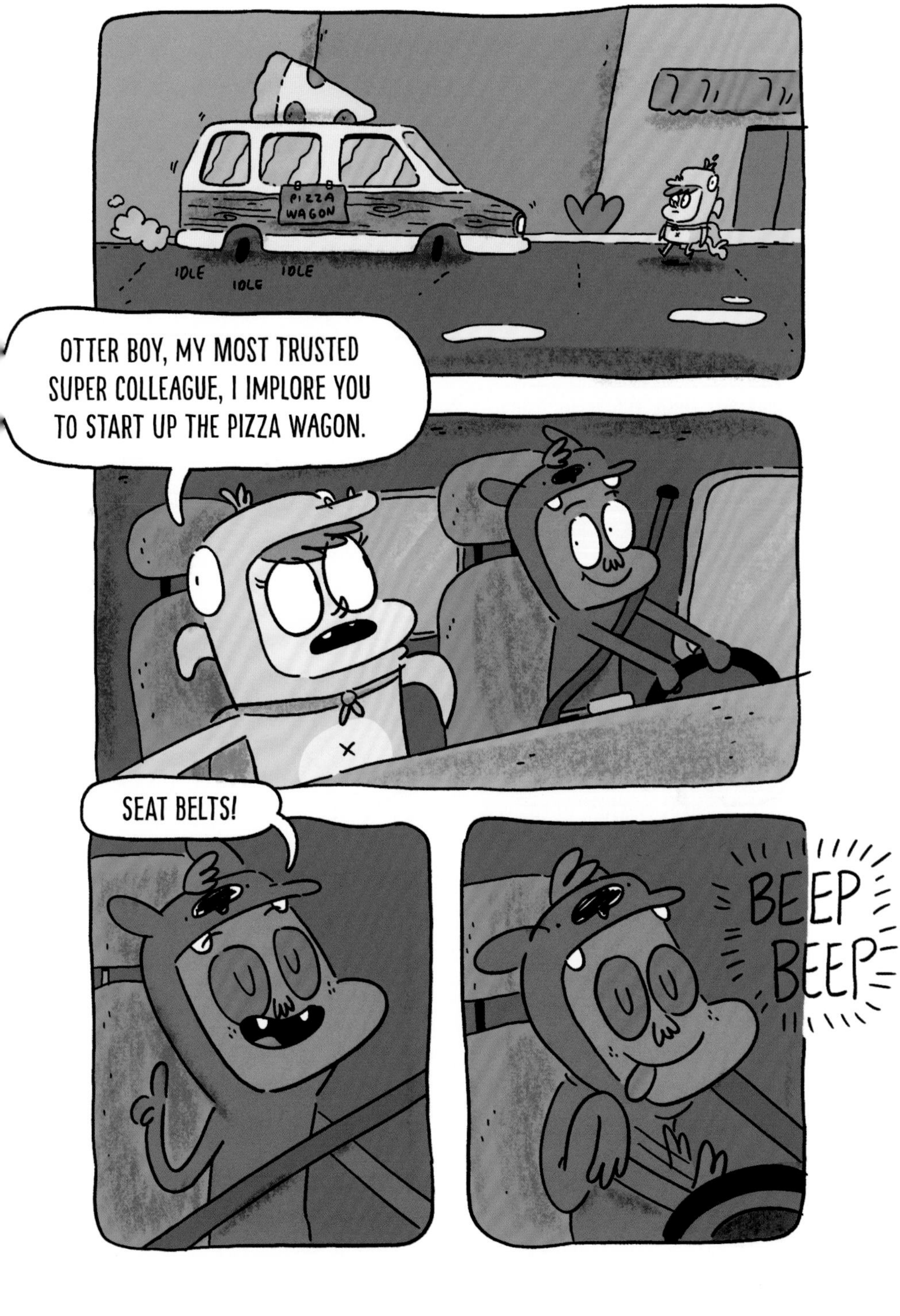
PIZZA WAGON
IDLE IDLE IDLE
OTTER BOY, MY MOST TRUSTED SUPER COLLEAGUE, I IMPLORE YOU TO START UP THE PIZZA WAGON.
SEAT BELTS!
BEEP BEEP

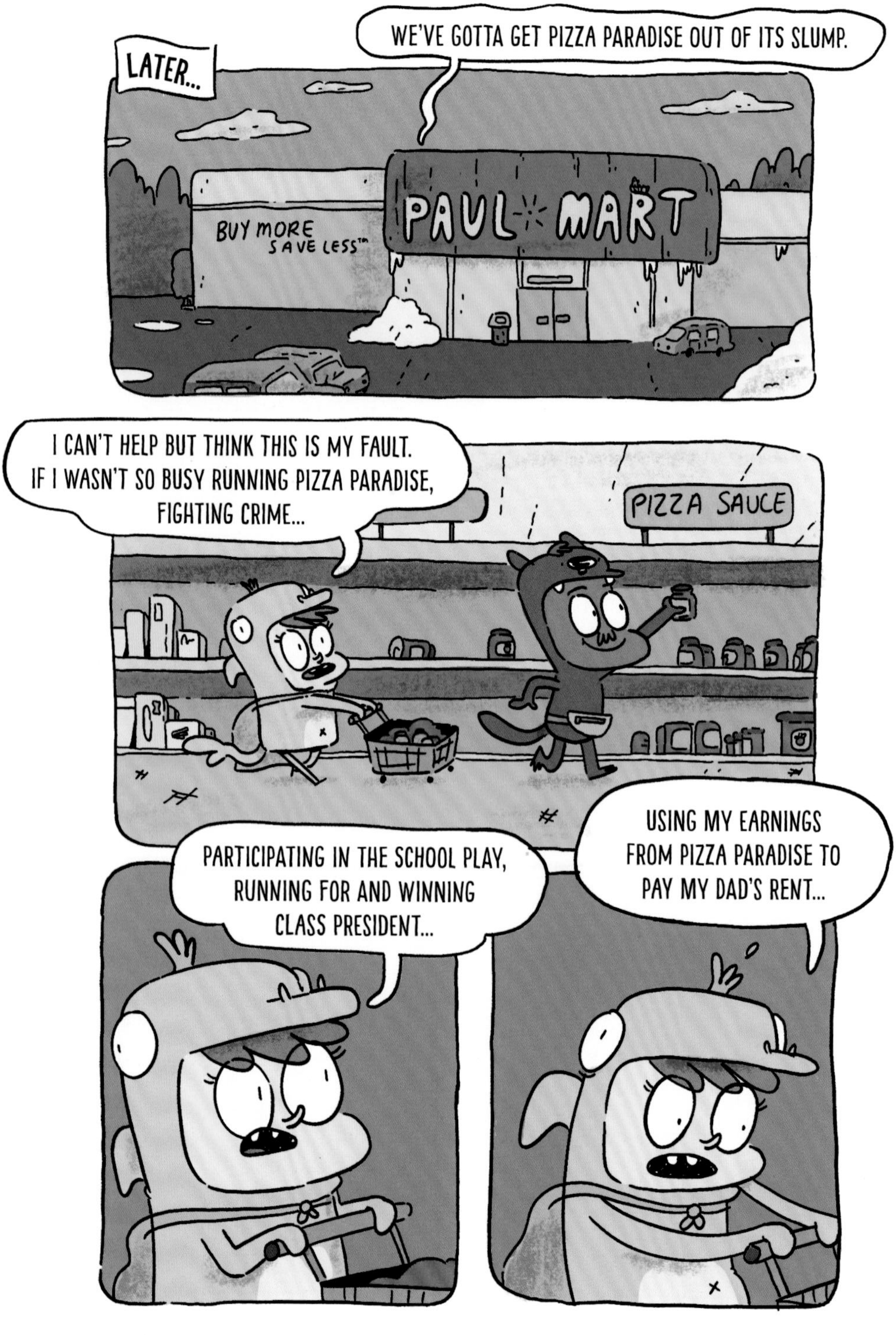
LATER...
WE'VE GOTTA GET PIZZA PARADISE OUT OF ITS SLUMP.
PAUL MART
BUY MORE SAVE LESS™
I CAN'T HELP BUT THINK THIS IS MY FAULT. IF I WASN'T SO BUSY RUNNING PIZZA PARADISE, FIGHTING CRIME...
PIZZA SAUCE
PARTICIPATING IN THE SCHOOL PLAY, RUNNING FOR AND WINNING CLASS PRESIDENT...
USING MY EARNINGS FROM PIZZA PARADISE TO PAY MY DAD'S RENT...

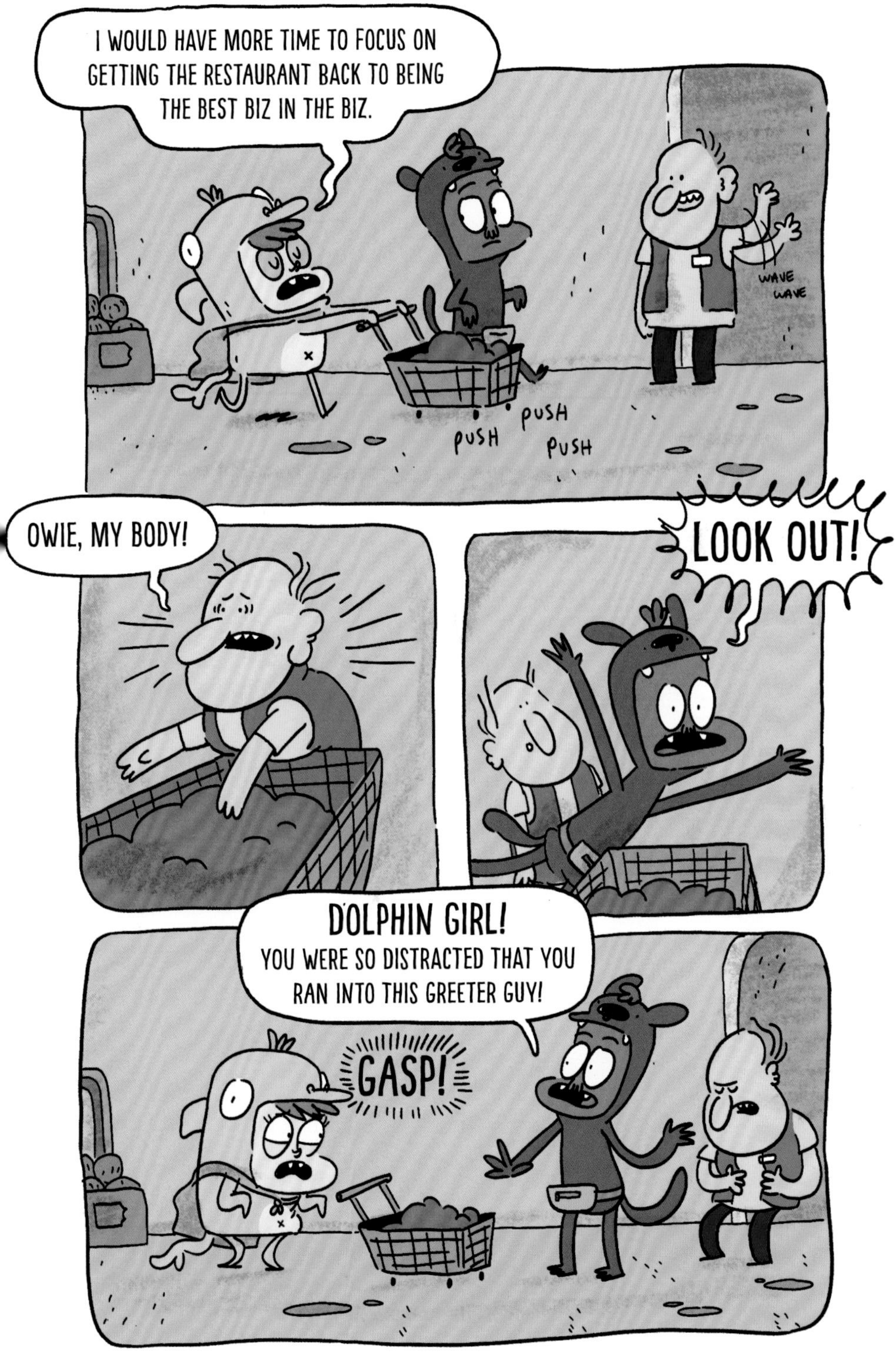
I WOULD HAVE MORE TIME TO FOCUS ON GETTING THE RESTAURANT BACK TO BEING THE BEST BIZ IN THE BIZ.
WAVE WAVE
PUSH PUSH PUSH
OWIE, MY BODY!
LOOK OUT!
DOLPHIN GIRL! YOU WERE SO DISTRACTED THAT YOU RAN INTO THIS GREETER GUY!
GASP!

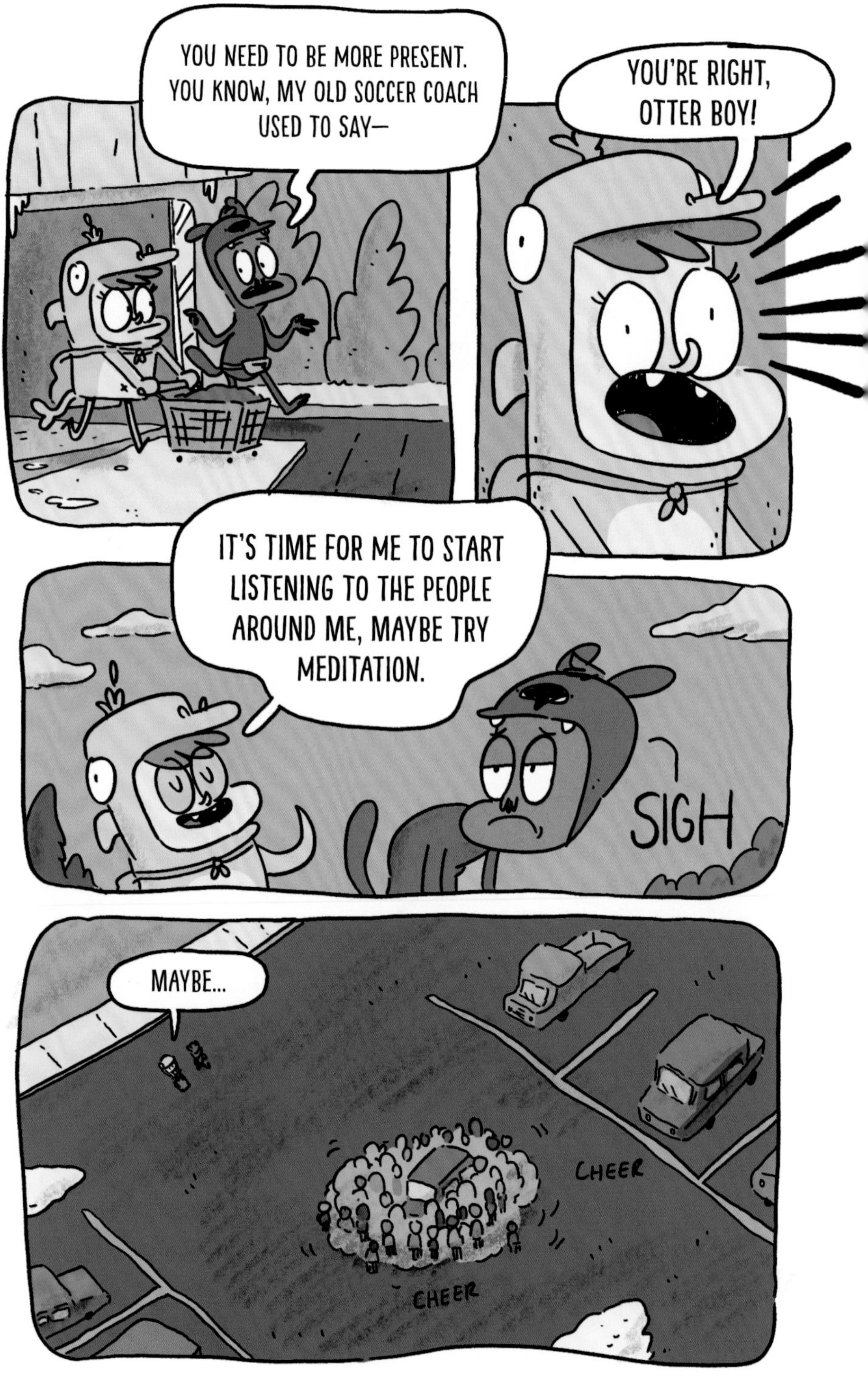
YOU NEED TO BE MORE PRESENT. YOU KNOW, MY OLD SOCCER COACH USED TO SAY—
YOU'RE RIGHT, OTTER BOY!
IT'S TIME FOR ME TO START LISTENING TO THE PEOPLE AROUND ME, MAYBE TRY MEDITATION.
SIGH
MAYBE...
CHEER
CHEER

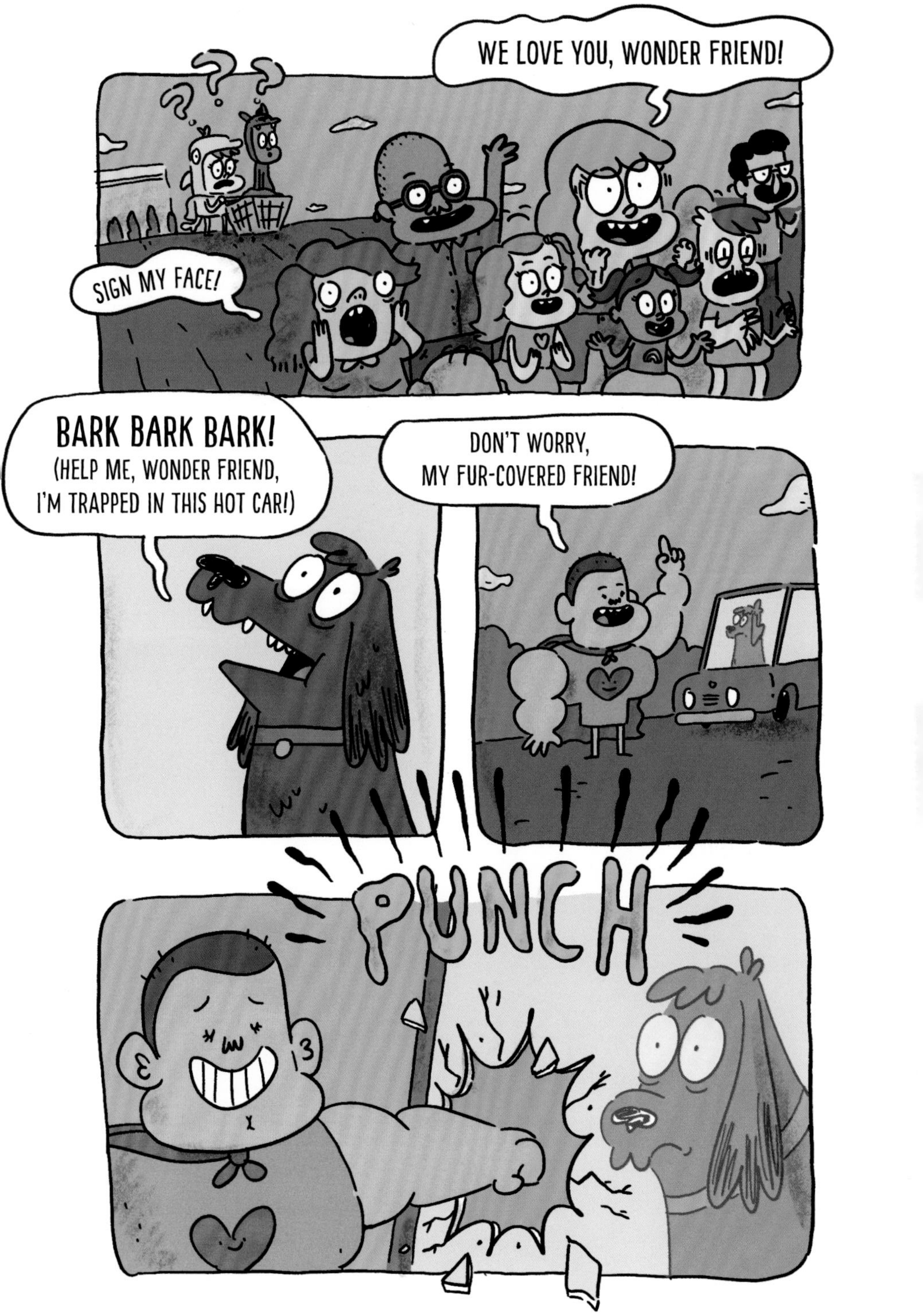
WE LOVE YOU, WONDER FRIEND!
SIGN MY FACE!
BARK BARK BARK!
(HELP ME, WONDER FRIEND, I'M TRAPPED IN THIS HOT CAR!)
DON'T WORRY, MY FUR-COVERED FRIEND!
PUNCH

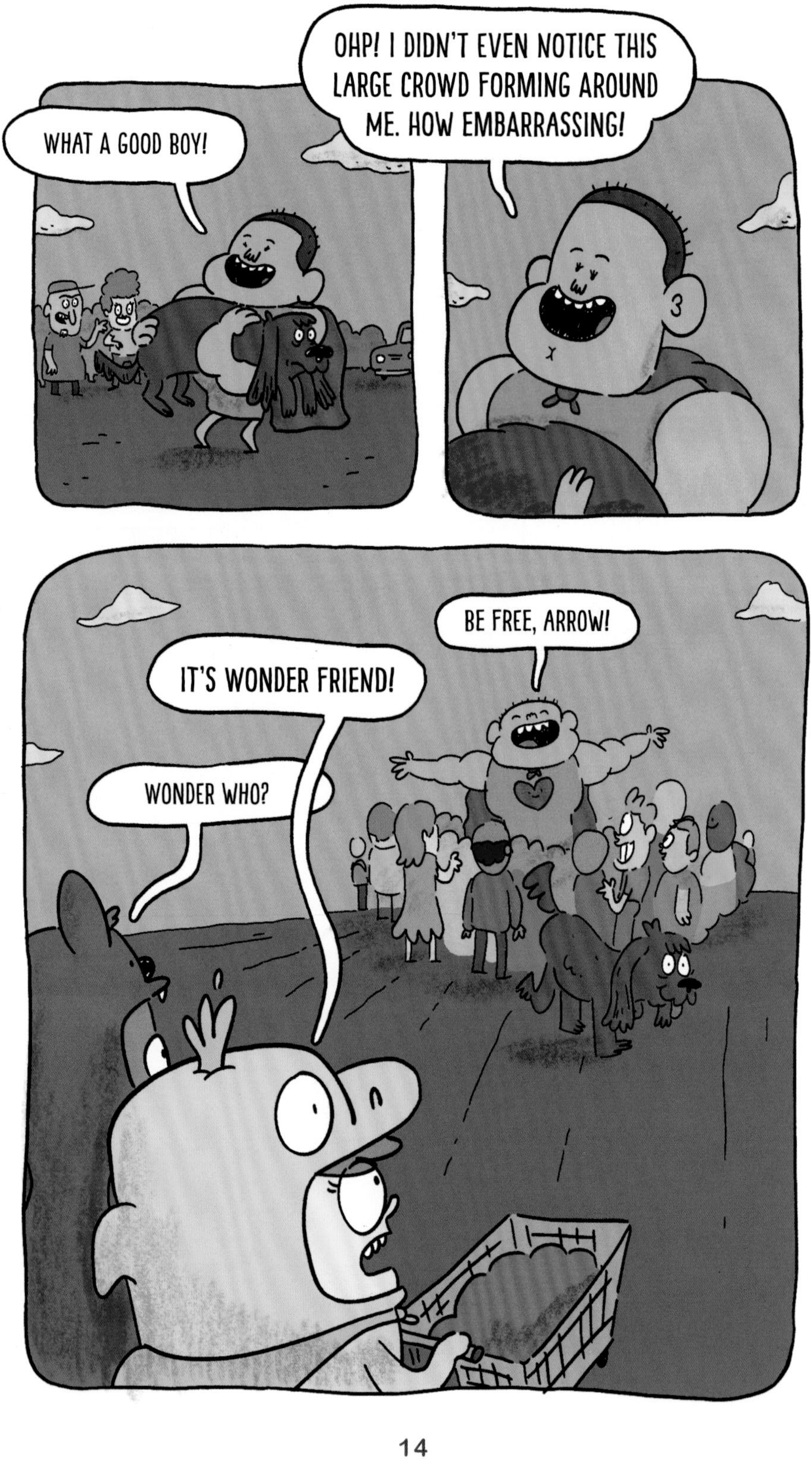
WHAT A GOOD BOY!
OHP! I DIDN'T EVEN NOTICE THIS LARGE CROWD FORMING AROUND ME. HOW EMBARRASSING!
BE FREE, ARROW!
IT'S WONDER FRIEND!
WONDER WHO?

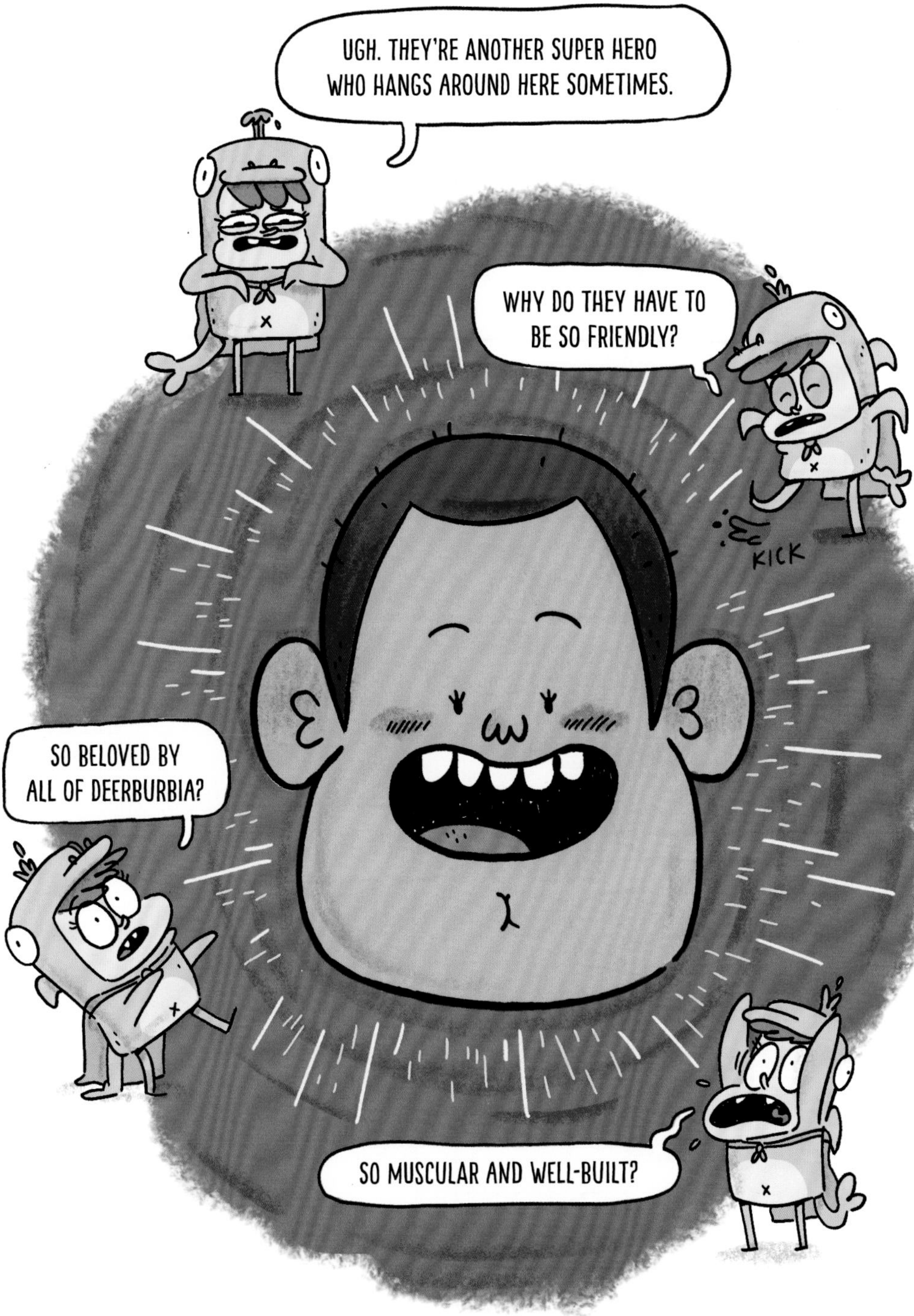
UGH. THEY'RE ANOTHER SUPER HERO WHO HANGS AROUND HERE SOMETIMES.
WHY DO THEY HAVE TO BE SO FRIENDLY?
KICK
SO BELOVED BY ALL OF DEERBURBIA?
SO MUSCULAR AND WELL-BUILT?

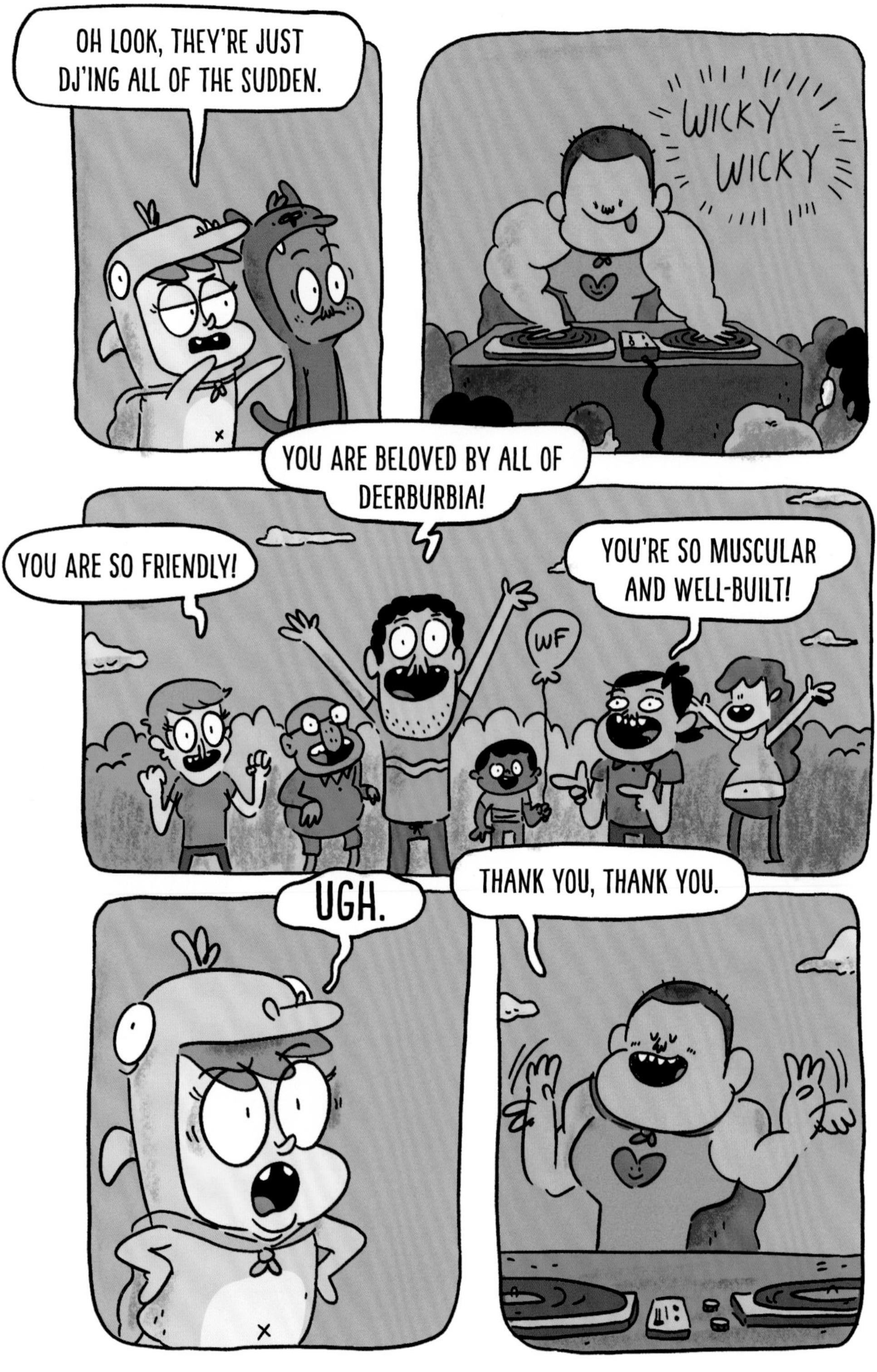
OH LOOK, THEY'RE JUST DJ'ING ALL OF THE SUDDEN.
WICKY WICKY
YOU ARE BELOVED BY ALL OF DEERBURBIA!
YOU ARE SO FRIENDLY!
YOU'RE SO MUSCULAR AND WELL-BUILT!
WF
UGH.
THANK YOU, THANK YOU.

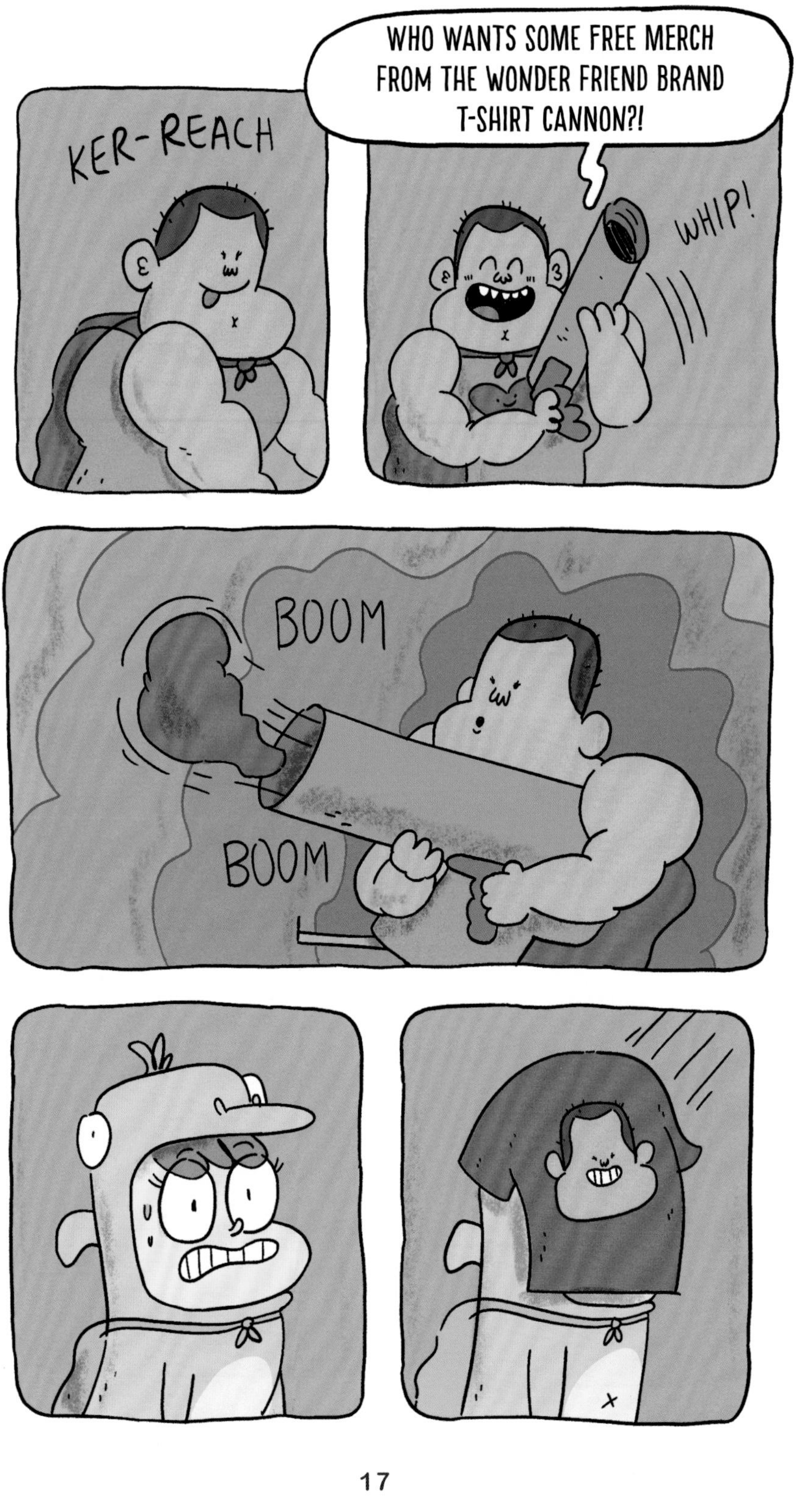

KER-REACH
WHO WANTS SOME FREE MERCH FROM THE WONDER FRIEND BRAND T-SHIRT CANNON?!
WHIP!
BOOM
BOOM

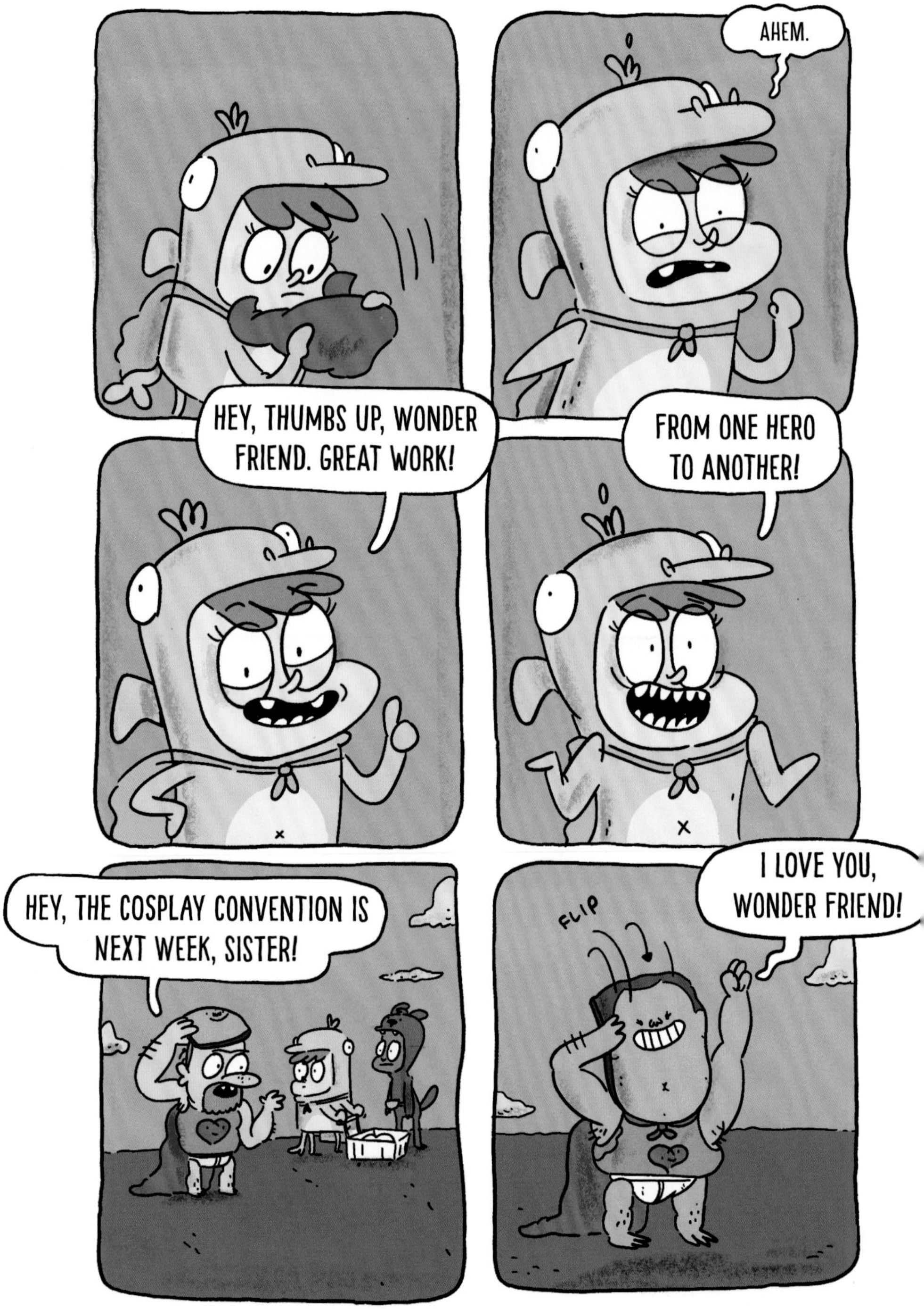
AHEM.
HEY, THUMBS UP, WONDER FRIEND. GREAT WORK!
FROM ONE HERO TO ANOTHER!
HEY, THE COSPLAY CONVENTION IS NEXT WEEK, SISTER!
FLIP
I LOVE YOU, WONDER FRIEND!

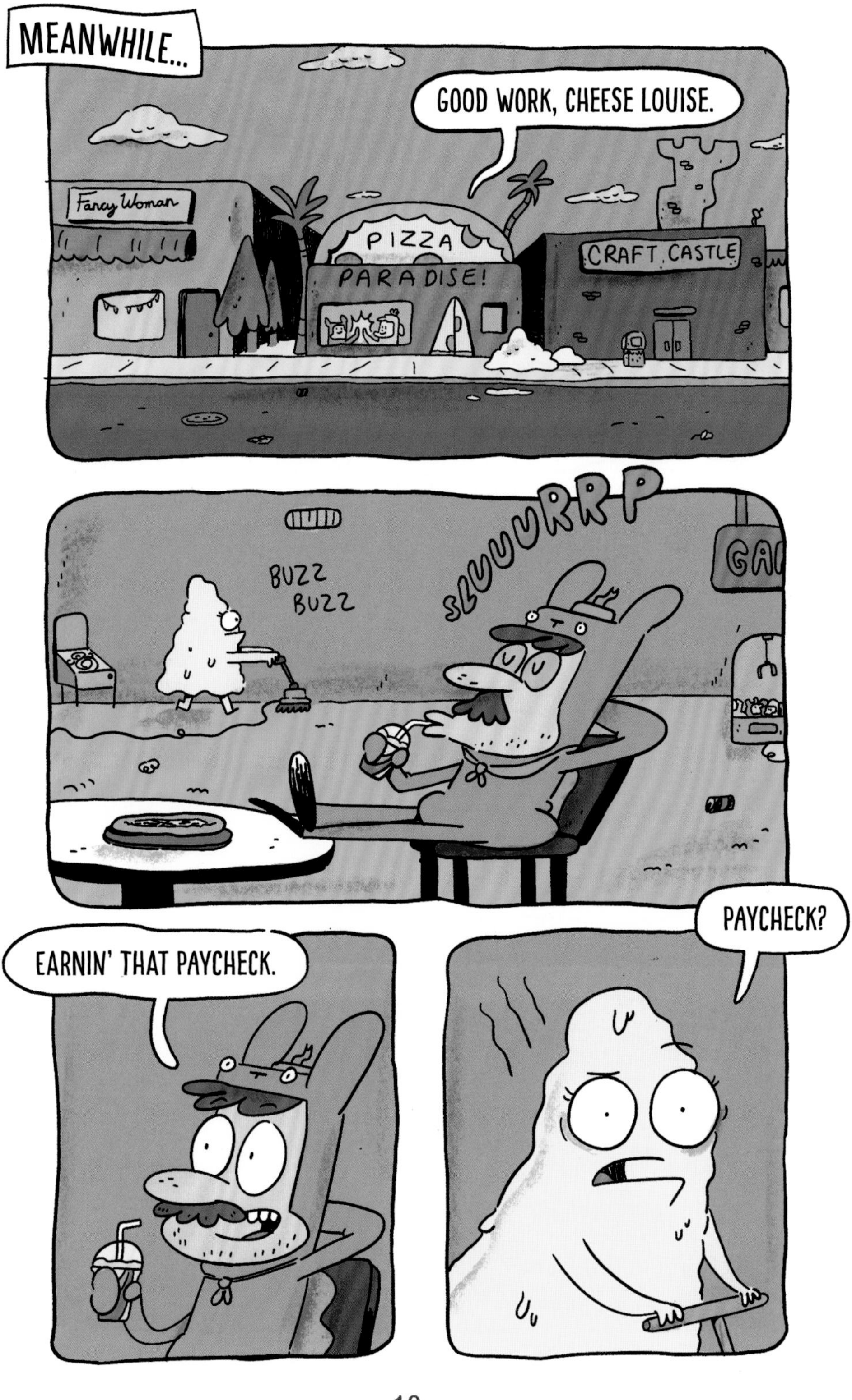
MEANWHILE...
GOOD WORK, CHEESE LOUISE.
Fancy Woman
PIZZA
PARADISE!
CRAFT CASTLE
BUZZ
BUZZ
SLUUURRP
EARNIN' THAT PAYCHECK.
PAYCHECK?

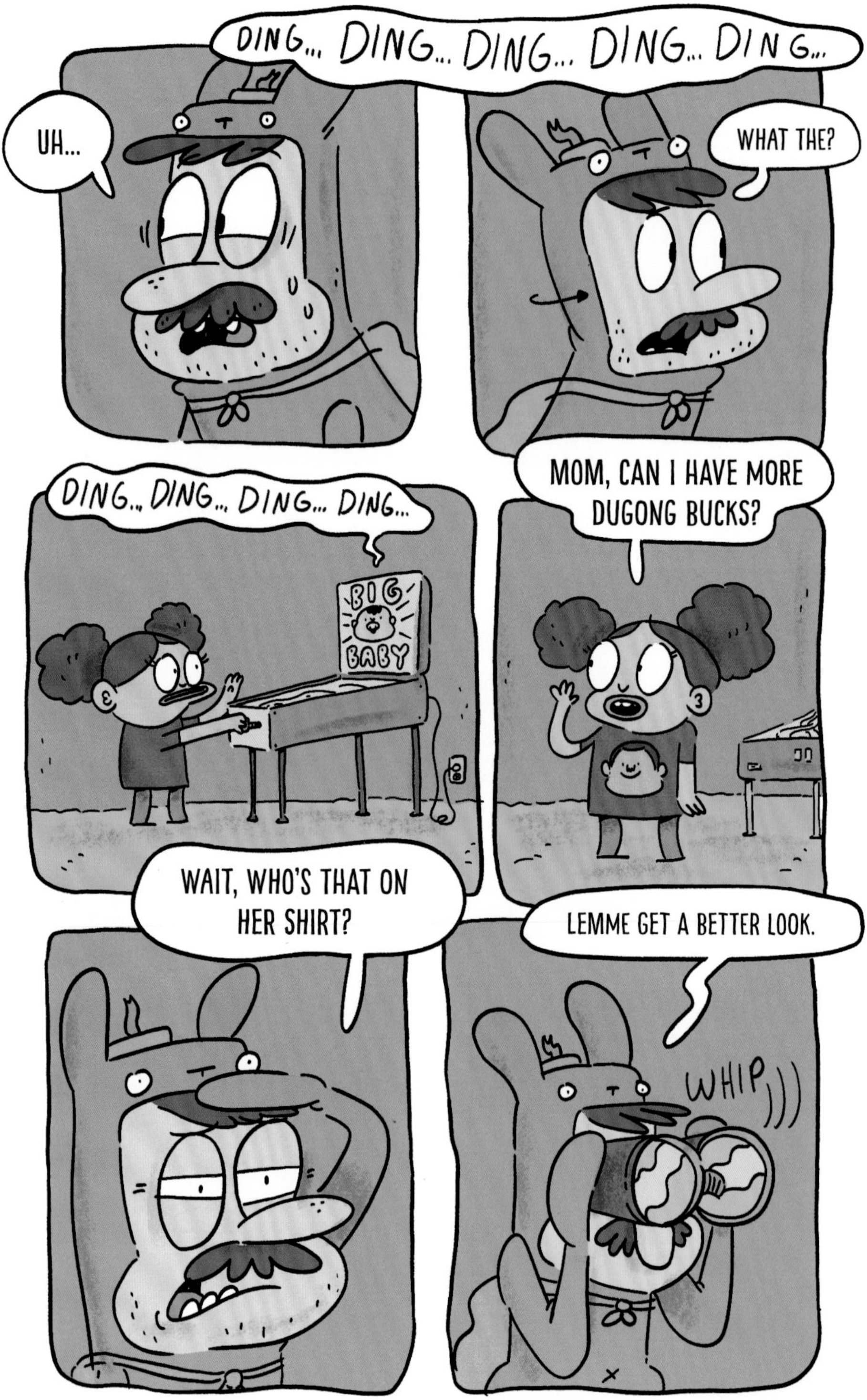
DING... DING... DING... DING... DING...
UH...
WHAT THE?
DING... DING... DING... DING...
BIG BABY
MOM, CAN I HAVE MORE DUGONG BUCKS?
WAIT, WHO'S THAT ON HER SHIRT?
LEMME GET A BETTER LOOK.
WHIP

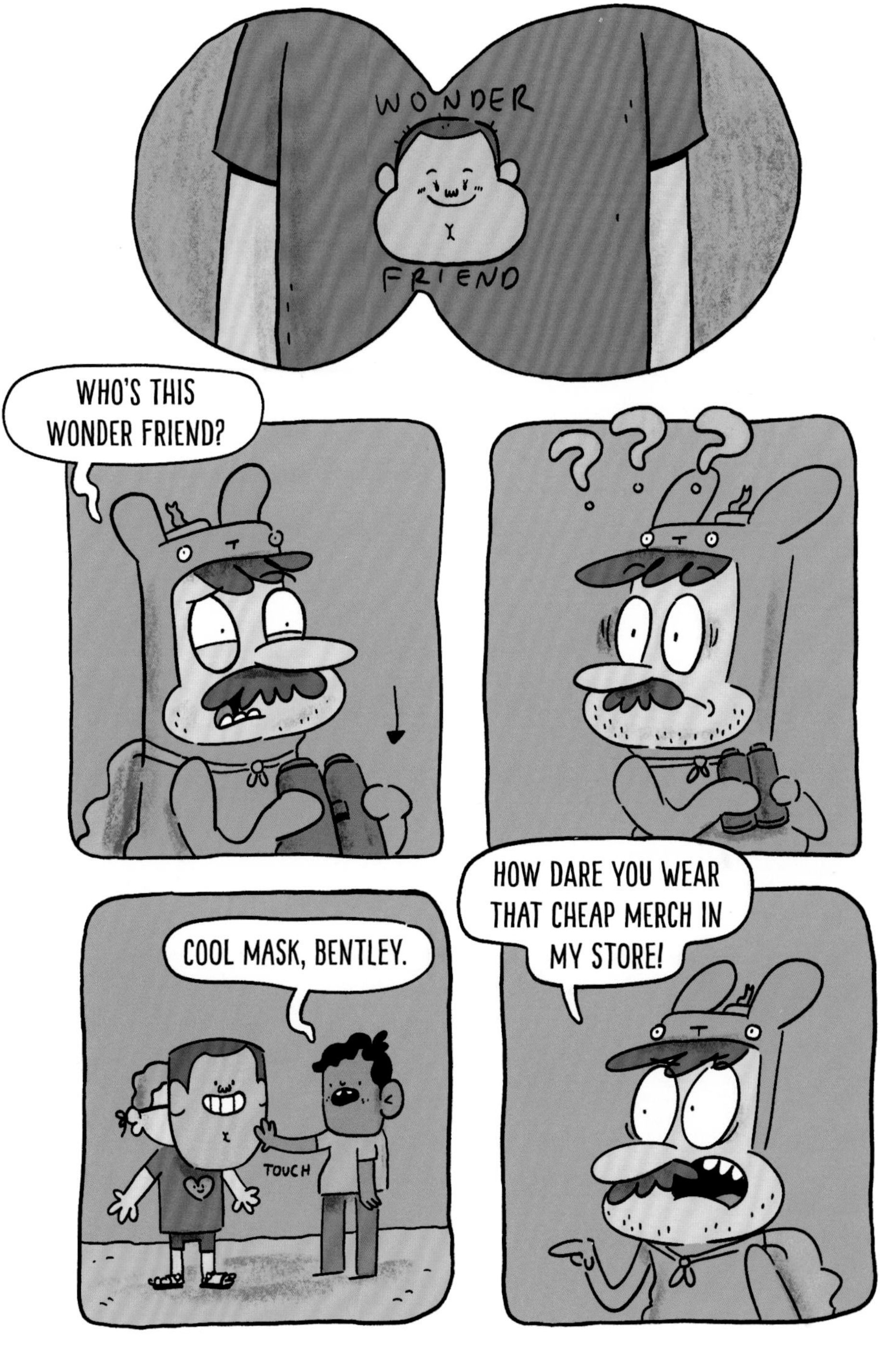
WONDER
FRIEND
WHO'S THIS WONDER FRIEND?
COOL MASK, BENTLEY.
TOUCH
HOW DARE YOU WEAR THAT CHEAP MERCH IN MY STORE!

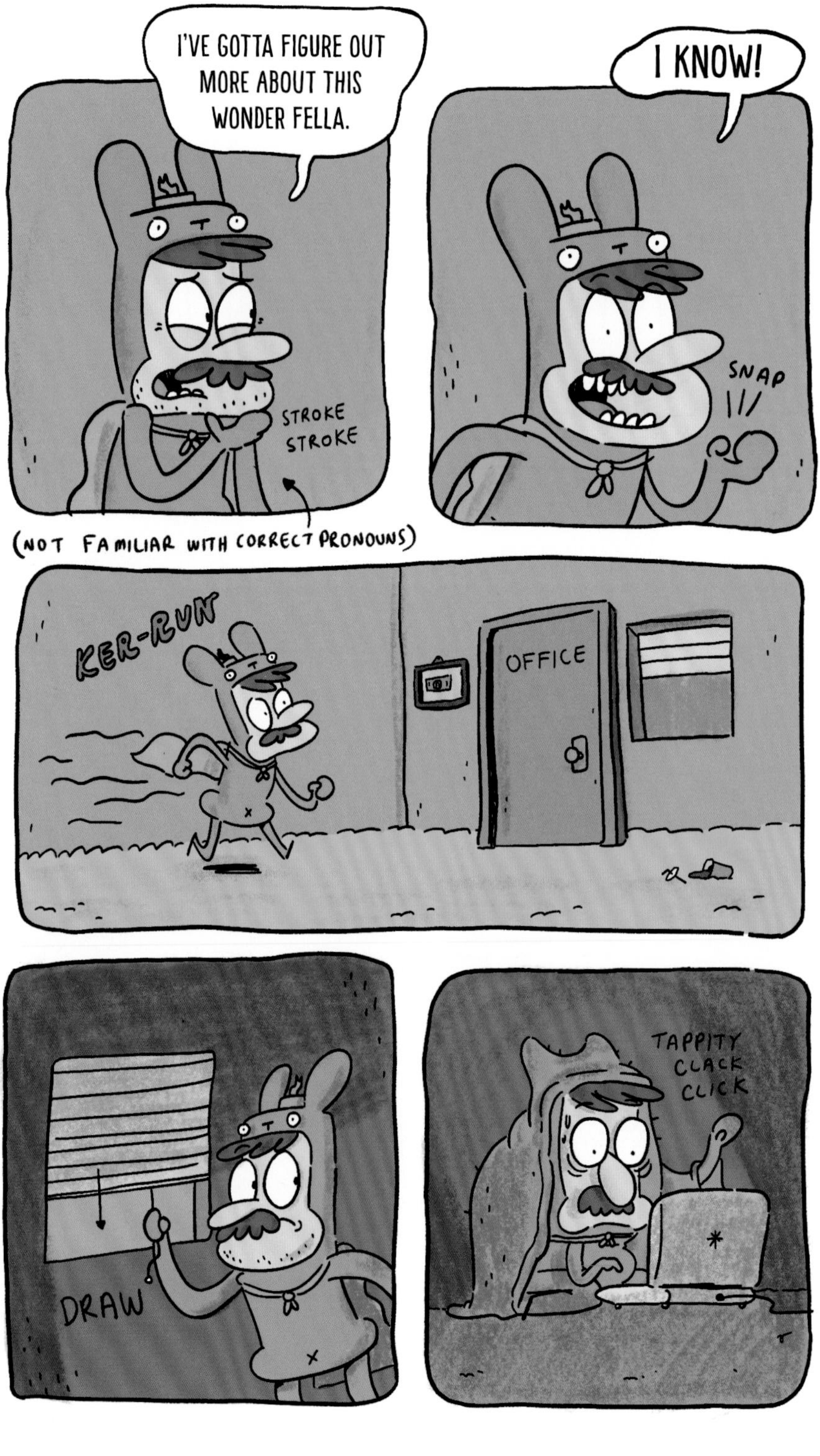
I'VE GOTTA FIGURE OUT MORE ABOUT THIS WONDER FELLA.
STROKE STROKE
(NOT FAMILIAR WITH CORRECT PRONOUNS)
I KNOW!
SNAP
KER-RUN
OFFICE
DRAW
TAPPITY CLACK CLICK

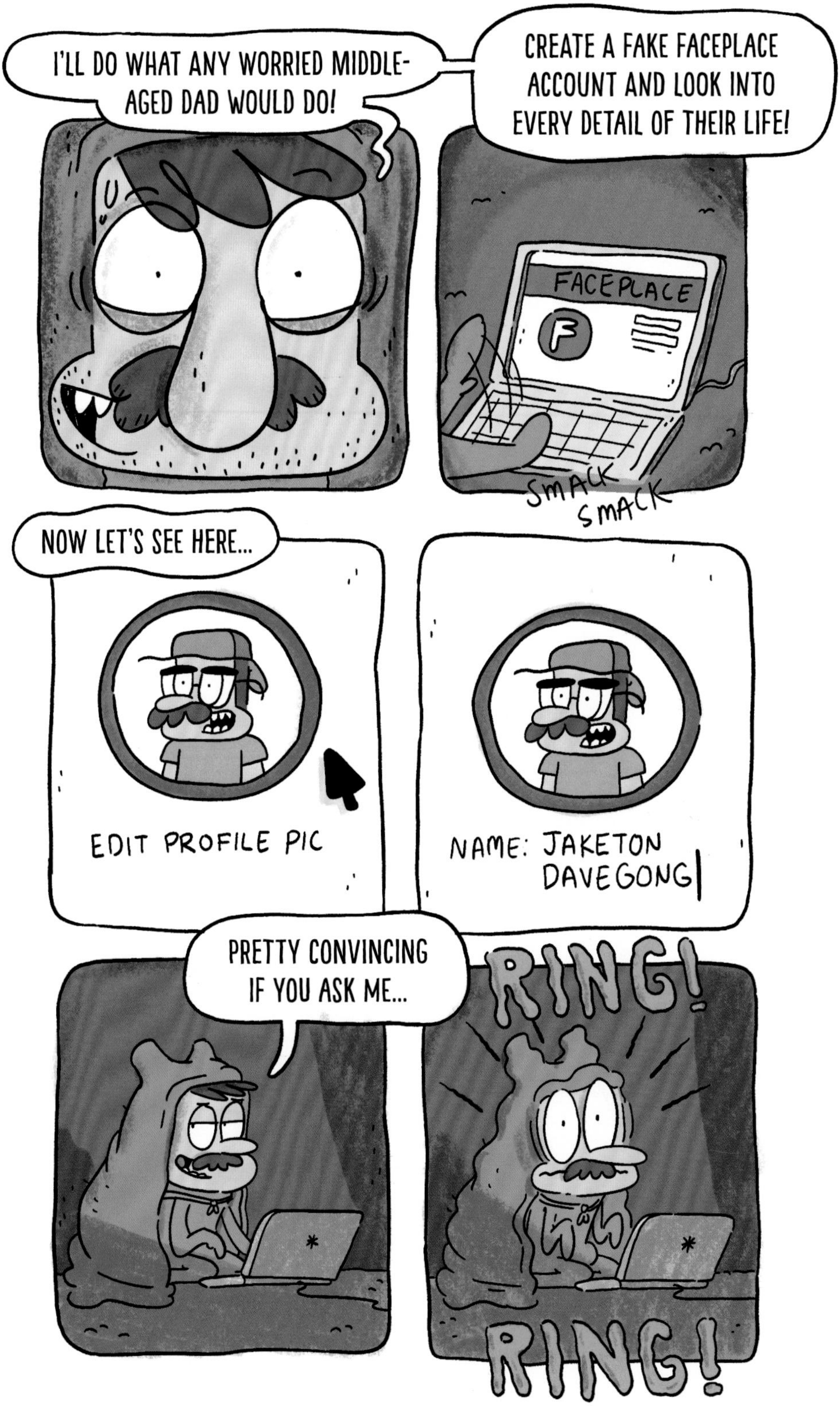
I'LL DO WHAT ANY WORRIED MIDDLE-AGED DAD WOULD DO!
CREATE A FAKE FACEPLACE ACCOUNT AND LOOK INTO EVERY DETAIL OF THEIR LIFE!
FACEPLACE
F
SMACK SMACK
NOW LET'S SEE HERE...
EDIT PROFILE PIC
NAME: JAKETON DAVEGONG
PRETTY CONVINCING IF YOU ASK ME...
RING!
RING!

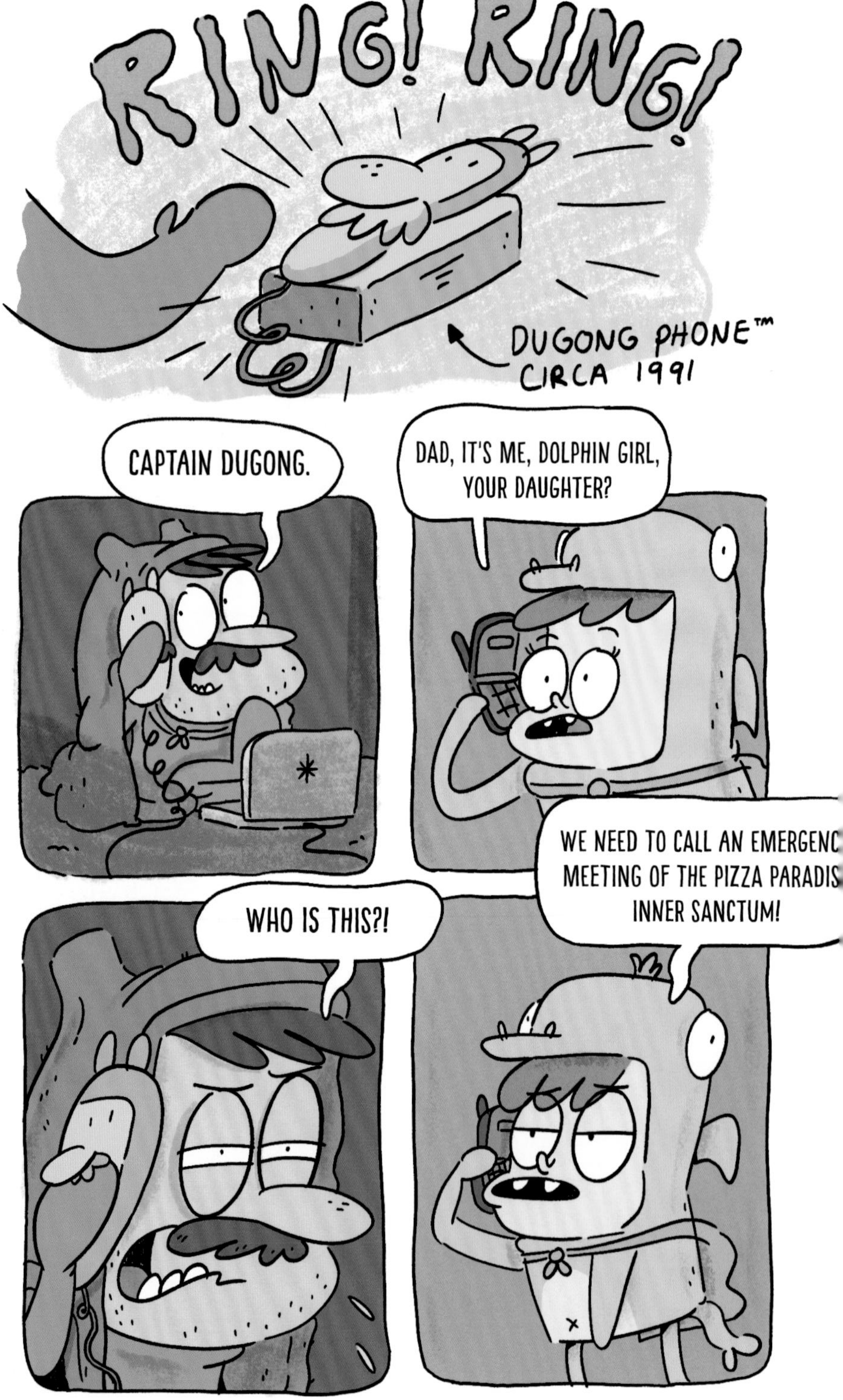
RING! RING!
DUGONG PHONE™ CIRCA 1991
CAPTAIN DUGONG.
DAD, IT'S ME, DOLPHIN GIRL, YOUR DAUGHTER?
WHO IS THIS?!
WE NEED TO CALL AN EMERGENC MEETING OF THE PIZZA PARADIS INNER SANCTUM!

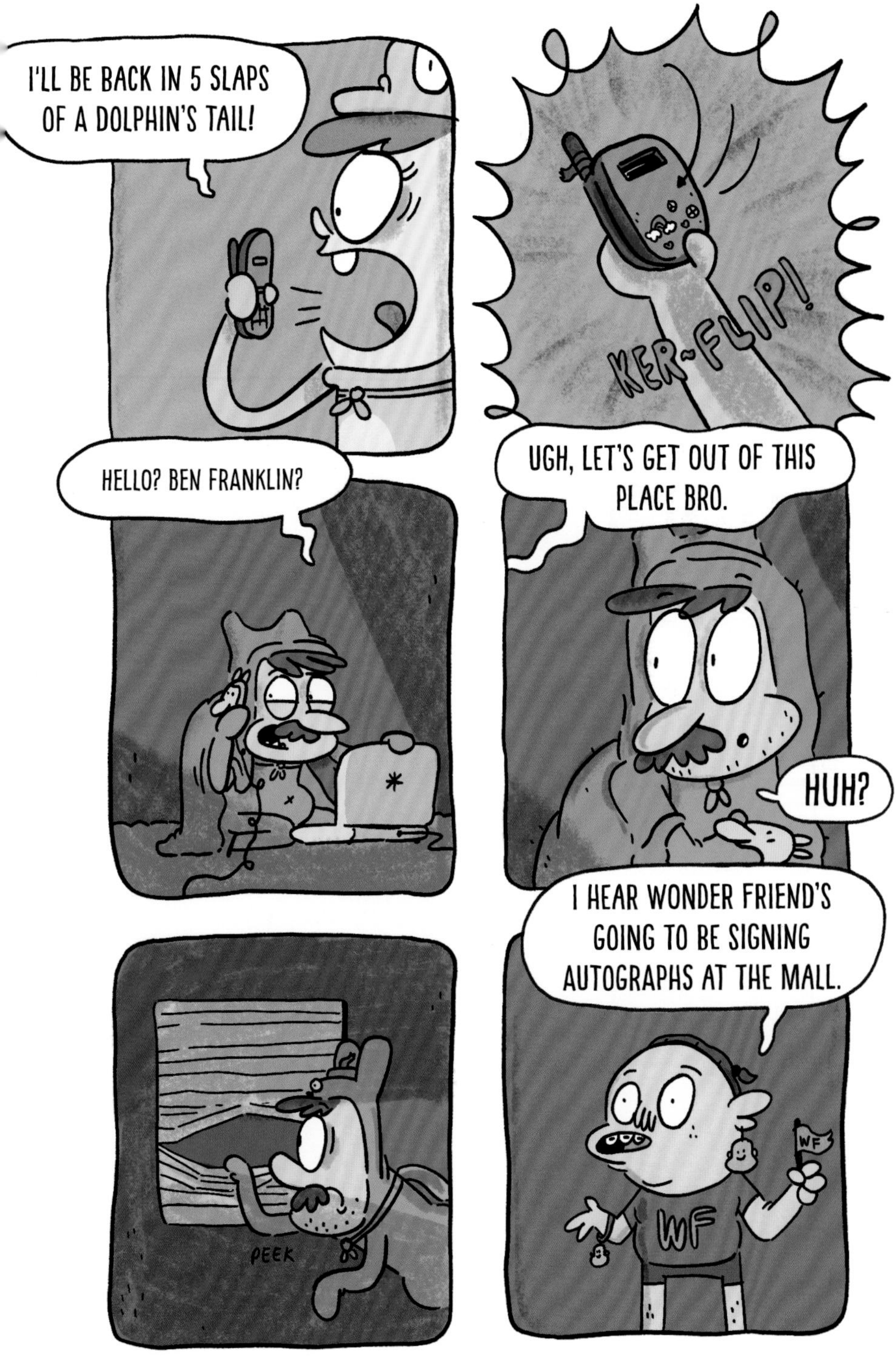
I'LL BE BACK IN 5 SLAPS OF A DOLPHIN'S TAIL!
KER-FLIP!
HELLO? BEN FRANKLIN?
UGH, LET'S GET OUT OF THIS PLACE BRO.
HUH?
PEEK
I HEAR WONDER FRIEND'S GOING TO BE SIGNING AUTOGRAPHS AT THE MALL.
WF
WF

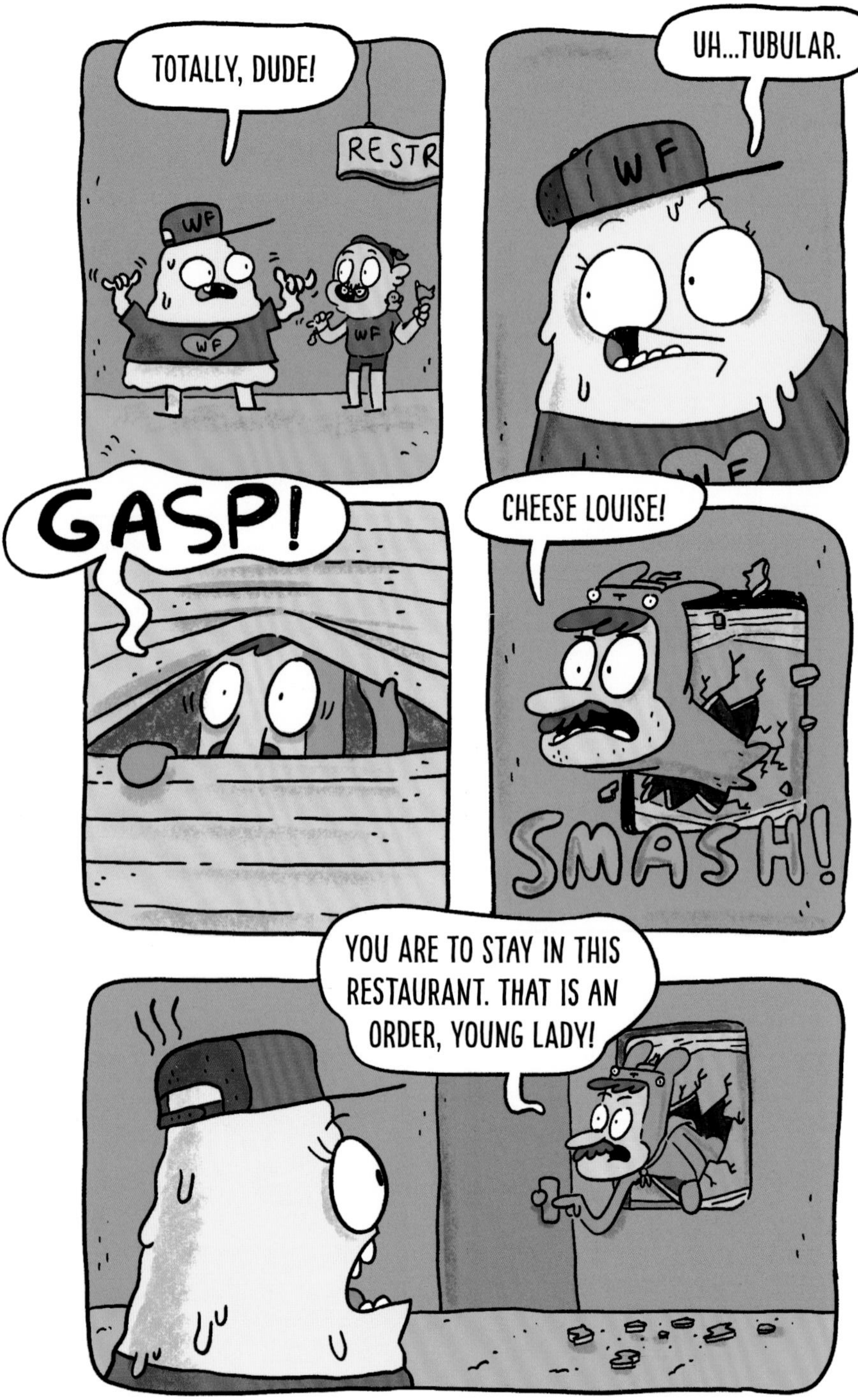
TOTALLY, DUDE!
RESTR
WF
WF
WF
WF
UH...TUBULAR.
WF
GASP!
CHEESE LOUISE!
SMASH!
YOU ARE TO STAY IN THIS RESTAURANT. THAT IS AN ORDER, YOUNG LADY!

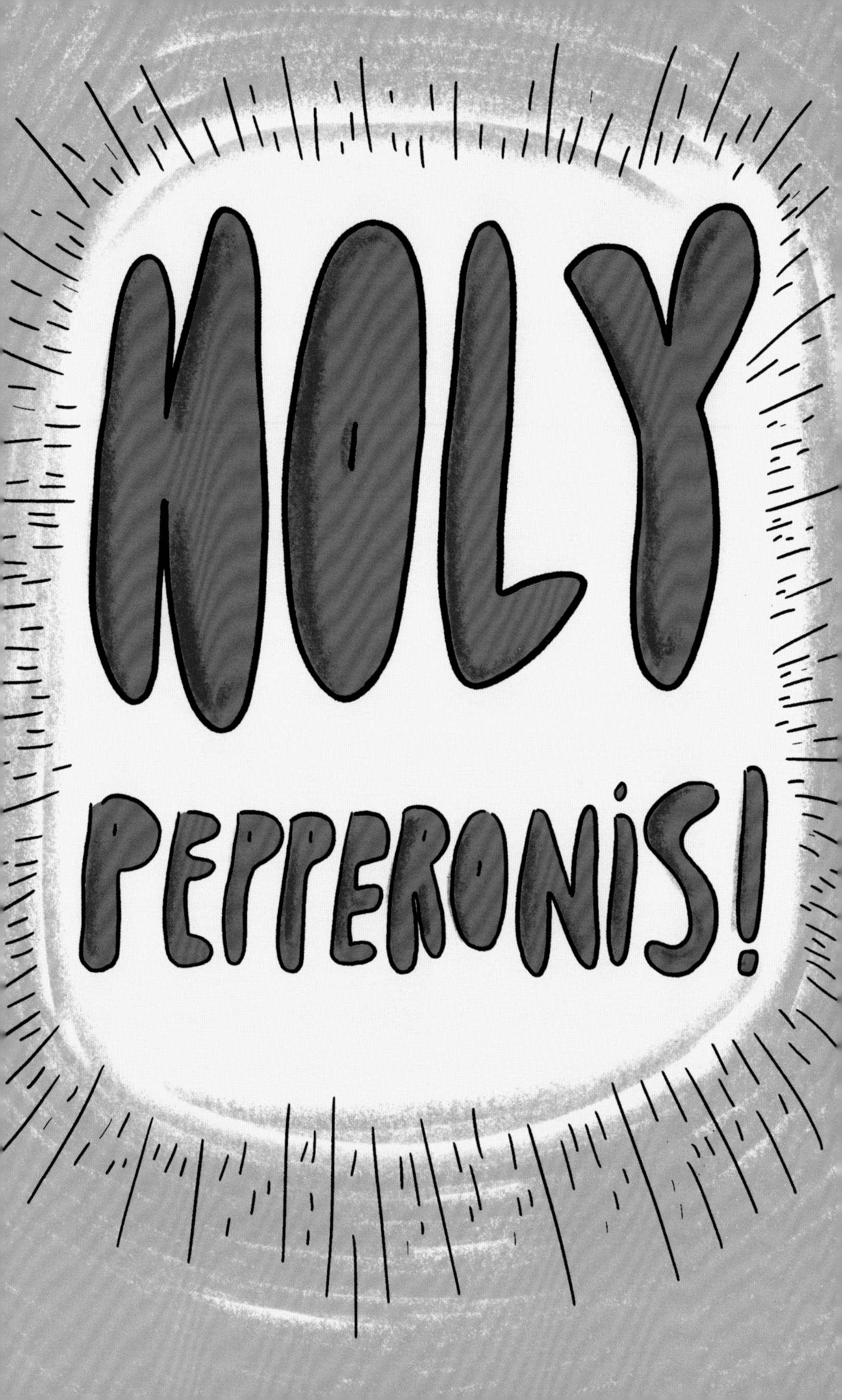
HOLY
PEPPERONIS!

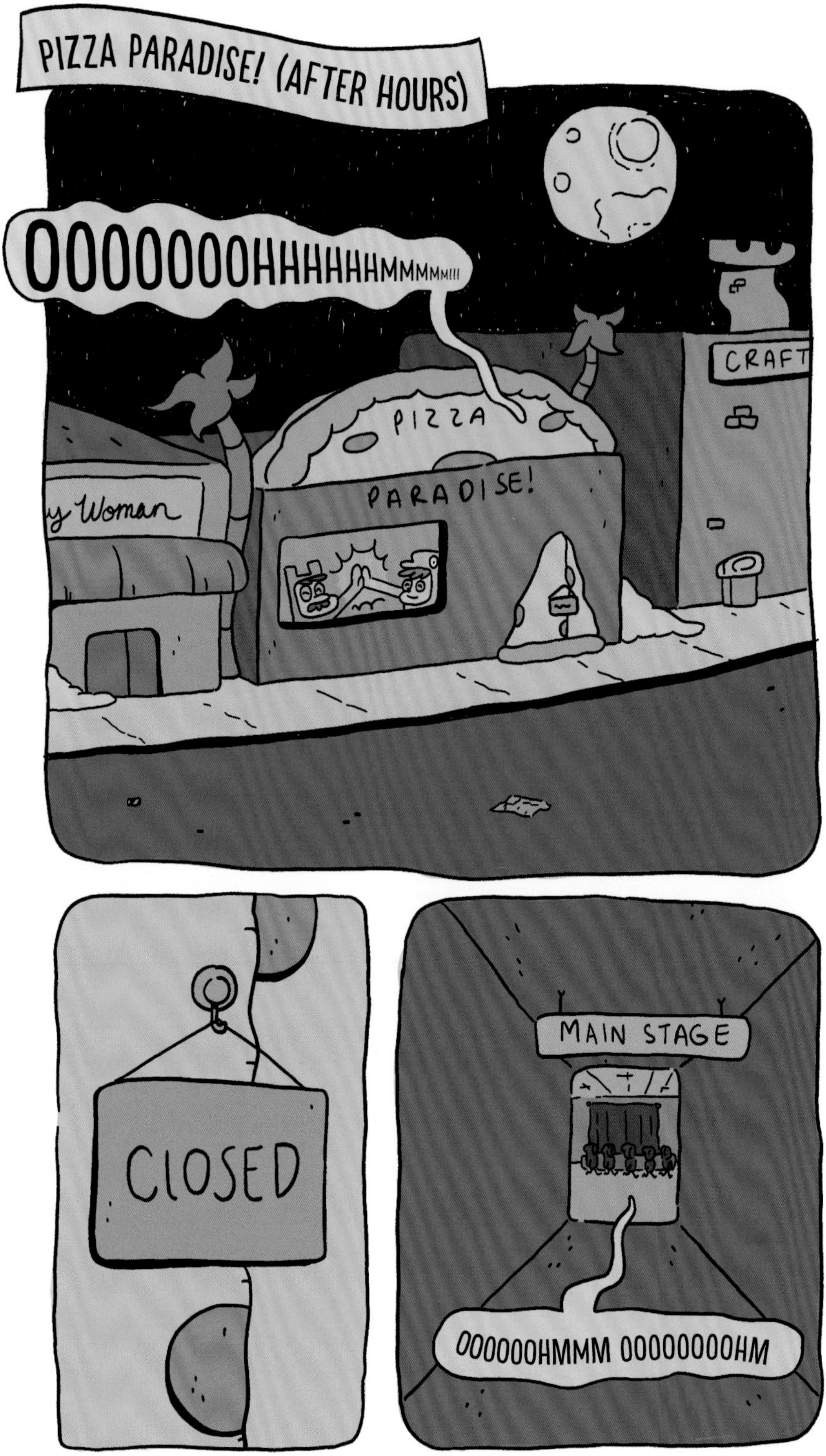
PIZZA PARADISE! (AFTER HOURS)
OOOOOOOHHHHHHMMMMM!!!
PIZZA
PARADISE!
y Woman
CRAFT
CLOSED
MAIN STAGE
OOOOOOHMMM OOOOOOOOHM

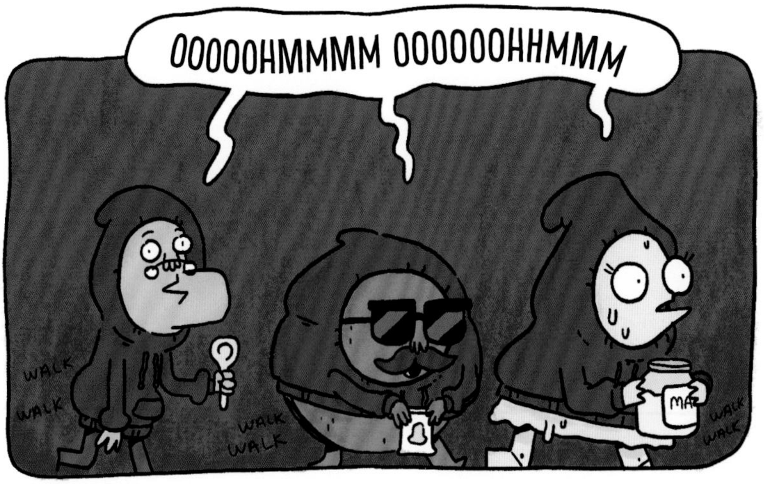
OOOOOHMMMM OOOOOOHHMMM
WALK WALK
WALK WALK
WALK WALK

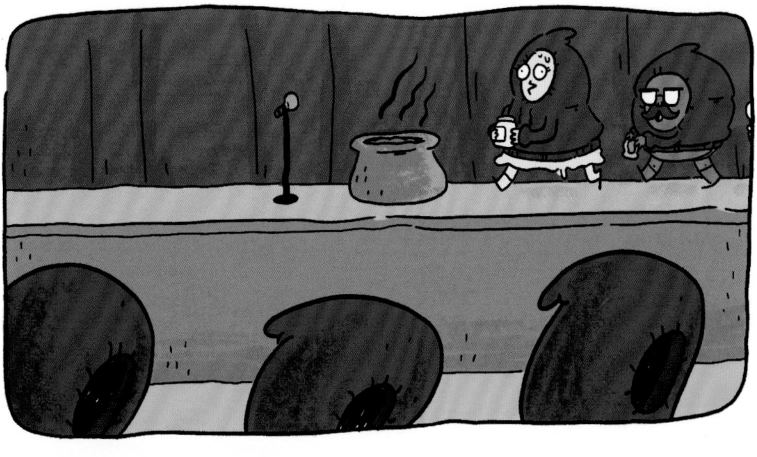

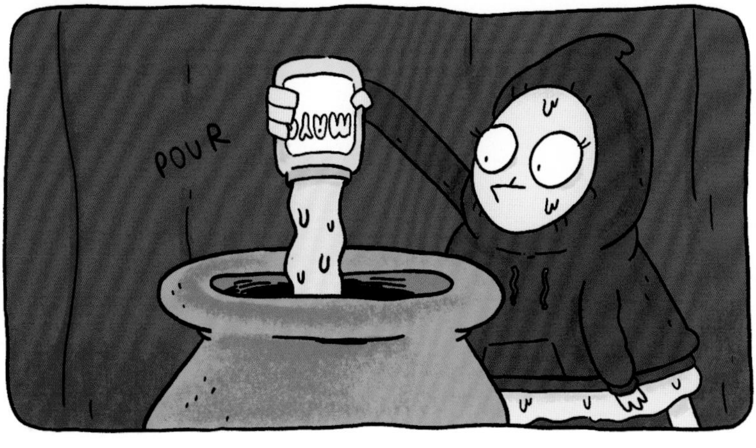
POUR

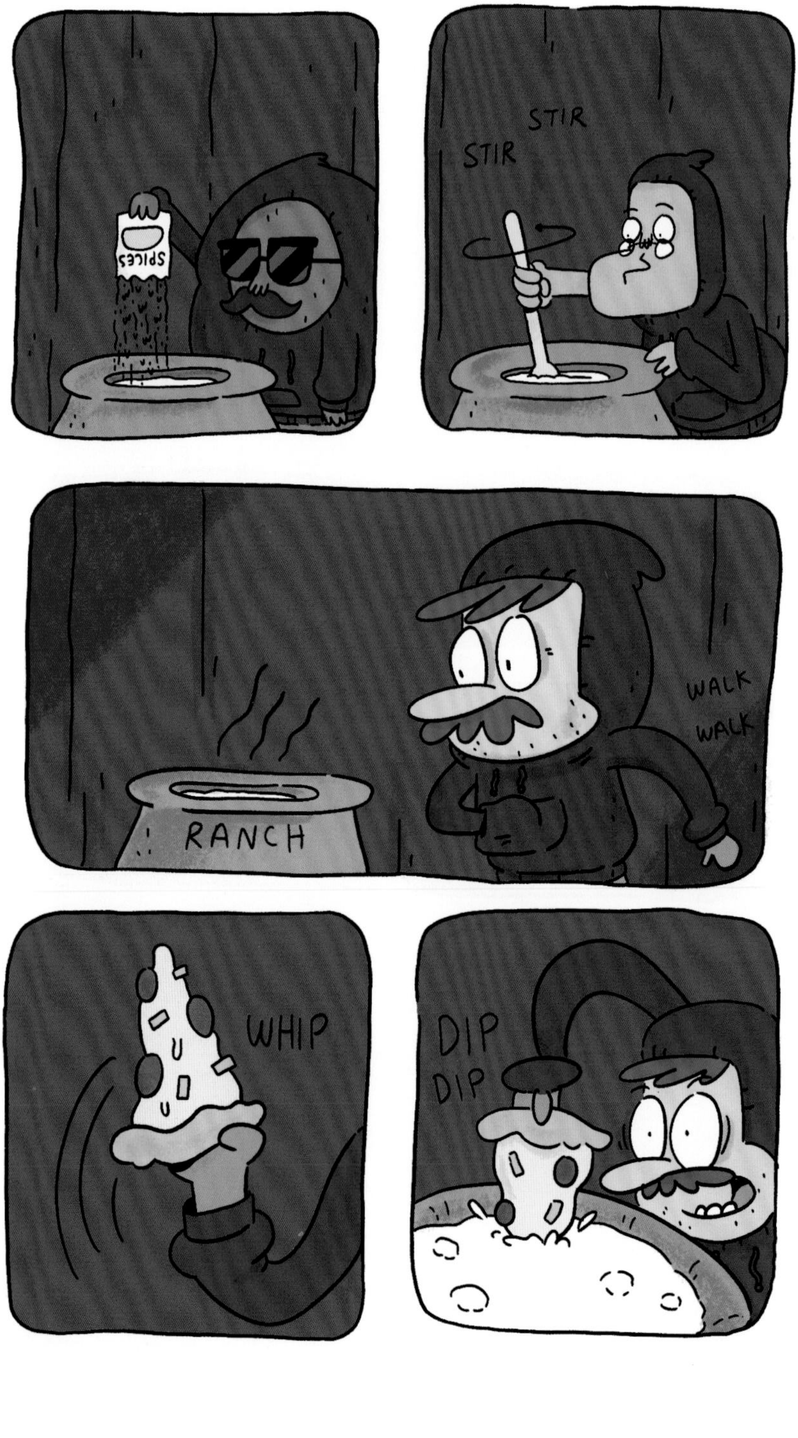
SPICES
STIR
STIR
WALK
WALK
RANCH
WHIP
DIP
DIP

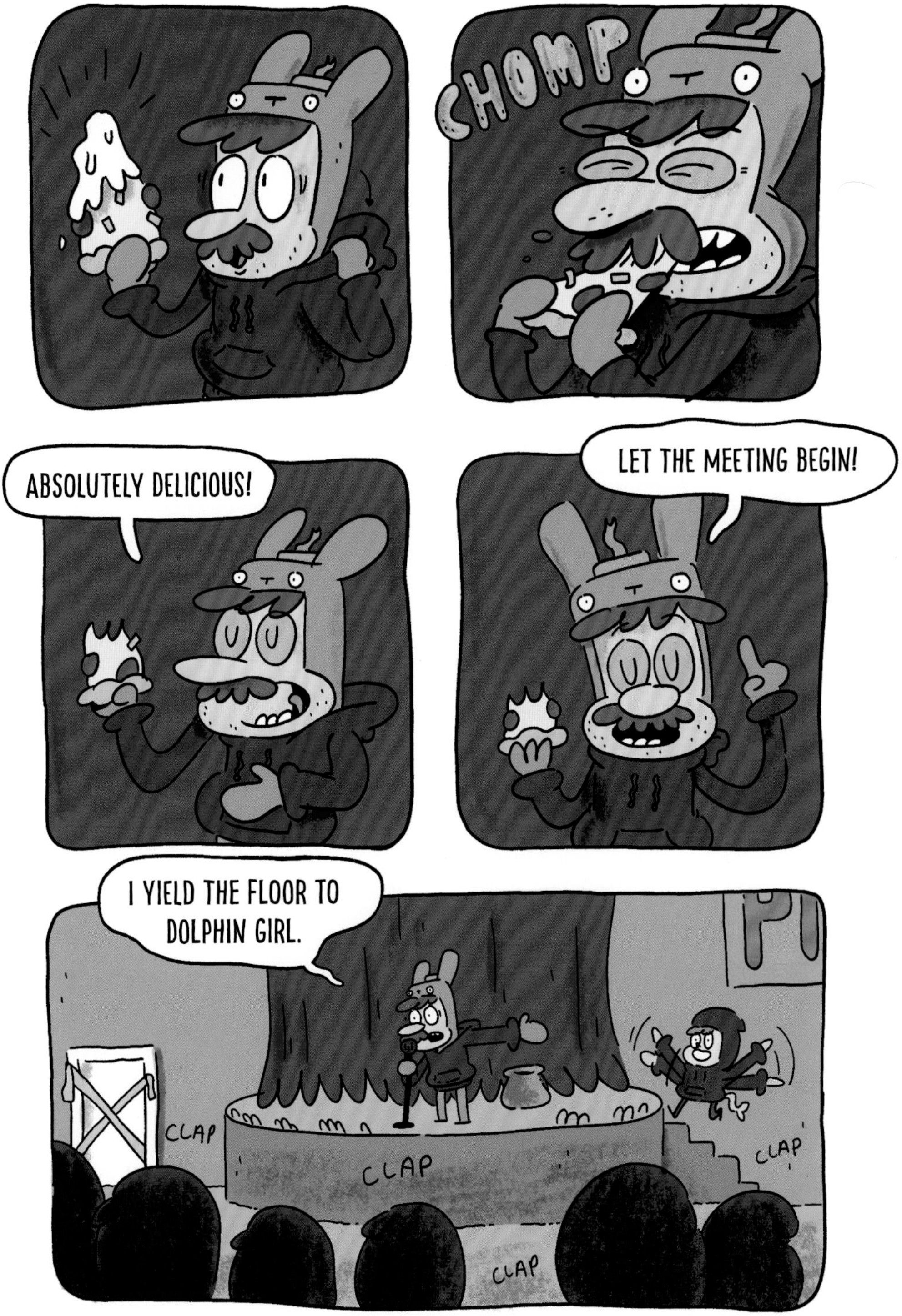
CHOMP
ABSOLUTELY DELICIOUS!
LET THE MEETING BEGIN!
I YIELD THE FLOOR TO DOLPHIN GIRL.
CLAP
CLAP
CLAP
CLAP

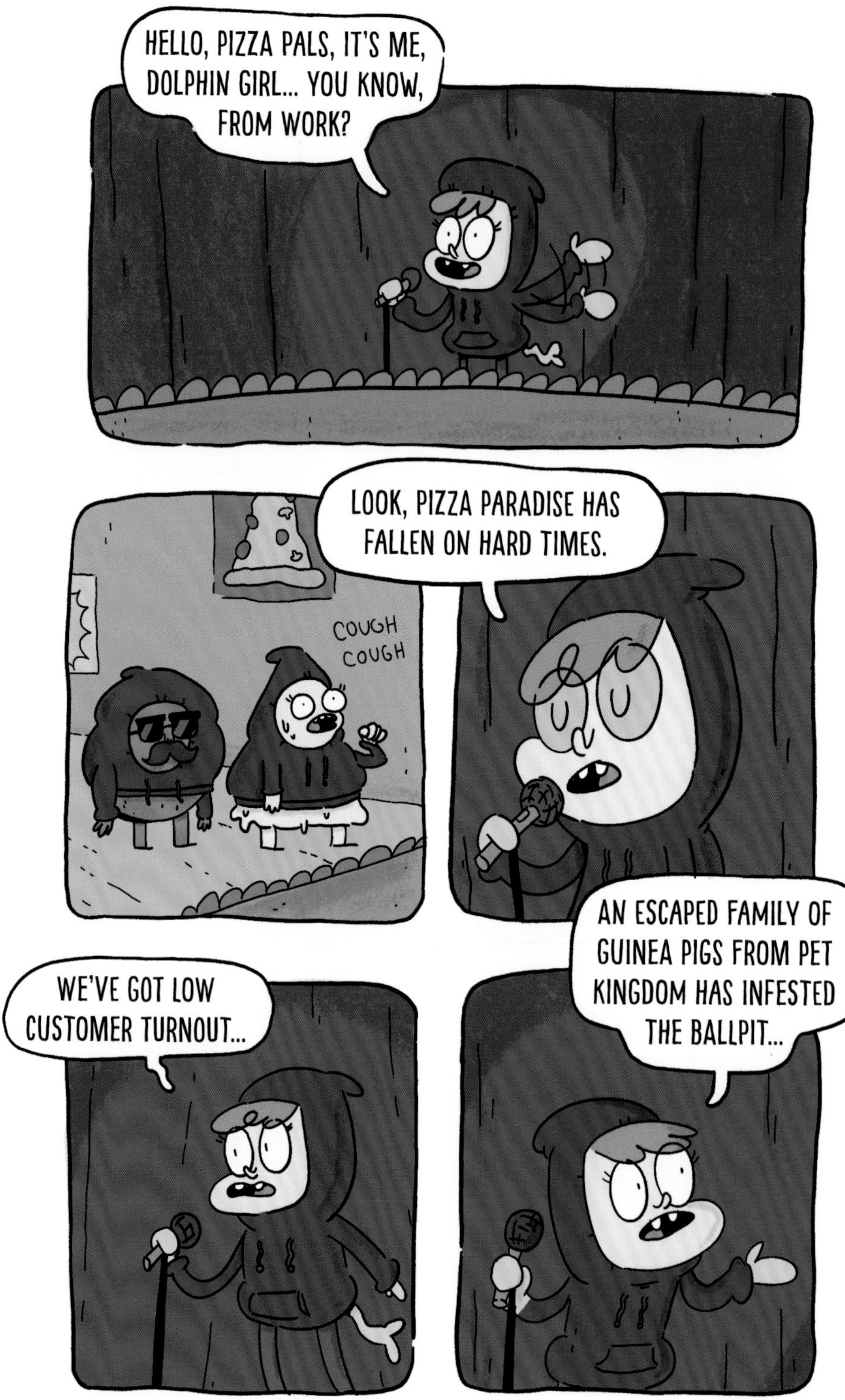
HELLO, PIZZA PALS, IT'S ME, DOLPHIN GIRL... YOU KNOW, FROM WORK?
LOOK, PIZZA PARADISE HAS FALLEN ON HARD TIMES.
COUGH COUGH
WE'VE GOT LOW CUSTOMER TURNOUT...
AN ESCAPED FAMILY OF GUINEA PIGS FROM PET KINGDOM HAS INFESTED THE BALLPIT...

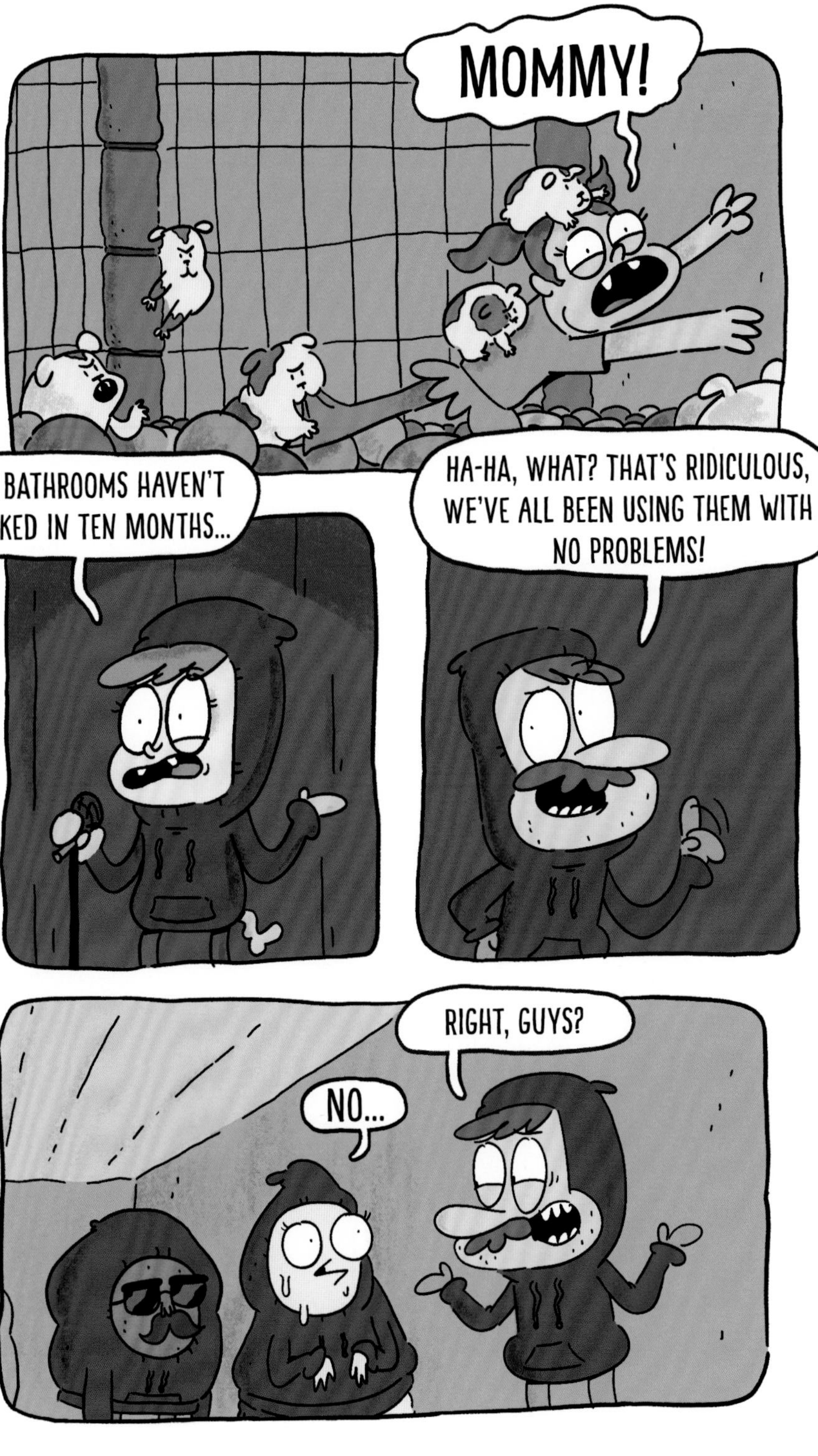
MOMMY!
THE BATHROOMS HAVEN'T WORKED IN TEN MONTHS...
HA-HA, WHAT? THAT'S RIDICULOUS, WE'VE ALL BEEN USING THEM WITH NO PROBLEMS!
RIGHT, GUYS?
NO...

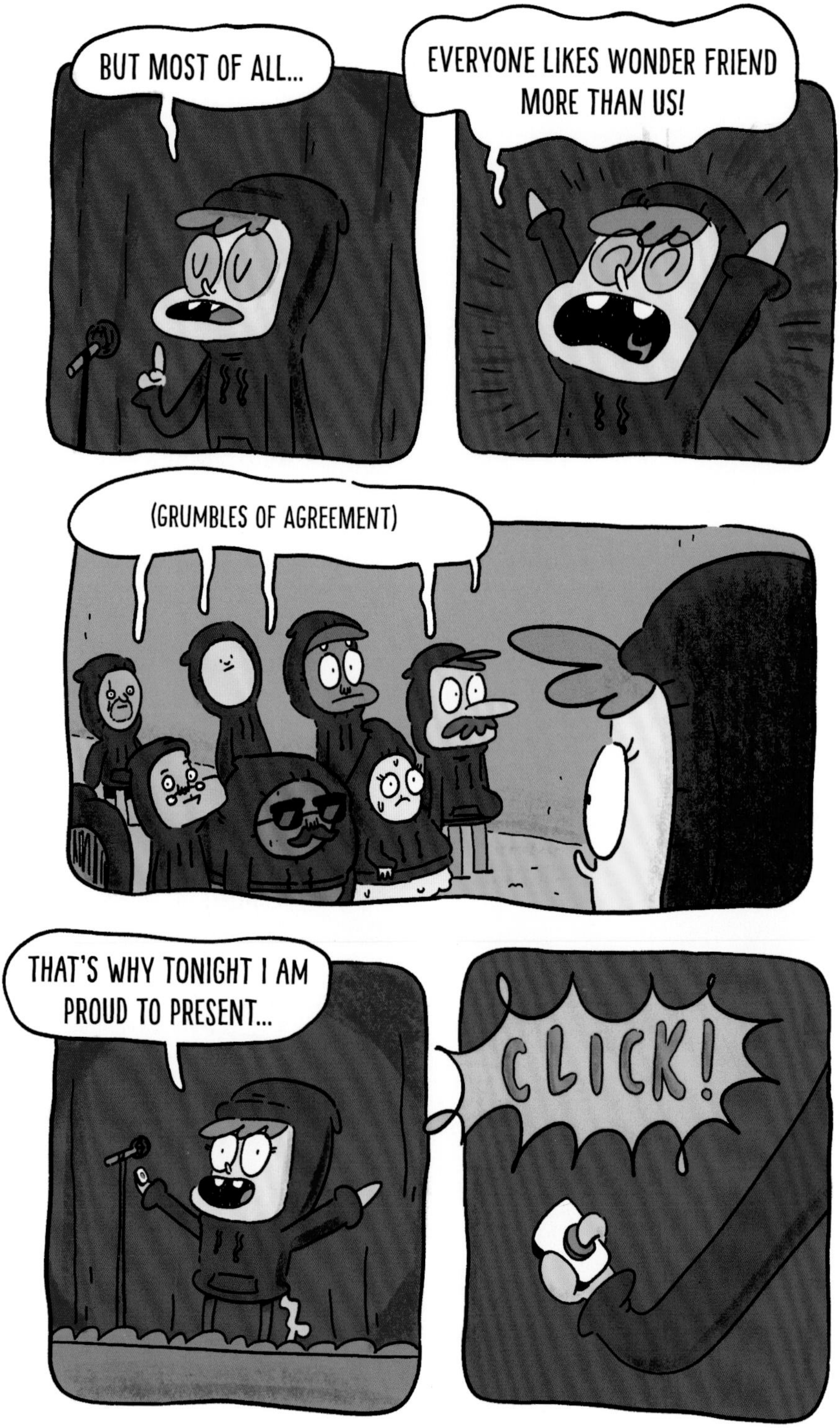

BUT MOST OF ALL...
EVERYONE LIKES WONDER FRIEND MORE THAN US!
(GRUMBLES OF AGREEMENT)
THAT'S WHY TONIGHT I AM PROUD TO PRESENT...
CLICK!

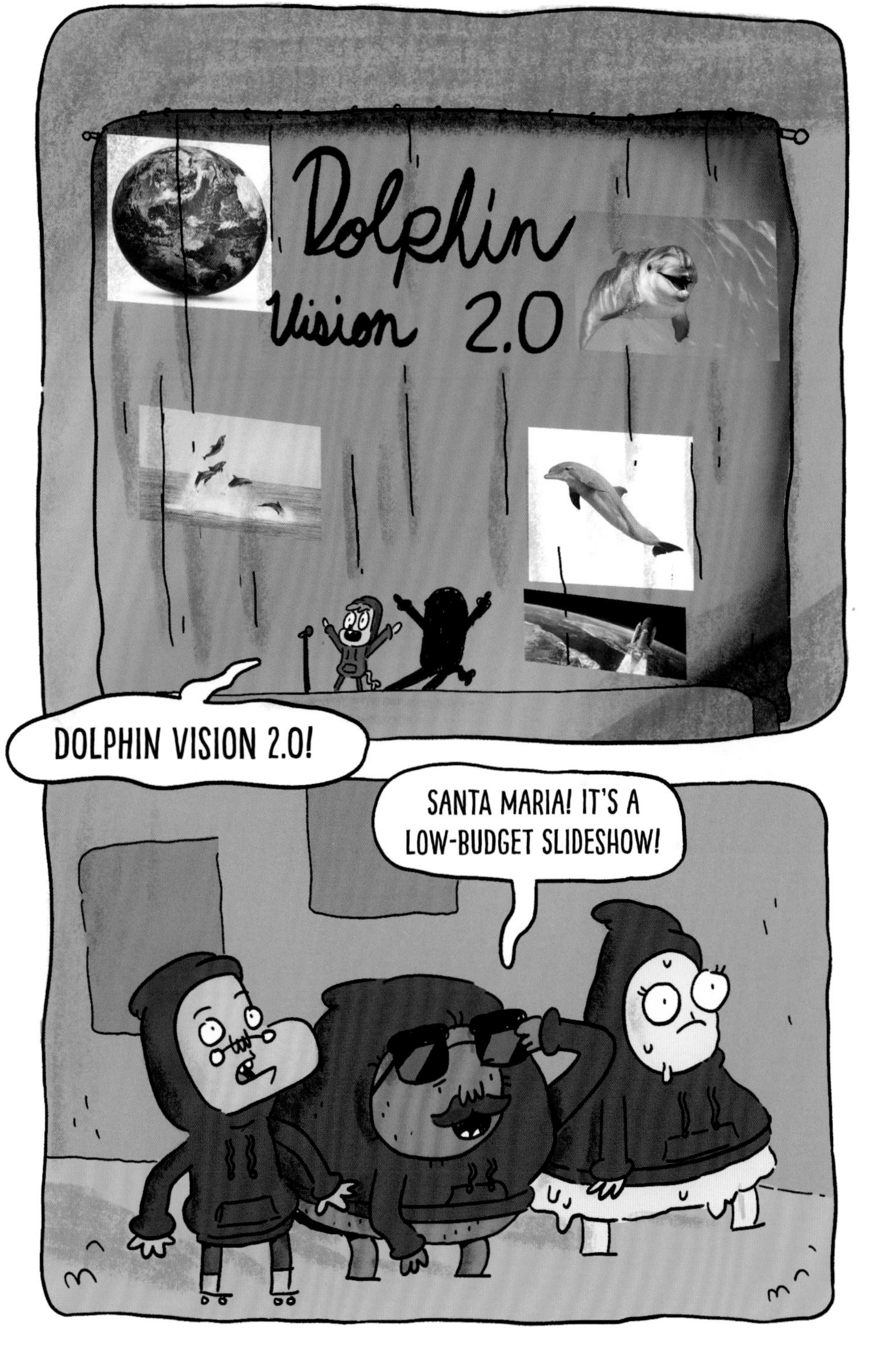
Dolphin Vision 2.0
DOLPHIN VISION 2.0!
SANTA MARIA! IT'S A LOW-BUDGET SLIDESHOW!

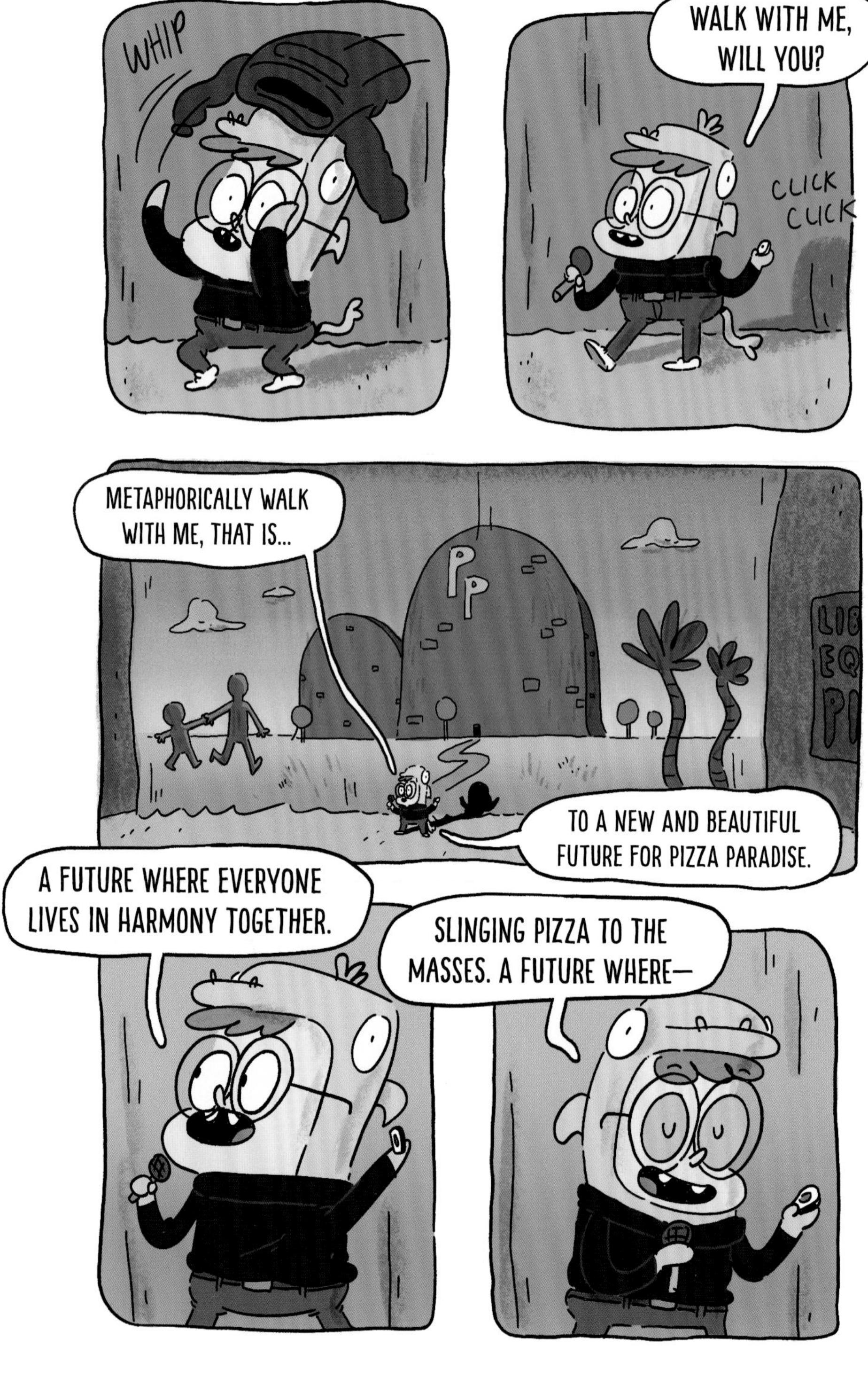
WHIP
WALK WITH ME, WILL YOU?
CLICK CLICK
METAPHORICALLY WALK WITH ME, THAT IS...
PP
TO A NEW AND BEAUTIFUL FUTURE FOR PIZZA PARADISE.
A FUTURE WHERE EVERYONE LIVES IN HARMONY TOGETHER.
SLINGING PIZZA TO THE MASSES. A FUTURE WHERE—

UH, LET'S CUT TO THE CHASE! HOW ARE YOU GONNA FIX PIZZA PARADISE, BABY?

THANKS FOR THE QUESTION, TONY THE PEPPERONI!

AS MENTIONED IN THE EMAIL, I WILL BE ANSWERING QUESTIONS AT THE END OF THE PRESENTATION.

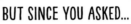

BUT SINCE YOU ASKED...

WE'RE ALL GOING TO HAVE TO CHANGE.

BIG TIME!

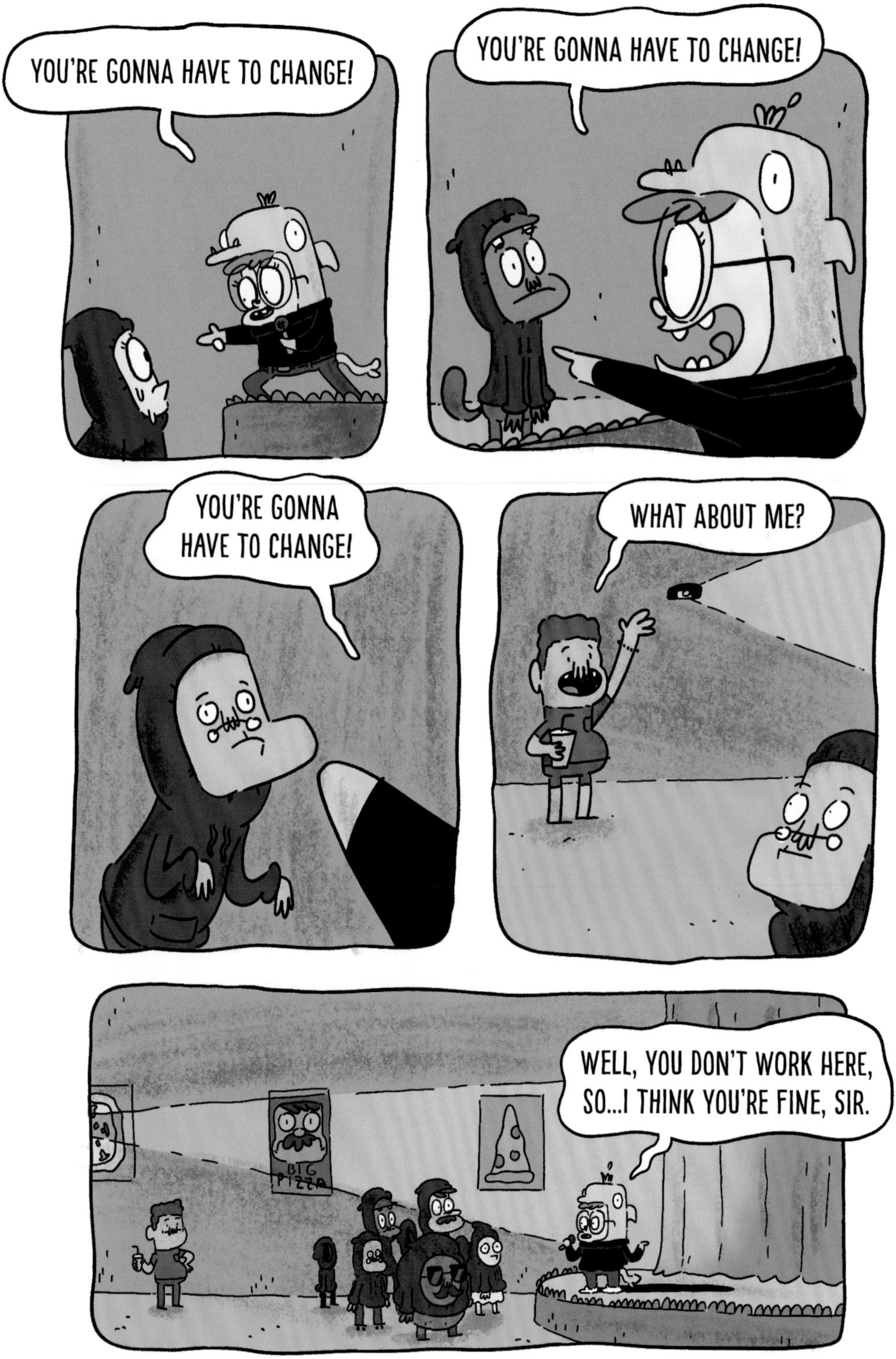
YOU'RE GONNA HAVE TO CHANGE!
YOU'RE GONNA HAVE TO CHANGE!
YOU'RE GONNA HAVE TO CHANGE!
WHAT ABOUT ME?
BIG PIZZA
WELL, YOU DON'T WORK HERE, SO...I THINK YOU'RE FINE, SIR.

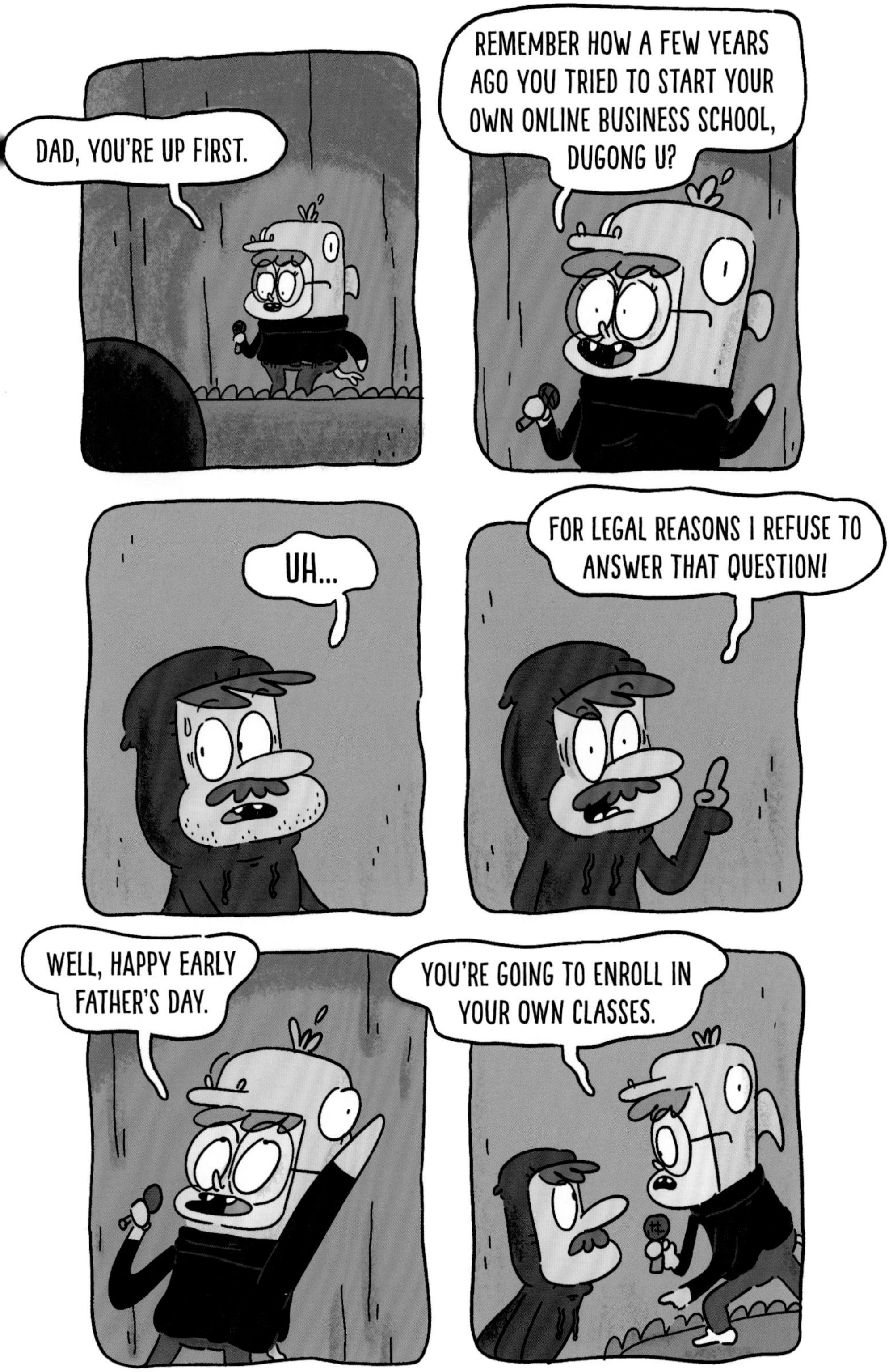
DAD, YOU'RE UP FIRST.
REMEMBER HOW A FEW YEARS AGO YOU TRIED TO START YOUR OWN ONLINE BUSINESS SCHOOL, DUGONG U?
UH...
FOR LEGAL REASONS I REFUSE TO ANSWER THAT QUESTION!
WELL, HAPPY EARLY FATHER'S DAY.
YOU'RE GOING TO ENROLL IN YOUR OWN CLASSES.

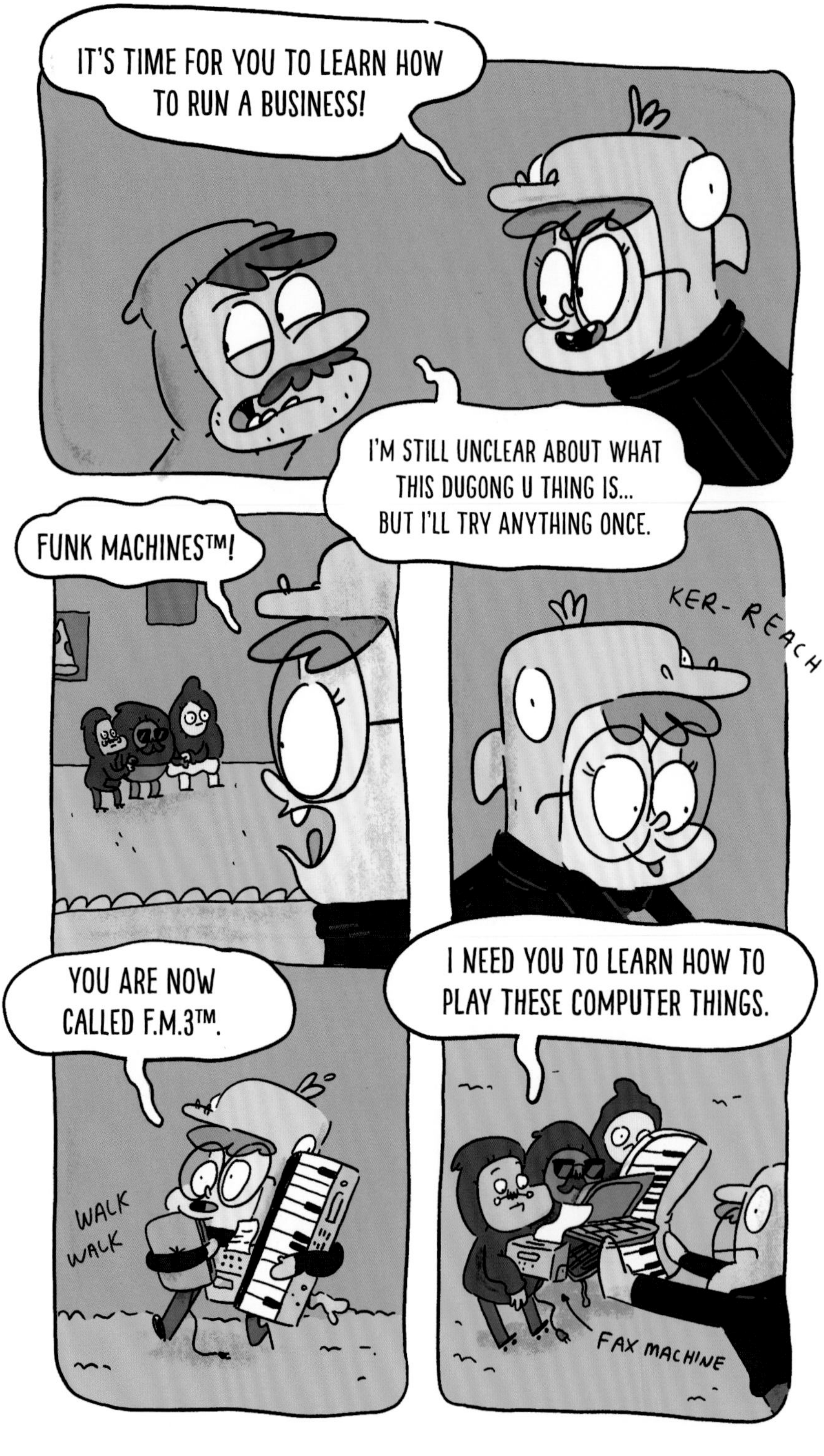
IT'S TIME FOR YOU TO LEARN HOW TO RUN A BUSINESS!
I'M STILL UNCLEAR ABOUT WHAT THIS DUGONG U THING IS... BUT I'LL TRY ANYTHING ONCE.
FUNK MACHINES™!
KER-REACH
YOU ARE NOW CALLED F.M.3™.
WALK WALK
I NEED YOU TO LEARN HOW TO PLAY THESE COMPUTER THINGS.
FAX MACHINE

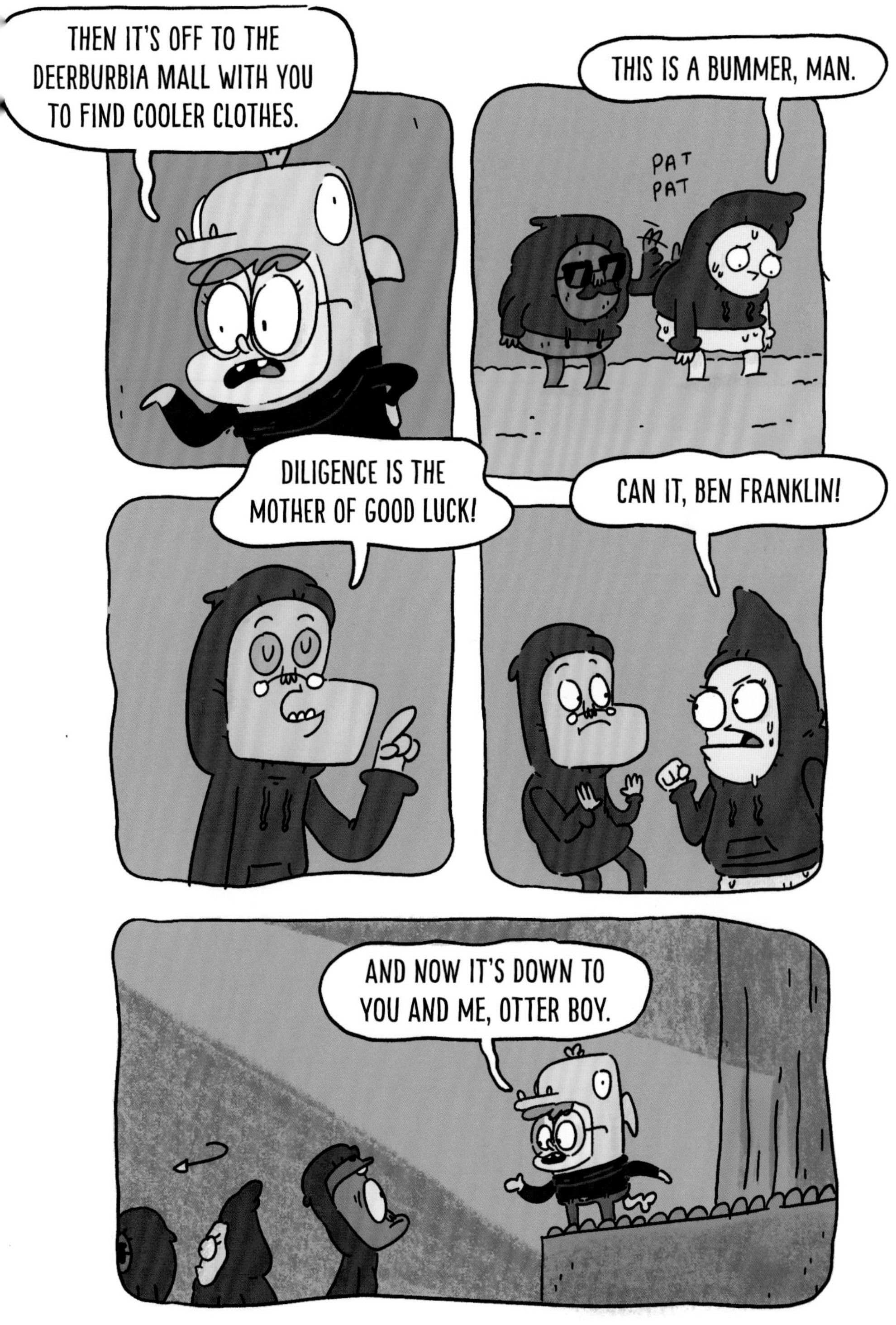
THEN IT'S OFF TO THE DEERBURBIA MALL WITH YOU TO FIND COOLER CLOTHES.
THIS IS A BUMMER, MAN.
PAT PAT
DILIGENCE IS THE MOTHER OF GOOD LUCK!
CAN IT, BEN FRANKLIN!
AND NOW IT'S DOWN TO YOU AND ME, OTTER BOY.

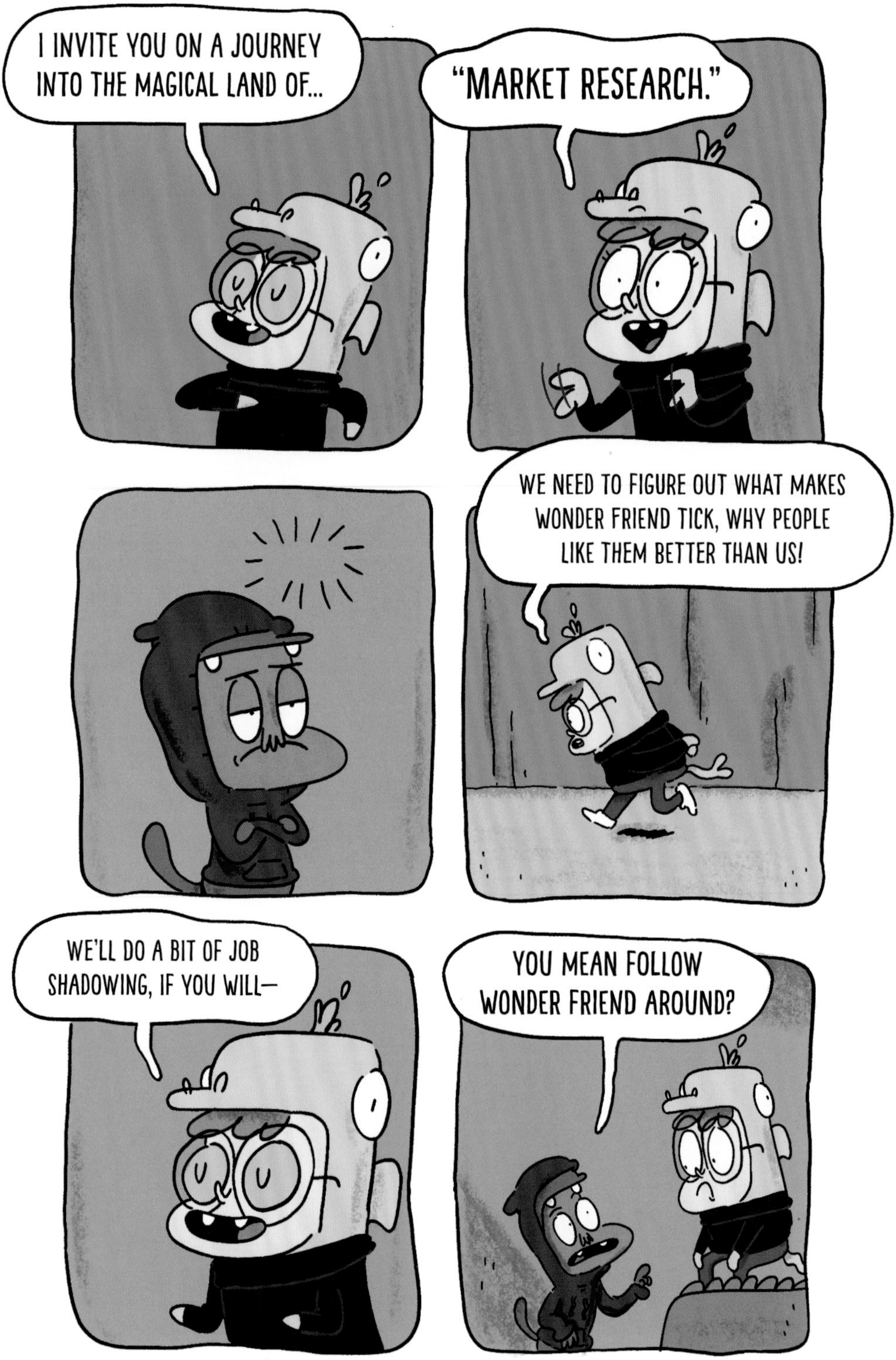
I INVITE YOU ON A JOURNEY INTO THE MAGICAL LAND OF...
"MARKET RESEARCH."
WE NEED TO FIGURE OUT WHAT MAKES WONDER FRIEND TICK, WHY PEOPLE LIKE THEM BETTER THAN US!
WE'LL DO A BIT OF JOB SHADOWING, IF YOU WILL—
YOU MEAN FOLLOW WONDER FRIEND AROUND?

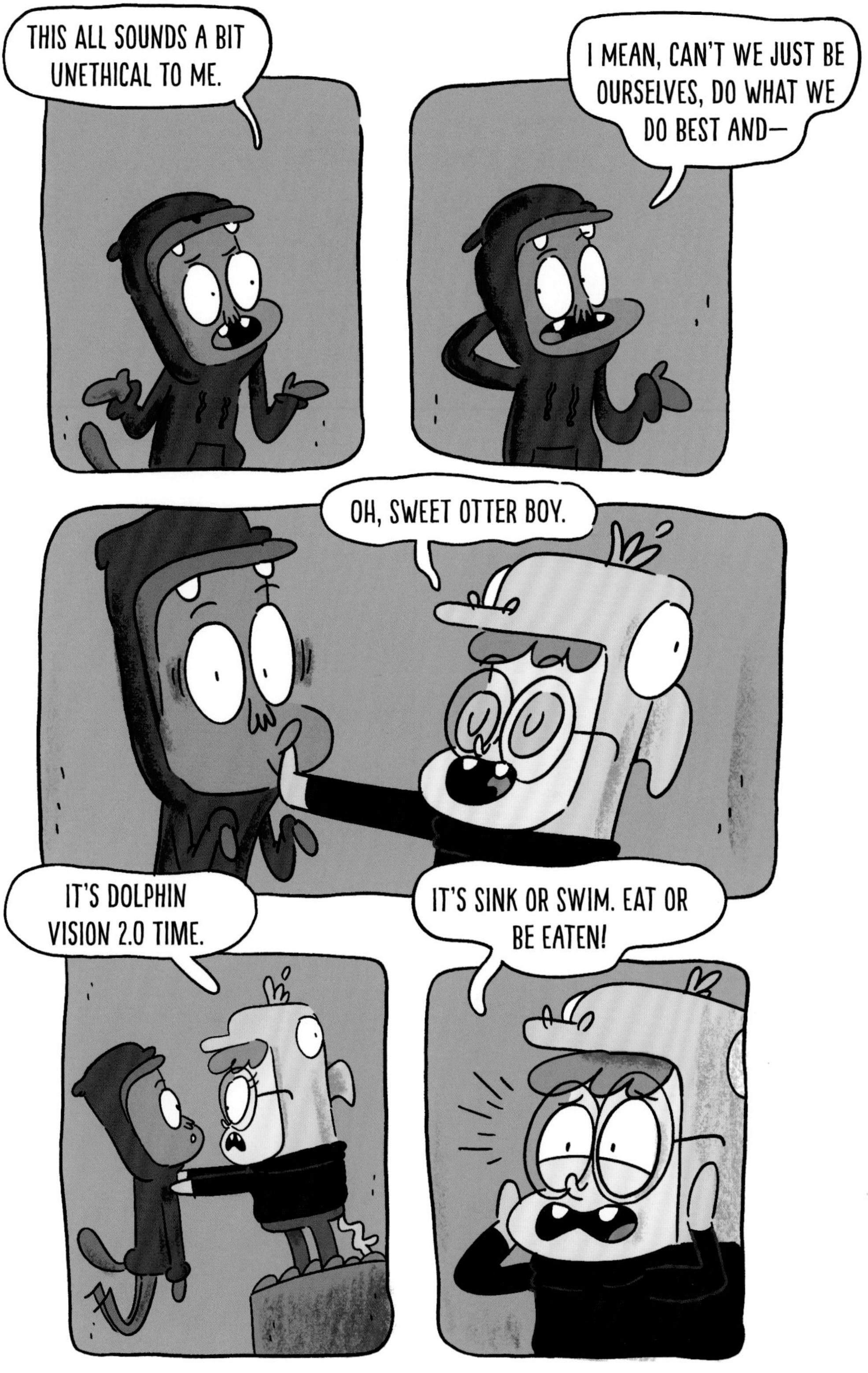
THIS ALL SOUNDS A BIT UNETHICAL TO ME.
I MEAN, CAN'T WE JUST BE OURSELVES, DO WHAT WE DO BEST AND—
OH, SWEET OTTER BOY.
IT'S DOLPHIN VISION 2.0 TIME.
IT'S SINK OR SWIM. EAT OR BE EATEN!

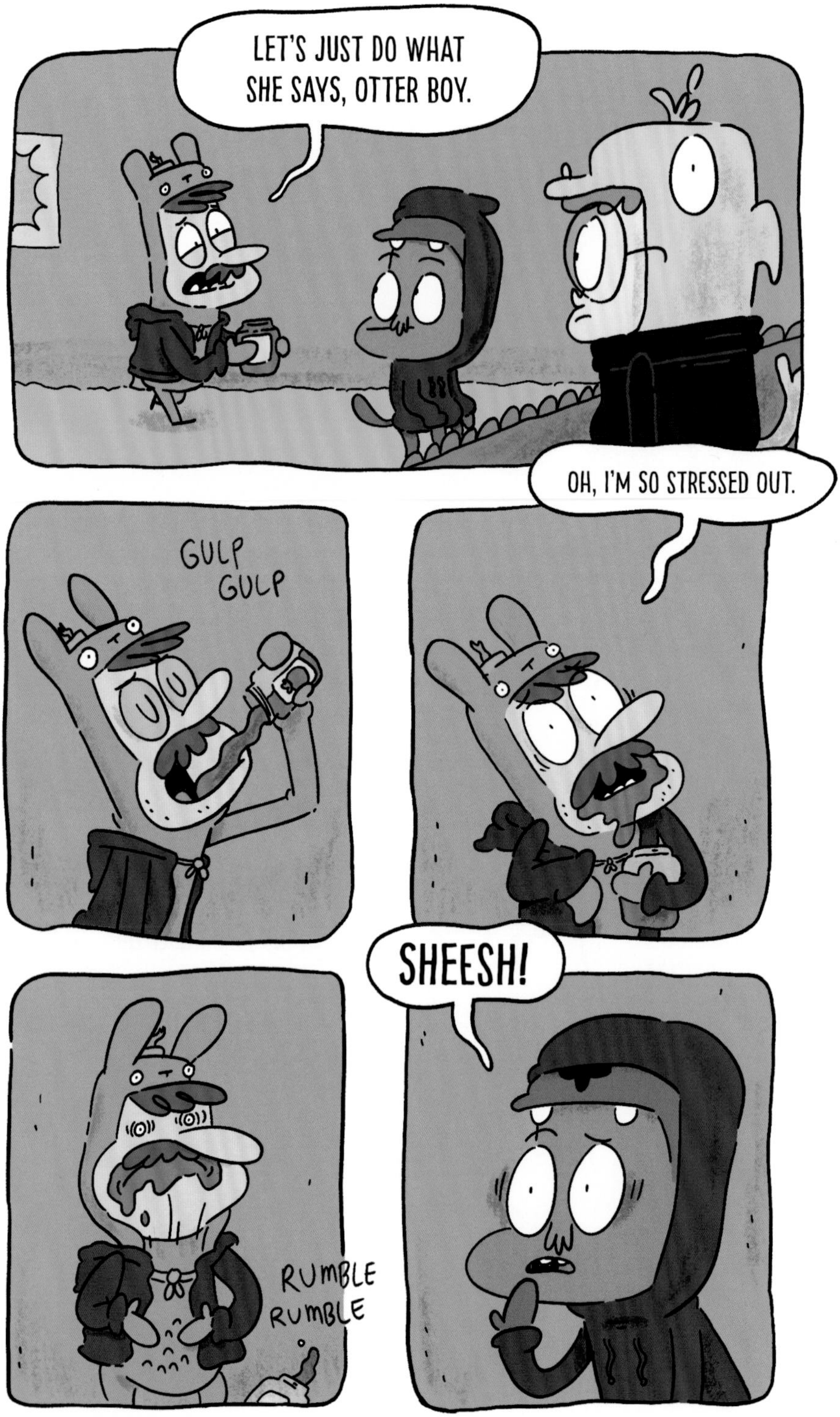
LET'S JUST DO WHAT SHE SAYS, OTTER BOY.
OH, I'M SO STRESSED OUT.
GULP GULP
SHEESH!
RUMBLE RUMBLE

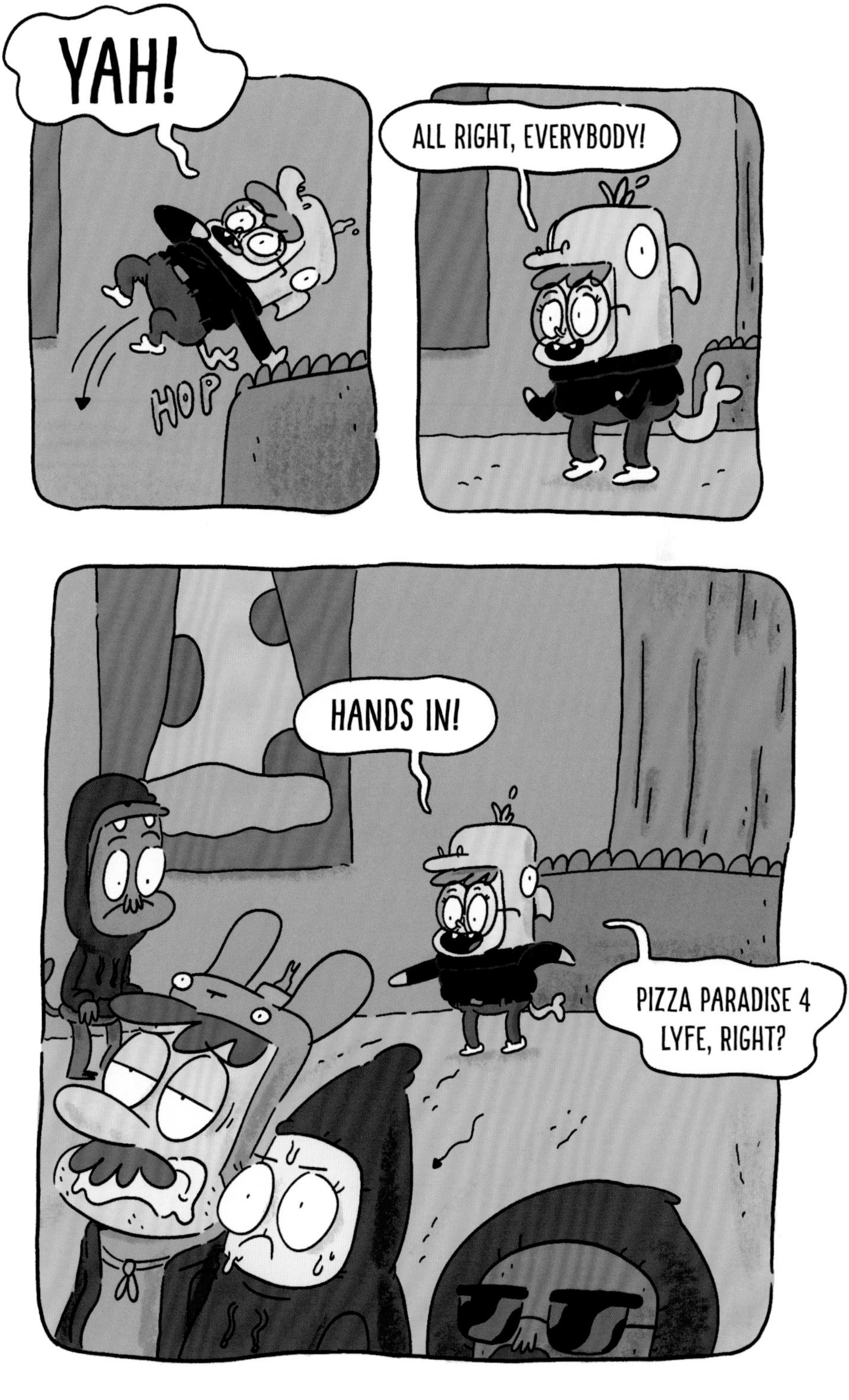
YAH!
HOP
ALL RIGHT, EVERYBODY!
HANDS IN!
PIZZA PARADISE 4 LYFE, RIGHT?

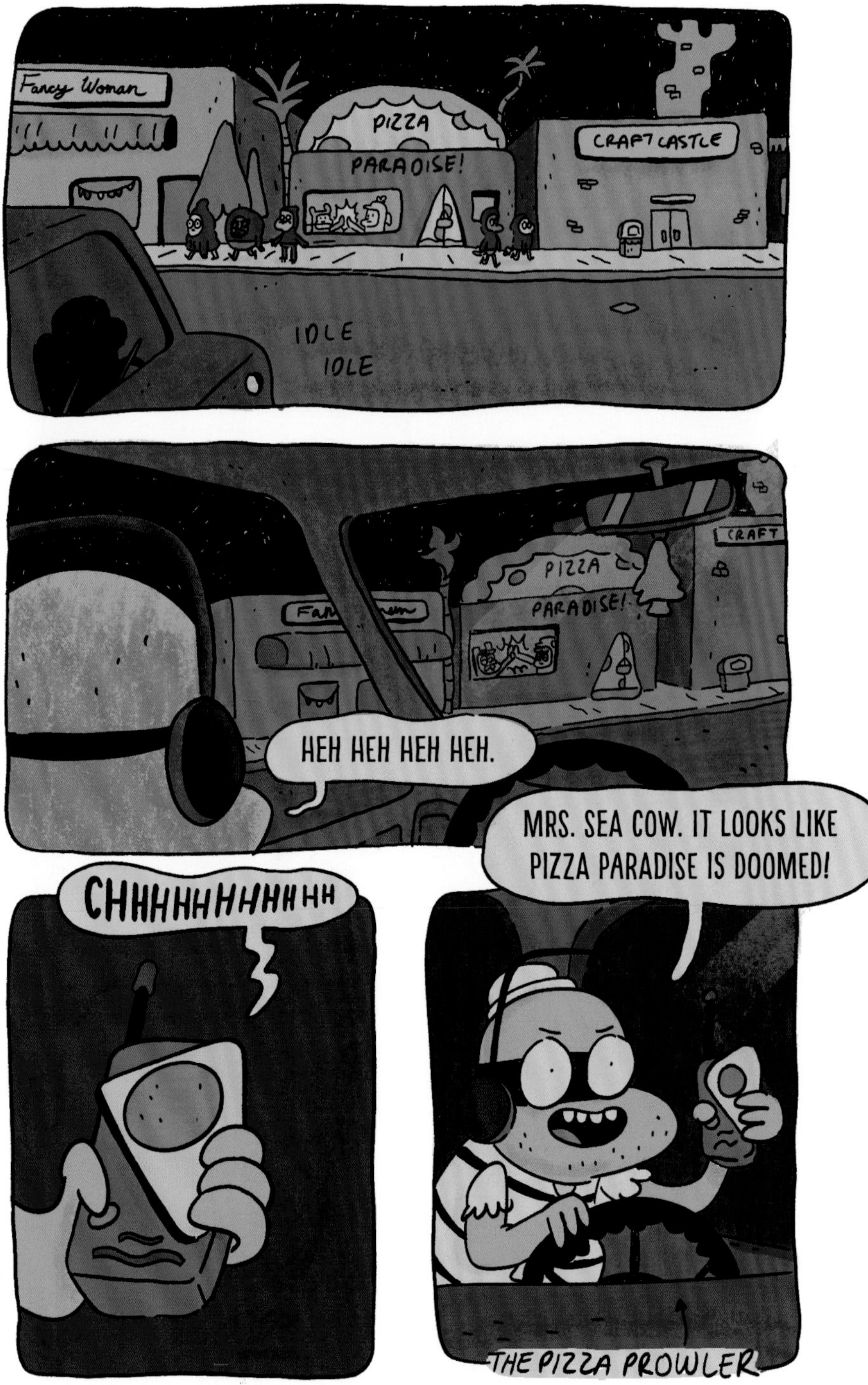
Fancy Woman
PIZZA
PARADISE!
CRAFT CASTLE
IDLE
IDLE
PIZZA
PARADISE!
CRAFT
HEH HEH HEH HEH.
MRS. SEA COW. IT LOOKS LIKE PIZZA PARADISE IS DOOMED!
CHHHHHHHHHHH
THE PIZZA PROWLER

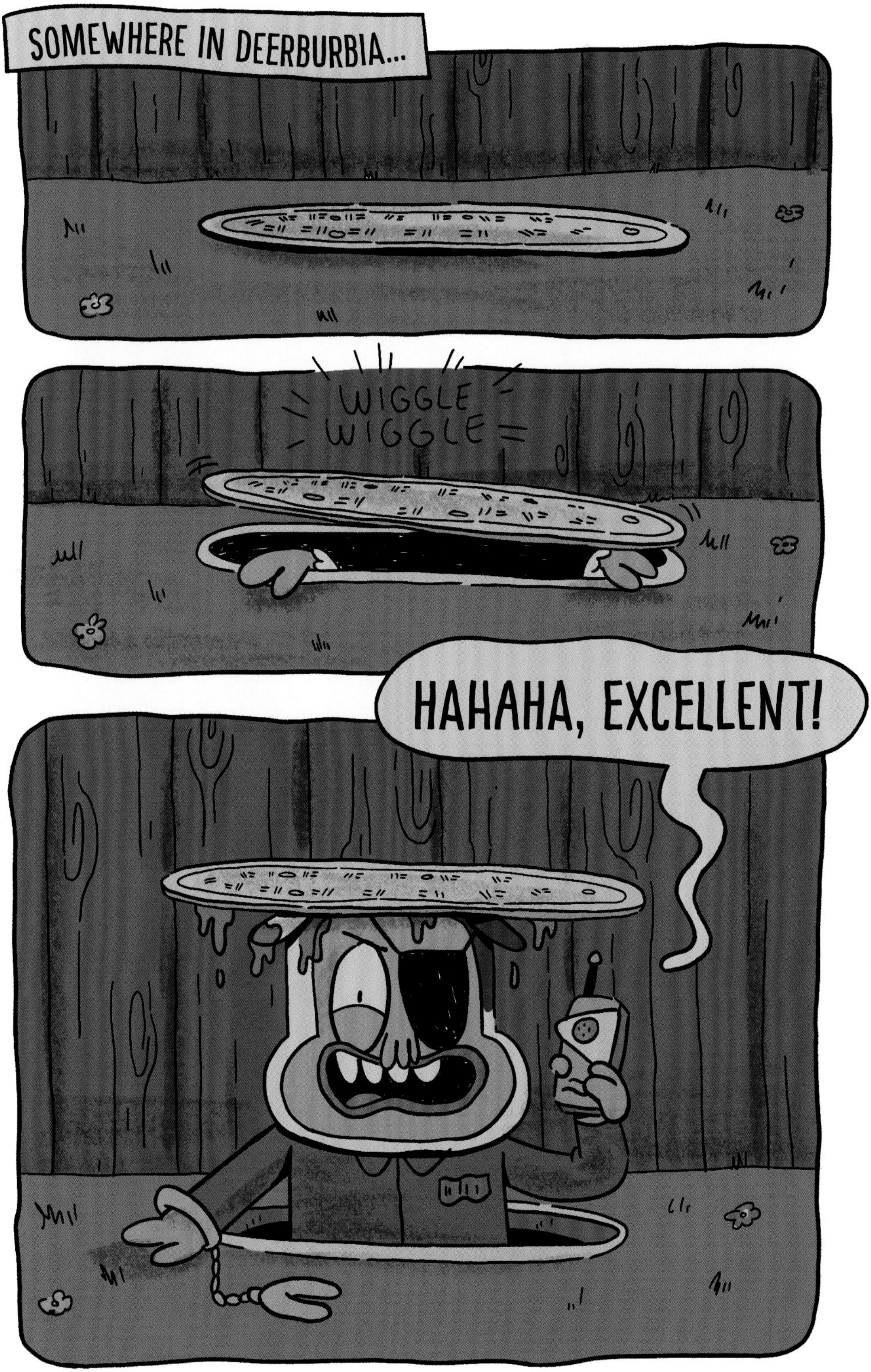
SOMEWHERE IN DEERBURBIA...
WIGGLE
WIGGLE
HAHAHA, EXCELLENT!

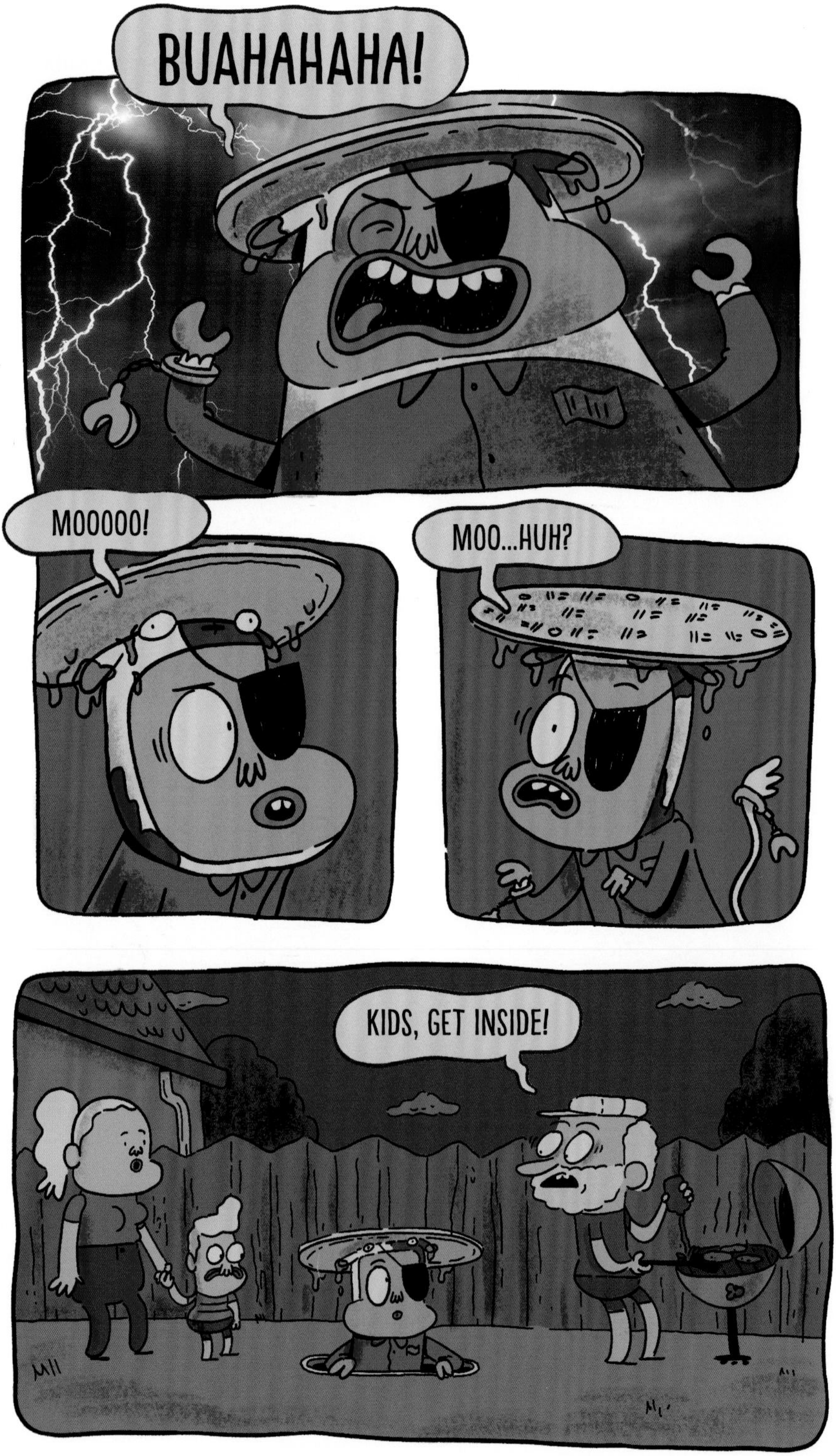
BUAHAHAHA!
MOOOOO!
MOO...HUH?
KIDS, GET INSIDE!

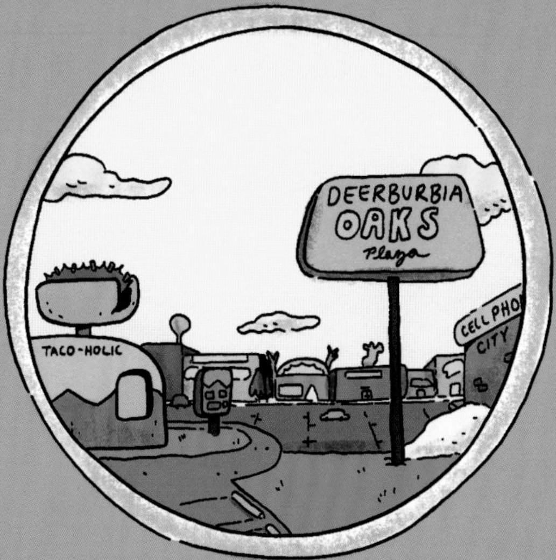
DEERBURBIA
OAKS
Plaza
TACO-HOLIC
CELL PHO
CITY

PART TWO

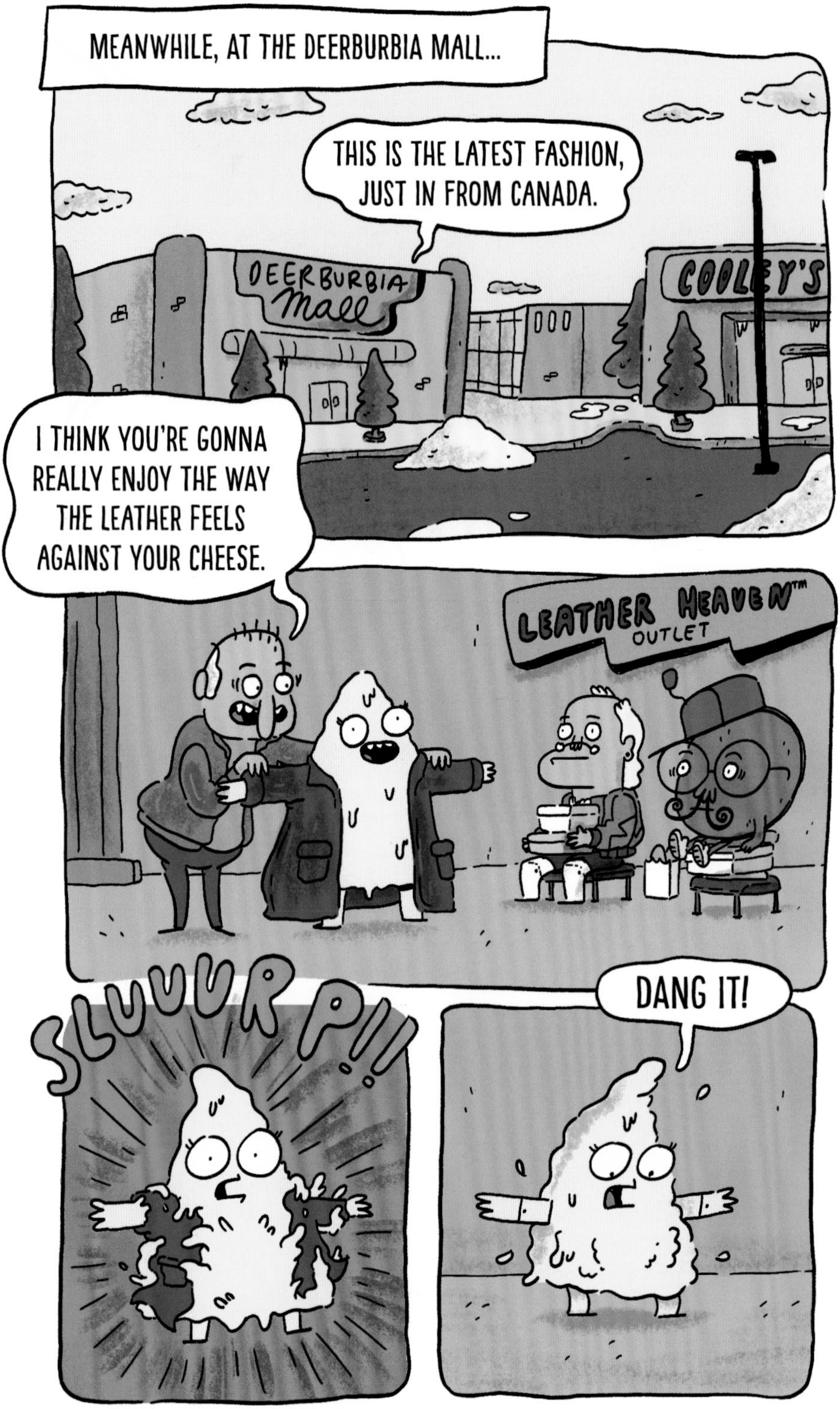
MEANWHILE, AT THE DEERBURBIA MALL...
THIS IS THE LATEST FASHION, JUST IN FROM CANADA.
DEERBURBIA Mall
I THINK YOU'RE GONNA REALLY ENJOY THE WAY THE LEATHER FEELS AGAINST YOUR CHEESE.
LEATHER HEAVEN™ OUTLET
SLUUURP!!
DANG IT!

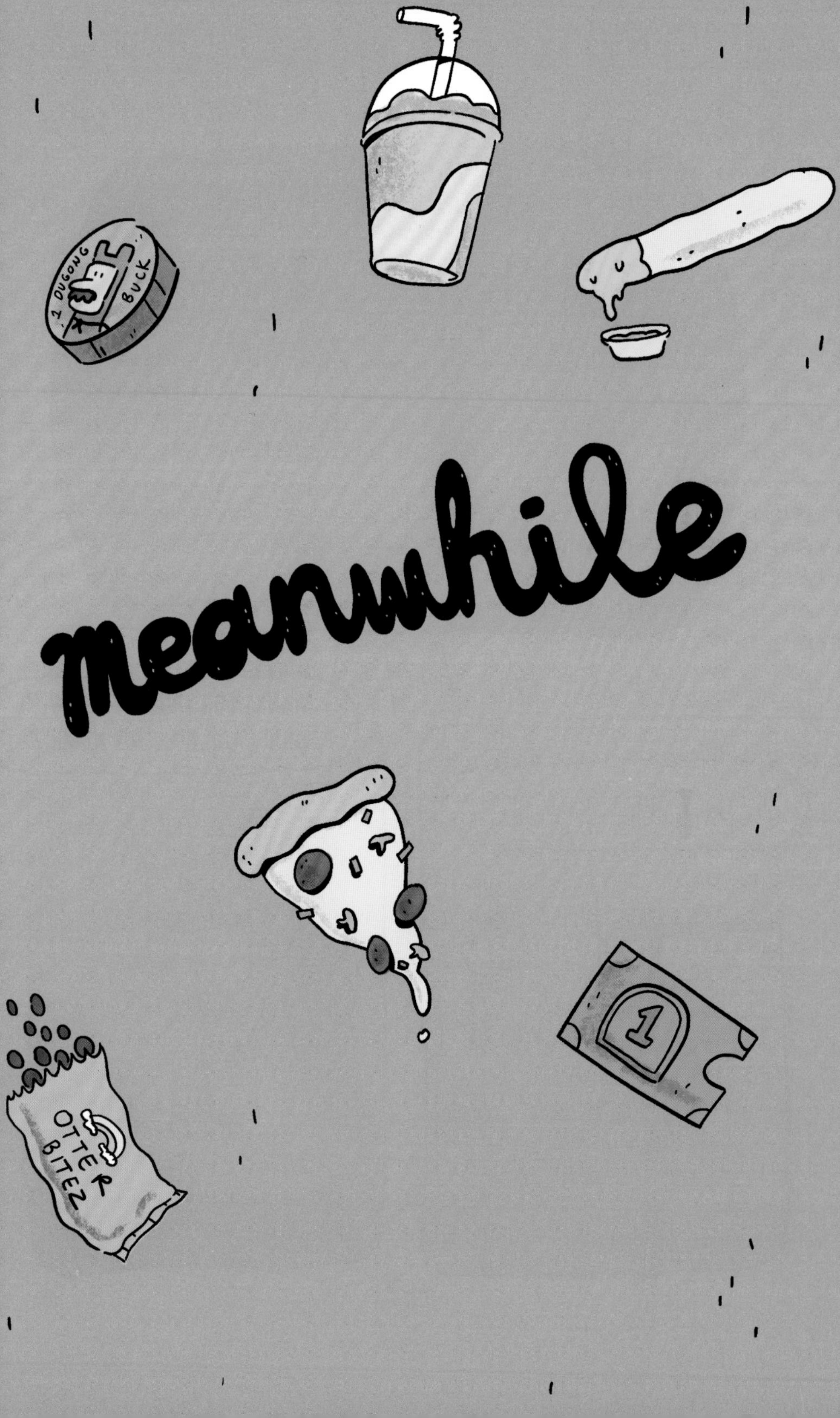
1 DUGONG BUCK
meanwhile
1
OTTER BITEZ

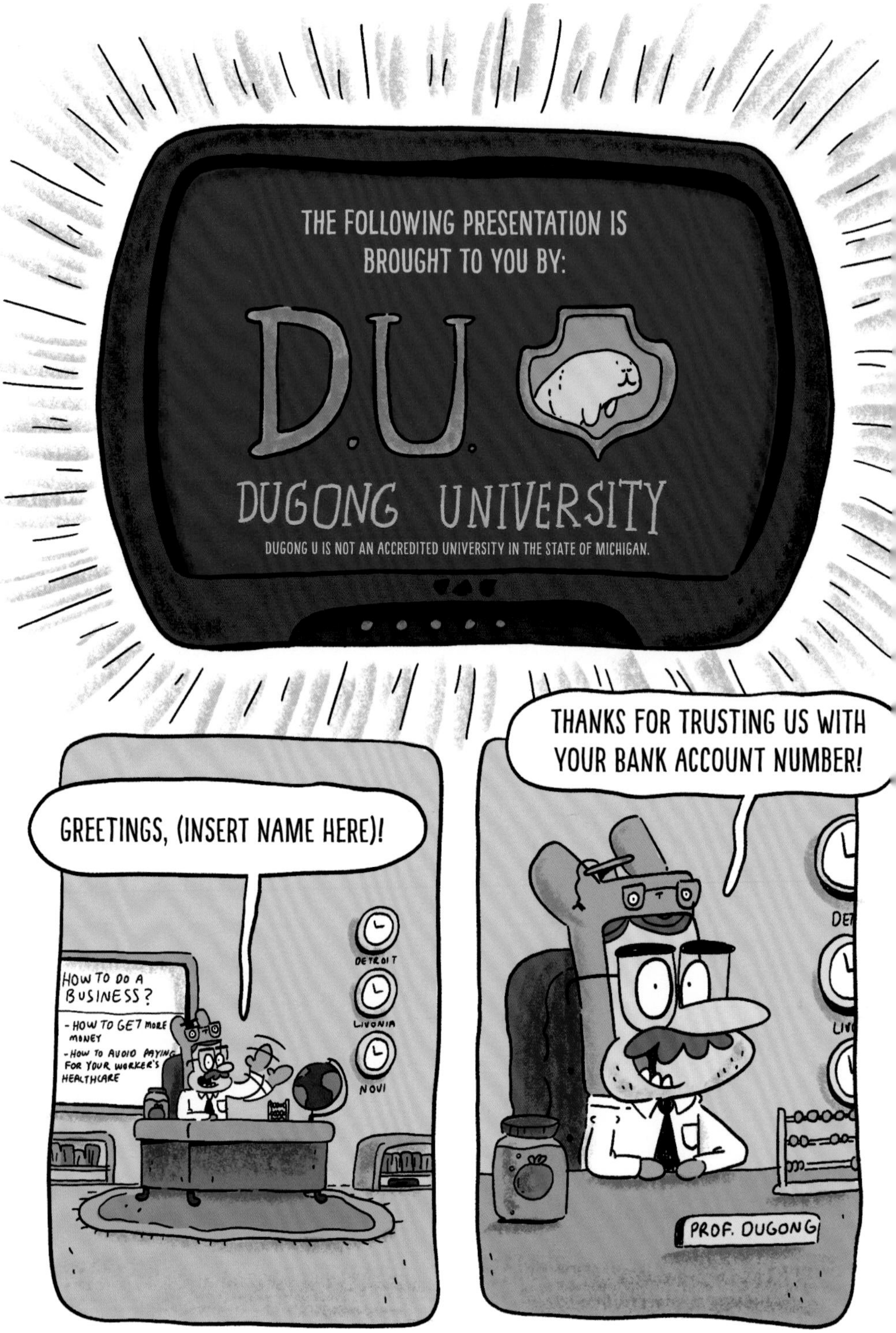
THE FOLLOWING PRESENTATION IS BROUGHT TO YOU BY:
D.U.
DUGONG UNIVERSITY
DUGONG U IS NOT AN ACCREDITED UNIVERSITY IN THE STATE OF MICHIGAN.
GREETINGS, (INSERT NAME HERE)!
HOW TO DO A BUSINESS?
- HOW TO GET MORE MONEY
- HOW TO AVOID PAYING FOR YOUR WORKER'S HEALTHCARE
DETROIT
LIVONIA
NOVI
THANKS FOR TRUSTING US WITH YOUR BANK ACCOUNT NUMBER!
PROF. DUGONG

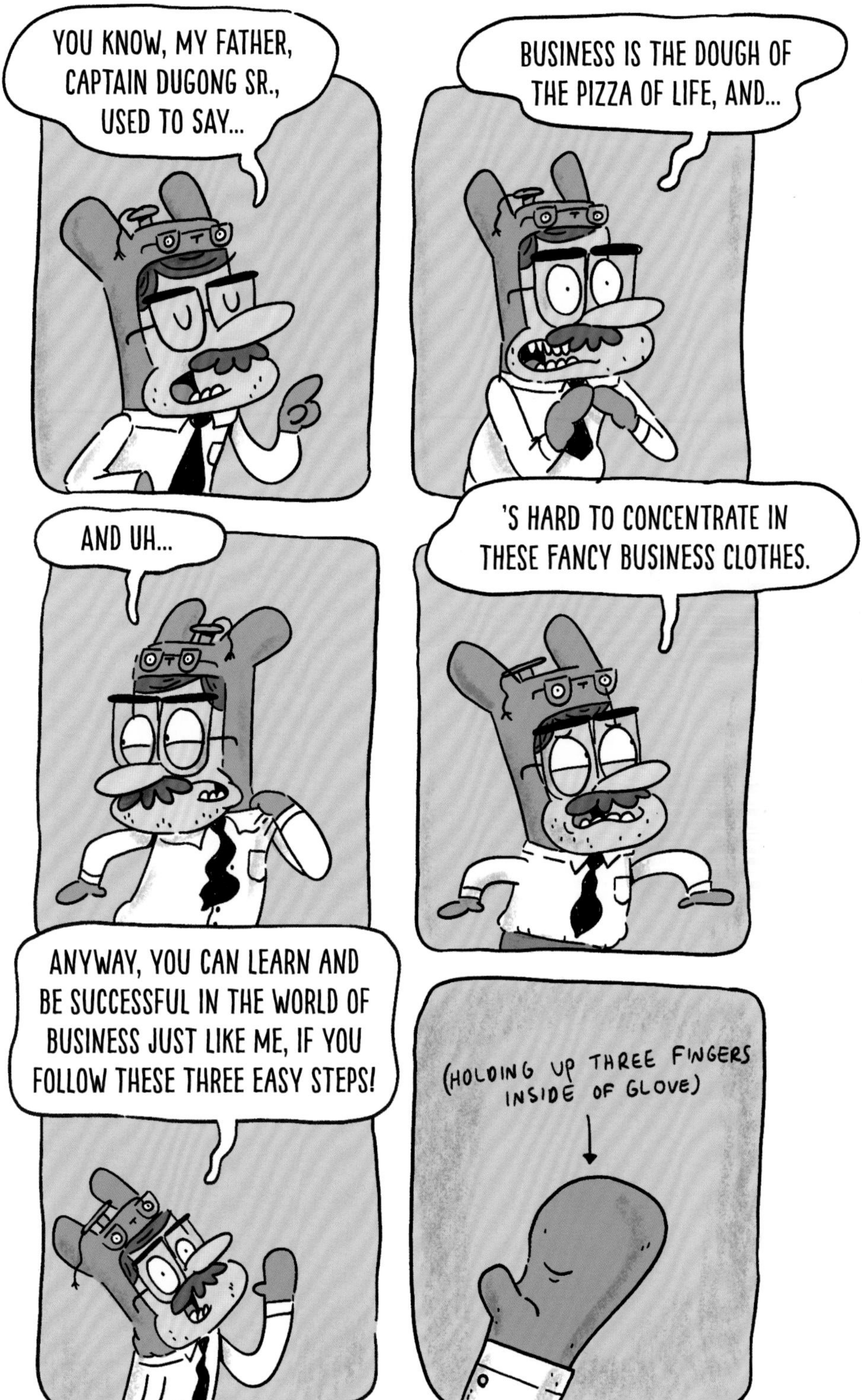
YOU KNOW, MY FATHER, CAPTAIN DUGONG SR., USED TO SAY...
BUSINESS IS THE DOUGH OF THE PIZZA OF LIFE, AND...
AND UH...
'S HARD TO CONCENTRATE IN THESE FANCY BUSINESS CLOTHES.
ANYWAY, YOU CAN LEARN AND BE SUCCESSFUL IN THE WORLD OF BUSINESS JUST LIKE ME, IF YOU FOLLOW THESE THREE EASY STEPS!
(HOLDING UP THREE FINGERS INSIDE OF GLOVE)

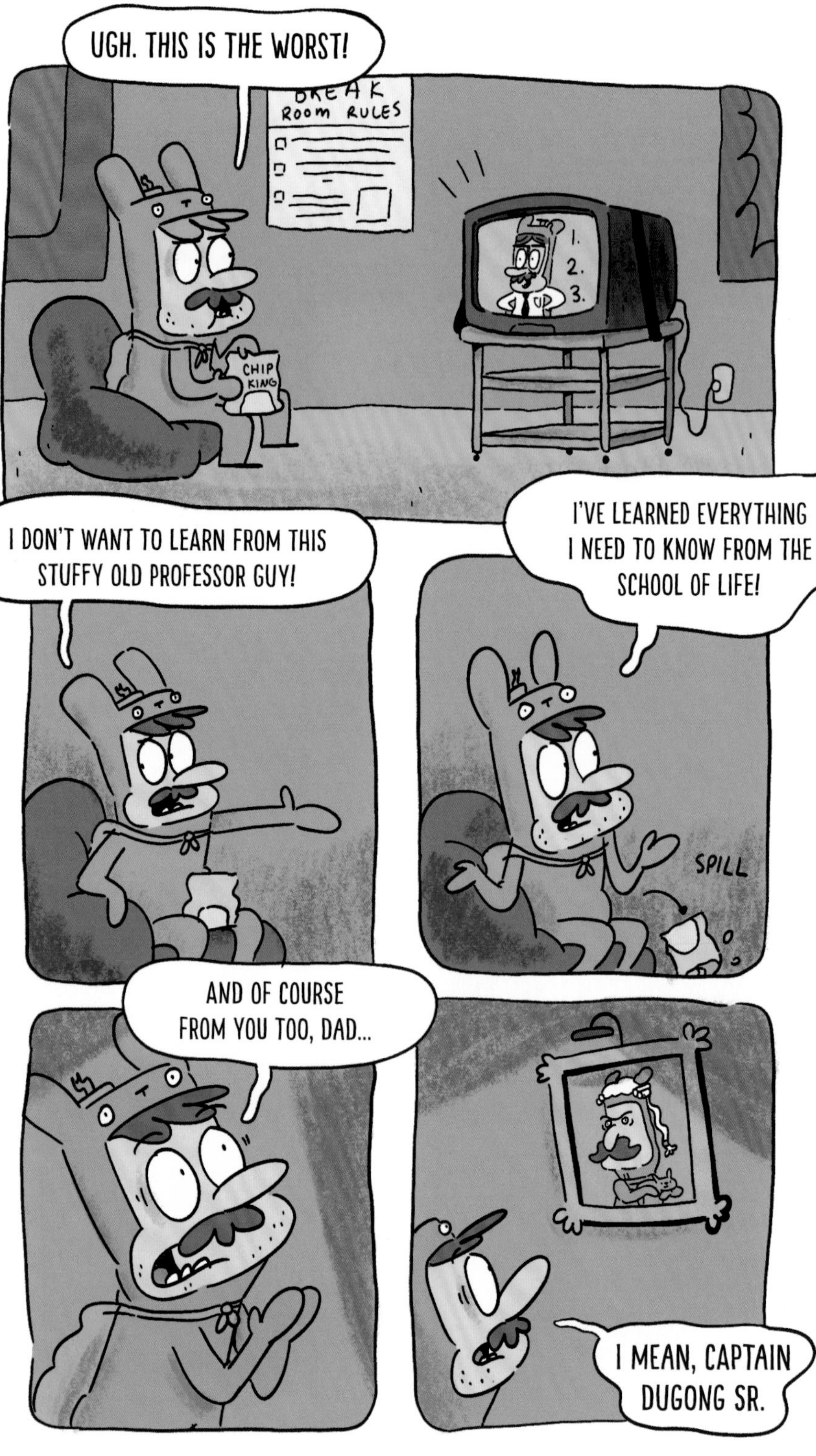
UGH. THIS IS THE WORST!
BREAK ROOM RULES
1.
2.
3.
CHIP KING
I DON'T WANT TO LEARN FROM THIS STUFFY OLD PROFESSOR GUY!
I'VE LEARNED EVERYTHING I NEED TO KNOW FROM THE SCHOOL OF LIFE!
SPILL
AND OF COURSE FROM YOU TOO, DAD...
I MEAN, CAPTAIN DUGONG SR.

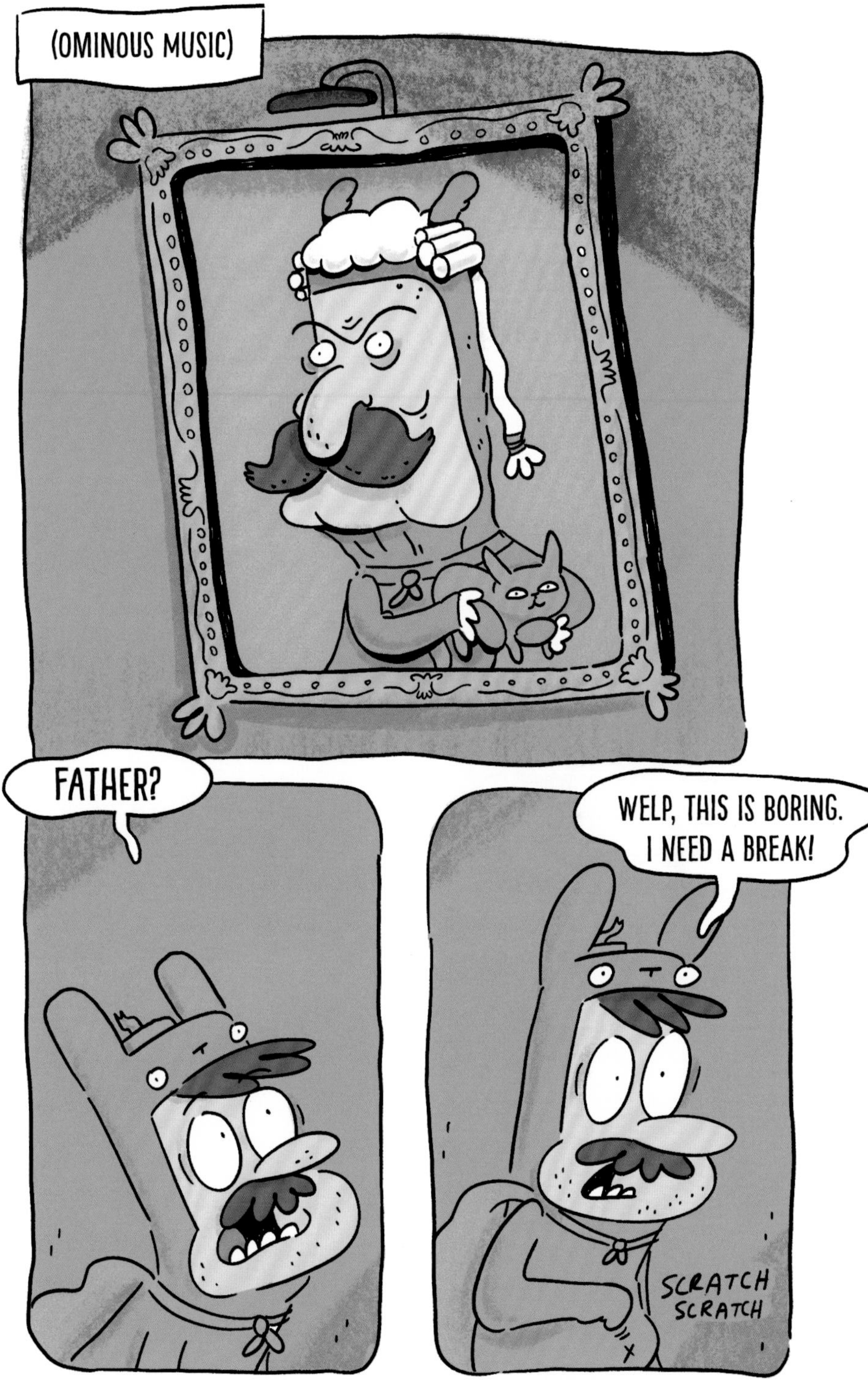
(OMINOUS MUSIC)
FATHER?
WELP, THIS IS BORING. I NEED A BREAK!
SCRATCH SCRATCH

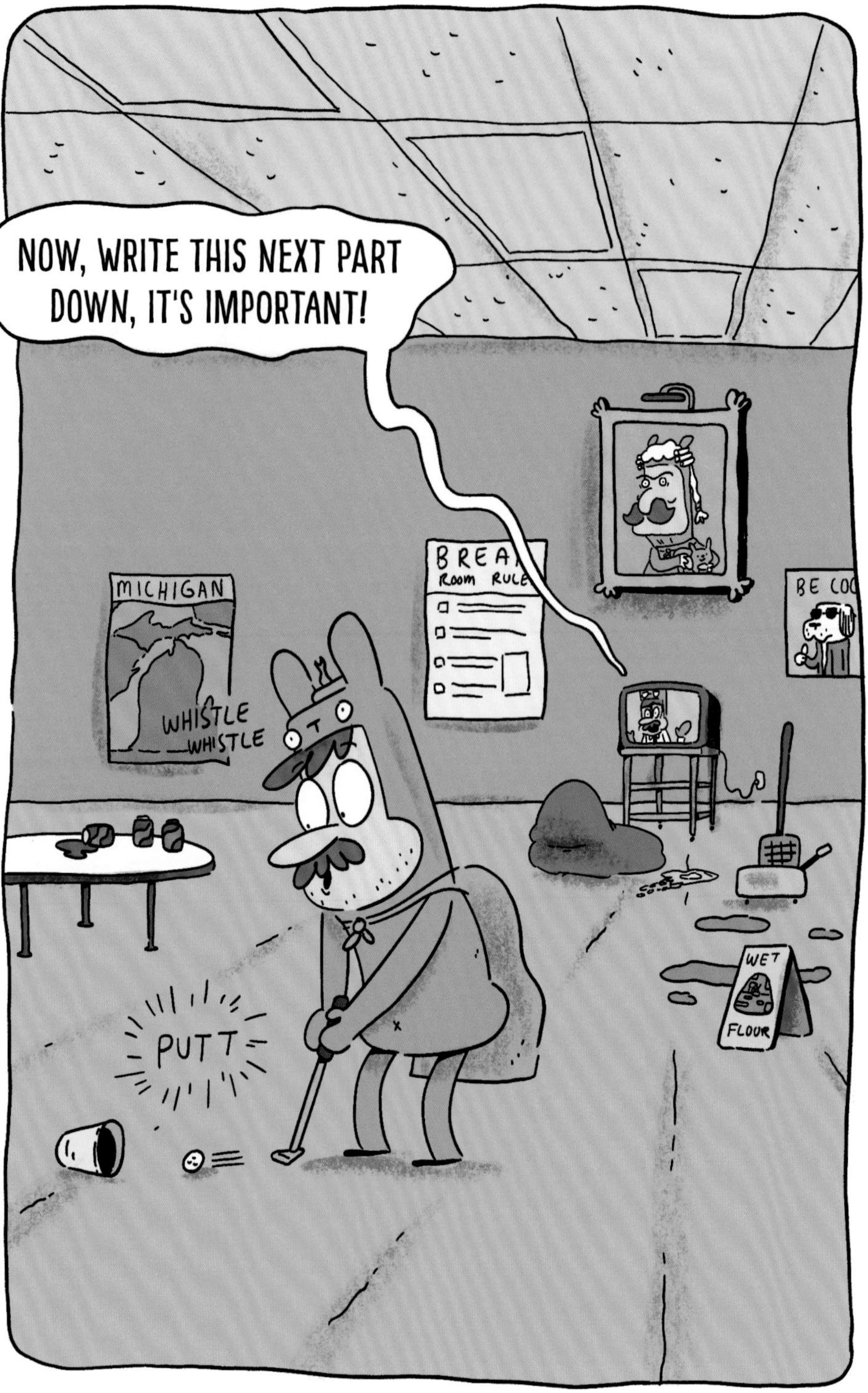
NOW, WRITE THIS NEXT PART DOWN, IT'S IMPORTANT!
MICHIGAN
WHISTLE
WHISTLE
BREA
Room RULE
BE CO
PUTT
WET
FLOUR

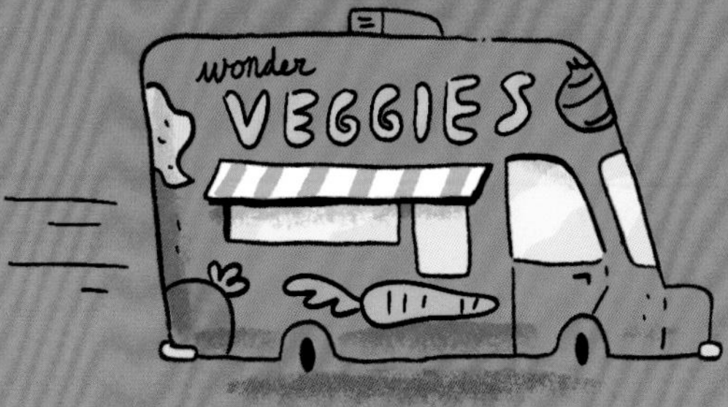
wonder
VEGGIES

ALSO meanwhile

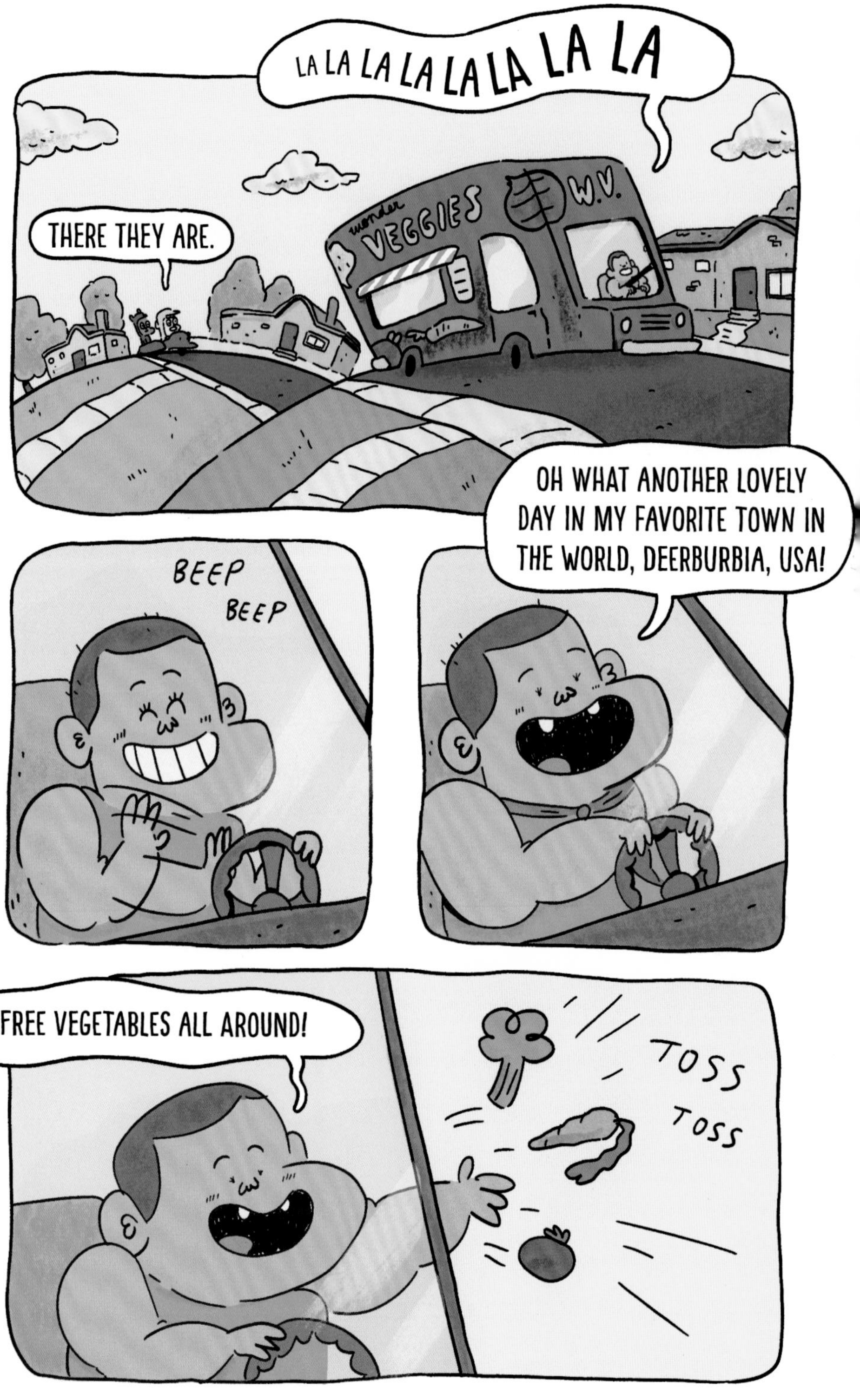
LA LA LA LA LA LA LA LA
THERE THEY ARE.
wonder VEGGIES W.V.
BEEP BEEP
OH WHAT ANOTHER LOVELY DAY IN MY FAVORITE TOWN IN THE WORLD, DEERBURBIA, USA!
FREE VEGETABLES ALL AROUND!
TOSS TOSS

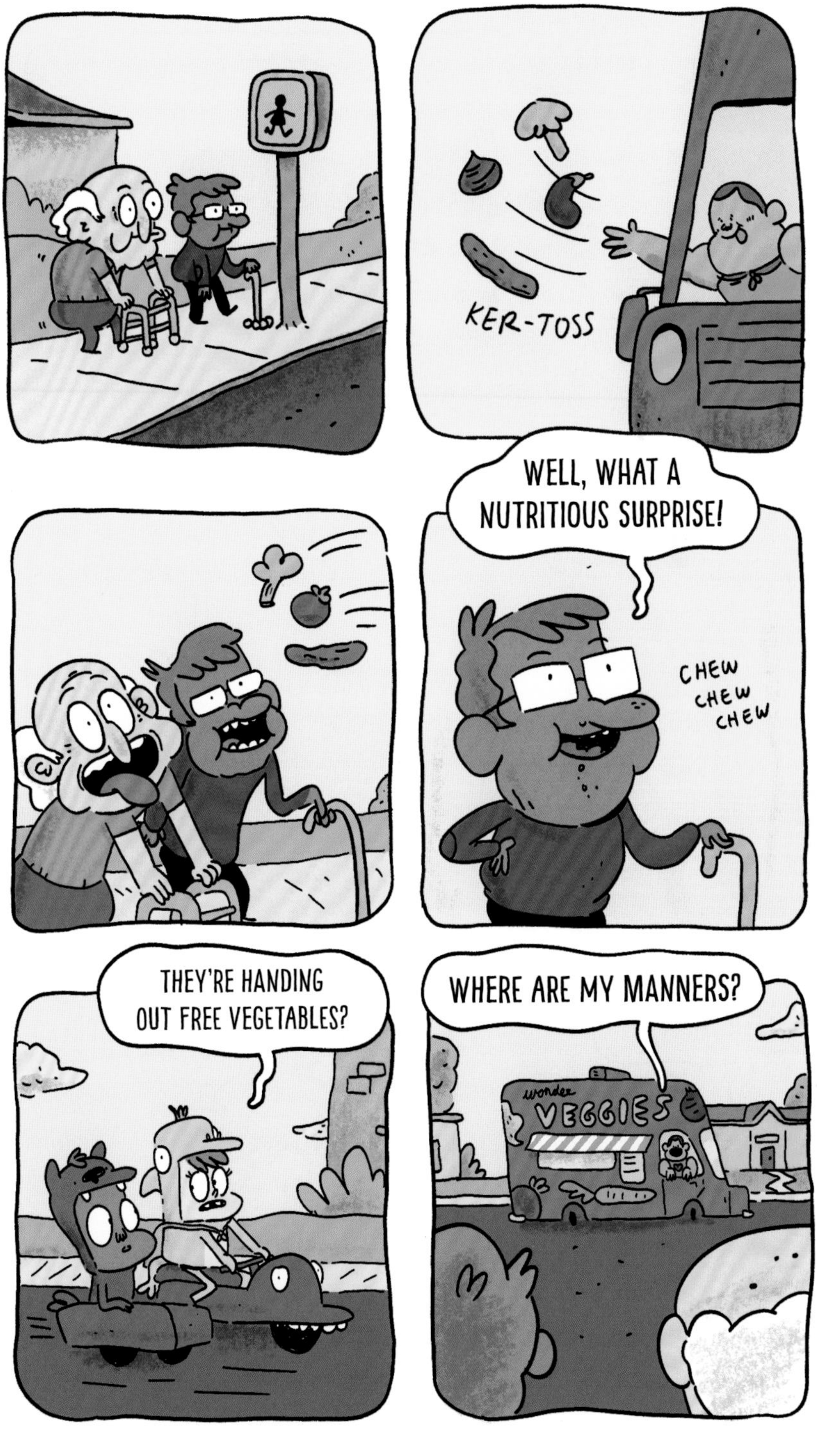
KER-TOSS
WELL, WHAT A NUTRITIOUS SURPRISE!
CHEW CHEW CHEW
THEY'RE HANDING OUT FREE VEGETABLES?
WHERE ARE MY MANNERS?
wonder VEGGIES

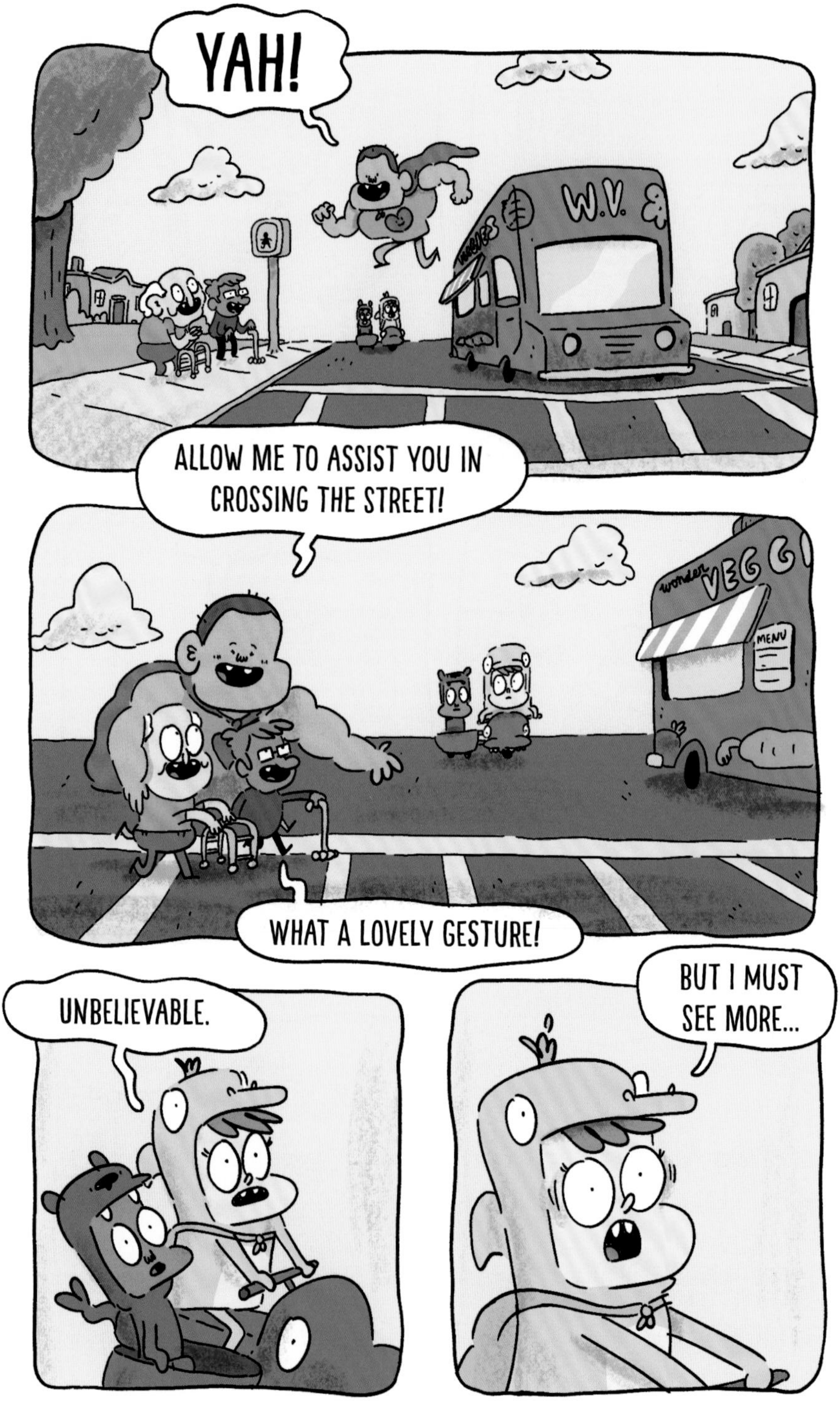
YAH!
W.V.
ALLOW ME TO ASSIST YOU IN CROSSING THE STREET!
VEGG
MENU
WHAT A LOVELY GESTURE!
UNBELIEVABLE.
BUT I MUST SEE MORE...

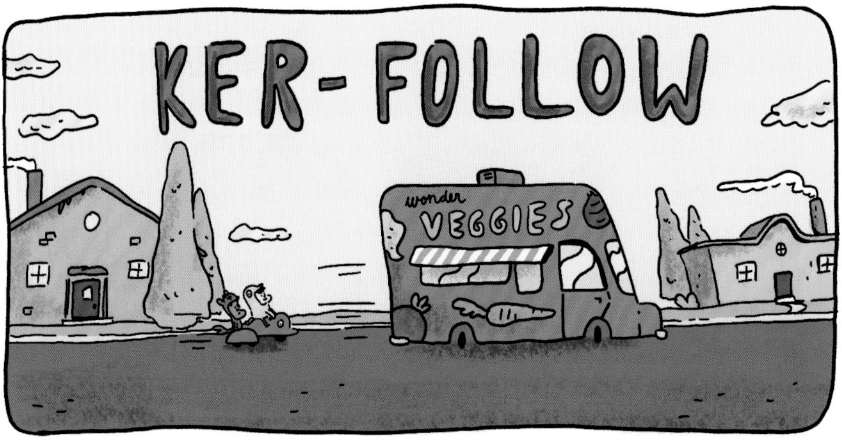
KER-FOLLOW
wonder
VEGGIES

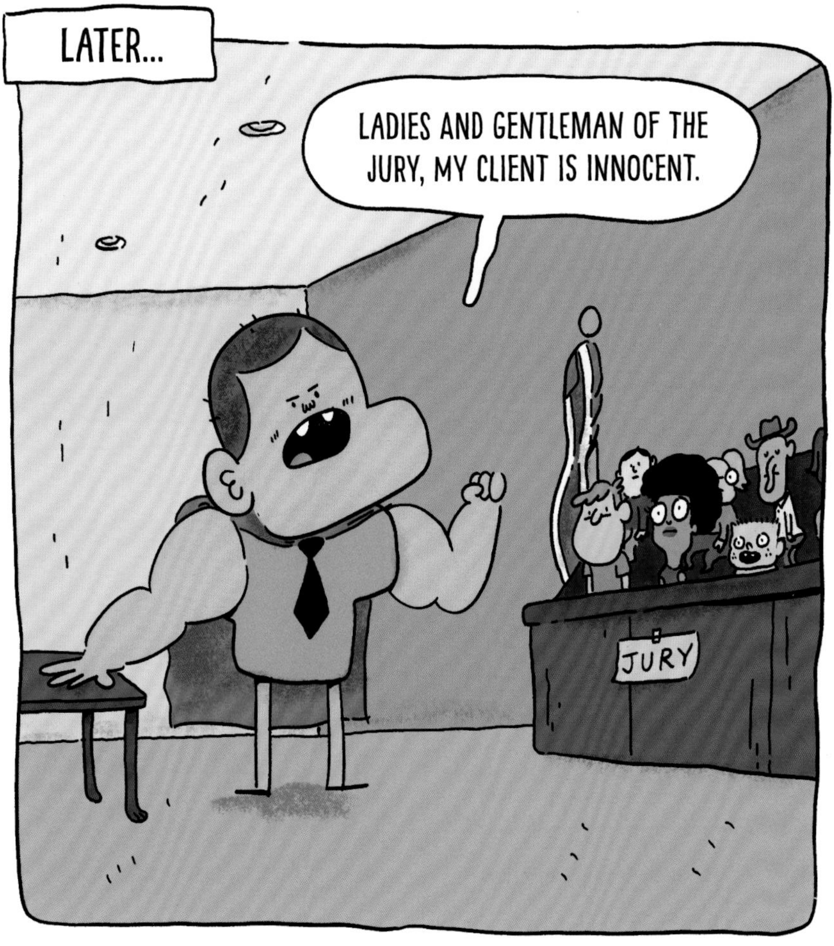
LATER...
LADIES AND GENTLEMAN OF THE JURY, MY CLIENT IS INNOCENT.
JURY

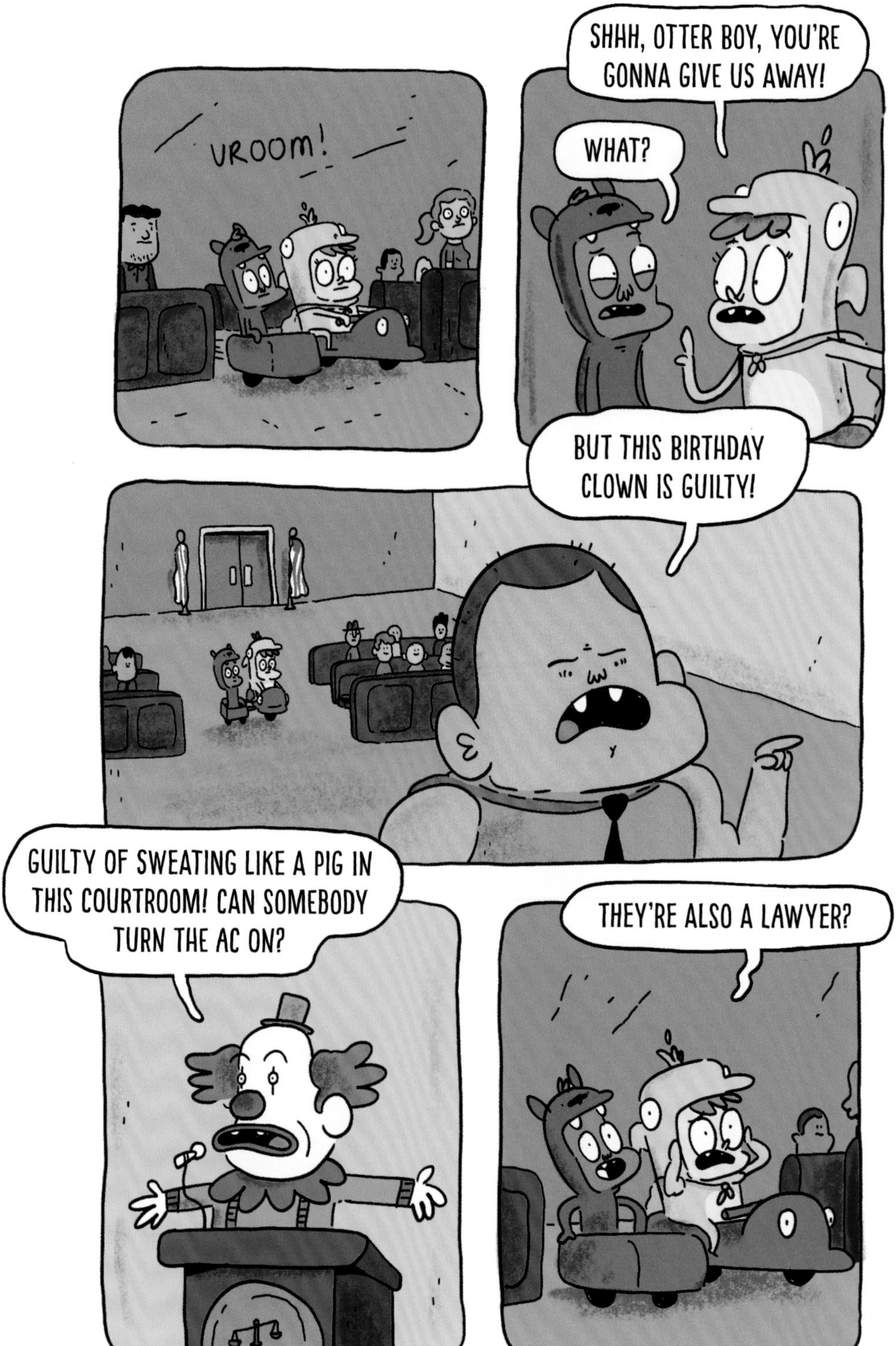
VROOM!
SHHH, OTTER BOY, YOU'RE GONNA GIVE US AWAY!
WHAT?
BUT THIS BIRTHDAY CLOWN IS GUILTY!
GUILTY OF SWEATING LIKE A PIG IN THIS COURTROOM! CAN SOMEBODY TURN THE AC ON?
THEY'RE ALSO A LAWYER?

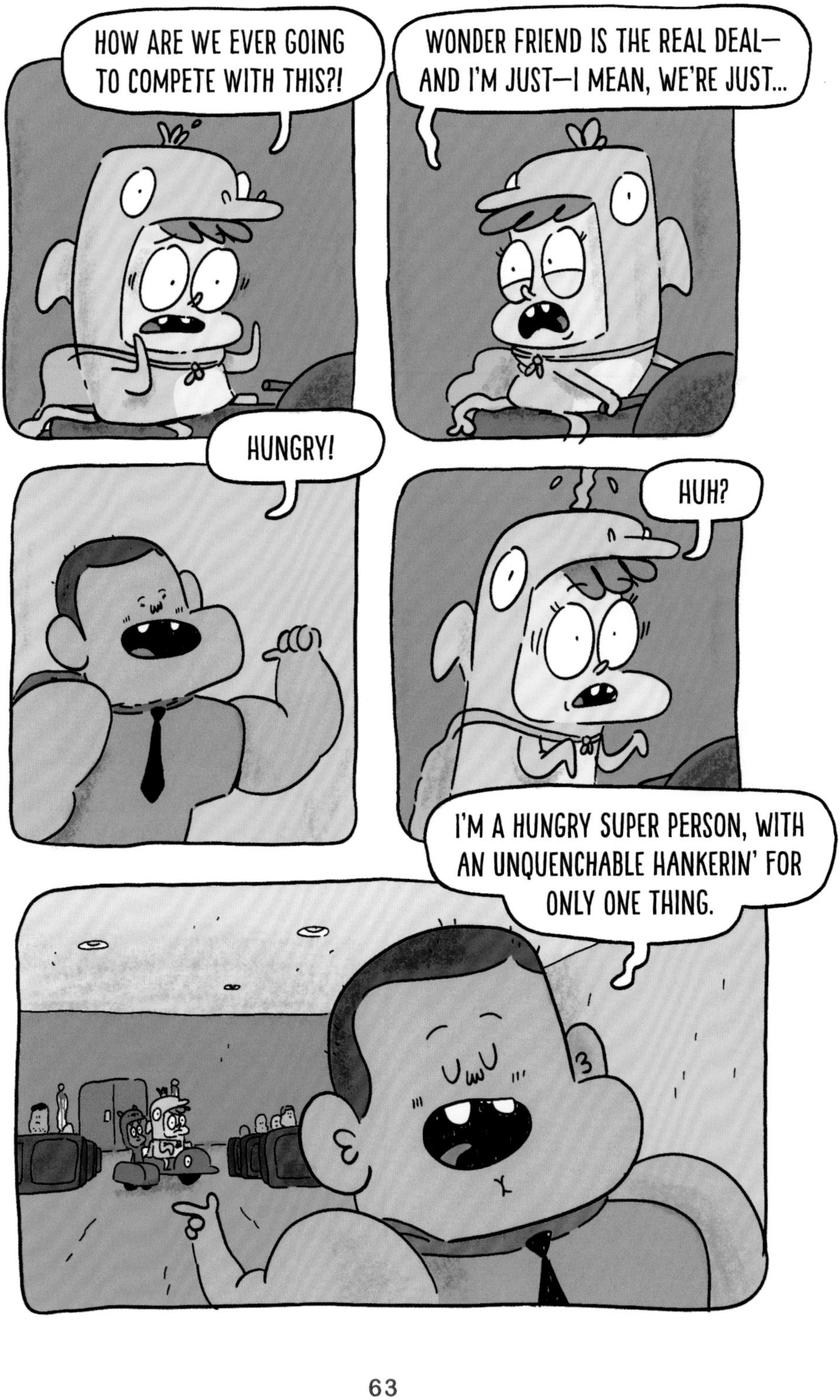
HOW ARE WE EVER GOING TO COMPETE WITH THIS?!
WONDER FRIEND IS THE REAL DEAL—AND I'M JUST—I MEAN, WE'RE JUST...
HUNGRY!
HUH?
I'M A HUNGRY SUPER PERSON, WITH AN UNQUENCHABLE HANKERIN' FOR ONLY ONE THING.

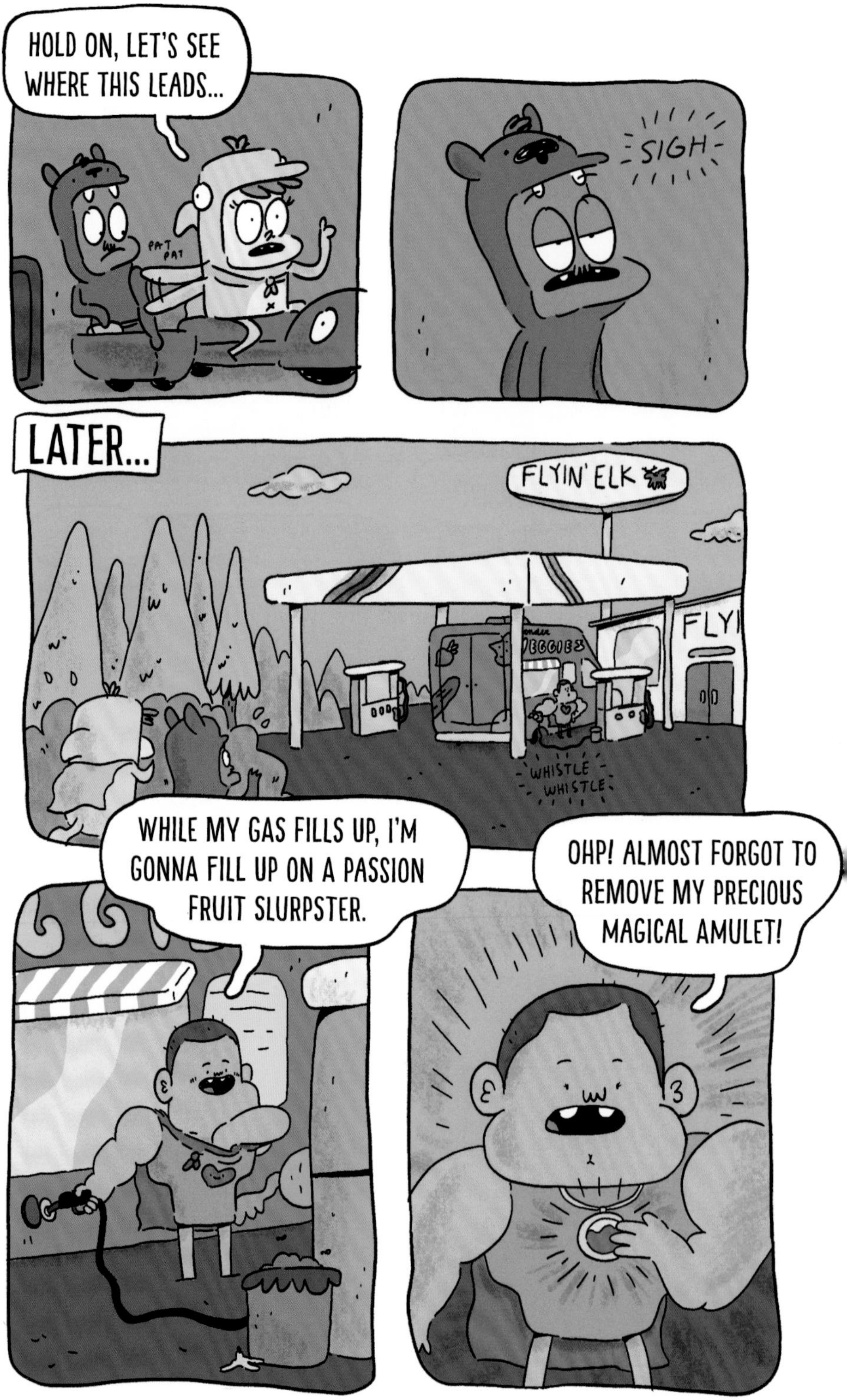
HOLD ON, LET'S SEE WHERE THIS LEADS...
PAT PAT
SIGH
LATER...
FLYIN' ELK
FLY
WHISTLE WHISTLE
WHILE MY GAS FILLS UP, I'M GONNA FILL UP ON A PASSION FRUIT SLURPSTER.
OHP! ALMOST FORGOT TO REMOVE MY PRECIOUS MAGICAL AMULET!

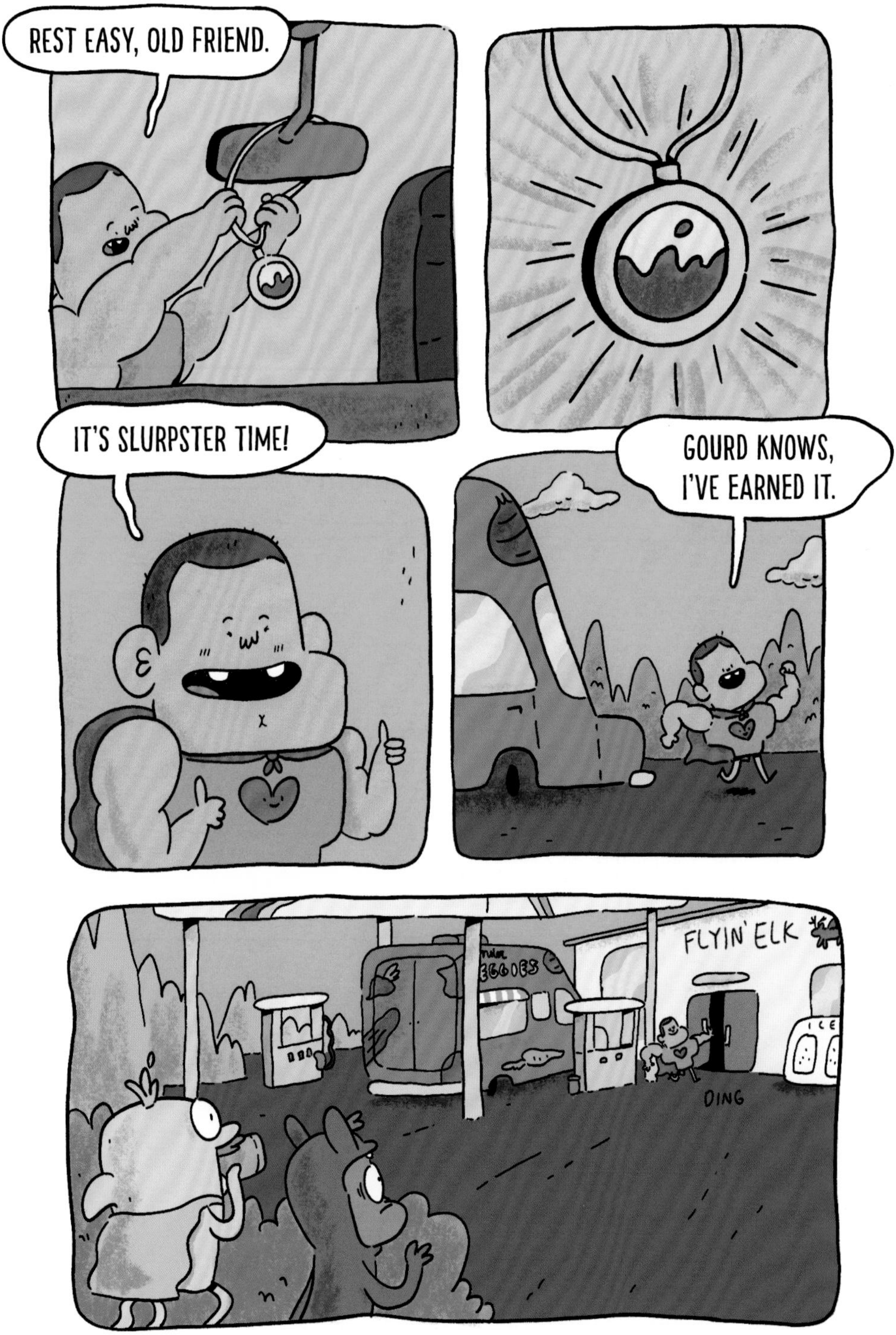
REST EASY, OLD FRIEND.
IT'S SLURPSTER TIME!
GOURD KNOWS, I'VE EARNED IT.
FLYIN' ELK
VEGGIES
ICE
DING

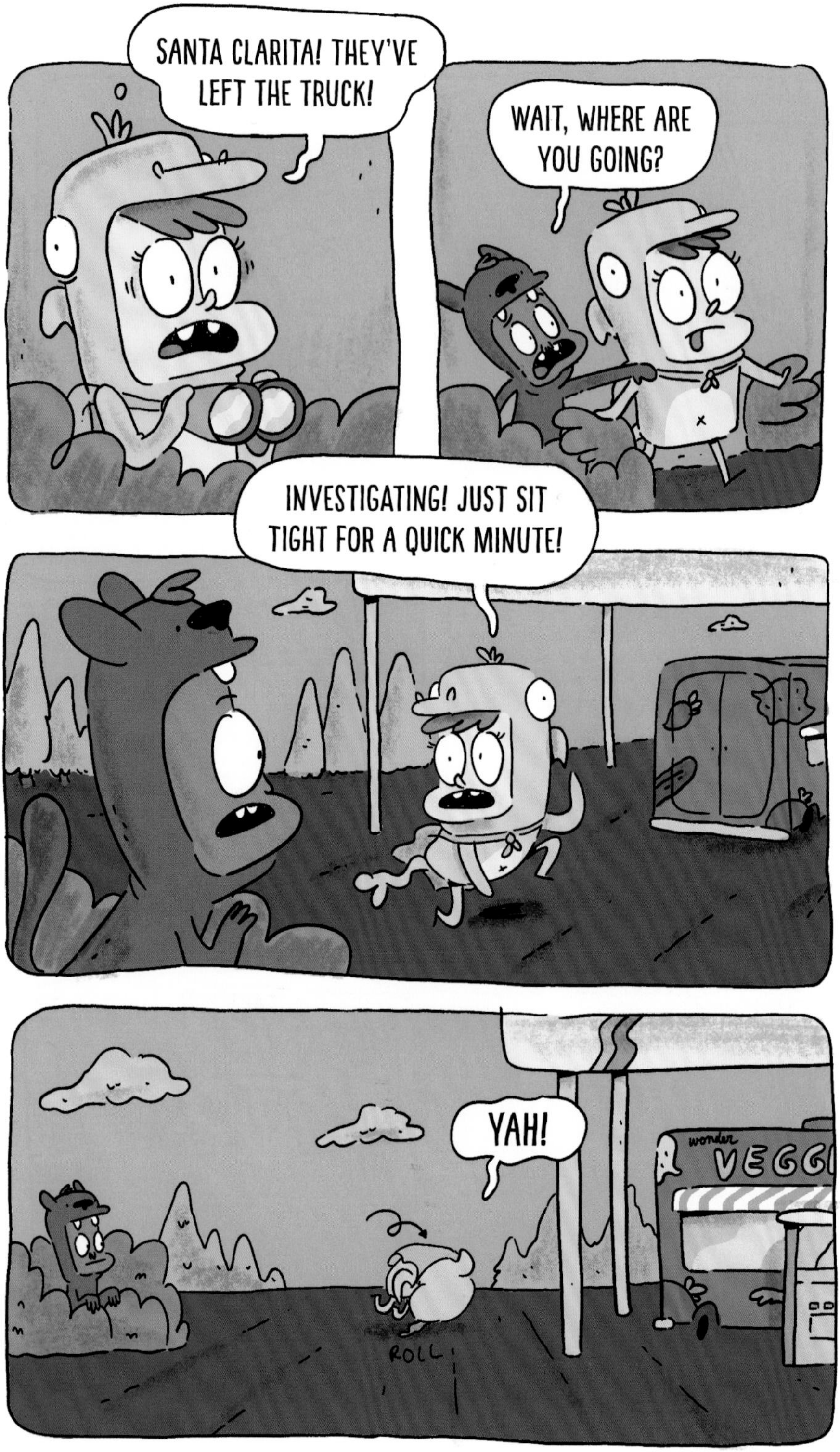
SANTA CLARITA! THEY'VE LEFT THE TRUCK!
WAIT, WHERE ARE YOU GOING?
INVESTIGATING! JUST SIT TIGHT FOR A QUICK MINUTE!
YAH!
wonder
VEGG
ROLL

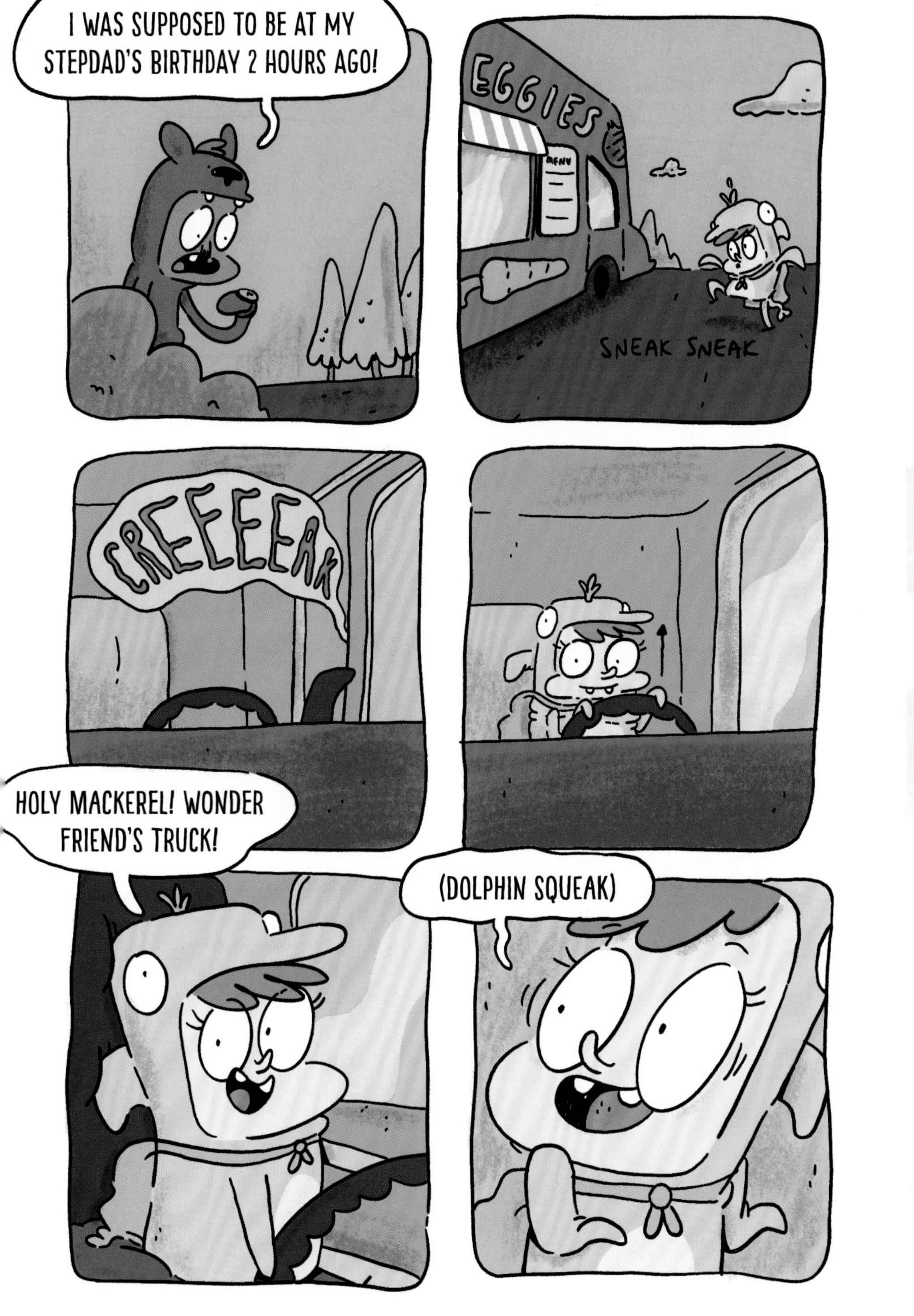
I WAS SUPPOSED TO BE AT MY STEPDAD'S BIRTHDAY 2 HOURS AGO!
EGGIES
MENU
SNEAK SNEAK
CREEEEAK
HOLY MACKEREL! WONDER FRIEND'S TRUCK!
(DOLPHIN SQUEAK)

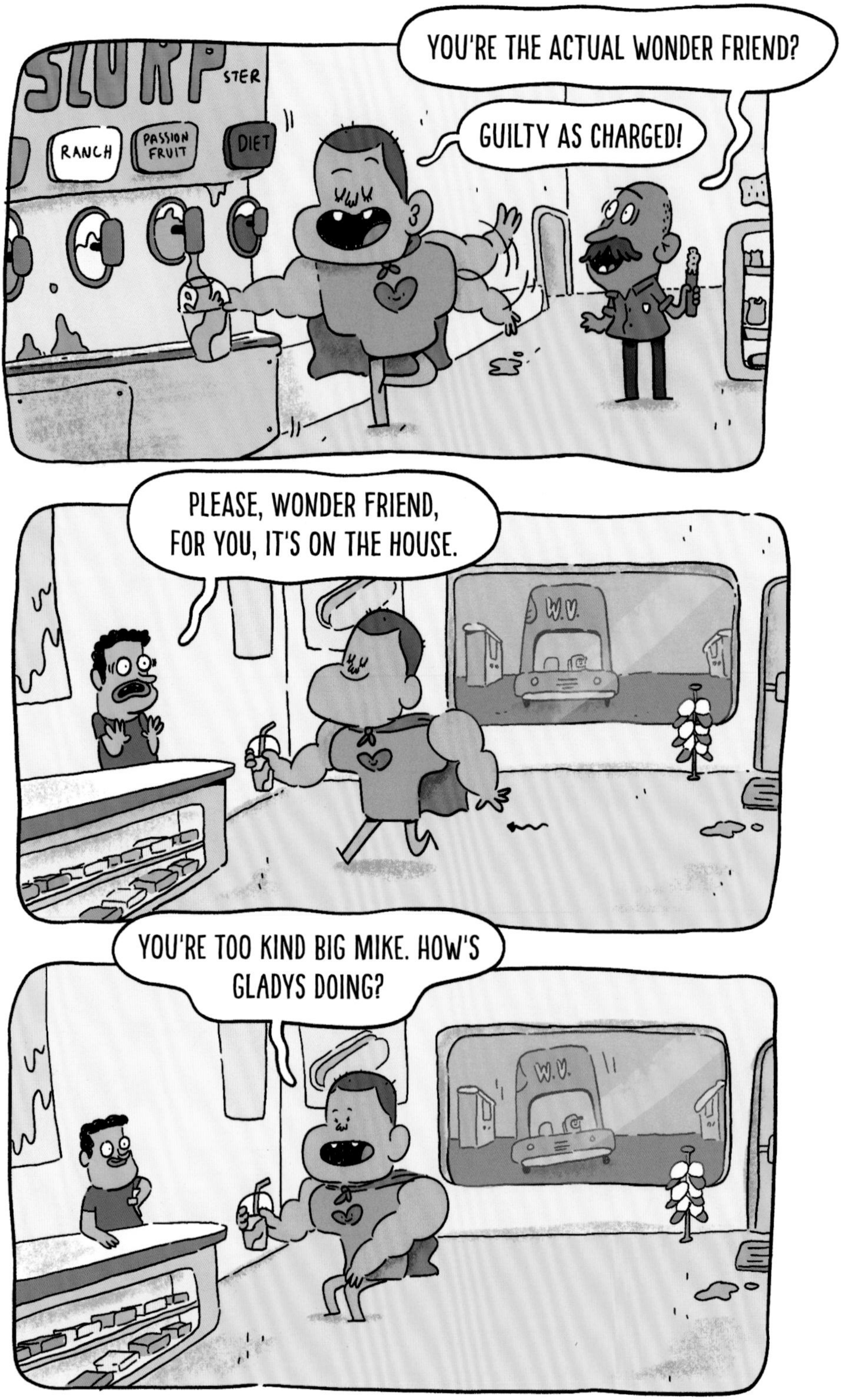
SLURPSTER
RANCH
PASSION FRUIT
DIET
YOU'RE THE ACTUAL WONDER FRIEND?
GUILTY AS CHARGED!
PLEASE, WONDER FRIEND, FOR YOU, IT'S ON THE HOUSE.
W.V.
YOU'RE TOO KIND BIG MIKE. HOW'S GLADYS DOING?
W.V.

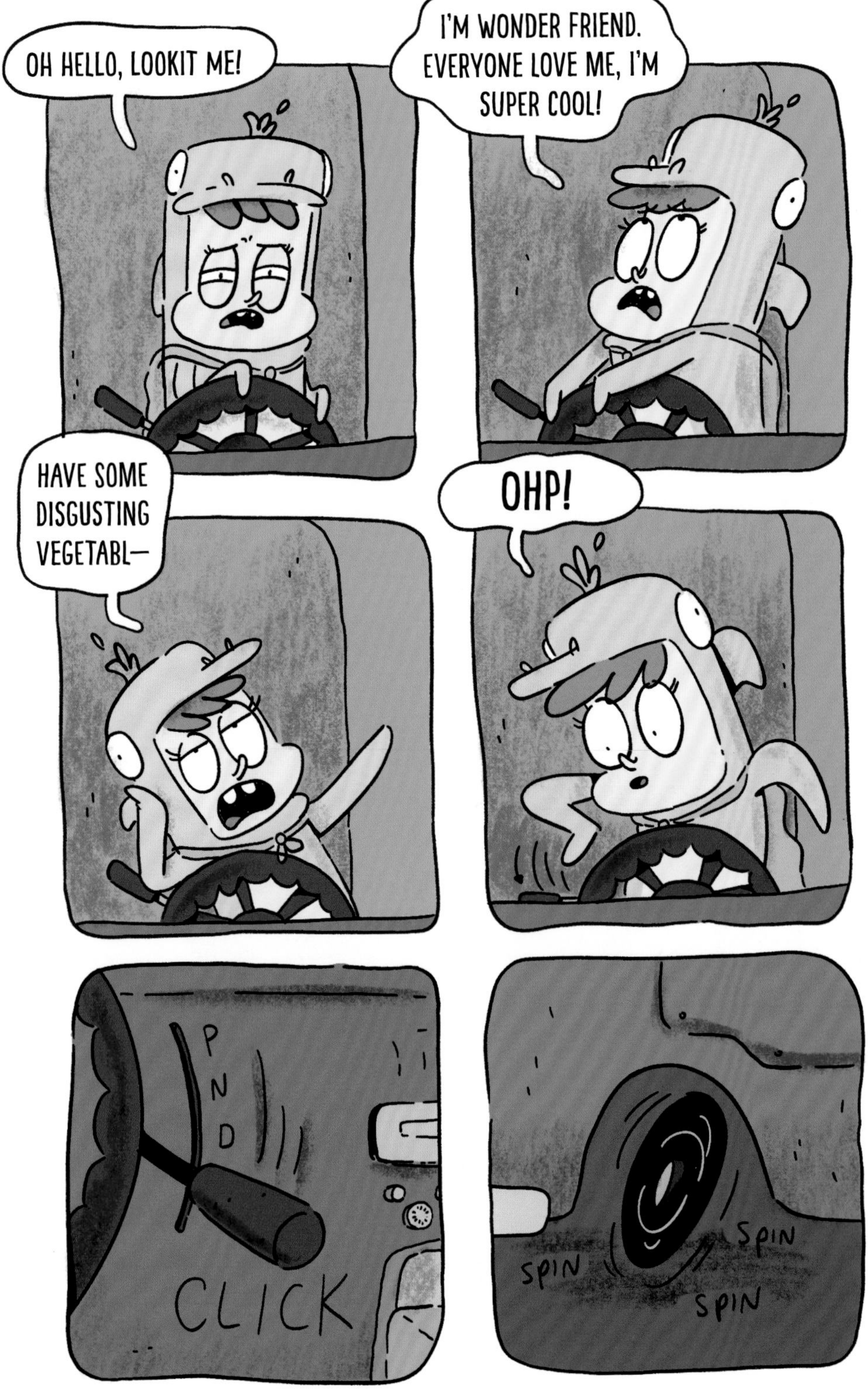
OH HELLO, LOOKIT ME!
I'M WONDER FRIEND. EVERYONE LOVE ME, I'M SUPER COOL!
HAVE SOME DISGUSTING VEGETABL—
OHP!
P
N
D
CLICK
SPIN
SPIN
SPIN

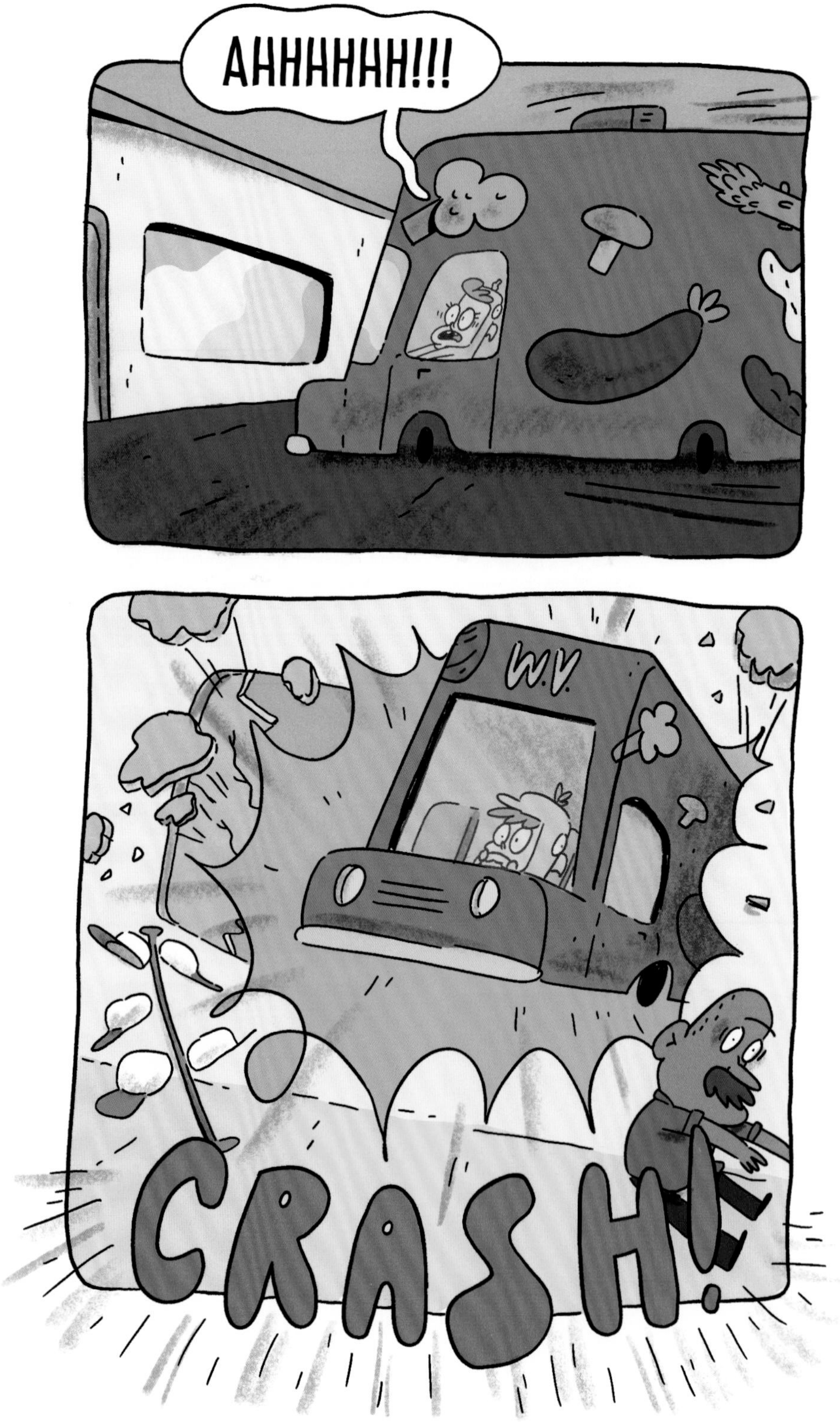
AHHHHHH!!!
W.V.
CRASH!

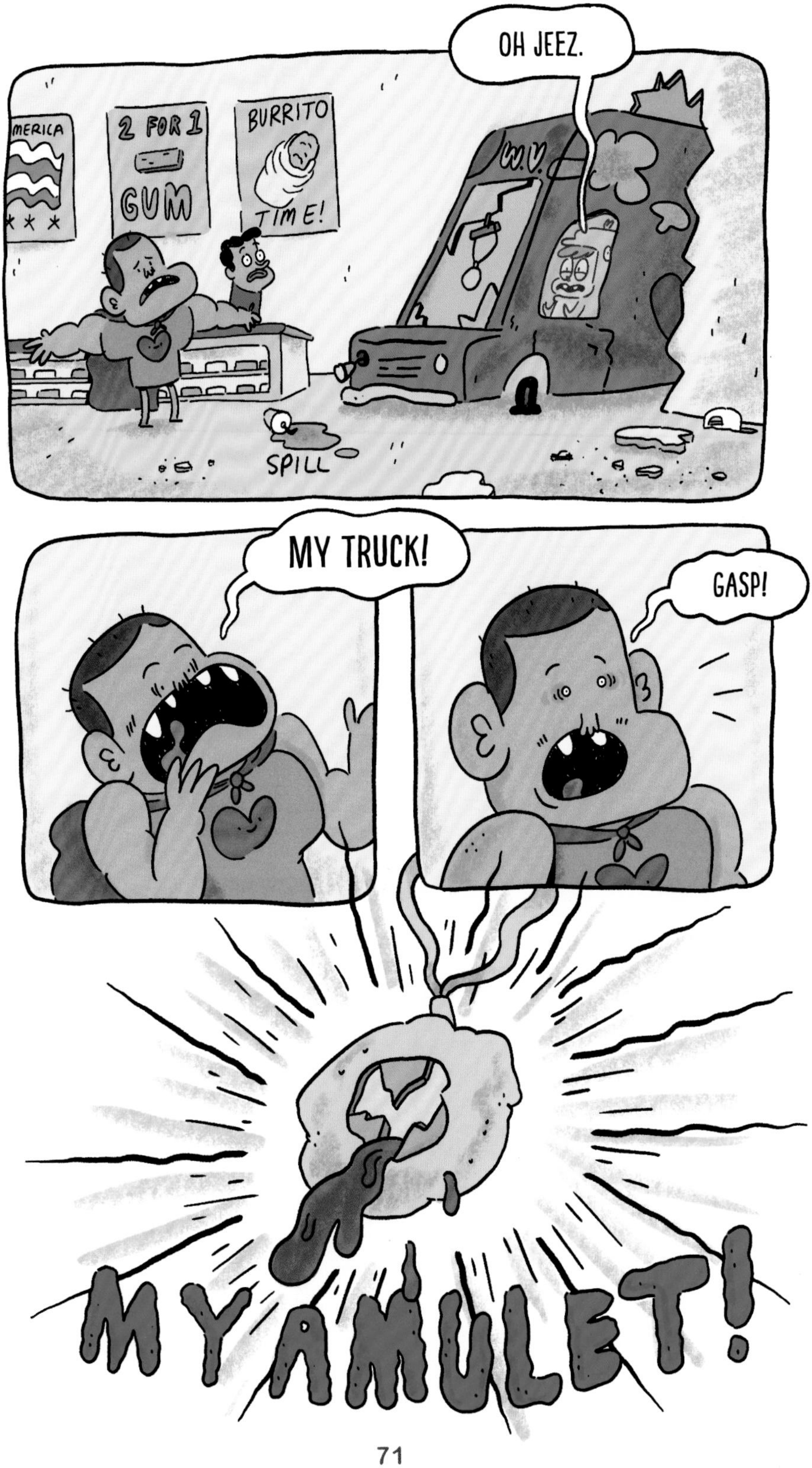

MERICA
2 FOR 1
GUM
BURRITO
TIME!
W.V.
OH JEEZ.
SPILL
MY TRUCK!
GASP!
MY AMULET!

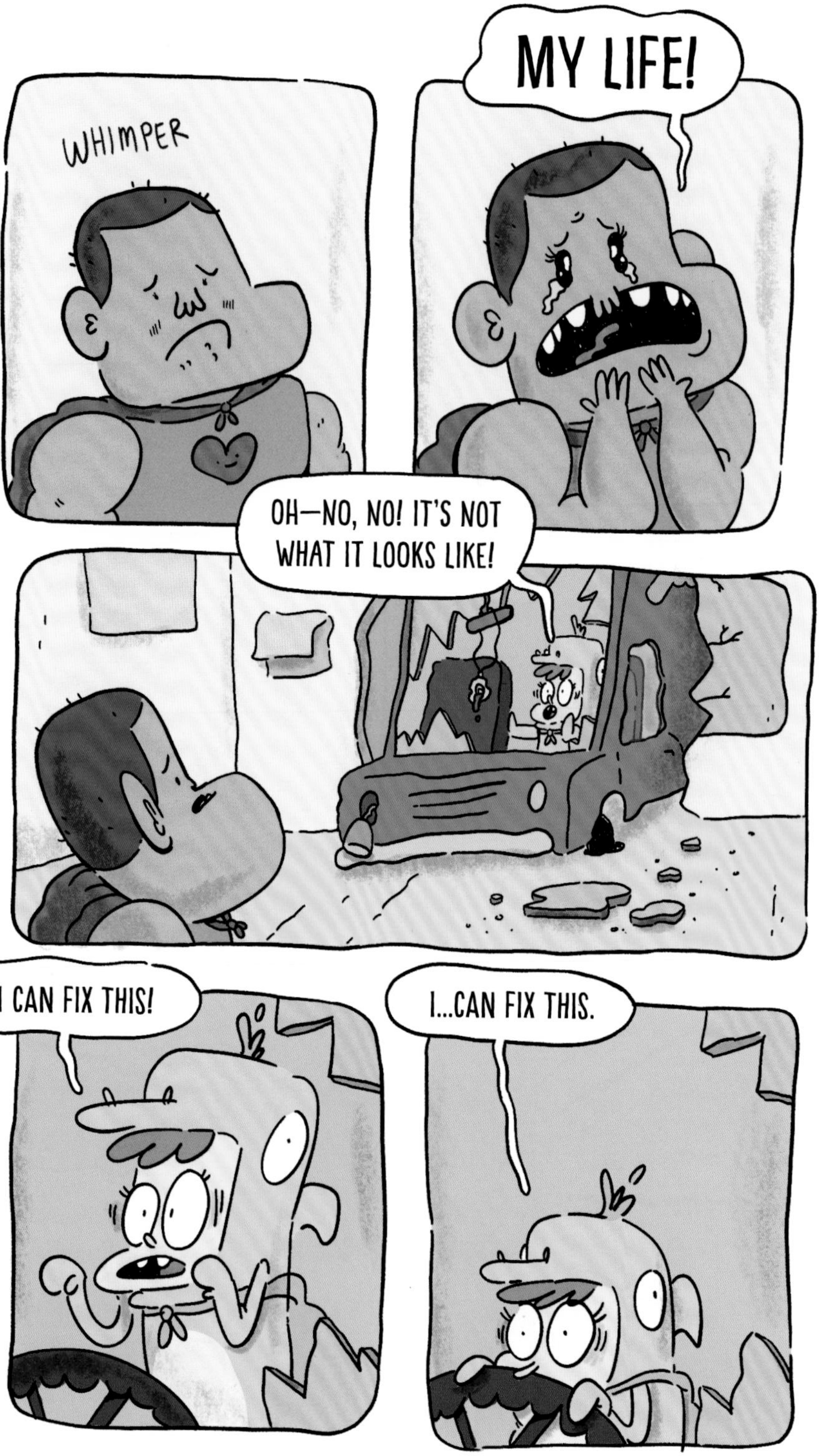
WHIMPER
MY LIFE!
OH—NO, NO! IT'S NOT WHAT IT LOOKS LIKE!
I CAN FIX THIS!
I...CAN FIX THIS.

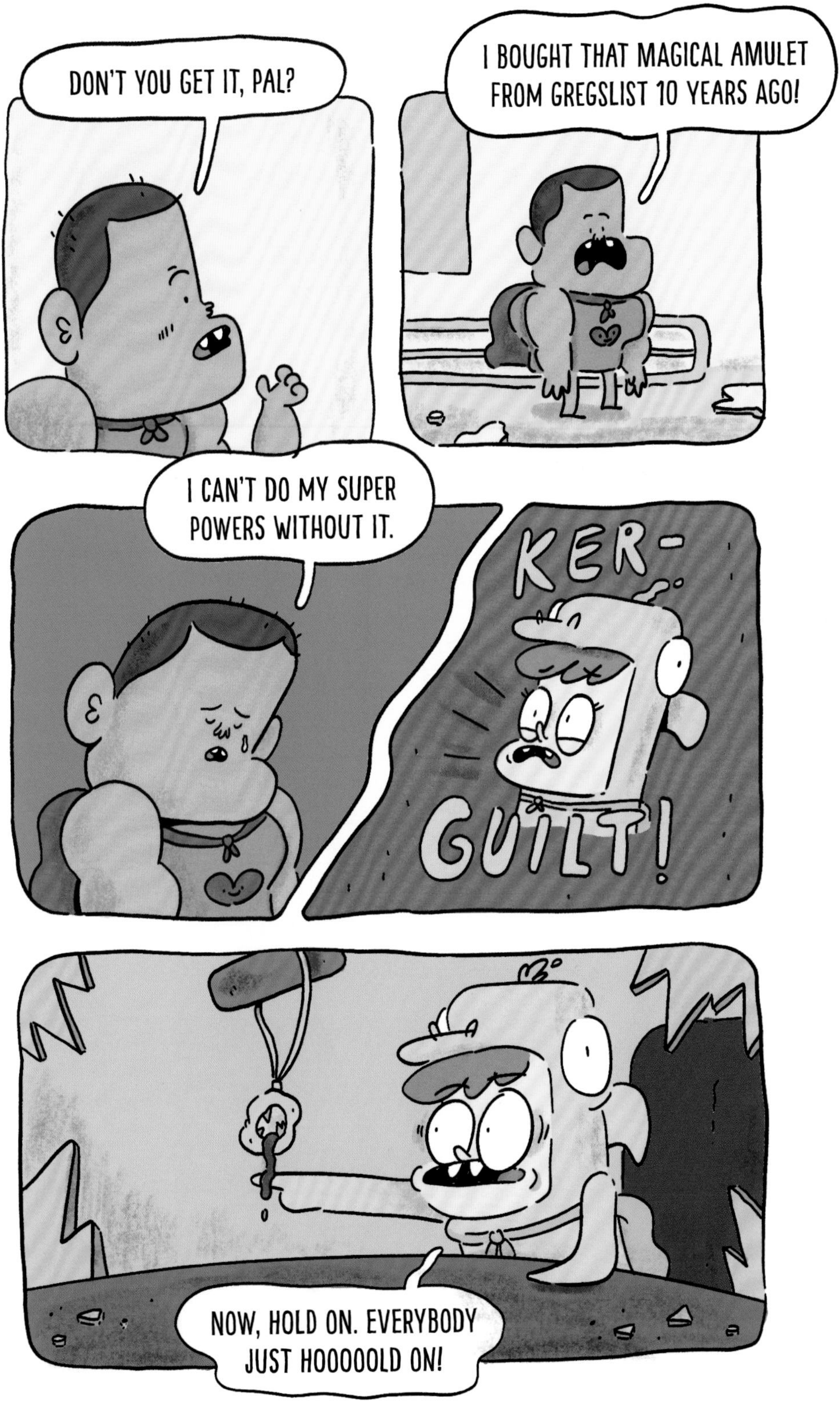
DON'T YOU GET IT, PAL?
I BOUGHT THAT MAGICAL AMULET FROM GREGSLIST 10 YEARS AGO!
I CAN'T DO MY SUPER POWERS WITHOUT IT.
KER-GUILT!
NOW, HOLD ON. EVERYBODY JUST HOOOOOLD ON!

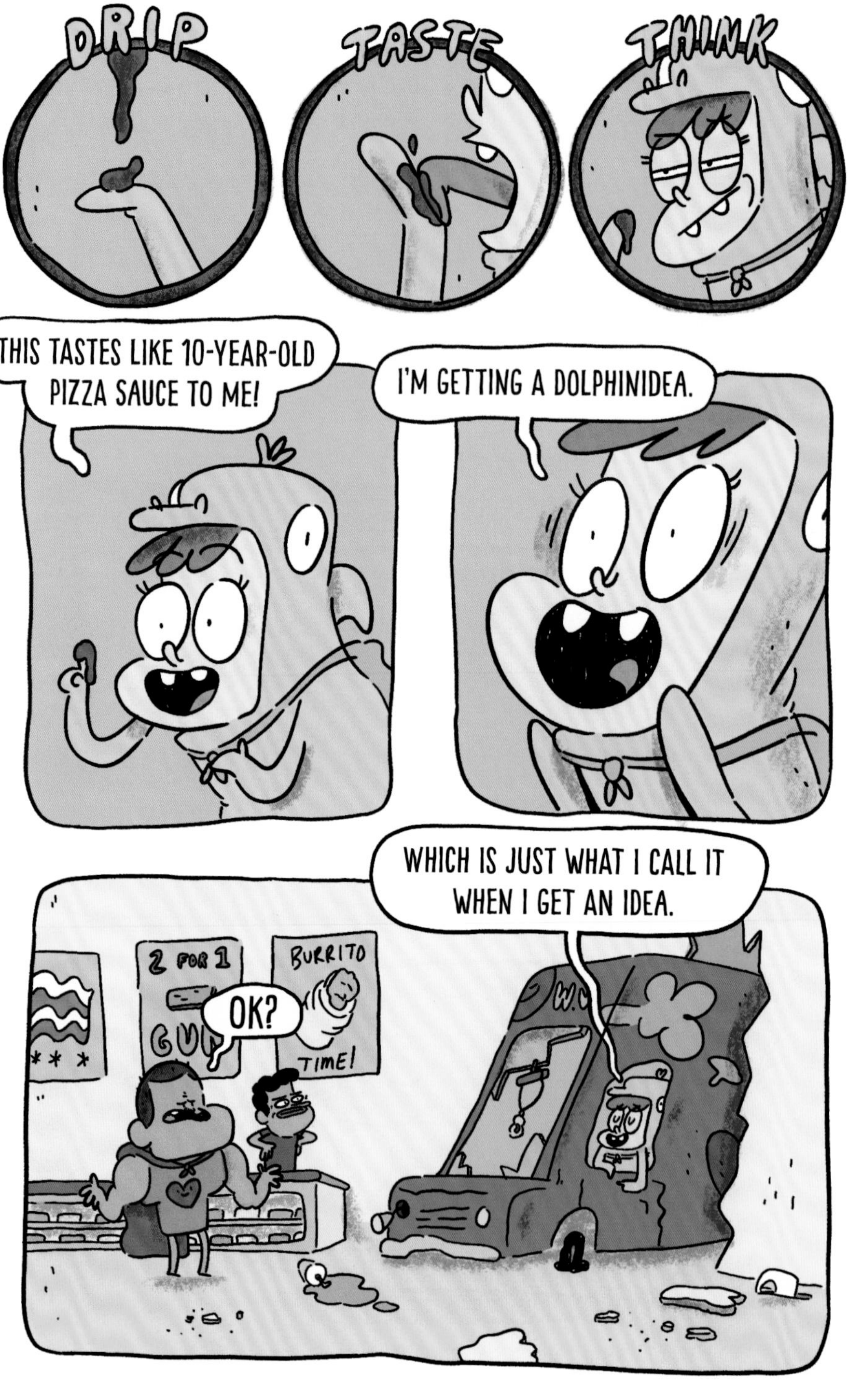
DRIP
TASTE
THINK
THIS TASTES LIKE 10-YEAR-OLD PIZZA SAUCE TO ME!
I'M GETTING A DOLPHINIDEA.
WHICH IS JUST WHAT I CALL IT WHEN I GET AN IDEA.
2 FOR 1
BURRITO TIME!
OK?

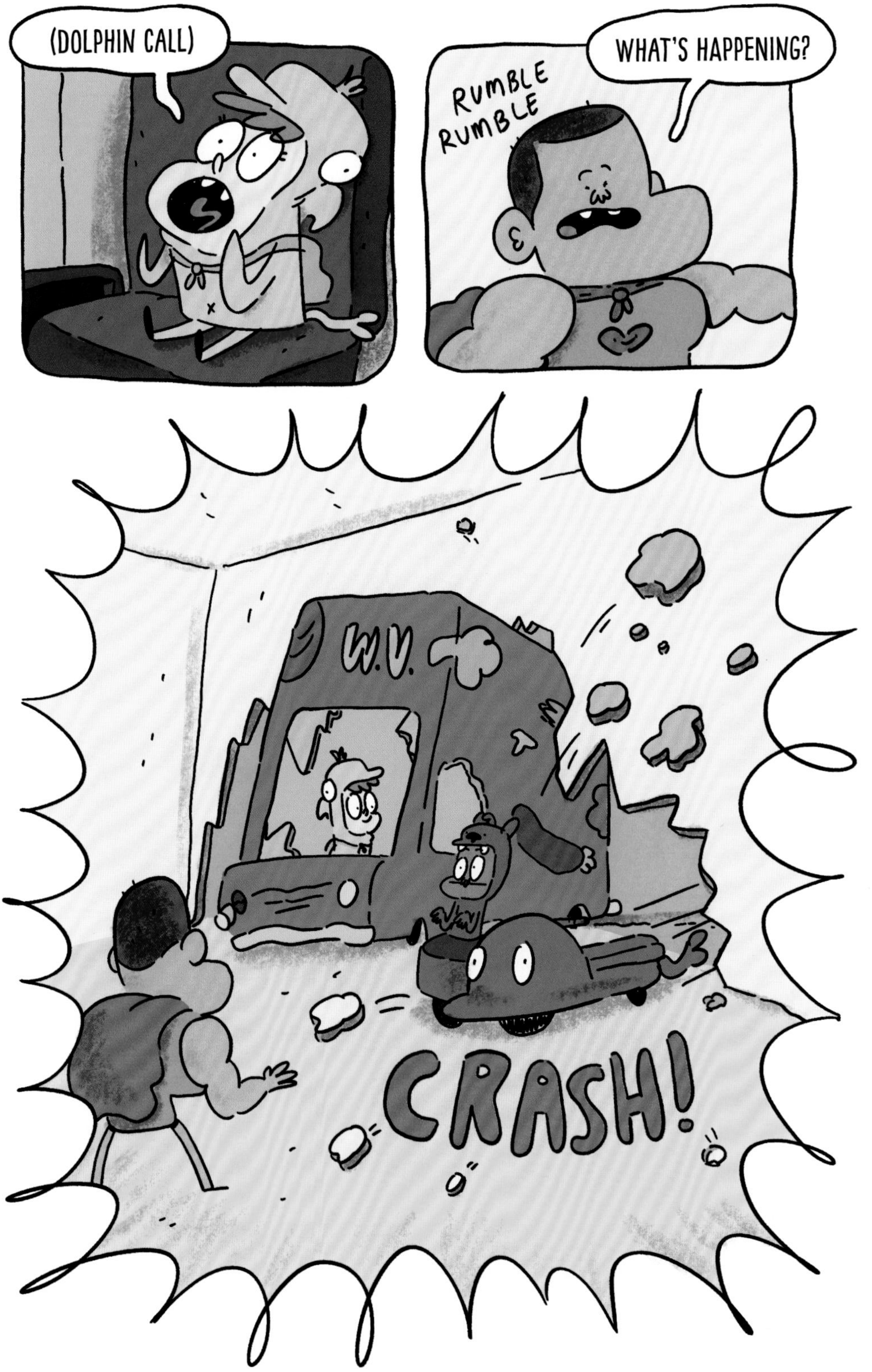
(DOLPHIN CALL)
RUMBLE RUMBLE
WHAT'S HAPPENING?
W.V.
CRASH!

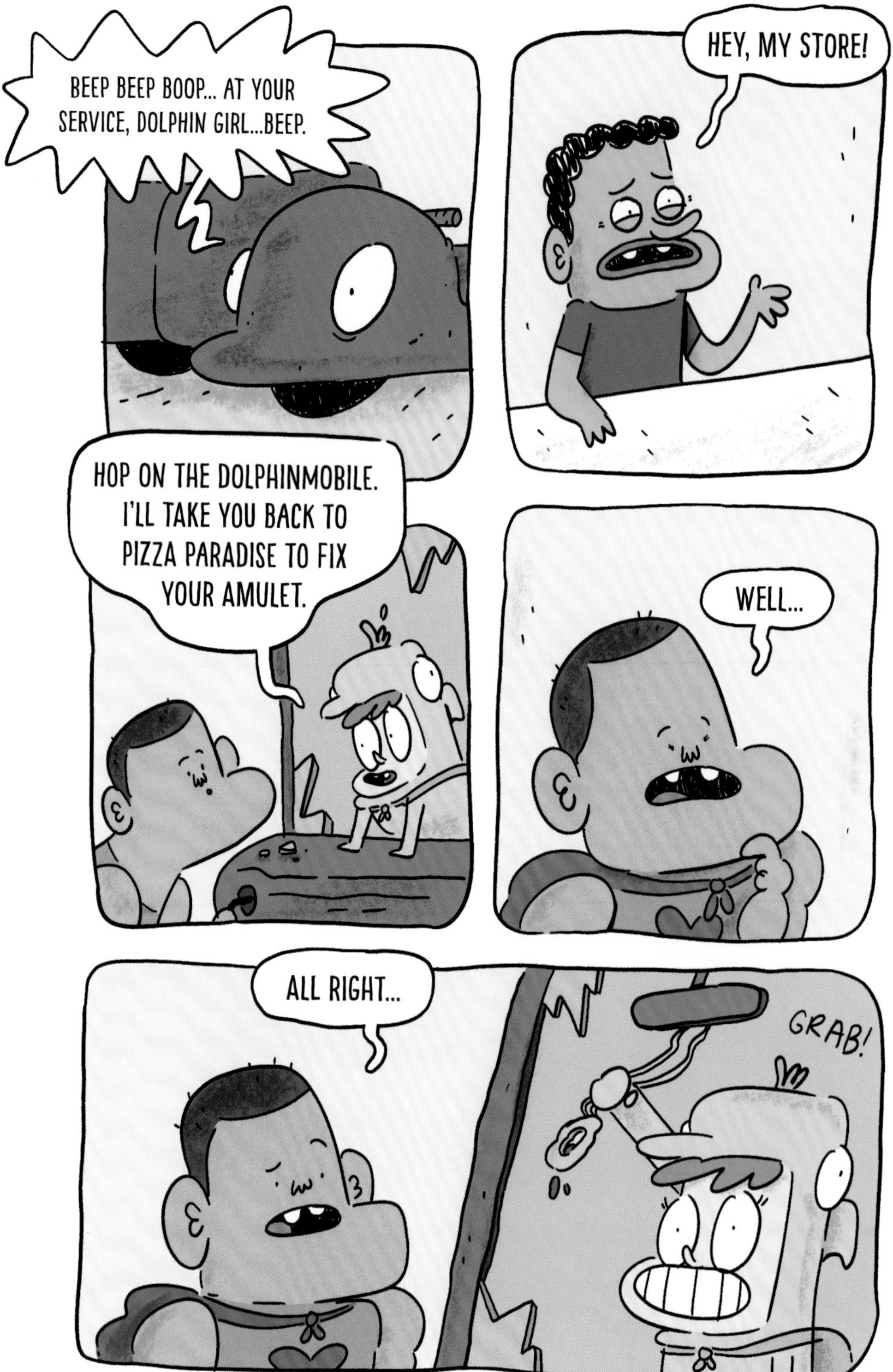
BEEP BEEP BOOP... AT YOUR SERVICE, DOLPHIN GIRL...BEEP.
HEY, MY STORE!
HOP ON THE DOLPHINMOBILE. I'LL TAKE YOU BACK TO PIZZA PARADISE TO FIX YOUR AMULET.
WELL...
ALL RIGHT...
GRAB!

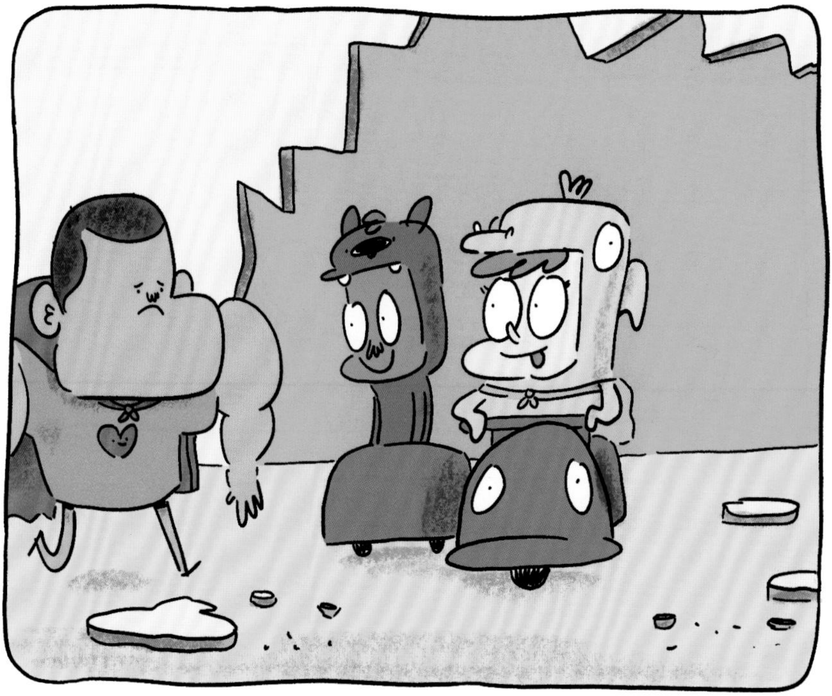

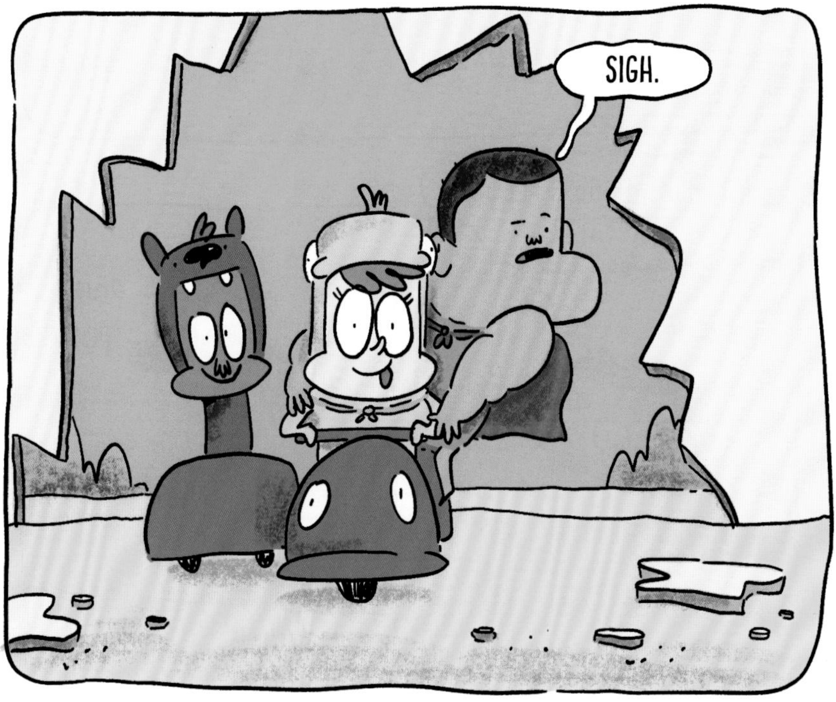
SIGH.

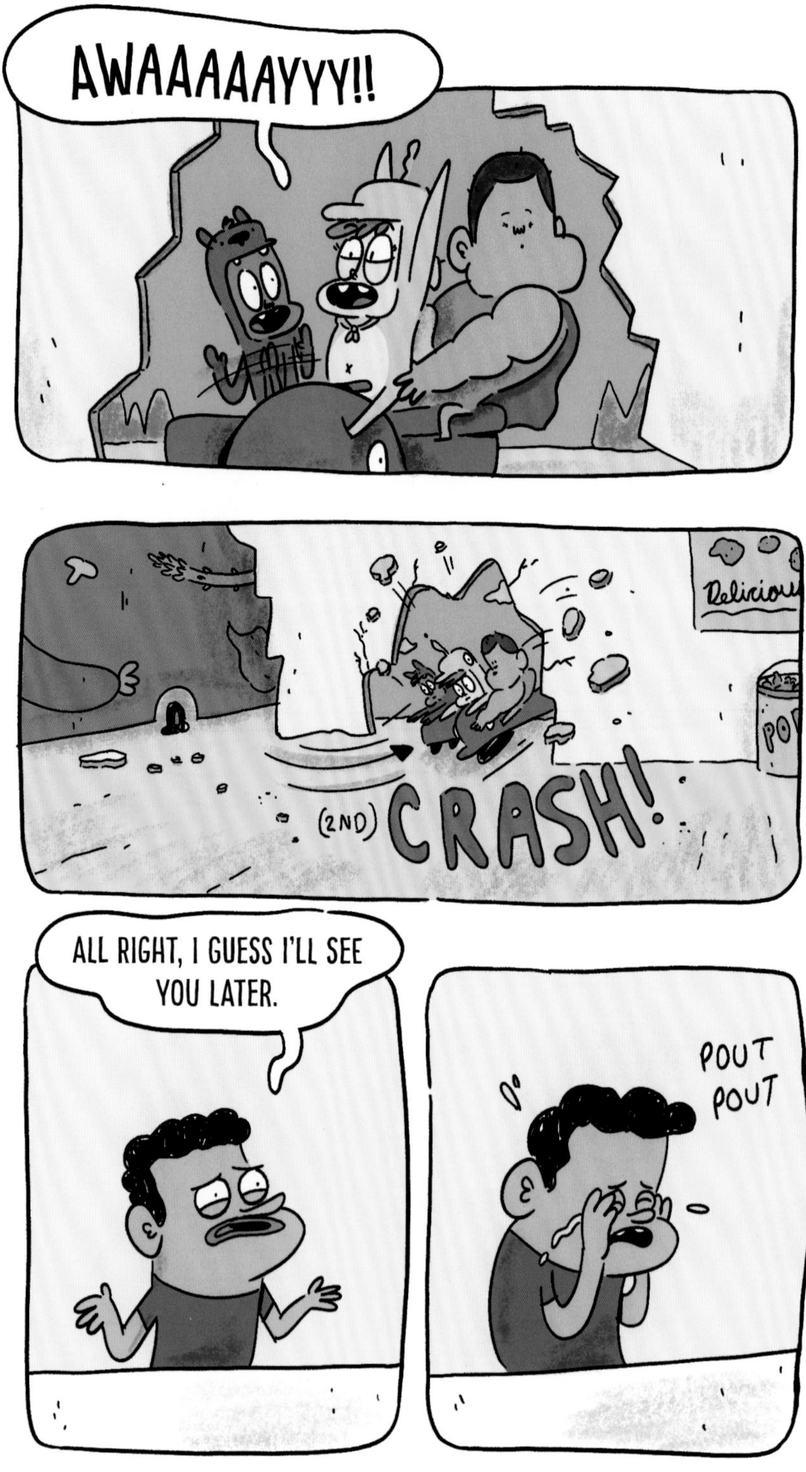
AWAAAAAYYY!!
Delicious
PO
(2ND) CRASH!
ALL RIGHT, I GUESS I'LL SEE YOU LATER.
POUT POUT

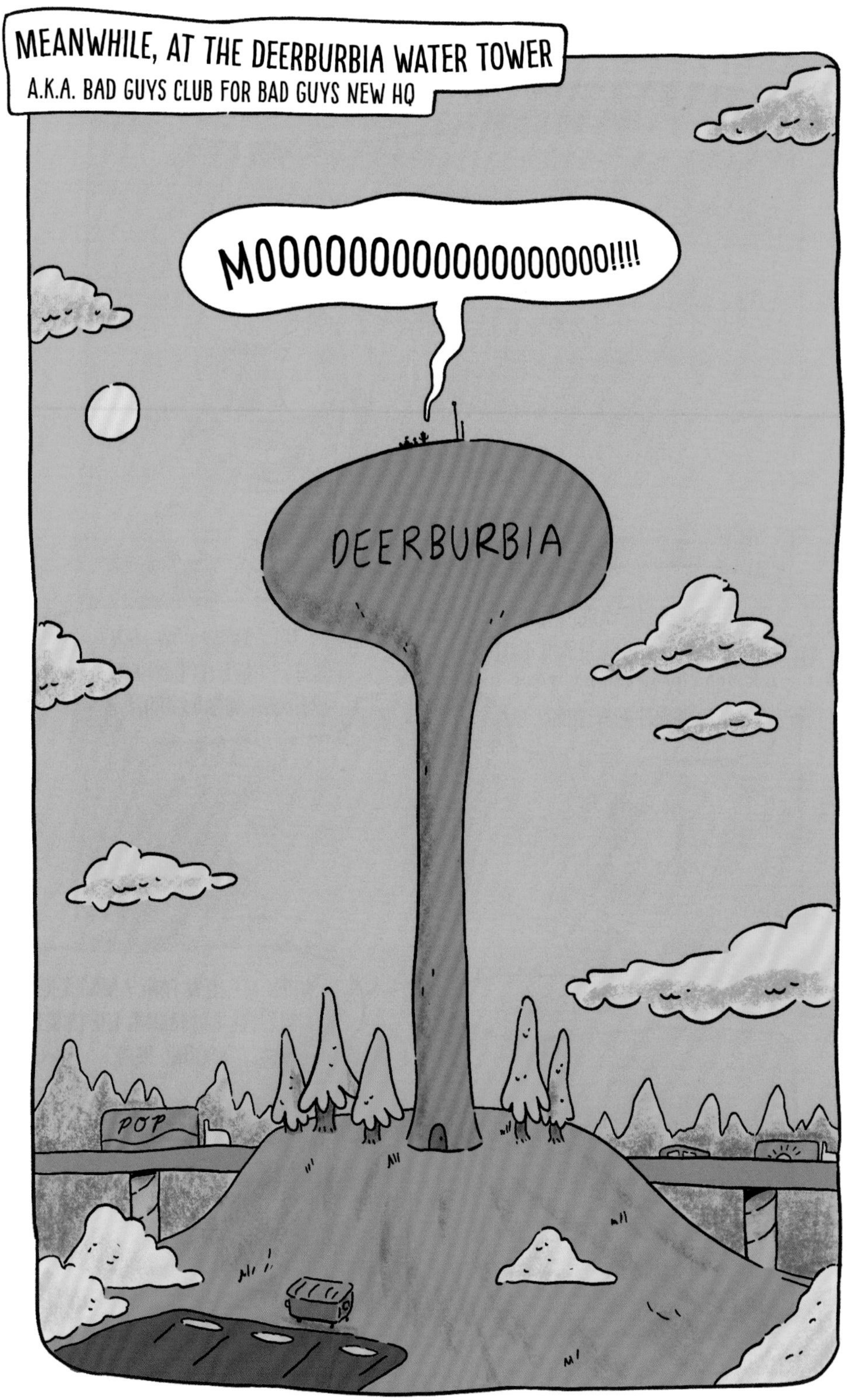

MEANWHILE, AT THE DEERBURBIA WATER TOWER
A.K.A. BAD GUYS CLUB FOR BAD GUYS NEW HQ
MOOOOOOOOOOOOOOOOOOO!!!!
DEERBURBIA
POP

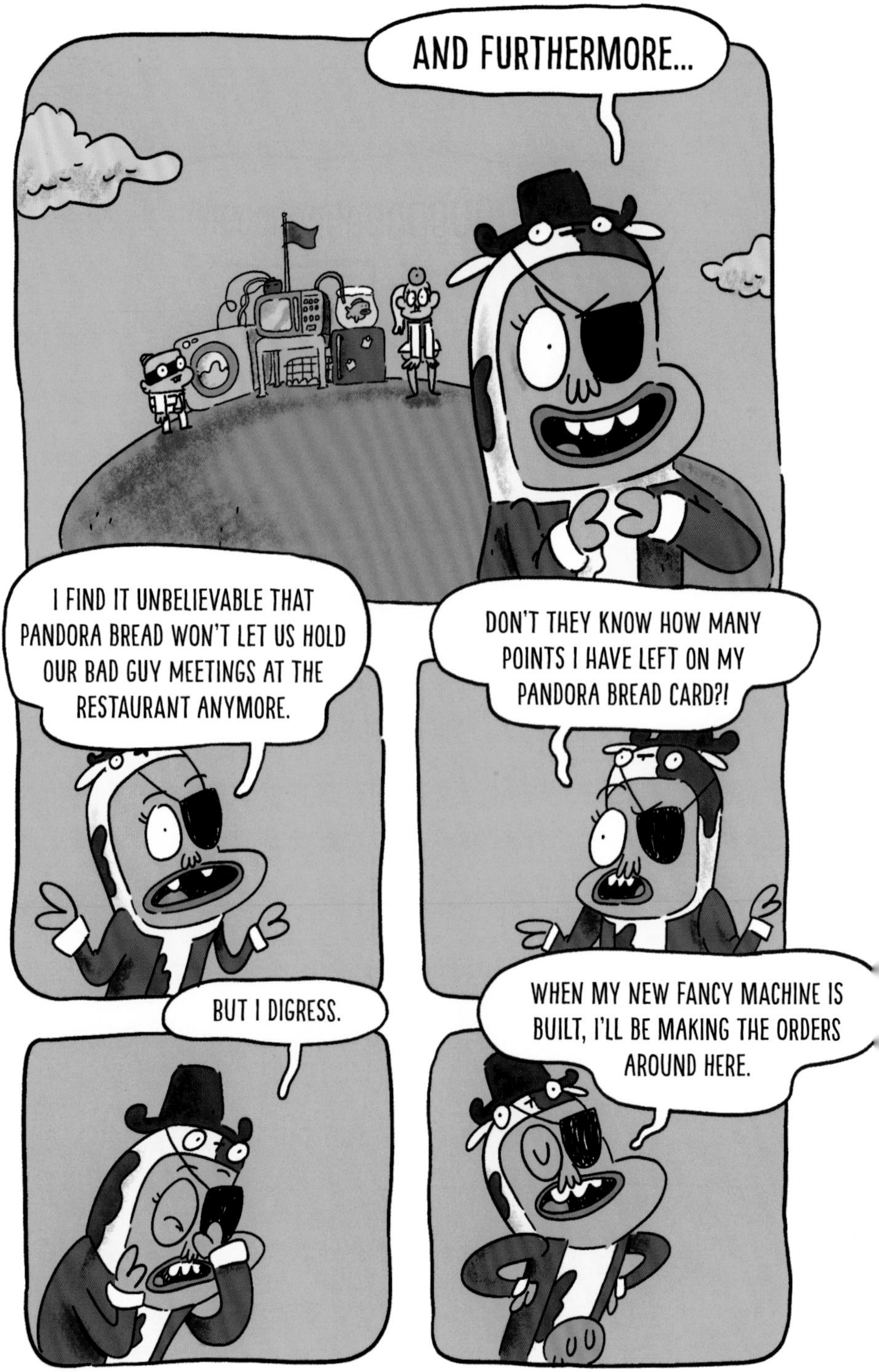
AND FURTHERMORE...
I FIND IT UNBELIEVABLE THAT PANDORA BREAD WON'T LET US HOLD OUR BAD GUY MEETINGS AT THE RESTAURANT ANYMORE.
DON'T THEY KNOW HOW MANY POINTS I HAVE LEFT ON MY PANDORA BREAD CARD?!
BUT I DIGRESS.
WHEN MY NEW FANCY MACHINE IS BUILT, I'LL BE MAKING THE ORDERS AROUND HERE.

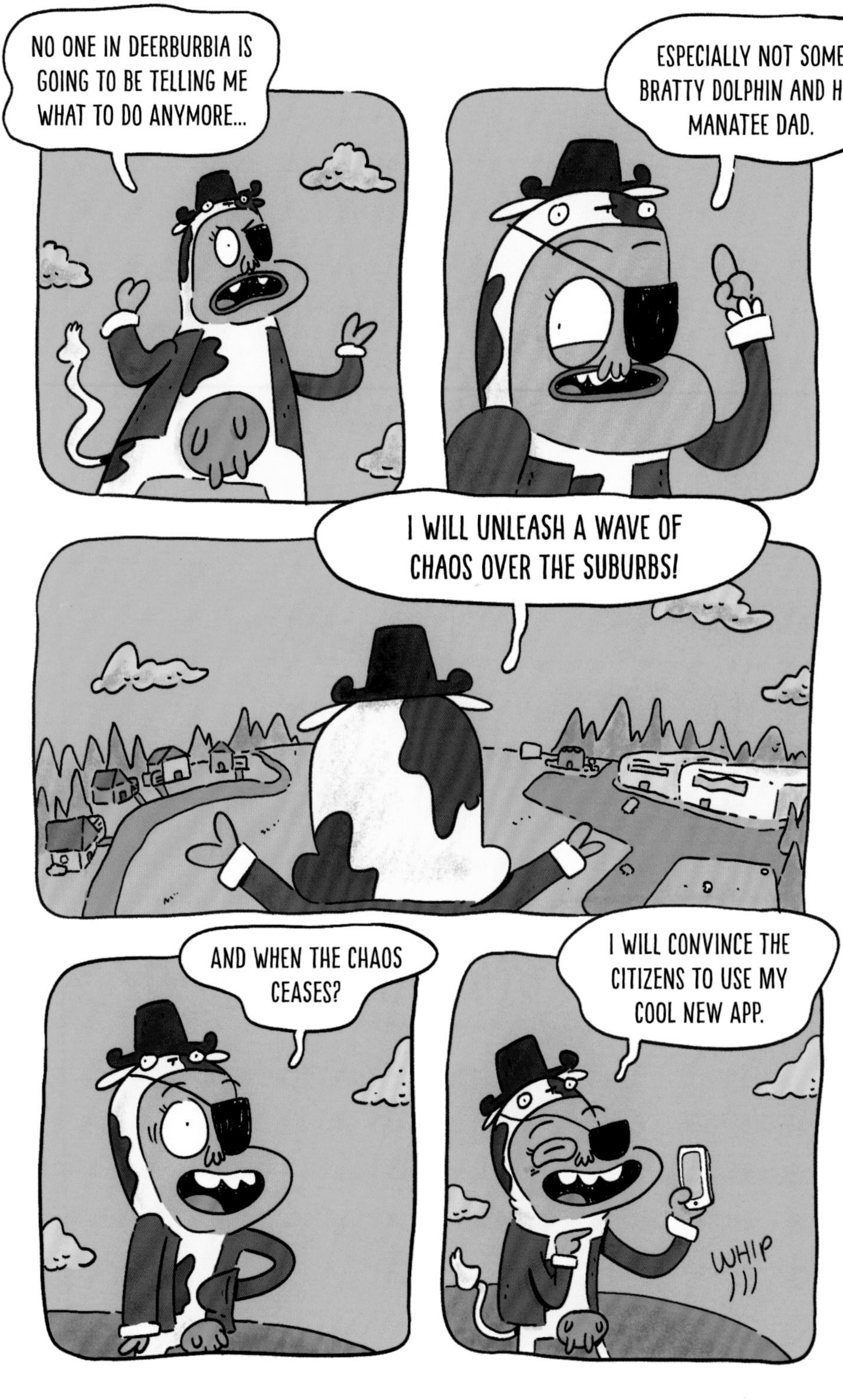
NO ONE IN DEERBURBIA IS GOING TO BE TELLING ME WHAT TO DO ANYMORE...
ESPECIALLY NOT SOME BRATTY DOLPHIN AND HER MANATEE DAD.
I WILL UNLEASH A WAVE OF CHAOS OVER THE SUBURBS!
AND WHEN THE CHAOS CEASES?
I WILL CONVINCE THE CITIZENS TO USE MY COOL NEW APP.
WHIP

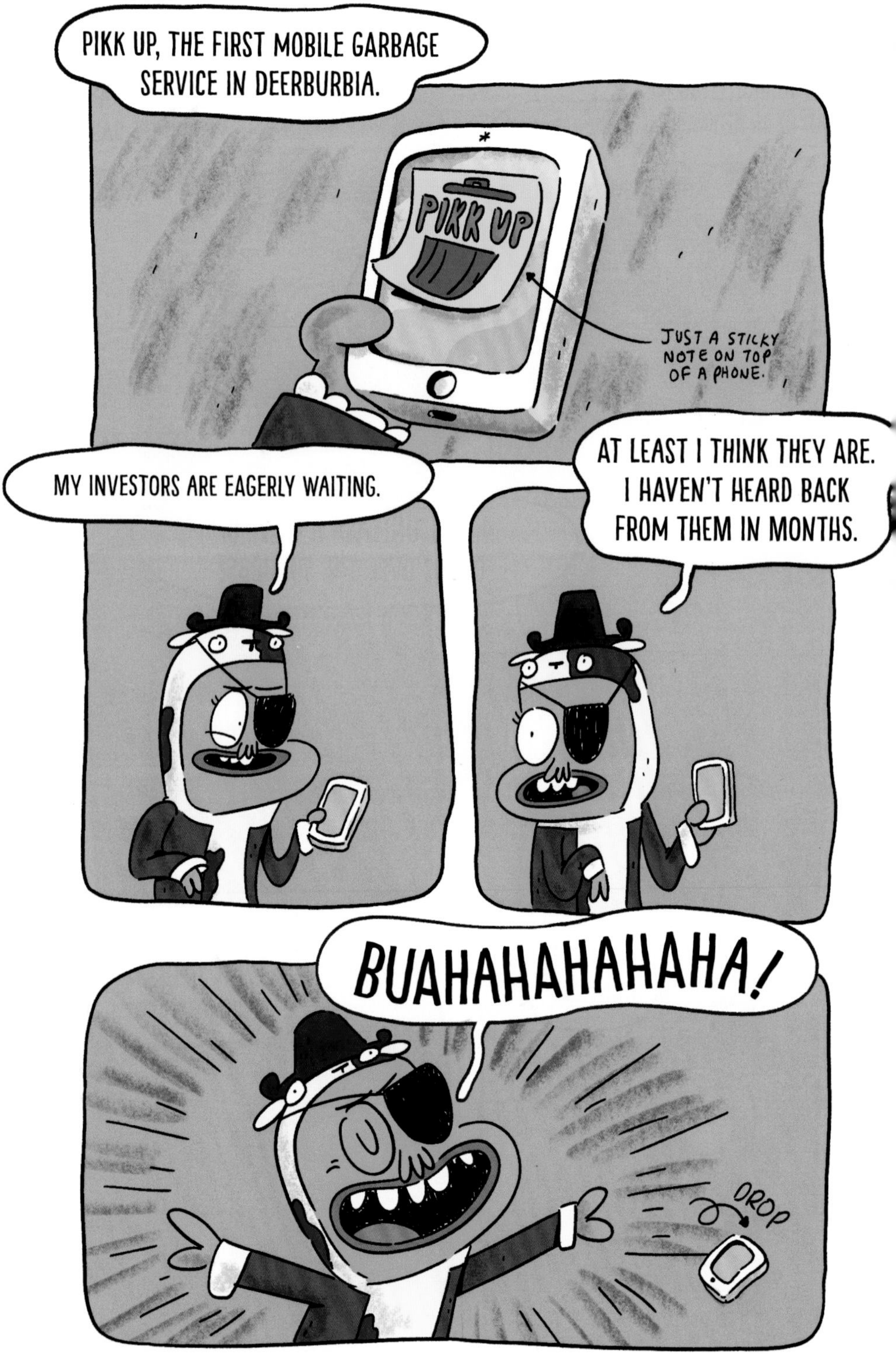
PIKK UP, THE FIRST MOBILE GARBAGE SERVICE IN DEERBURBIA.
PIKK UP
JUST A STICKY NOTE ON TOP OF A PHONE.
MY INVESTORS ARE EAGERLY WAITING.
AT LEAST I THINK THEY ARE. I HAVEN'T HEARD BACK FROM THEM IN MONTHS.
BUAHAHAHAHAHA!
DROP

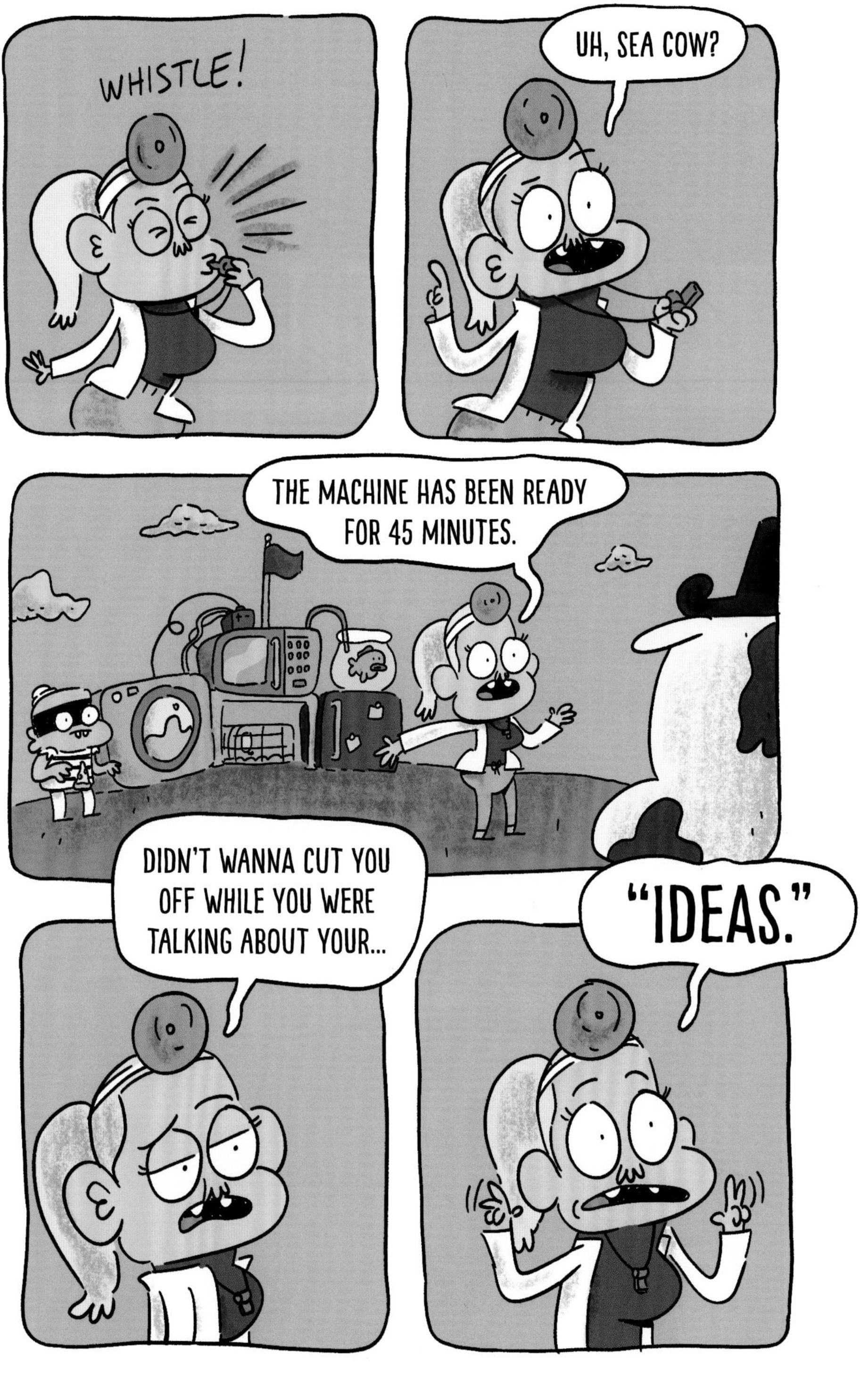
WHISTLE!
UH, SEA COW?
THE MACHINE HAS BEEN READY FOR 45 MINUTES.
DIDN'T WANNA CUT YOU OFF WHILE YOU WERE TALKING ABOUT YOUR...
"IDEAS."

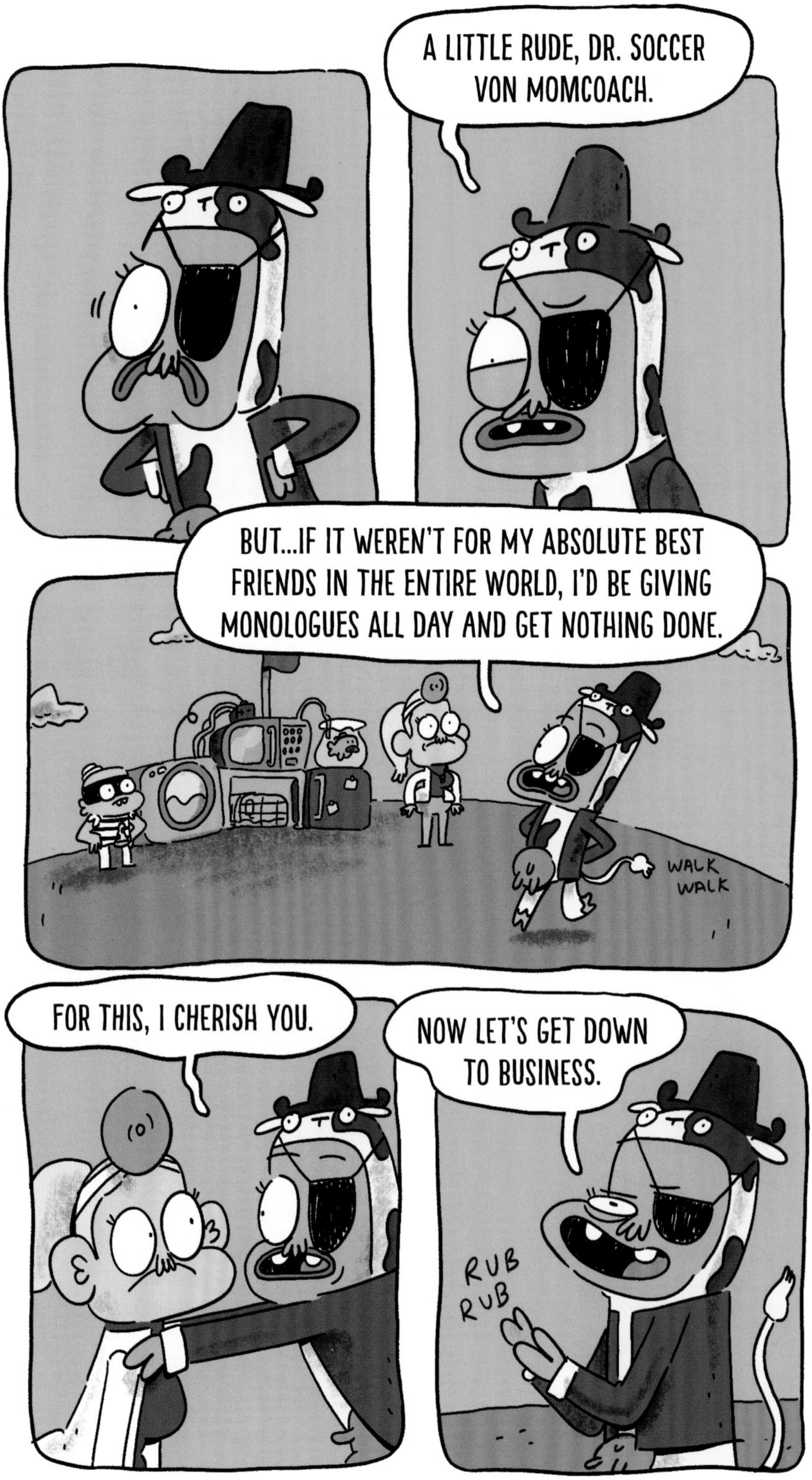
A LITTLE RUDE, DR. SOCCER VON MOMCOACH.
BUT...IF IT WEREN'T FOR MY ABSOLUTE BEST FRIENDS IN THE ENTIRE WORLD, I'D BE GIVING MONOLOGUES ALL DAY AND GET NOTHING DONE.
WALK WALK
FOR THIS, I CHERISH YOU.
NOW LET'S GET DOWN TO BUSINESS.
RUB RUB

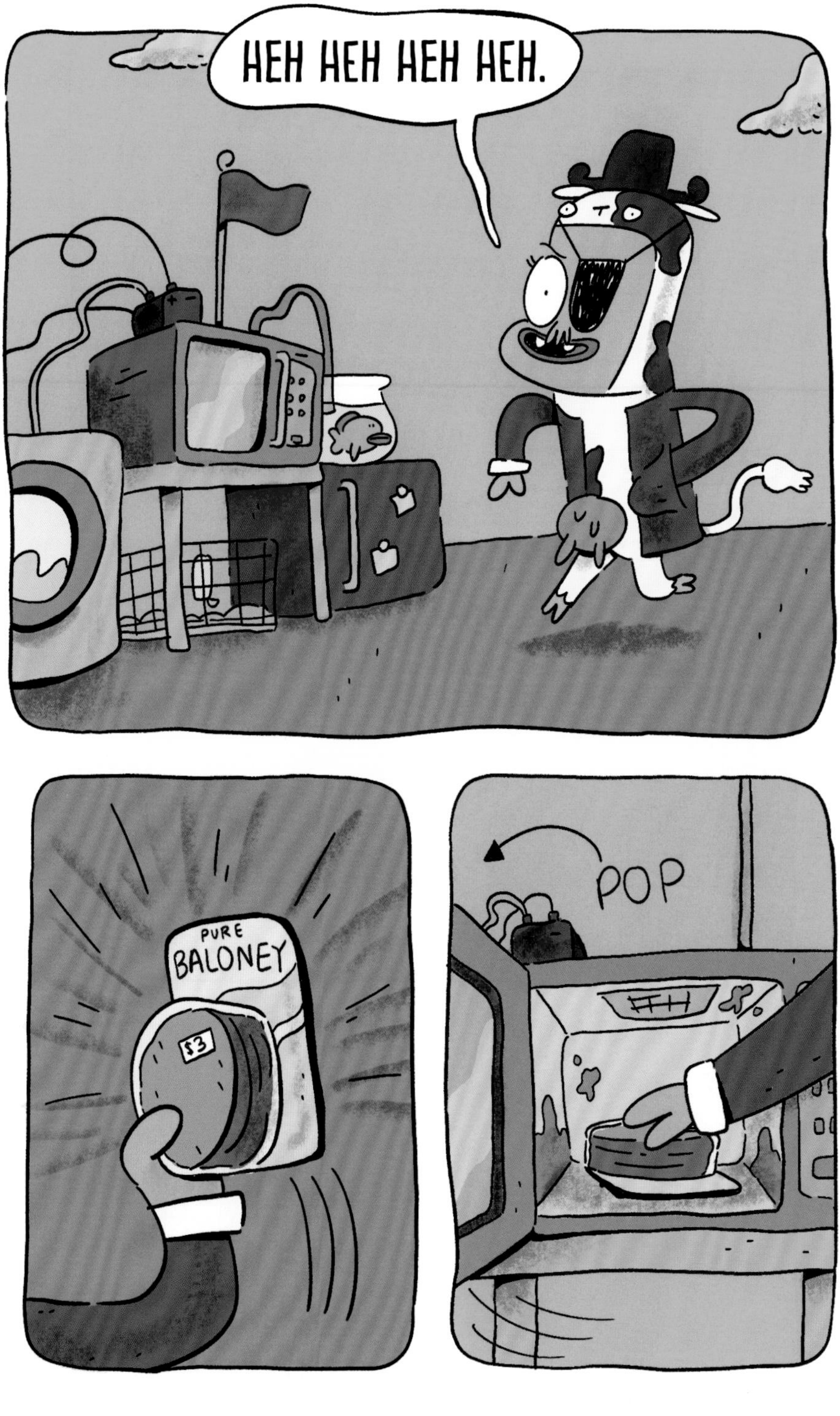
HEH HEH HEH HEH.
PURE
BALONEY
$3
POP

MY FELLOW BAD GUYS, I GIVE YOU **BALONEY STORM!**

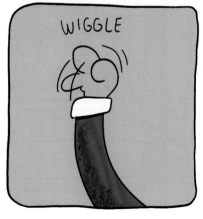

WIGGLE

PRESS

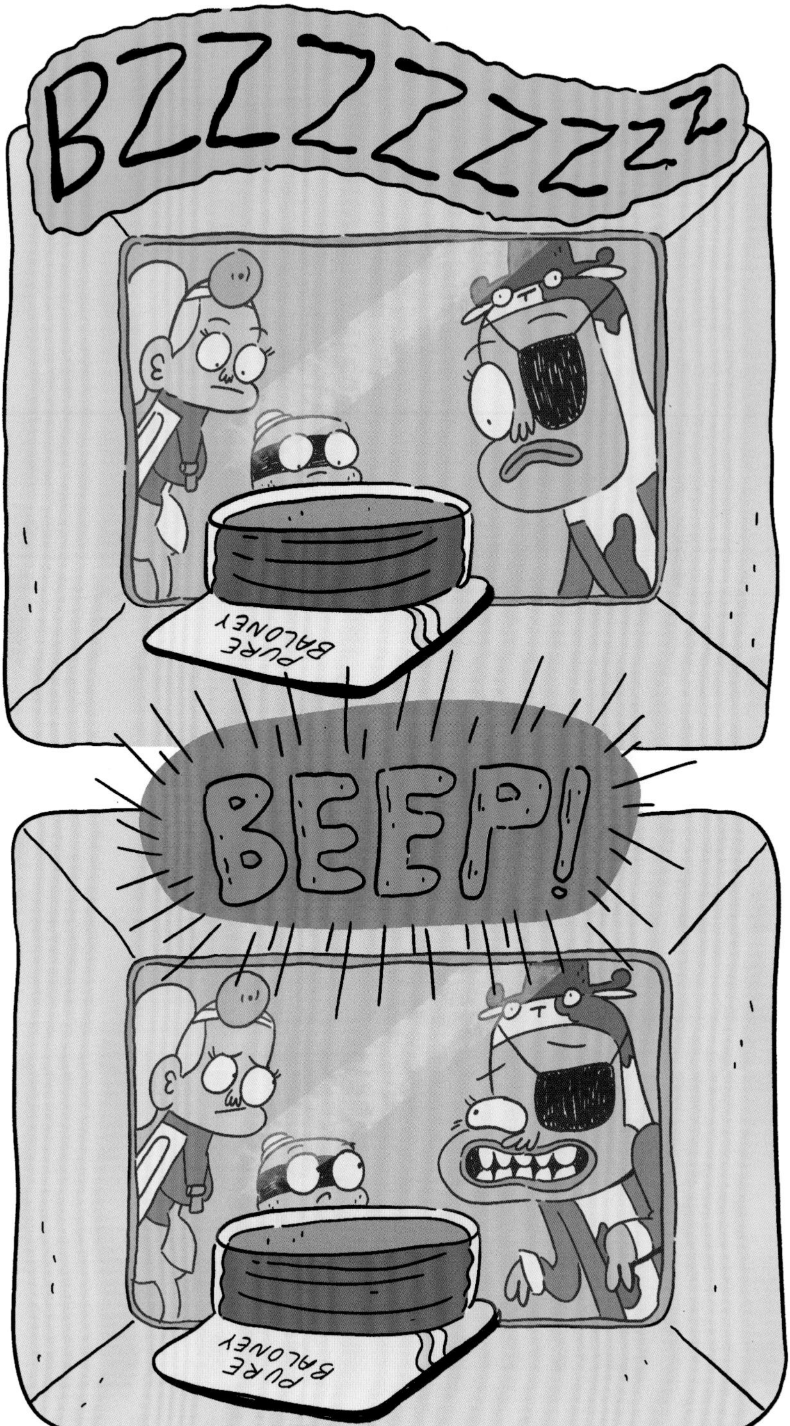
BZZZZZZZZ
PURE BALONEY
BEEP!
PURE BALONEY

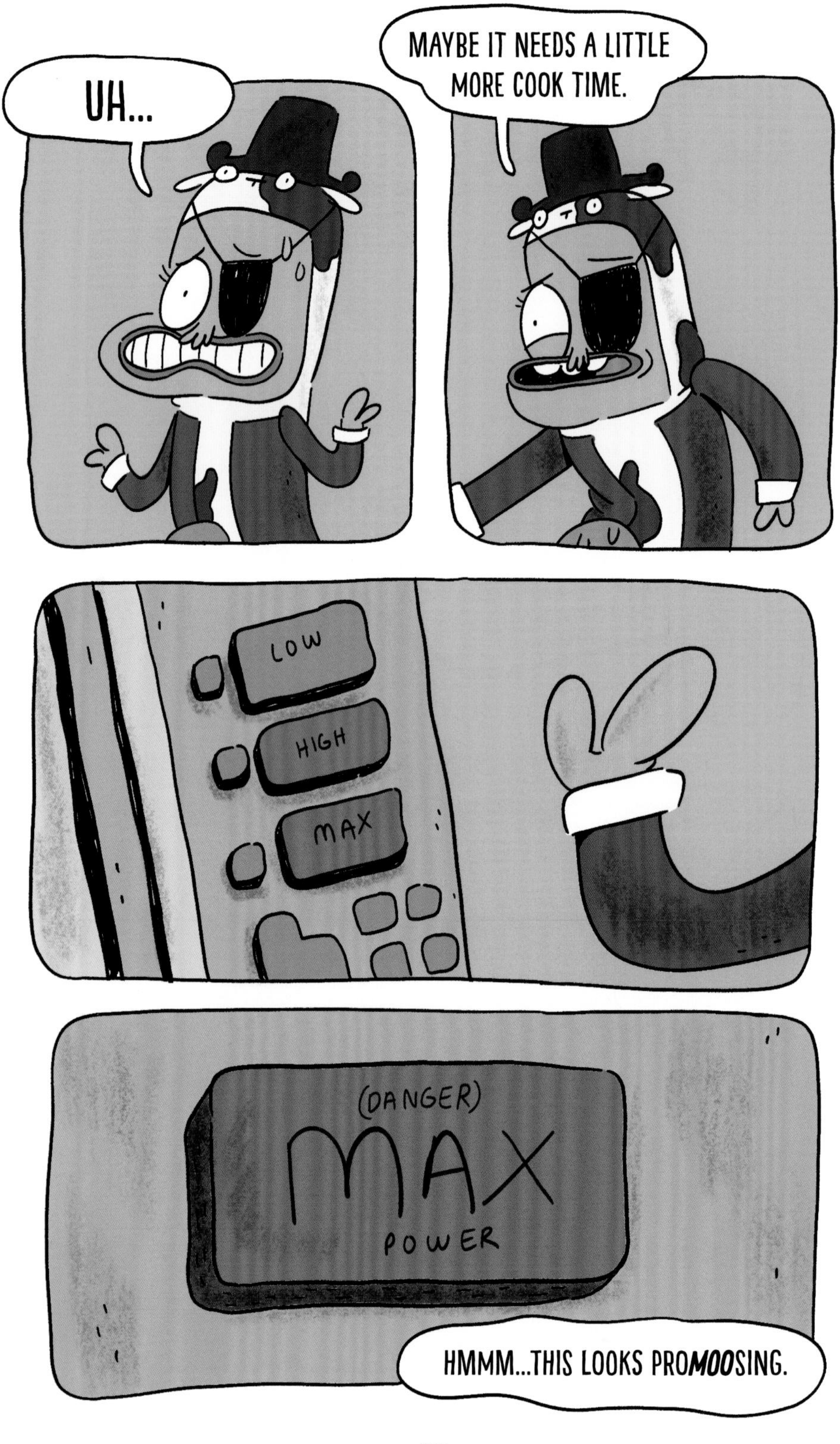
UH...
MAYBE IT NEEDS A LITTLE MORE COOK TIME.
LOW
HIGH
MAX
(DANGER)
MAX
POWER
HMMM...THIS LOOKS PRO*MOO*SING.

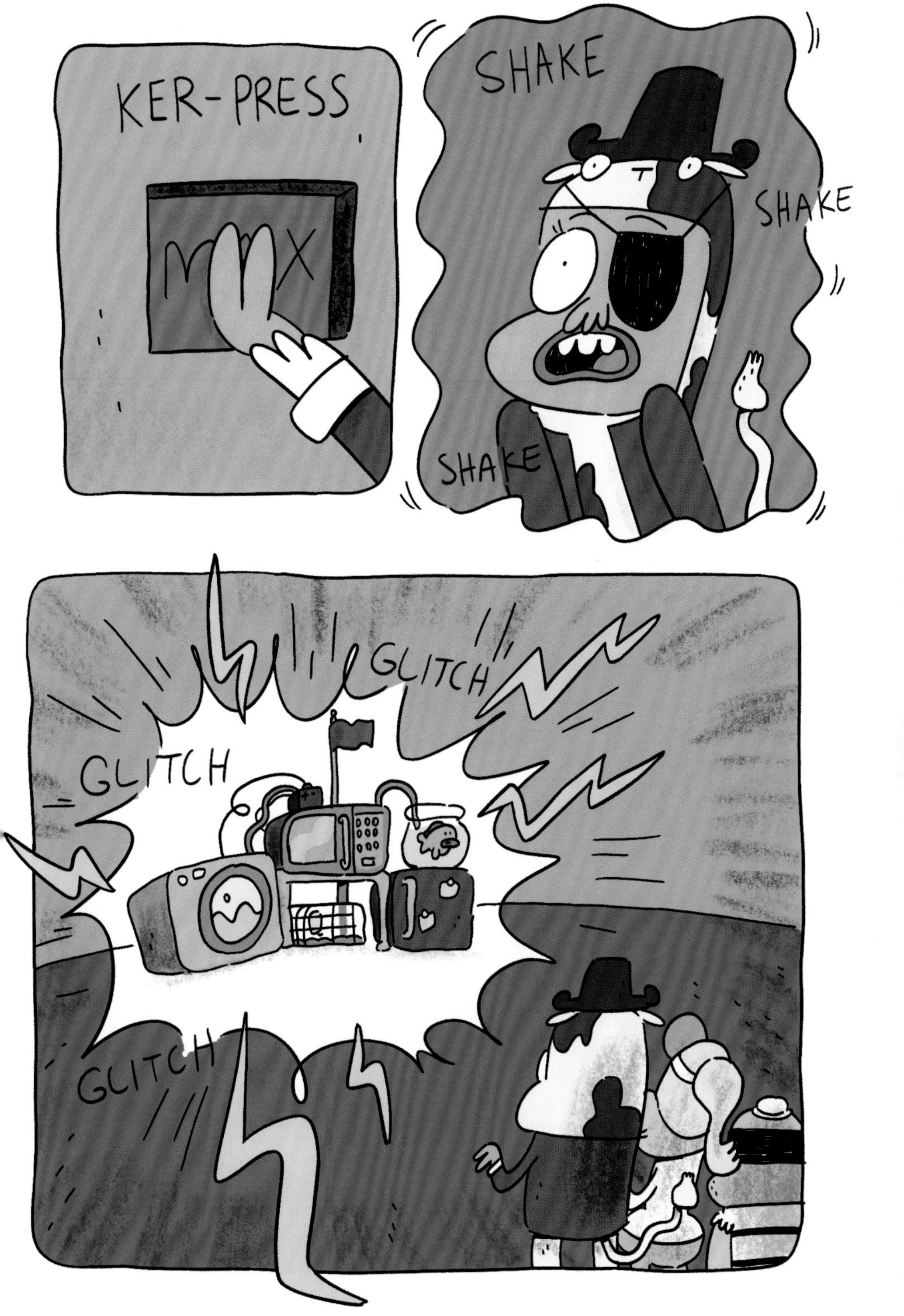
KER-PRESS
MAX
SHAKE
SHAKE
SHAKE
GLITCH
GLITCH
GLITCH

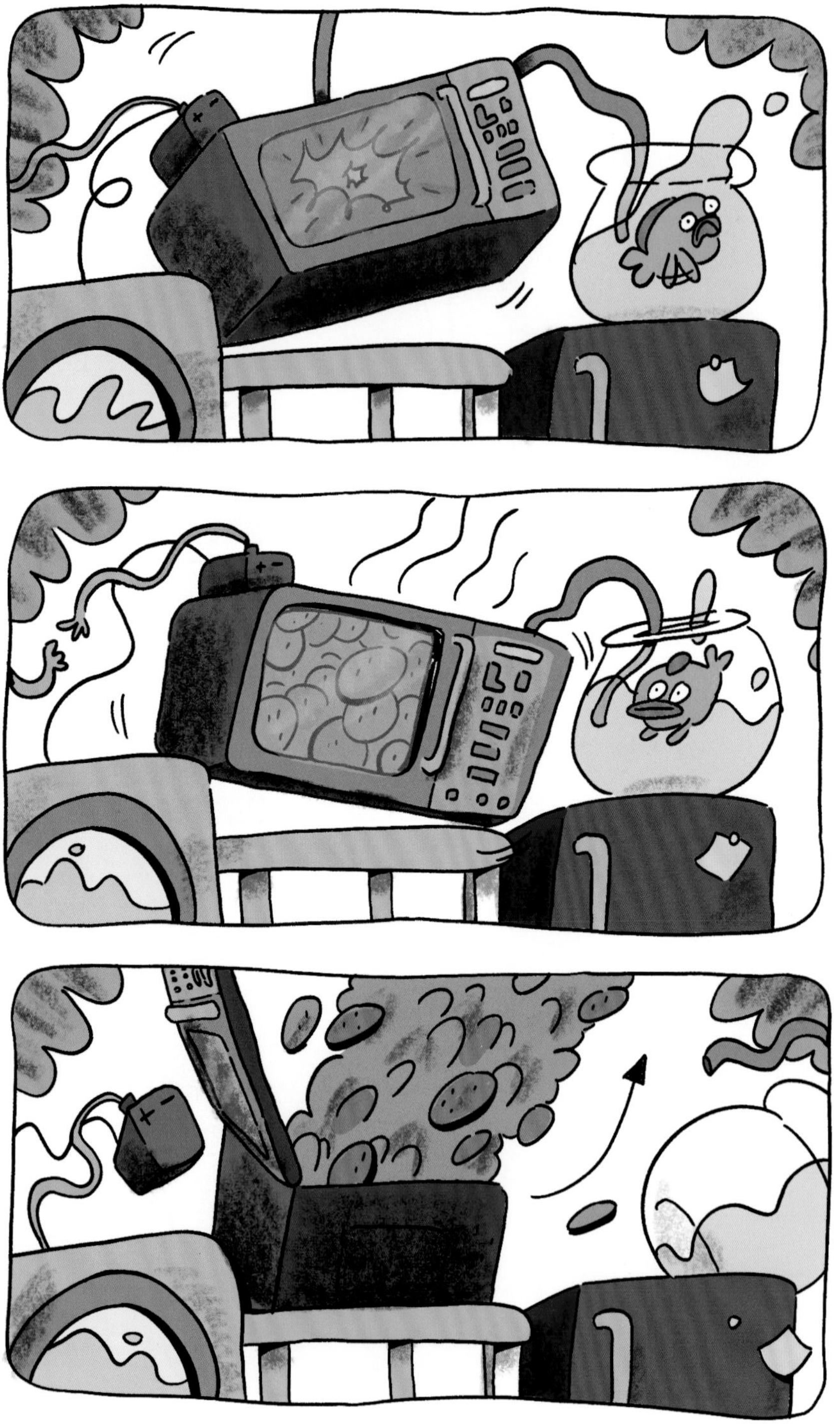

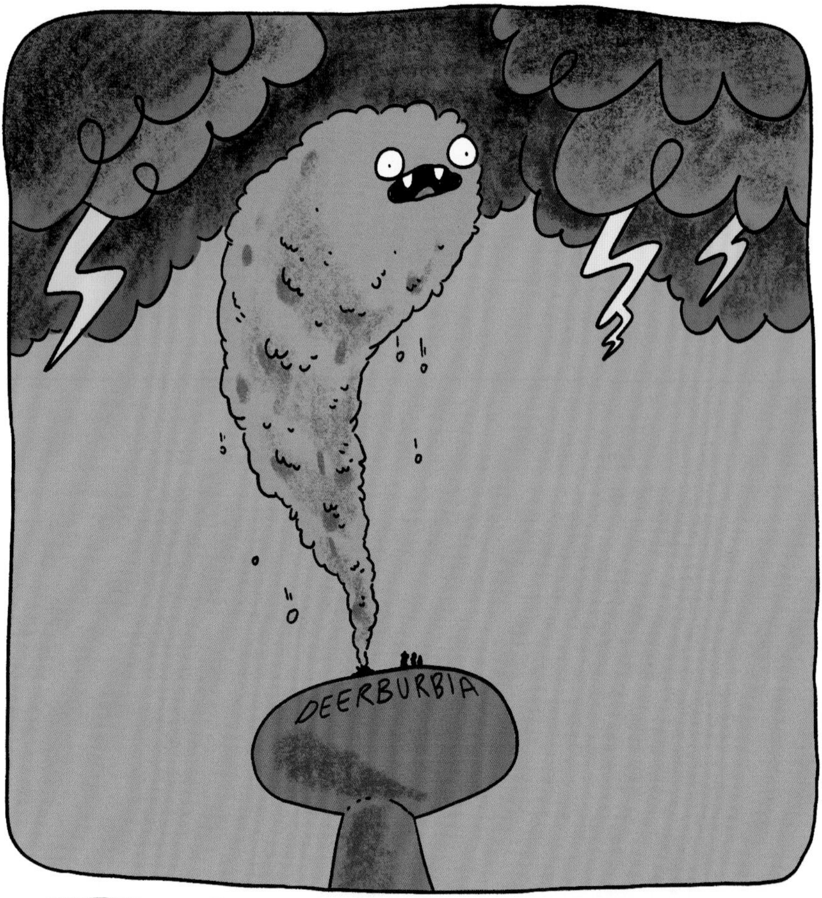

DEERBURBIA

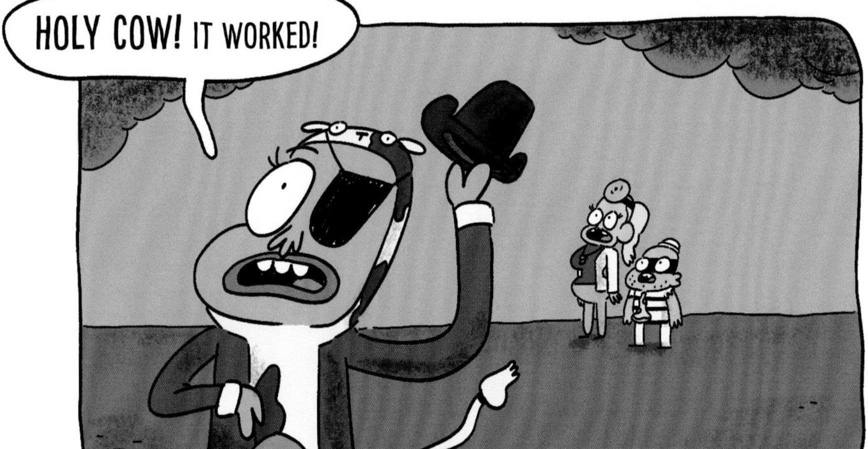

HOLY COW! IT WORKED!

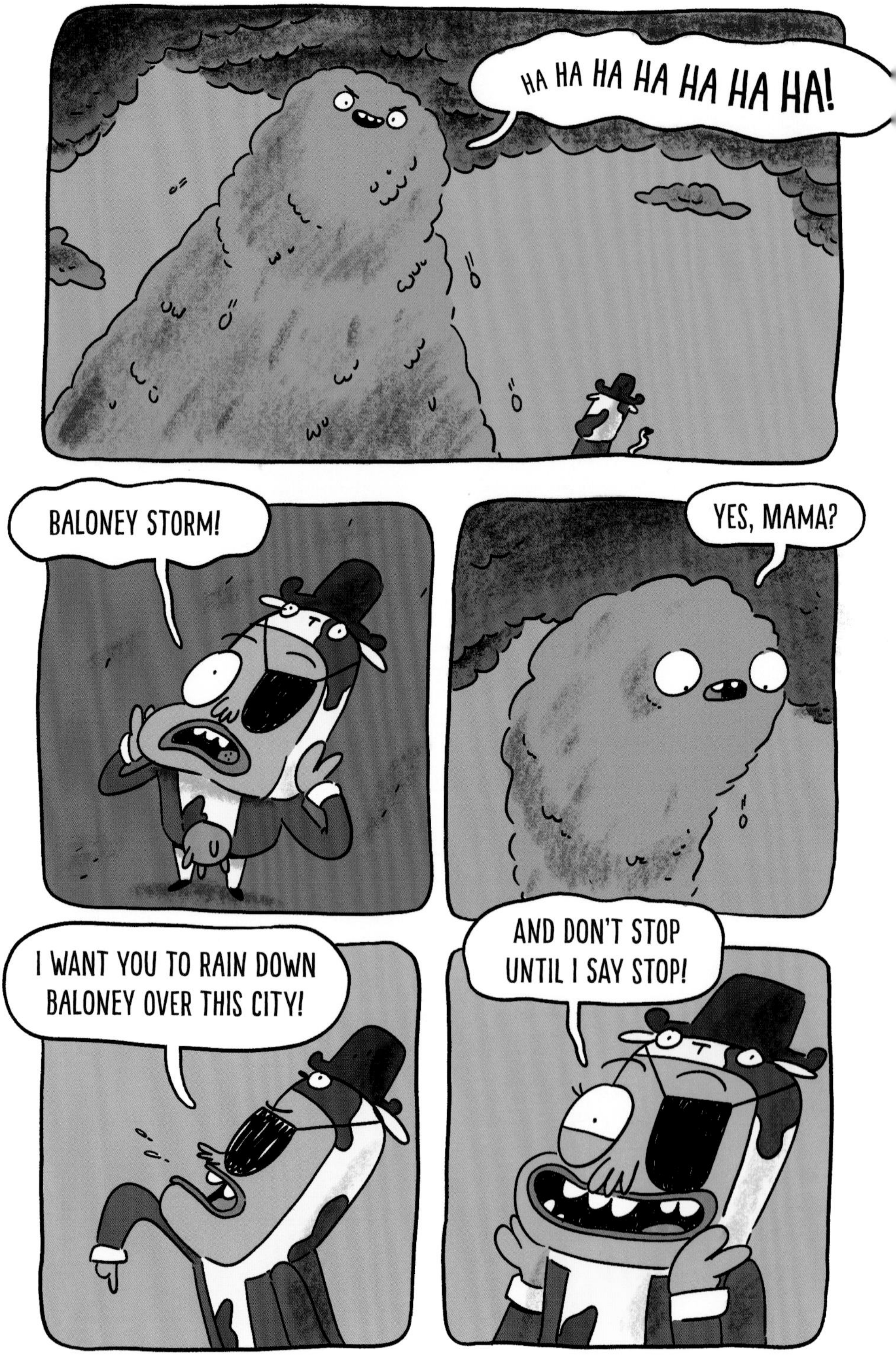
HA HA HA HA HA HA HA!
BALONEY STORM!
YES, MAMA?
I WANT YOU TO RAIN DOWN BALONEY OVER THIS CITY!
AND DON'T STOP UNTIL I SAY STOP!

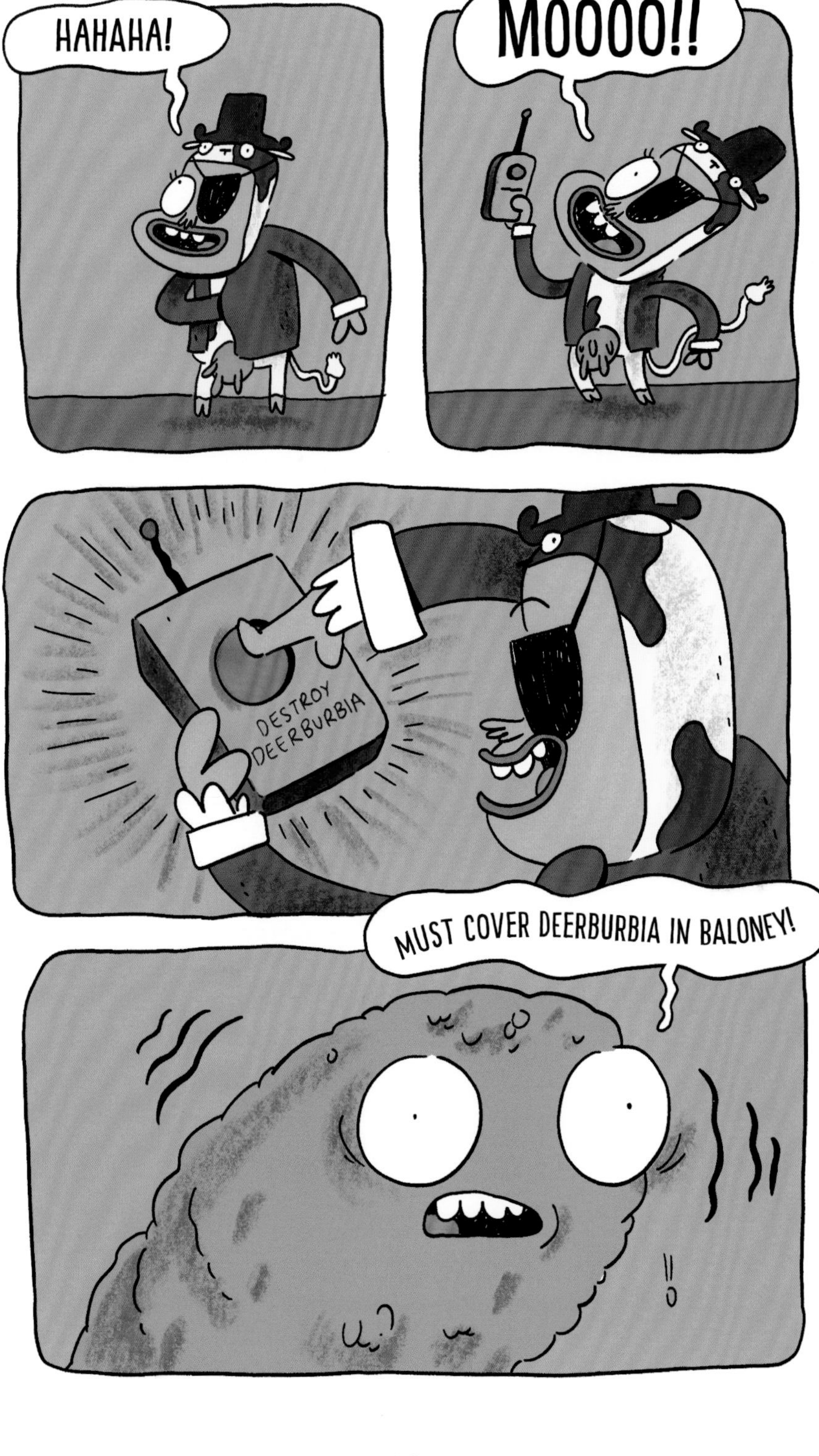
HAHAHA!
MOOOO!!
DESTROY DEERBURBIA
MUST COVER DEERBURBIA IN BALONEY!
!!

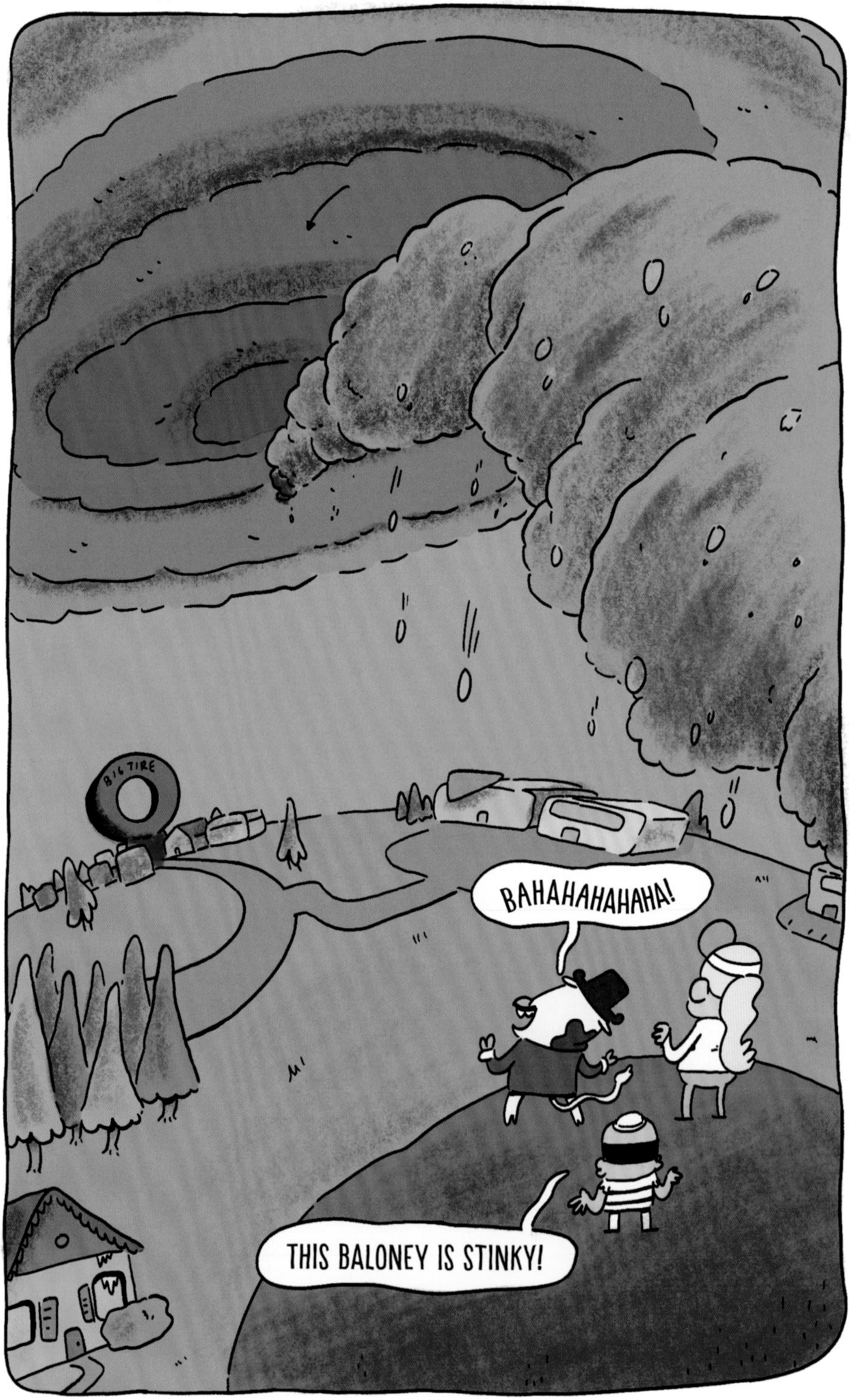
BIG TIRE
BAHAHAHAHAHA!
THIS BALONEY IS STINKY!

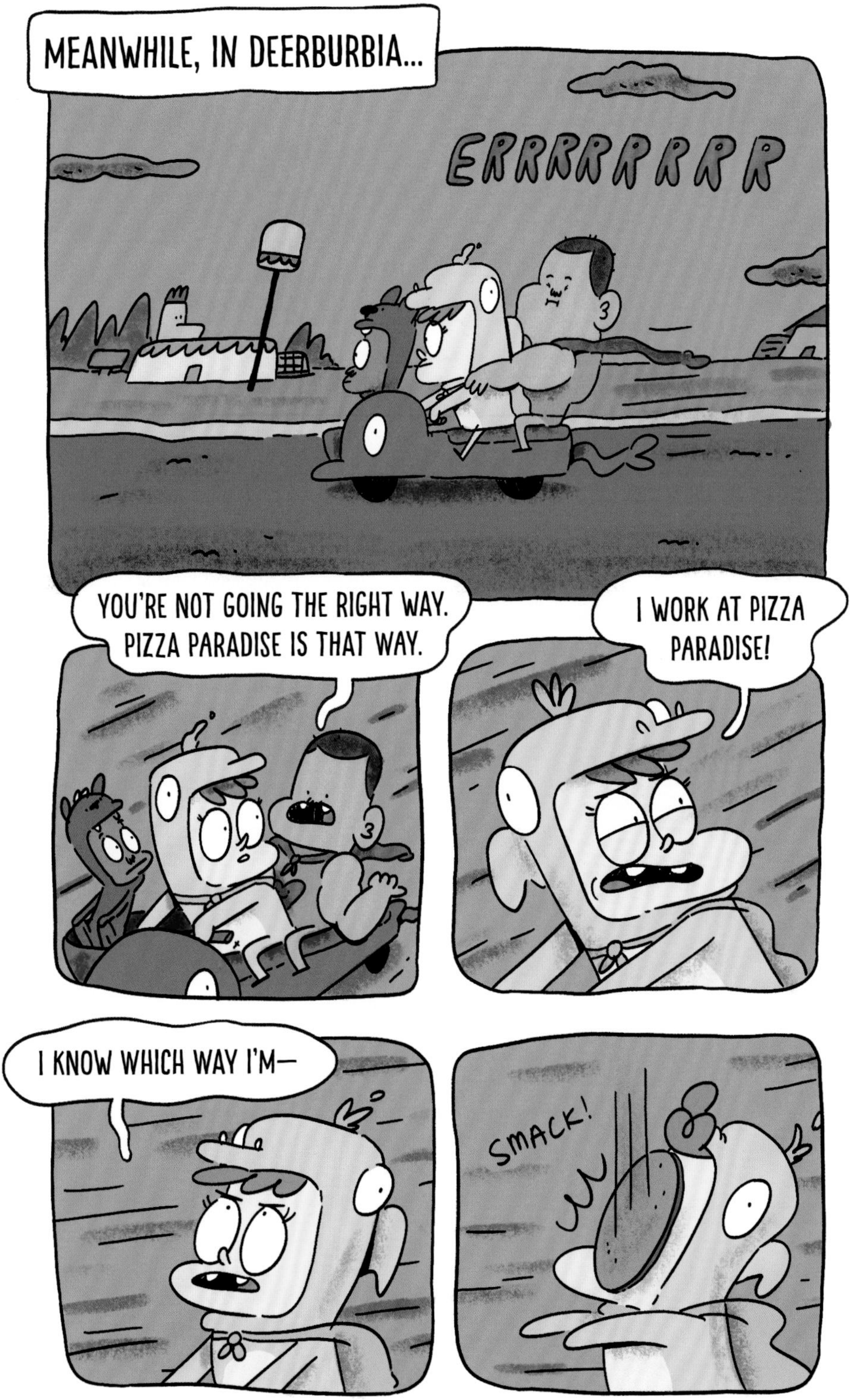
MEANWHILE, IN DEERBURBIA...
ERRRRRRRR
YOU'RE NOT GOING THE RIGHT WAY. PIZZA PARADISE IS THAT WAY.
I WORK AT PIZZA PARADISE!
I KNOW WHICH WAY I'M—
SMACK!

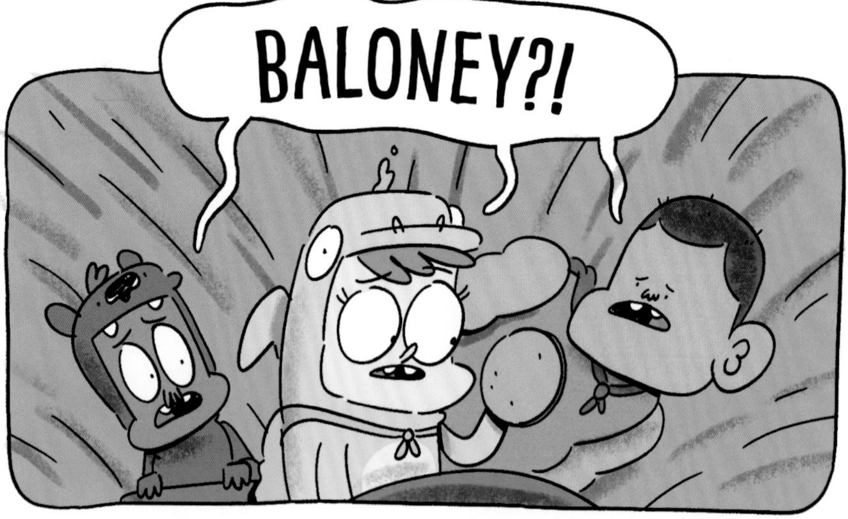
BALONEY?!

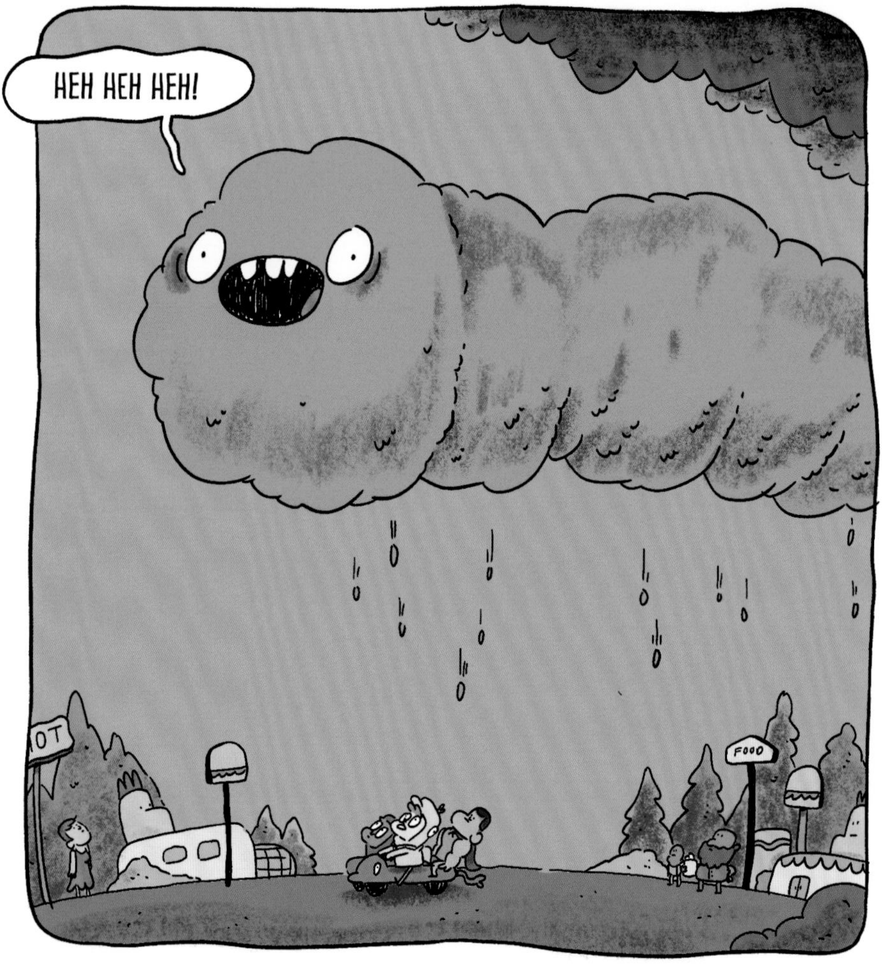
HEH HEH HEH!
OT
FOOD

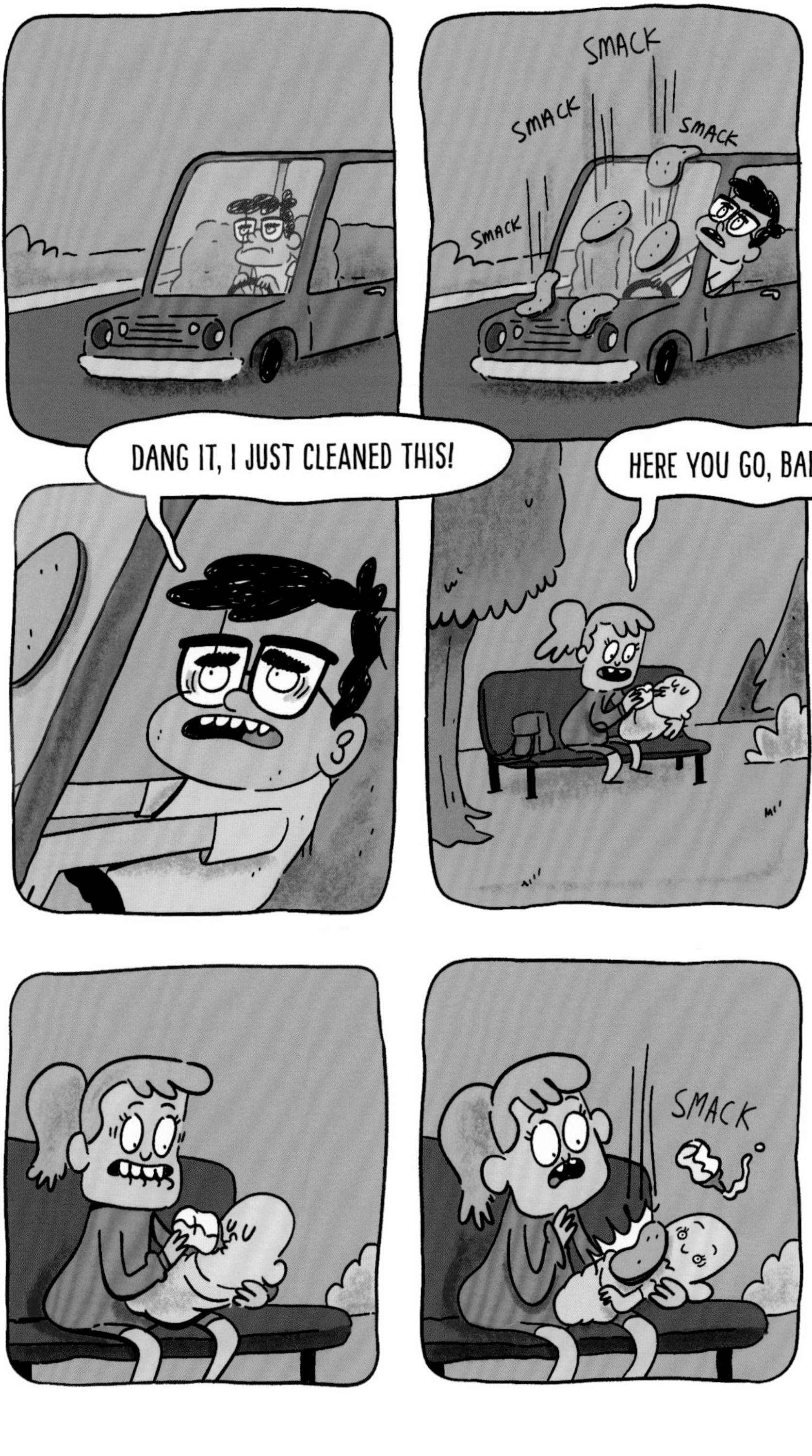
SMACK
SMACK
SMACK
SMACK
DANG IT, I JUST CLEANED THIS!
HERE YOU GO, BABY!
SMACK

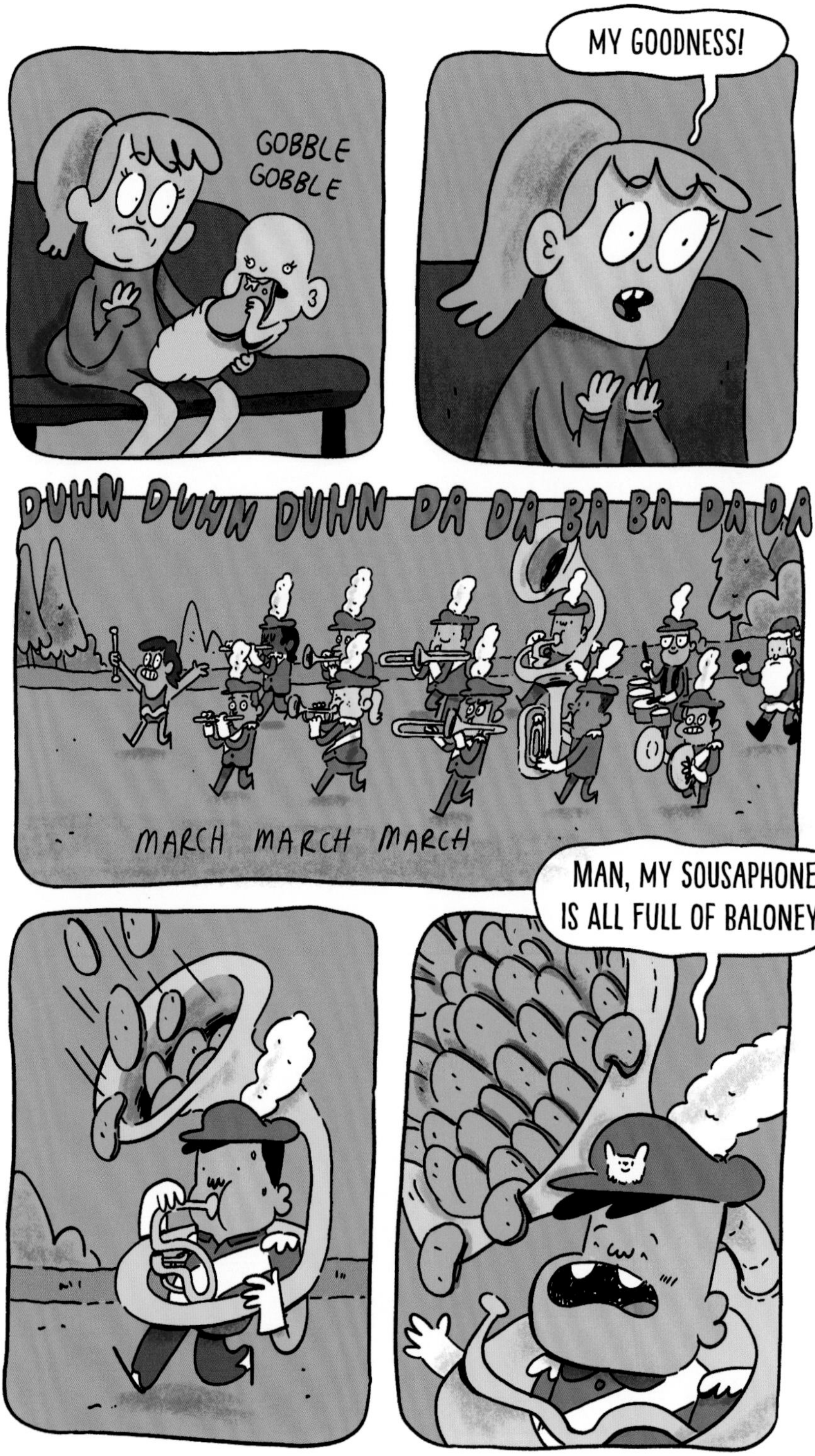
GOBBLE
GOBBLE
MY GOODNESS!
DUHN DUHN DUHN DA DA BA BA DA DA
MARCH MARCH MARCH
MAN, MY SOUSAPHONE IS ALL FULL OF BALONEY!

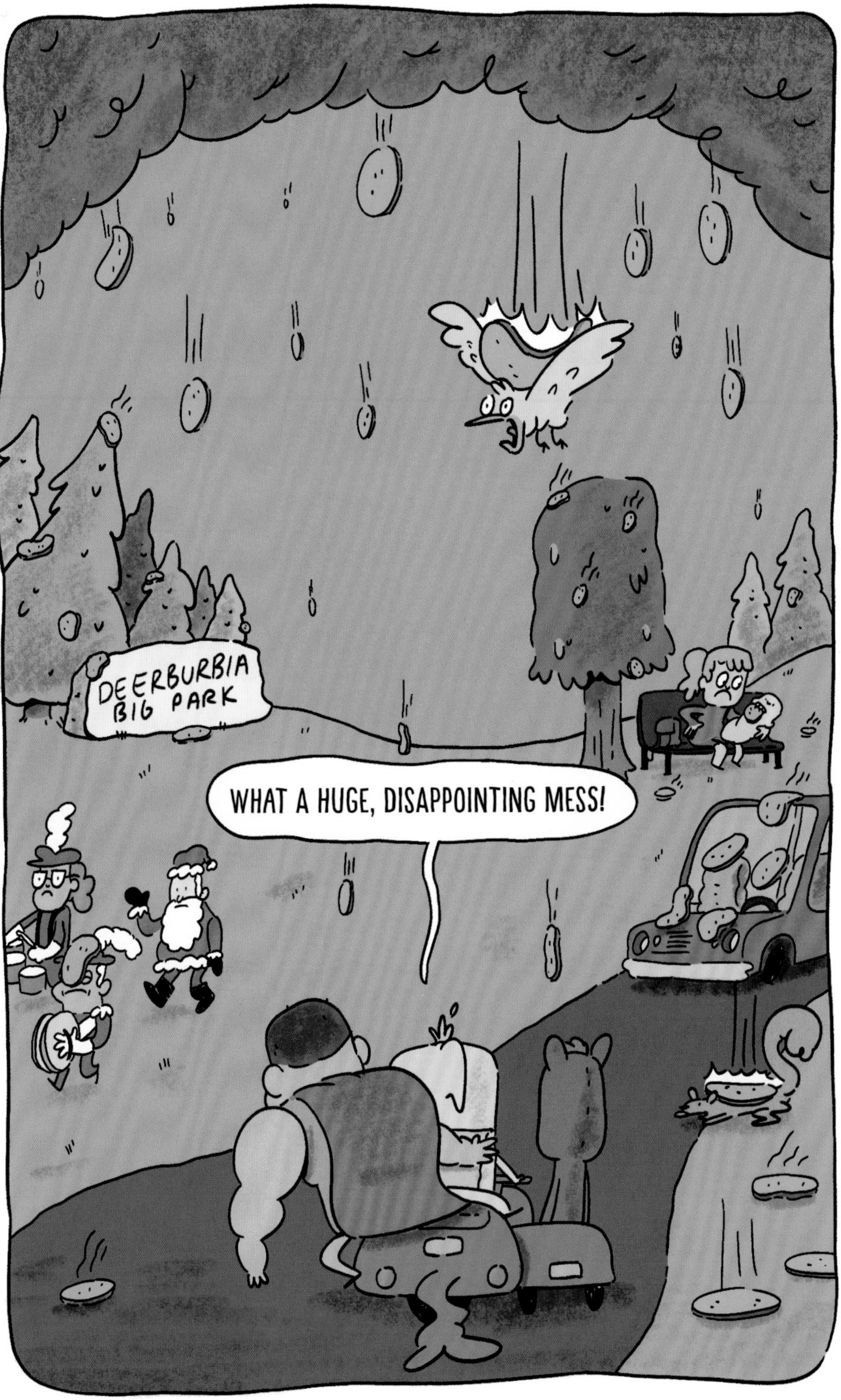
DEERBURBIA
BIG PARK
WHAT A HUGE, DISAPPOINTING MESS!

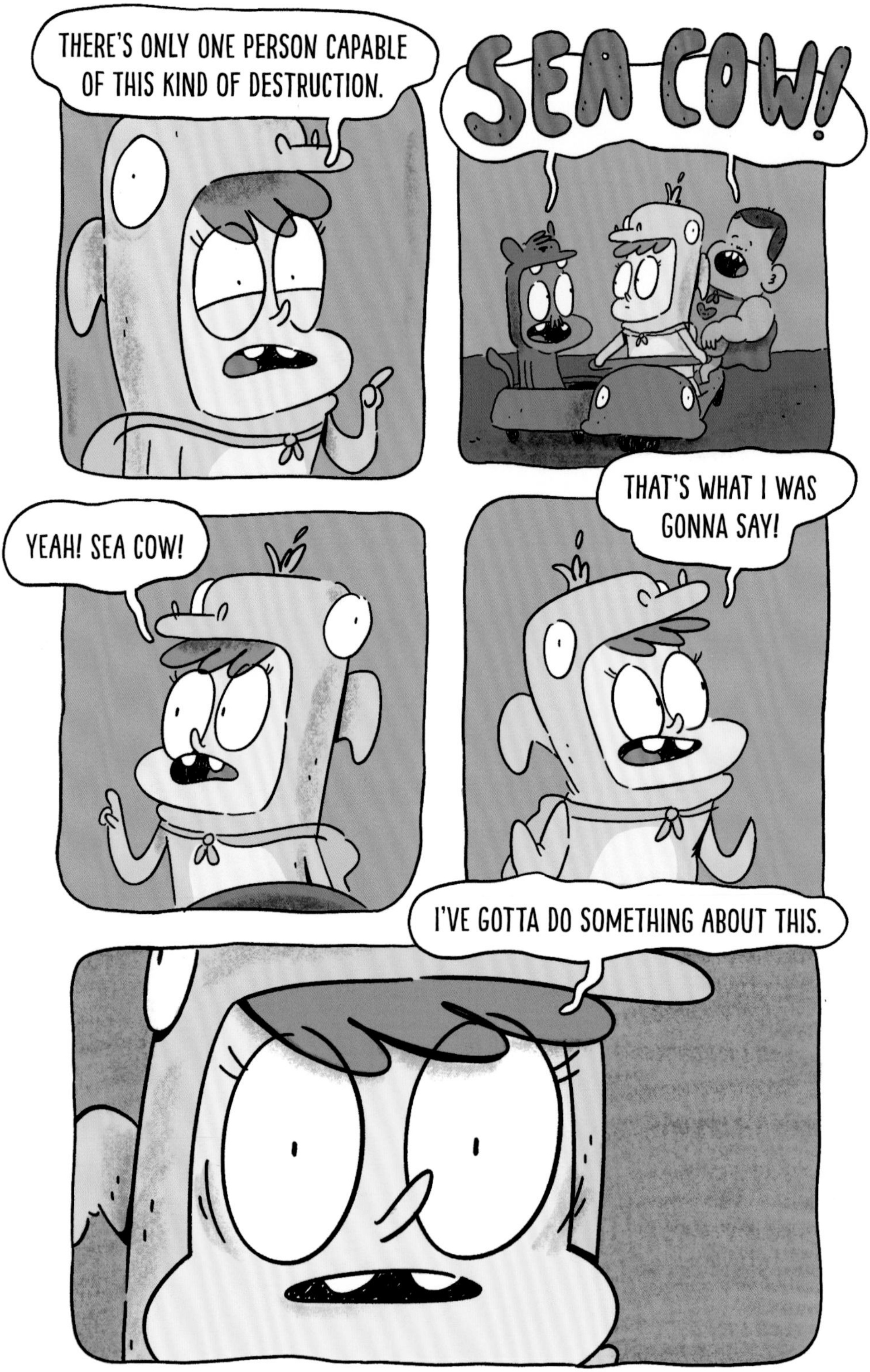
THERE'S ONLY ONE PERSON CAPABLE OF THIS KIND OF DESTRUCTION.
SEA COW!
YEAH! SEA COW!
THAT'S WHAT I WAS GONNA SAY!
I'VE GOTTA DO SOMETHING ABOUT THIS.

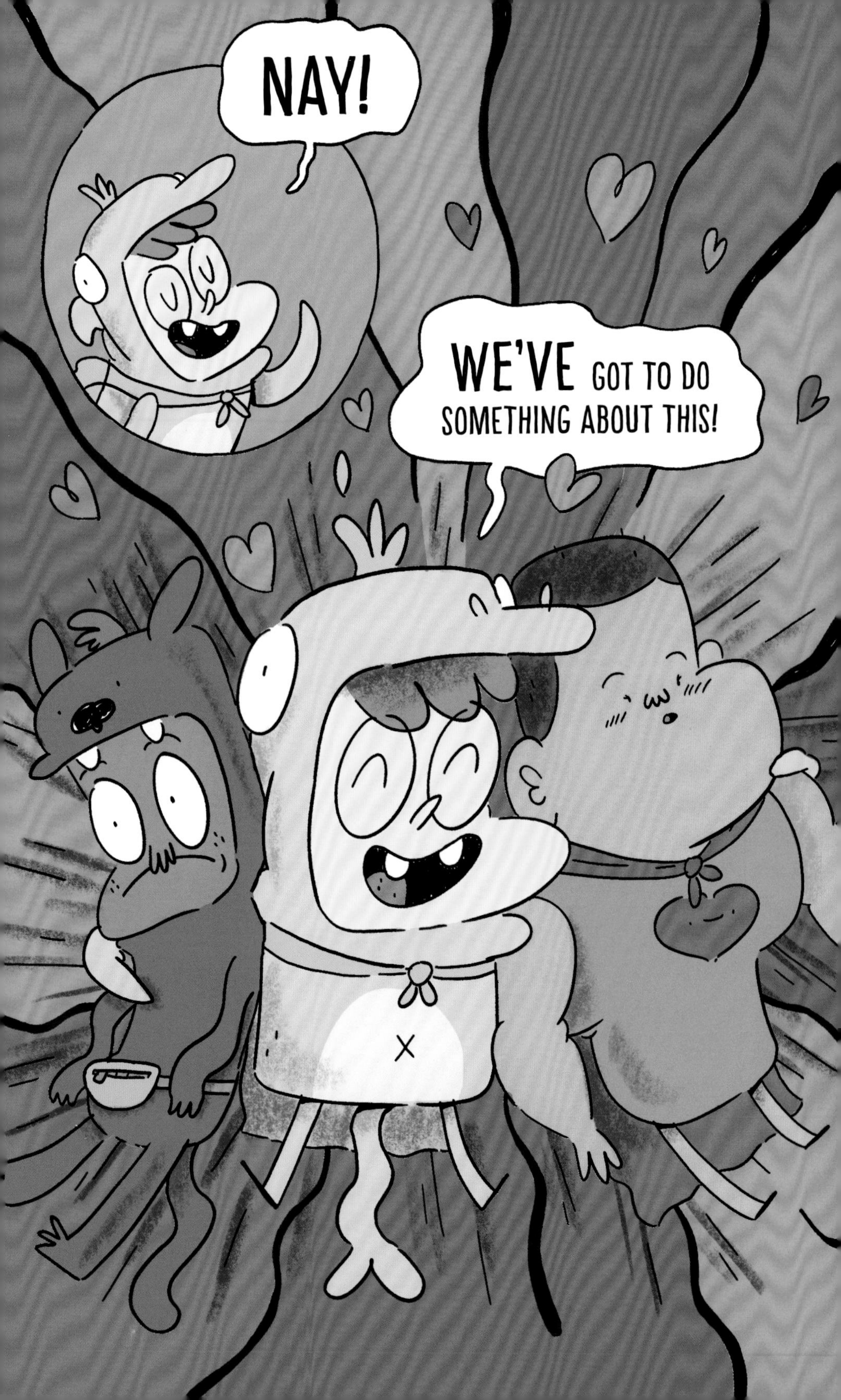
NAY!
WE'VE GOT TO DO SOMETHING ABOUT THIS!

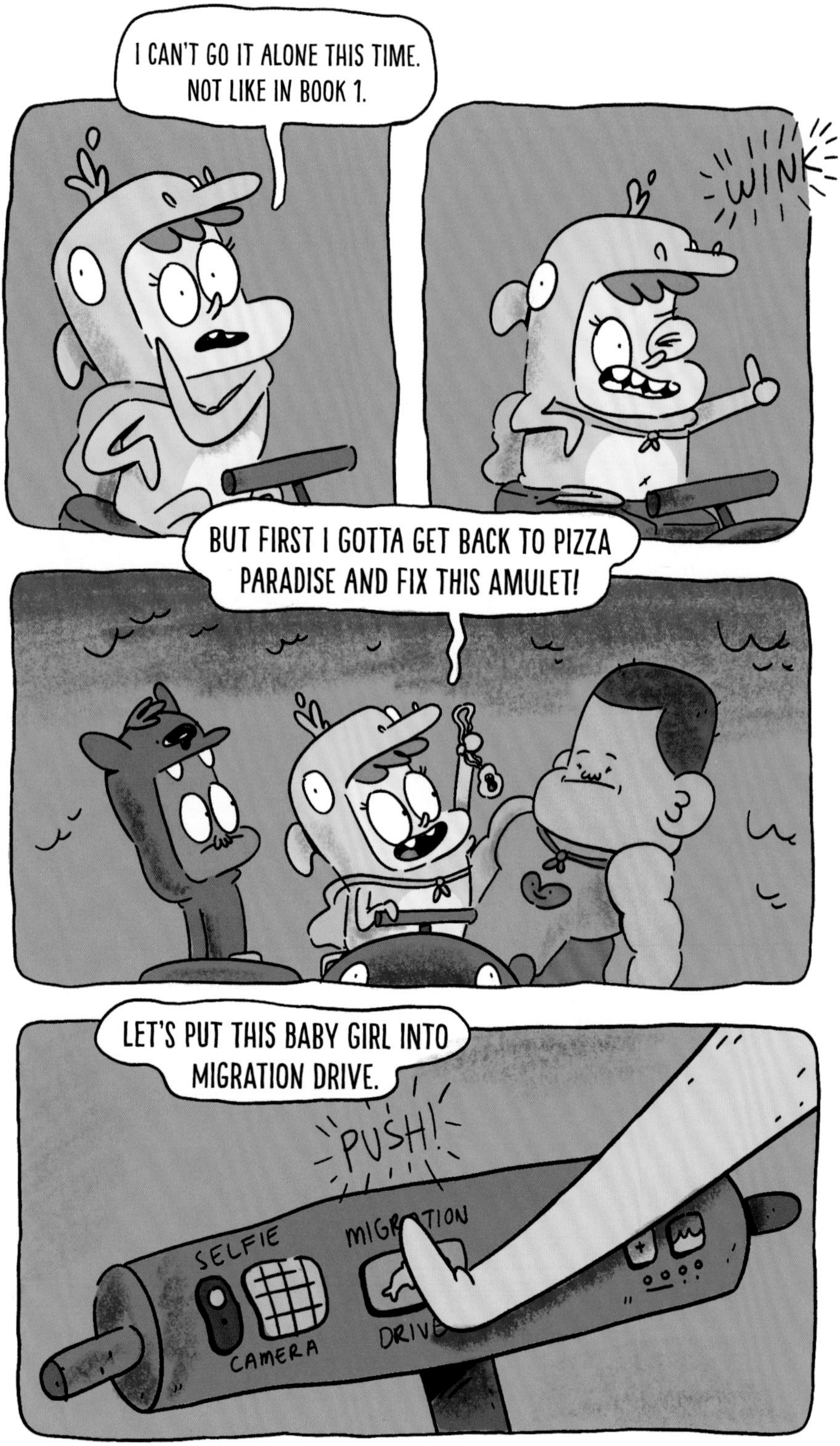
I CAN'T GO IT ALONE THIS TIME. NOT LIKE IN BOOK 1.
WINK
BUT FIRST I GOTTA GET BACK TO PIZZA PARADISE AND FIX THIS AMULET!
LET'S PUT THIS BABY GIRL INTO MIGRATION DRIVE.
PUSH!
SELFIE
CAMERA
MIGR
TION
DRIV

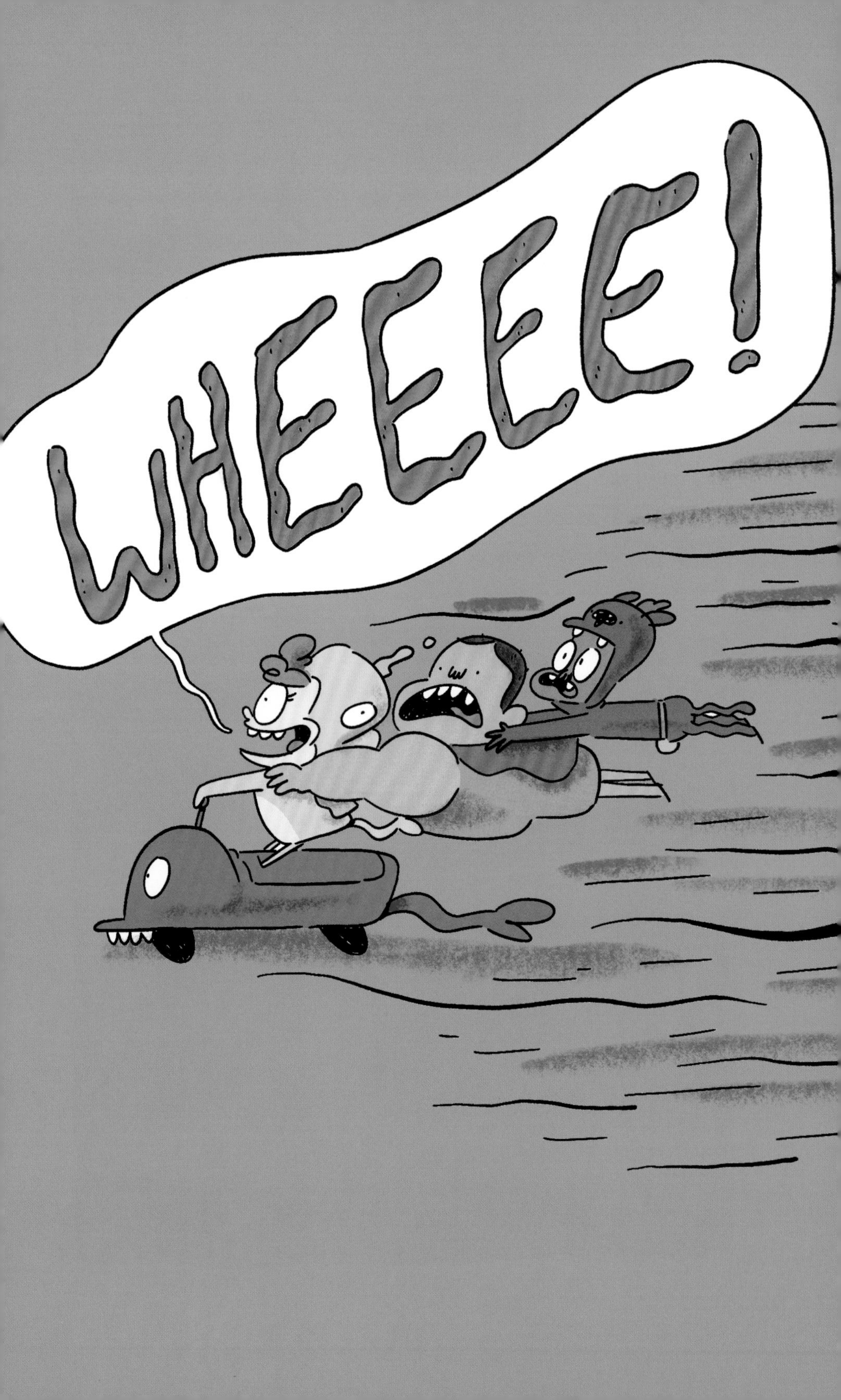
WHEEEE!

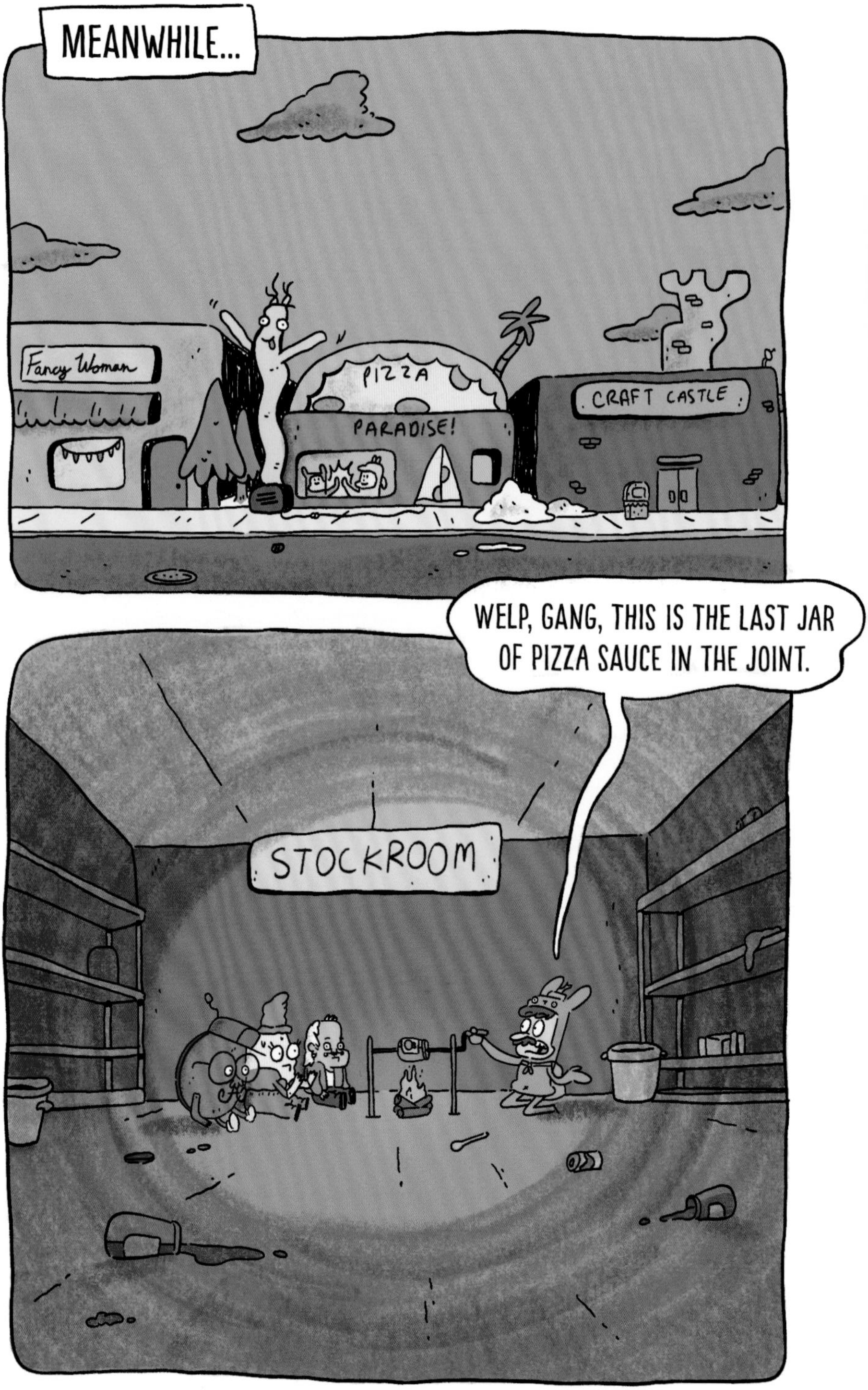
MEANWHILE...
Fancy Woman
PIZZA
PARADISE!
CRAFT CASTLE
WELP, GANG, THIS IS THE LAST JAR OF PIZZA SAUCE IN THE JOINT.
STOCKROOM

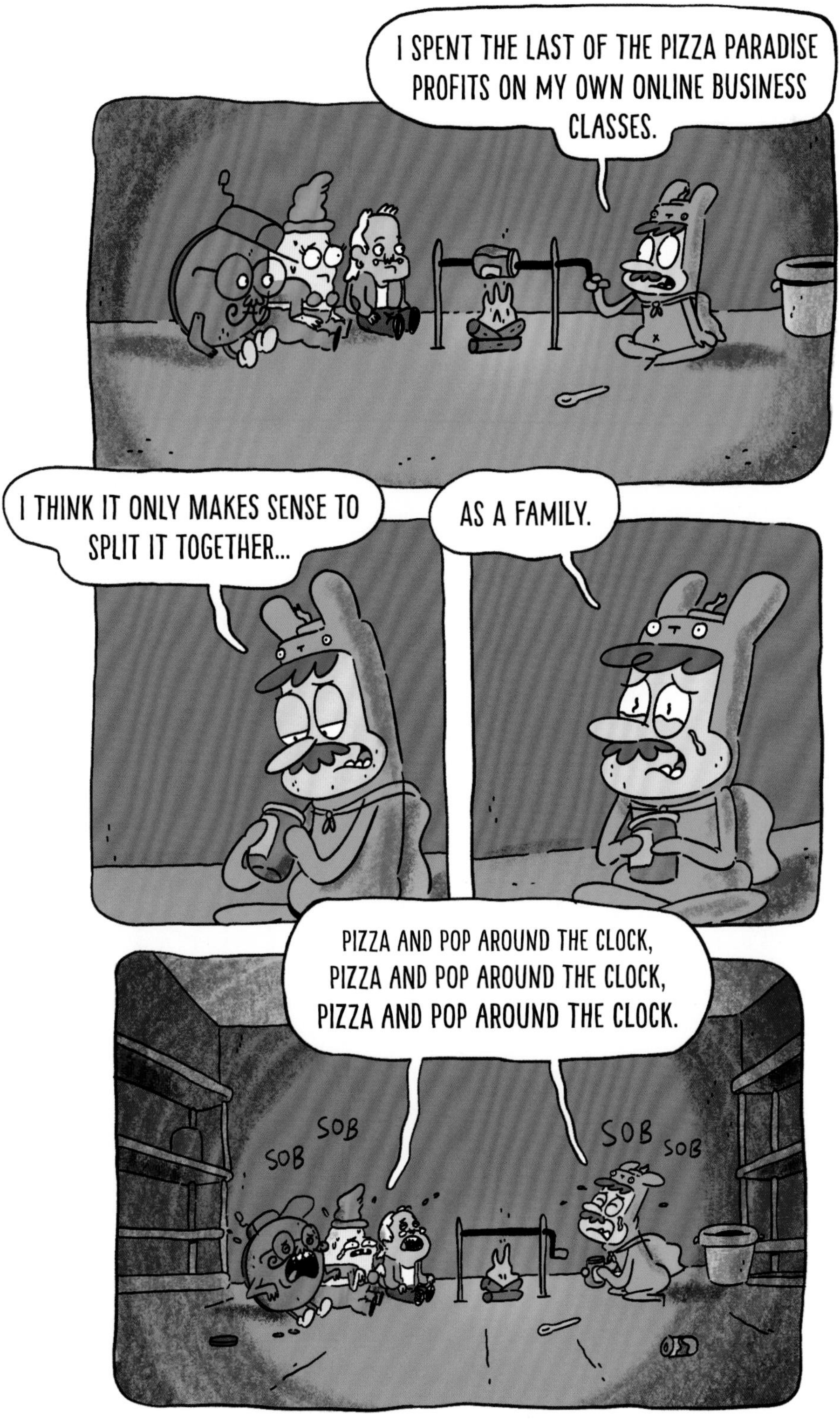
I SPENT THE LAST OF THE PIZZA PARADISE PROFITS ON MY OWN ONLINE BUSINESS CLASSES.
I THINK IT ONLY MAKES SENSE TO SPLIT IT TOGETHER...
AS A FAMILY.
PIZZA AND POP AROUND THE CLOCK, PIZZA AND POP AROUND THE CLOCK, PIZZA AND POP AROUND THE CLOCK.
SOB
SOB
SOB
SOB

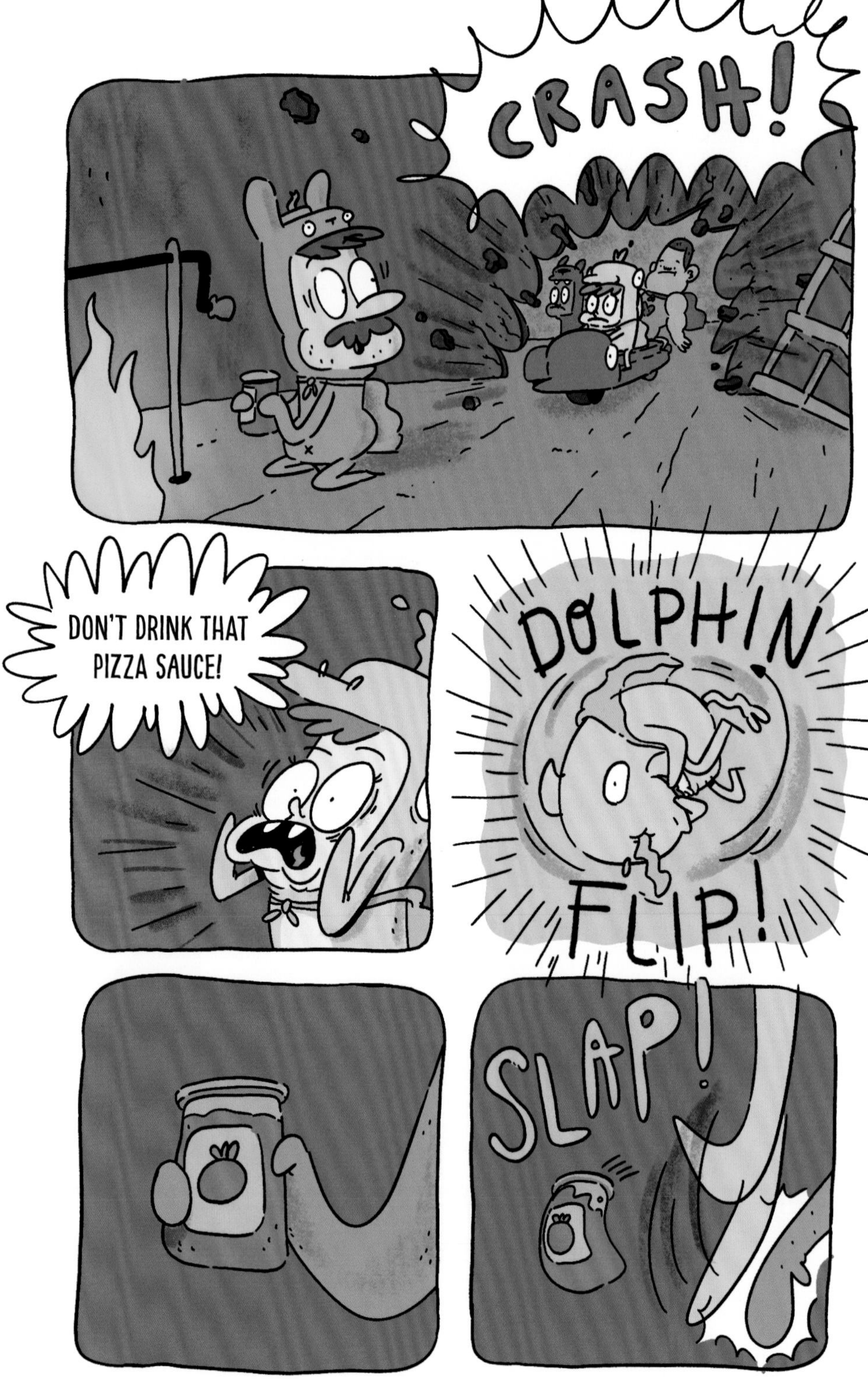
CRASH!
DON'T DRINK THAT PIZZA SAUCE!
DOLPHIN FLIP!
SLAP!

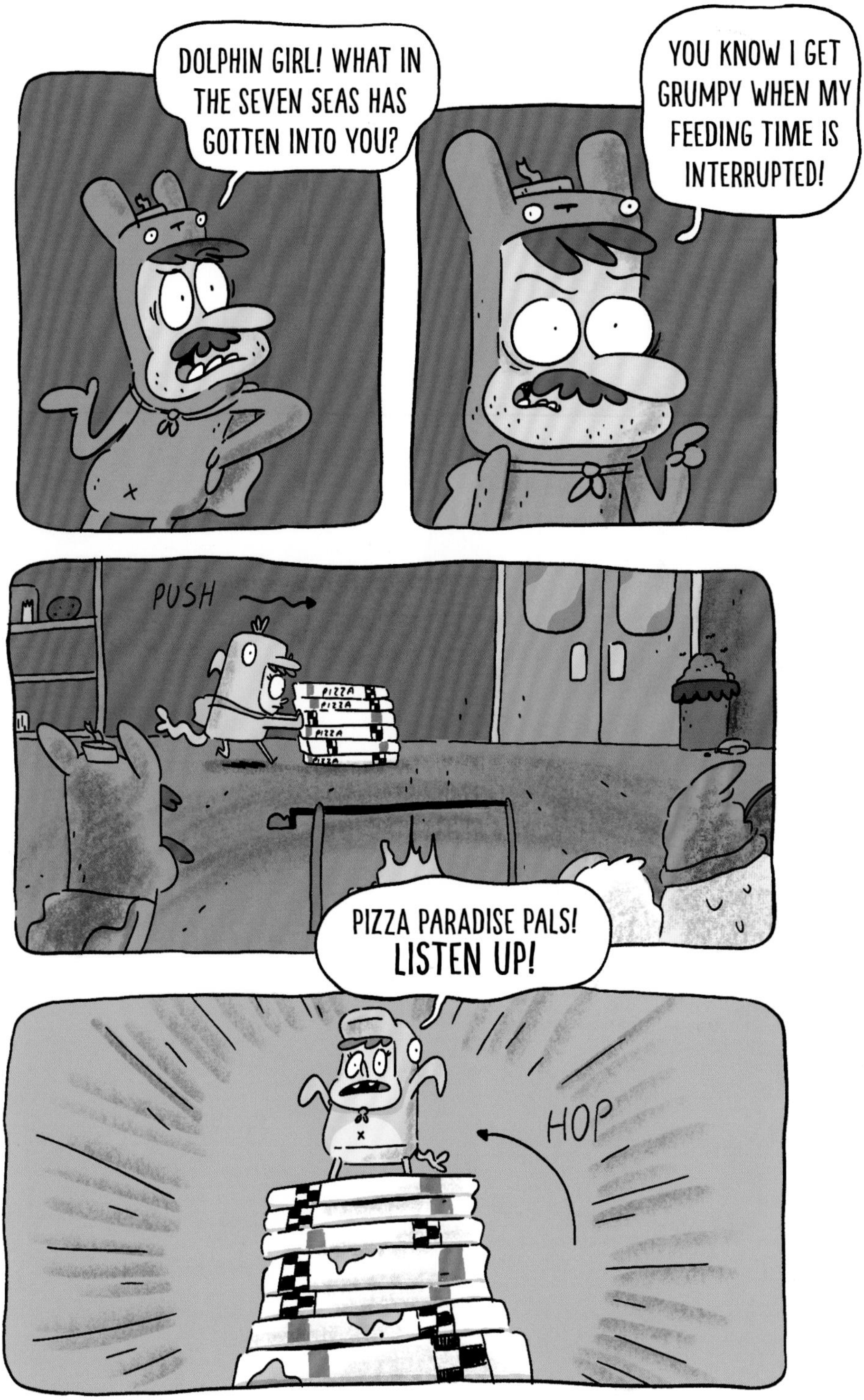
DOLPHIN GIRL! WHAT IN THE SEVEN SEAS HAS GOTTEN INTO YOU?
YOU KNOW I GET GRUMPY WHEN MY FEEDING TIME IS INTERRUPTED!
PUSH
PIZZA
PIZZA
PIZZA
PIZZA PARADISE PALS! LISTEN UP!
HOP

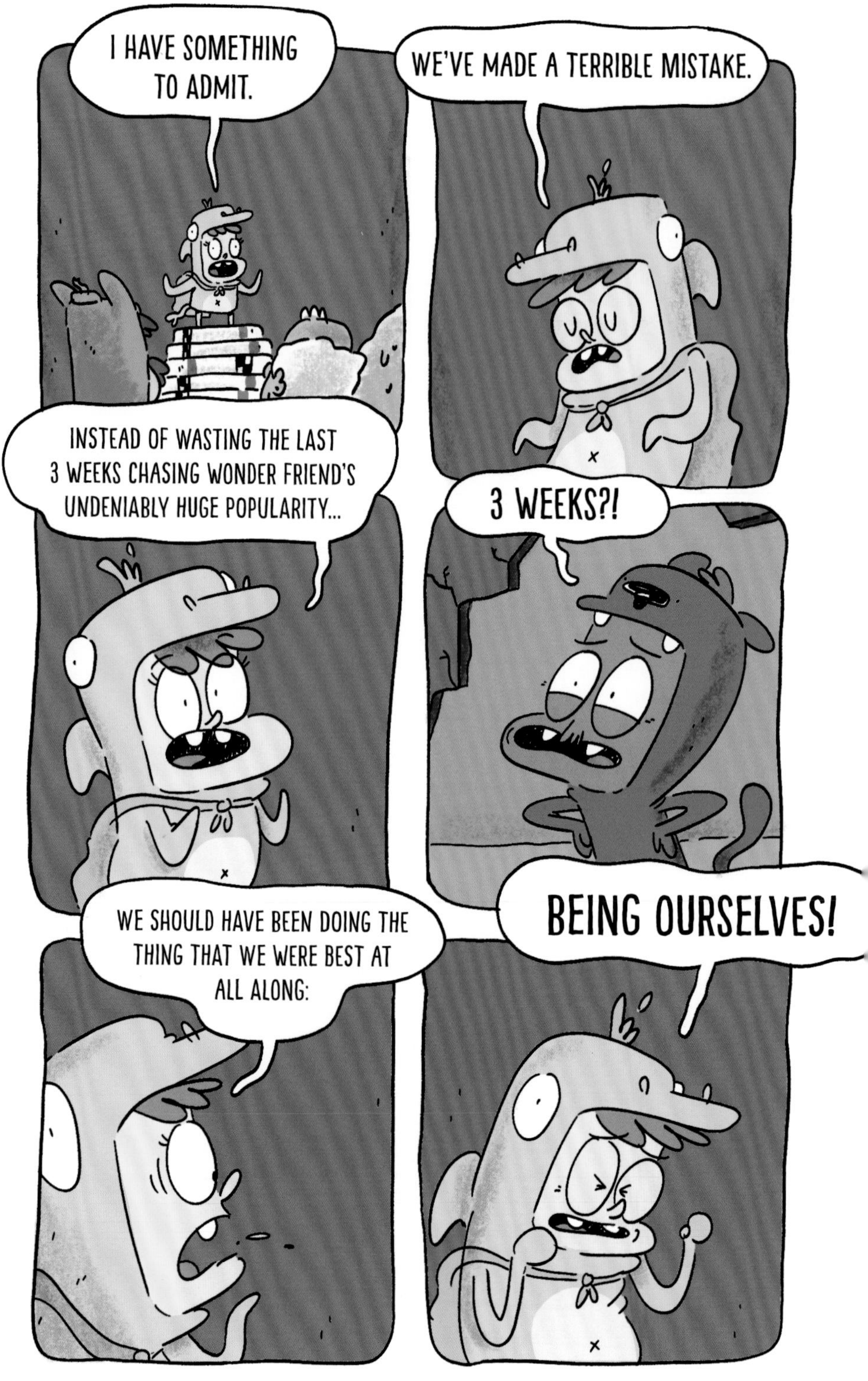
I HAVE SOMETHING TO ADMIT.
WE'VE MADE A TERRIBLE MISTAKE.
INSTEAD OF WASTING THE LAST 3 WEEKS CHASING WONDER FRIEND'S UNDENIABLY HUGE POPULARITY...
3 WEEKS?!
WE SHOULD HAVE BEEN DOING THE THING THAT WE WERE BEST AT ALL ALONG:
BEING OURSELVES!

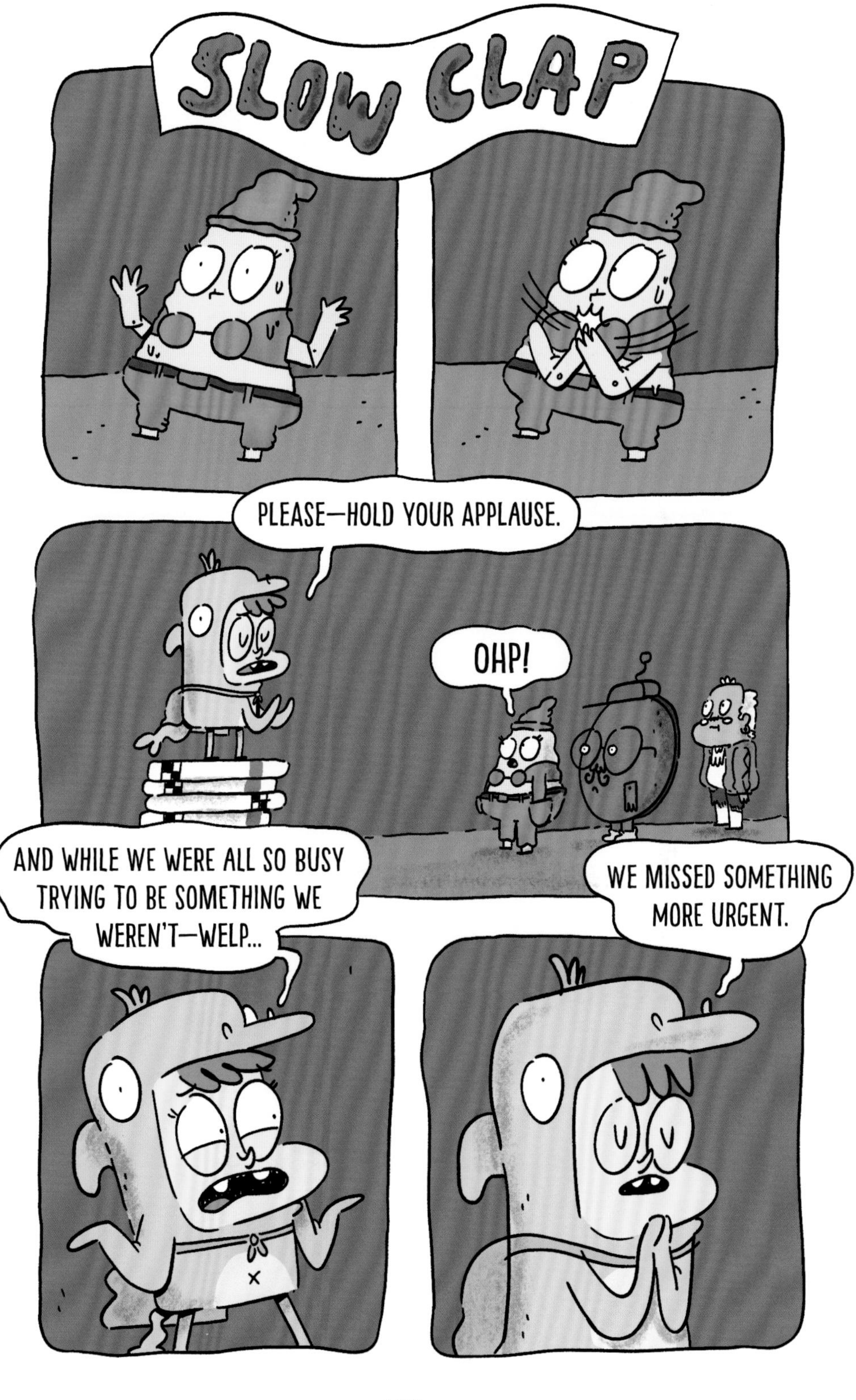
SLOW CLAP
PLEASE—HOLD YOUR APPLAUSE.
OHP!
AND WHILE WE WERE ALL SO BUSY TRYING TO BE SOMETHING WE WEREN'T—WELP...
WE MISSED SOMETHING MORE URGENT.

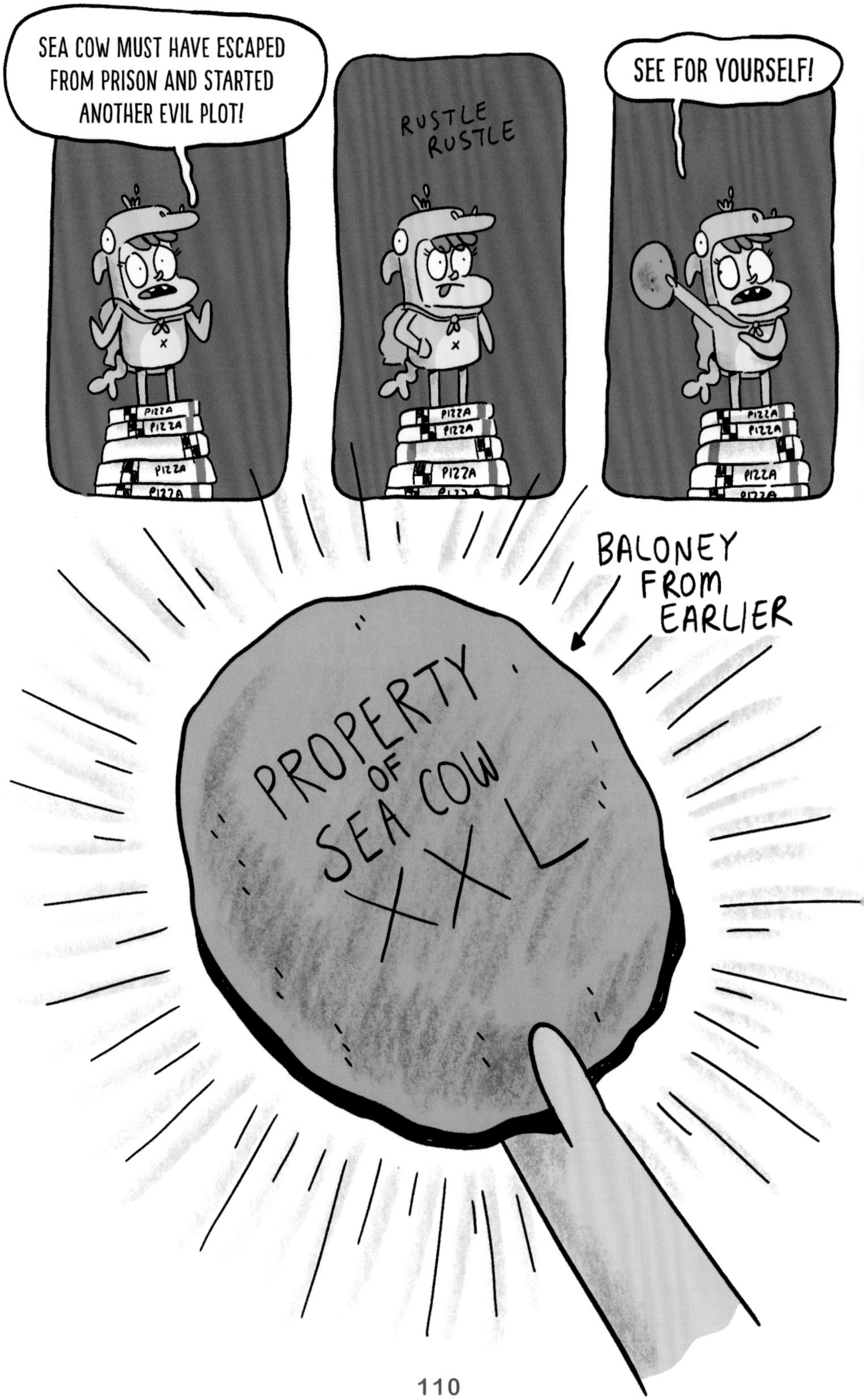
SEA COW MUST HAVE ESCAPED FROM PRISON AND STARTED ANOTHER EVIL PLOT!
RUSTLE RUSTLE
SEE FOR YOURSELF!
BALONEY FROM EARLIER
PROPERTY OF SEA COW
XXL

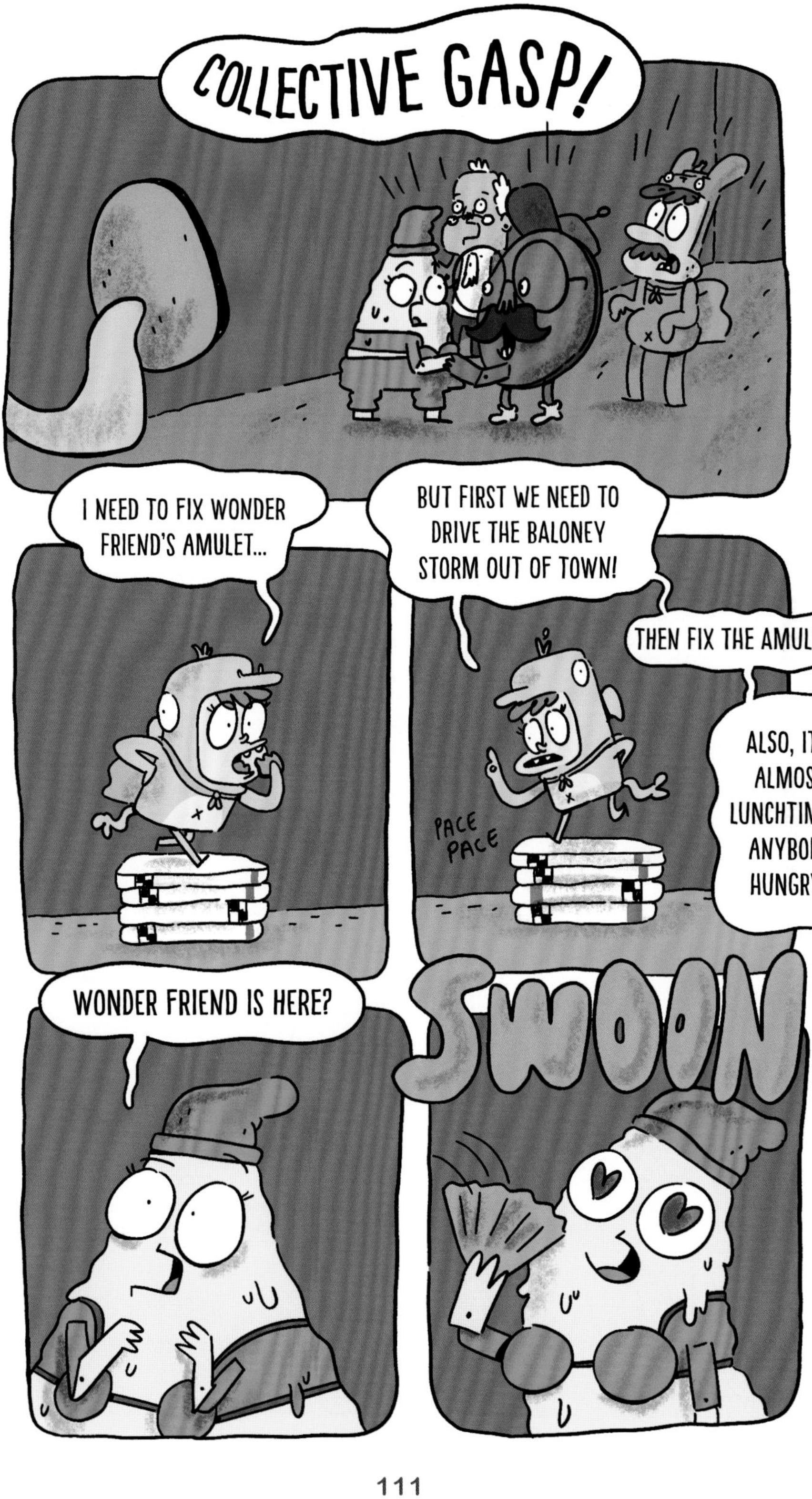
COLLECTIVE GASP!
I NEED TO FIX WONDER FRIEND'S AMULET...
BUT FIRST WE NEED TO DRIVE THE BALONEY STORM OUT OF TOWN!
THEN FIX THE AMULET!
ALSO, IT'S ALMOST LUNCHTIME—ANYBODY HUNGRY?
PACE PACE
WONDER FRIEND IS HERE?
SWOON

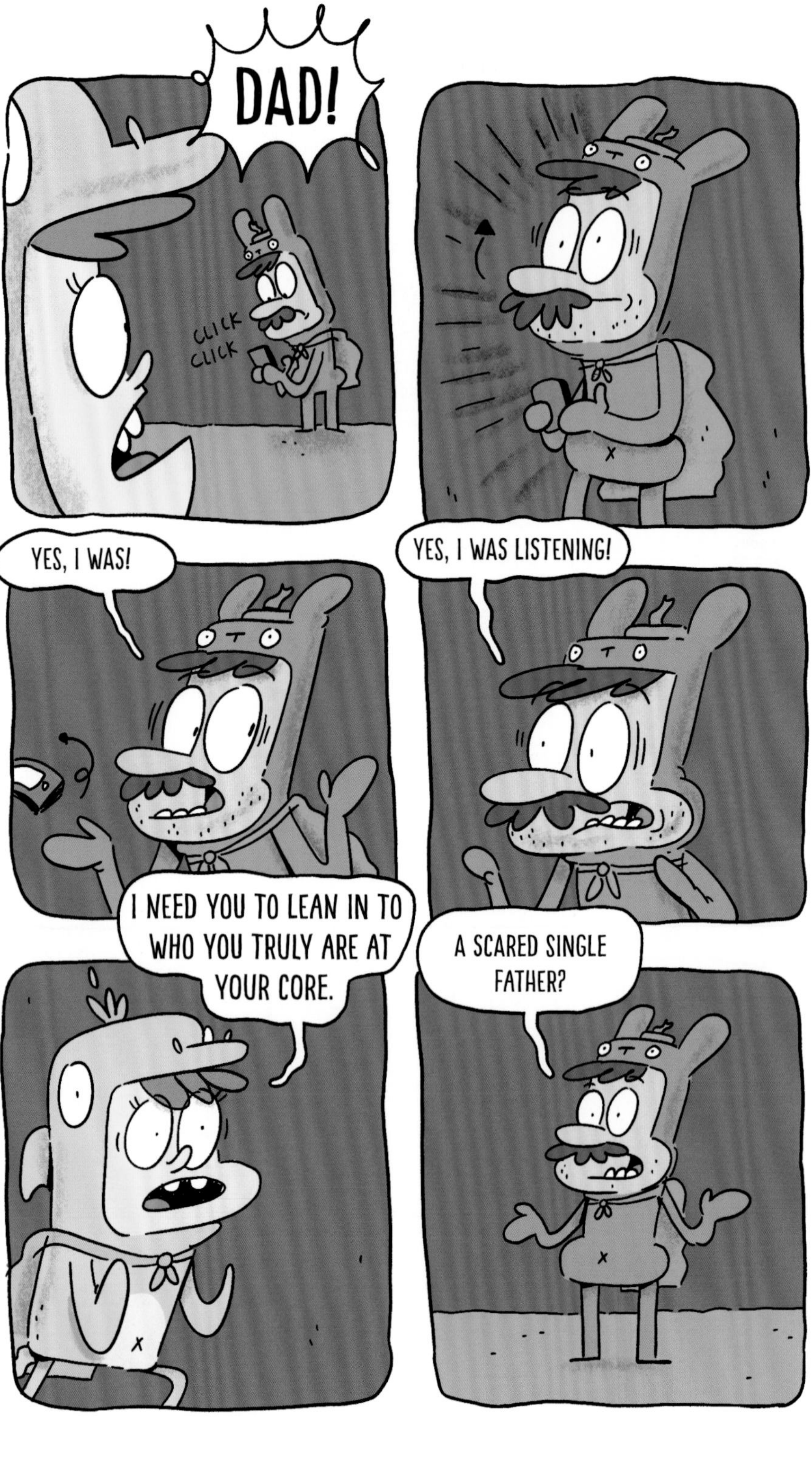
DAD!
CLICK CLICK
YES, I WAS!
YES, I WAS LISTENING!
I NEED YOU TO LEAN IN TO WHO YOU TRULY ARE AT YOUR CORE.
A SCARED SINGLE FATHER?

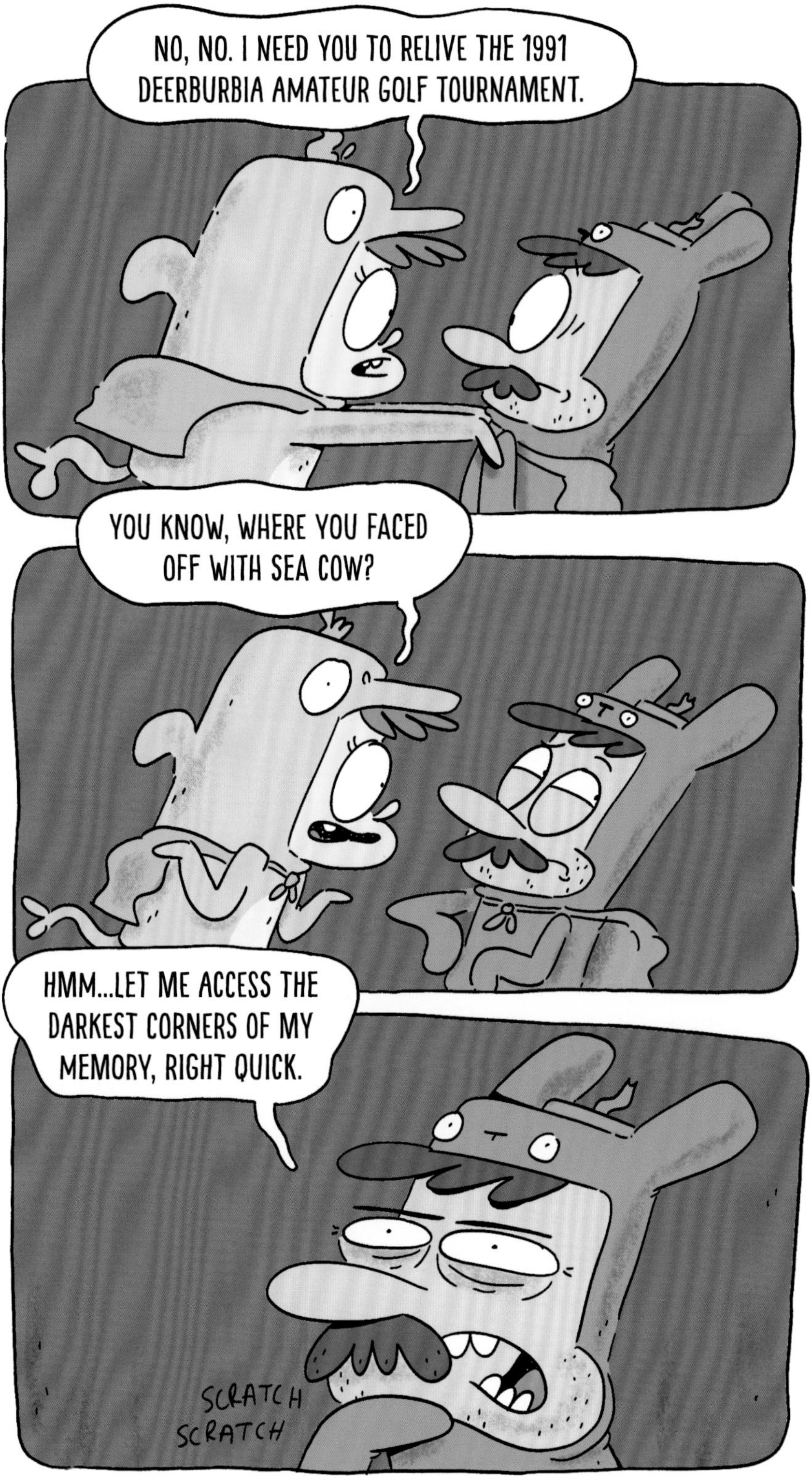
NO, NO. I NEED YOU TO RELIVE THE 1991 DEERBURBIA AMATEUR GOLF TOURNAMENT.
YOU KNOW, WHERE YOU FACED OFF WITH SEA COW?
HMM...LET ME ACCESS THE DARKEST CORNERS OF MY MEMORY, RIGHT QUICK.
SCRATCH SCRATCH

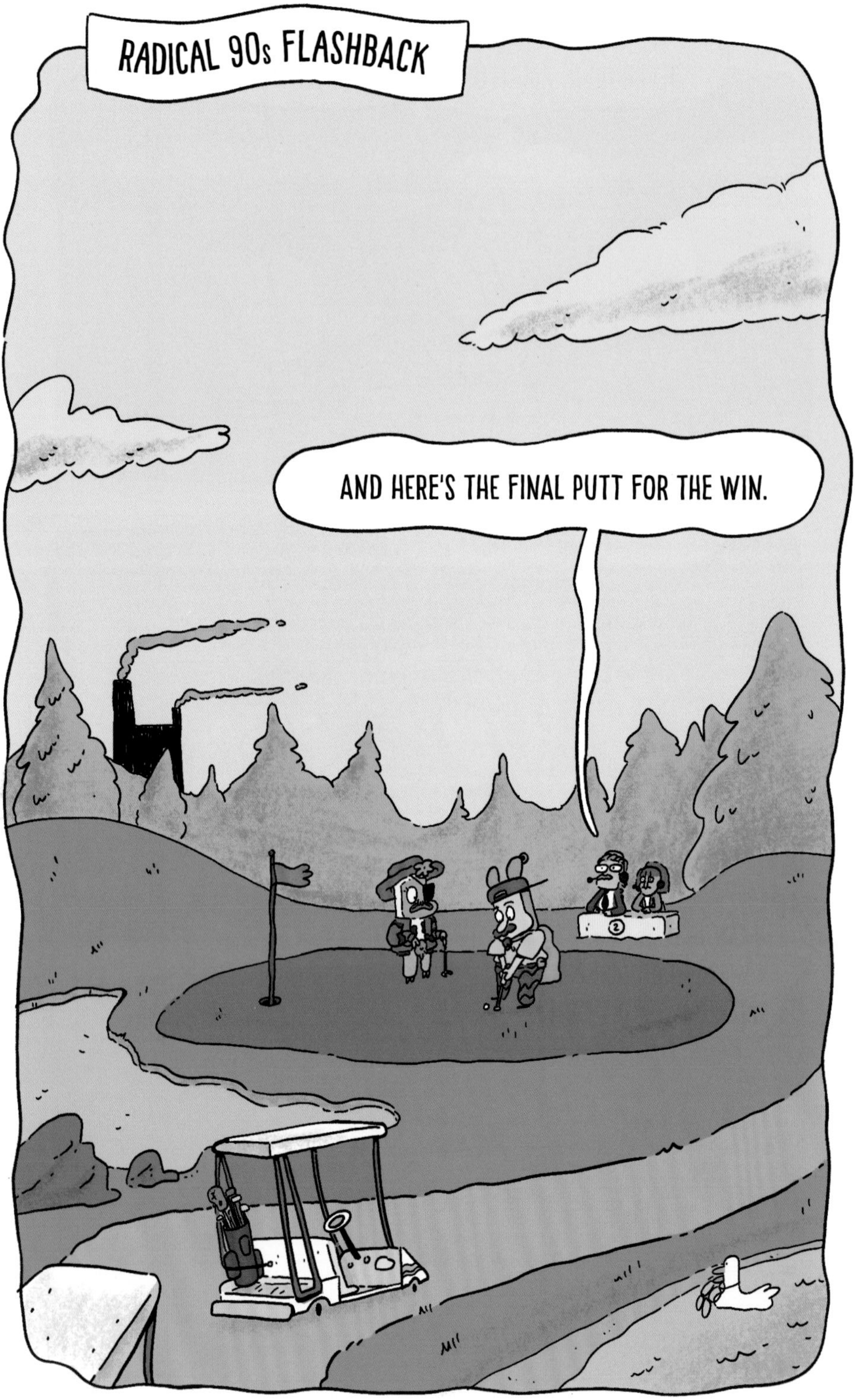
RADICAL 90s FLASHBACK
AND HERE'S THE FINAL PUTT FOR THE WIN.

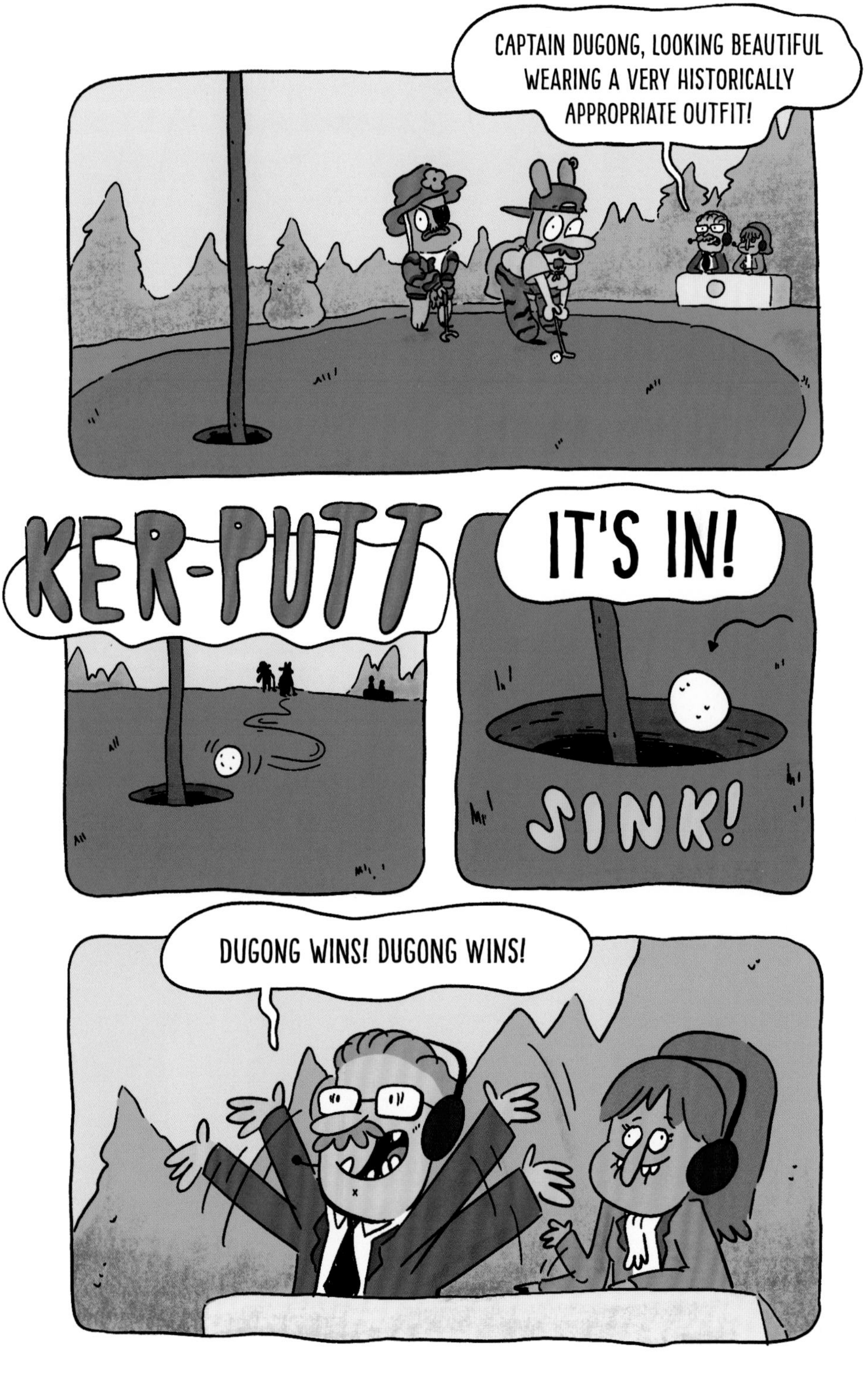
CAPTAIN DUGONG, LOOKING BEAUTIFUL WEARING A VERY HISTORICALLY APPROPRIATE OUTFIT!
KER-PUTT
IT'S IN!
SINK!
DUGONG WINS! DUGONG WINS!

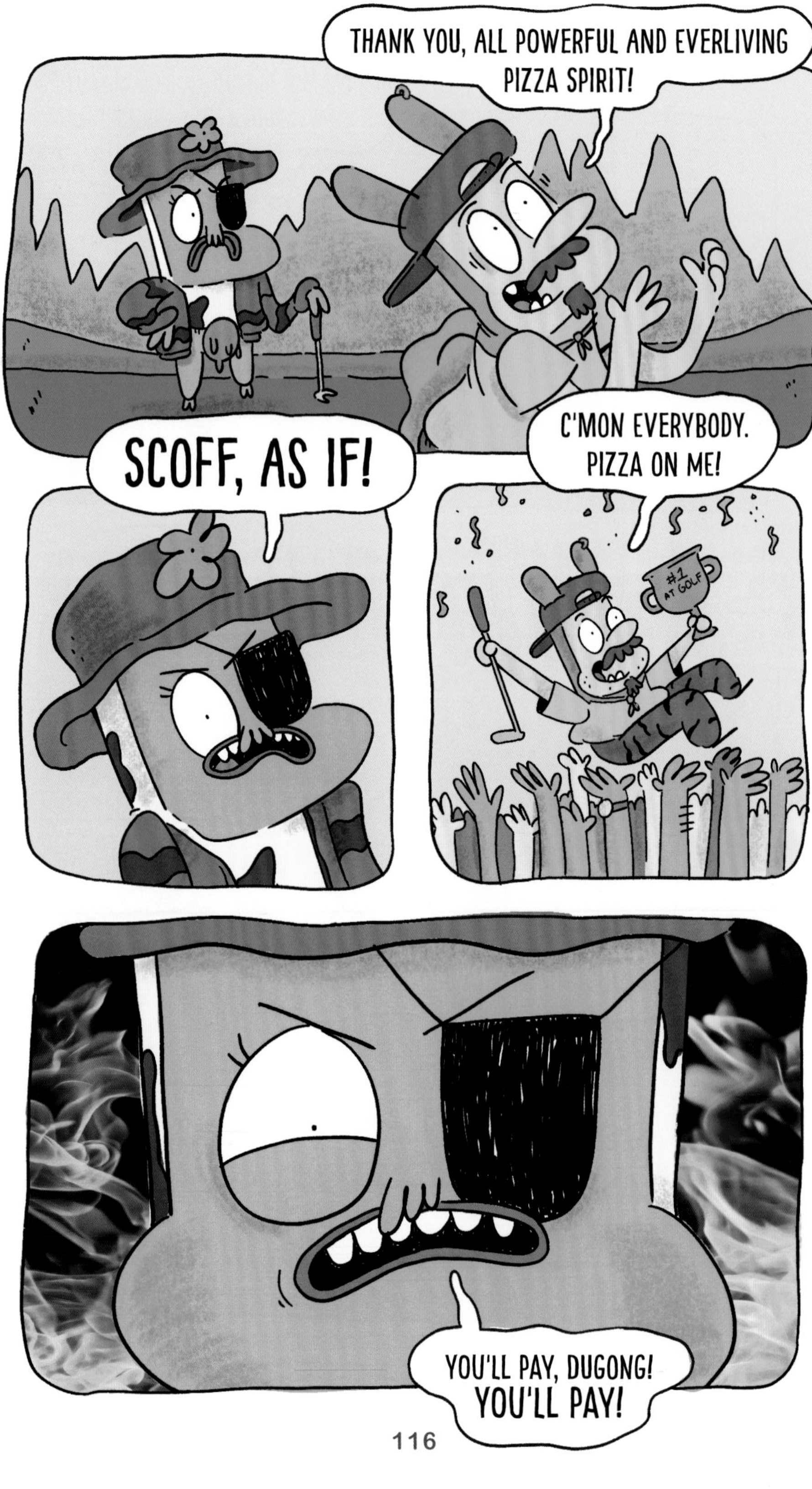
THANK YOU, ALL POWERFUL AND EVERLIVING PIZZA SPIRIT!
SCOFF, AS IF!
C'MON EVERYBODY. PIZZA ON ME!
#1 AT GOLF
YOU'LL PAY, DUGONG! YOU'LL PAY!

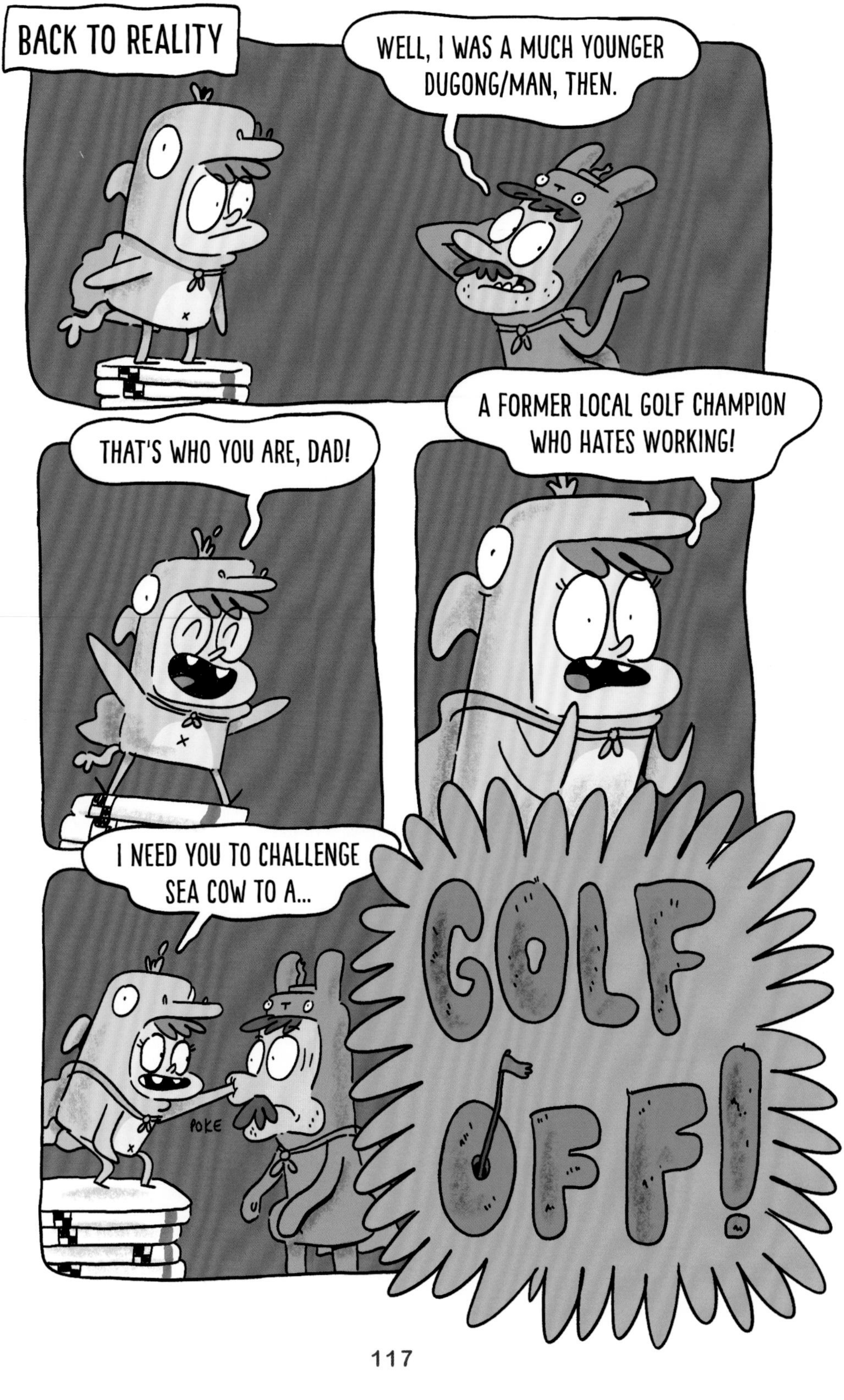

BACK TO REALITY
WELL, I WAS A MUCH YOUNGER DUGONG/MAN, THEN.
THAT'S WHO YOU ARE, DAD!
A FORMER LOCAL GOLF CHAMPION WHO HATES WORKING!
I NEED YOU TO CHALLENGE SEA COW TO A...
POKE
GOLF OFF!

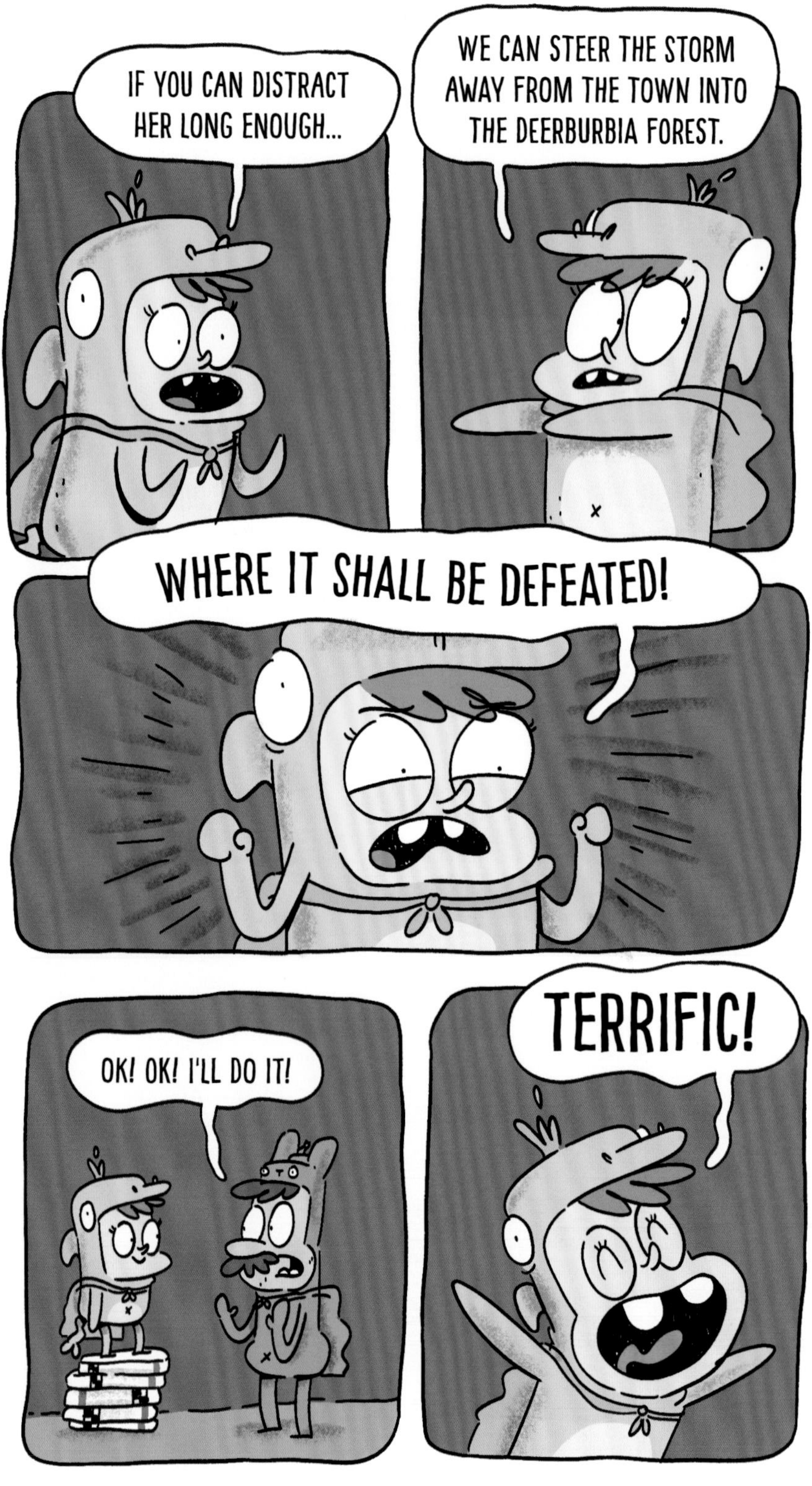
IF YOU CAN DISTRACT HER LONG ENOUGH...
WE CAN STEER THE STORM AWAY FROM THE TOWN INTO THE DEERBURBIA FOREST.
WHERE IT SHALL BE DEFEATED!
OK! OK! I'LL DO IT!
TERRIFIC!

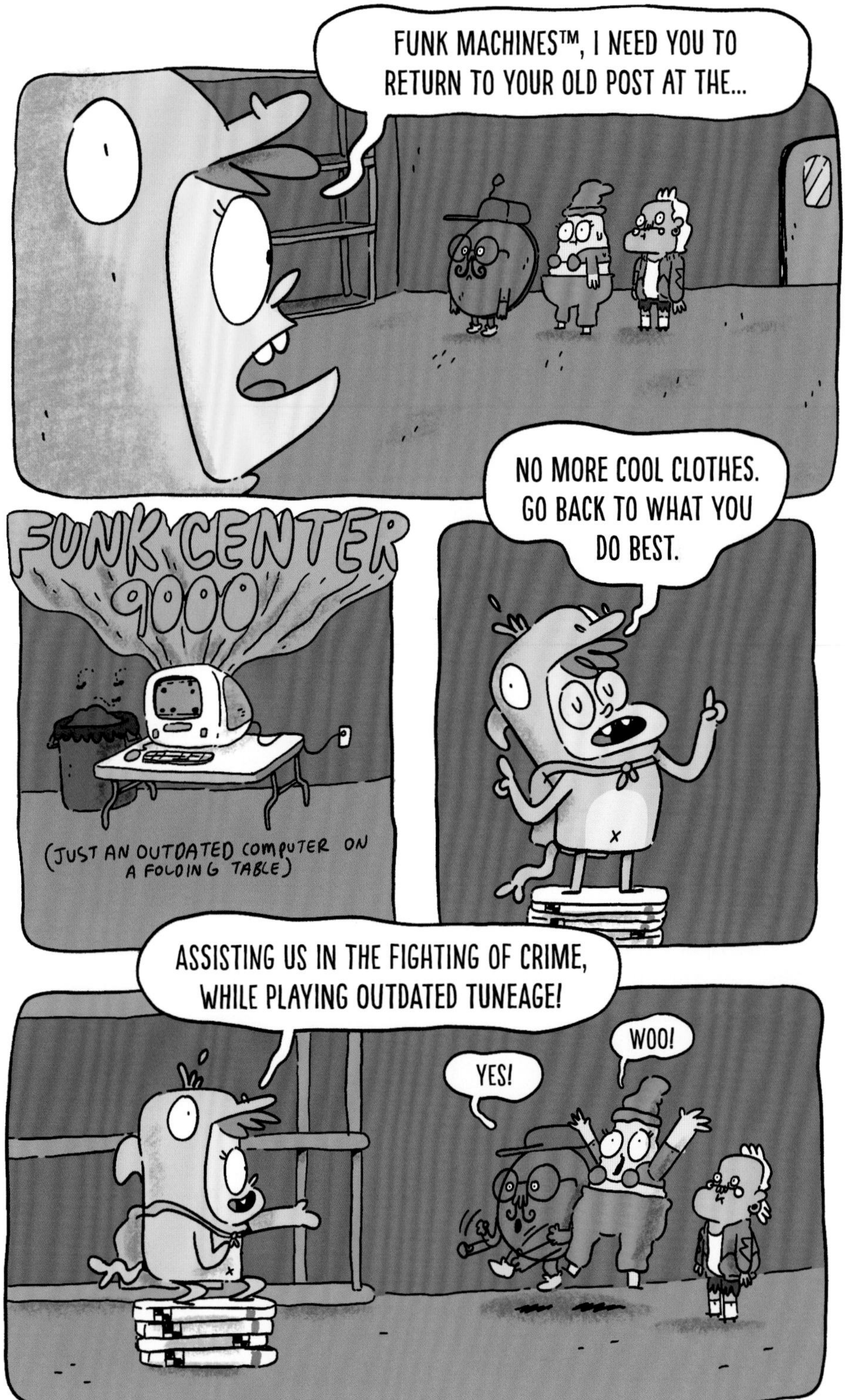
FUNK MACHINES™, I NEED YOU TO RETURN TO YOUR OLD POST AT THE...
FUNK CENTER 9000
(JUST AN OUTDATED COMPUTER ON A FOLDING TABLE)
NO MORE COOL CLOTHES. GO BACK TO WHAT YOU DO BEST.
ASSISTING US IN THE FIGHTING OF CRIME, WHILE PLAYING OUTDATED TUNEAGE!
YES!
WOO!

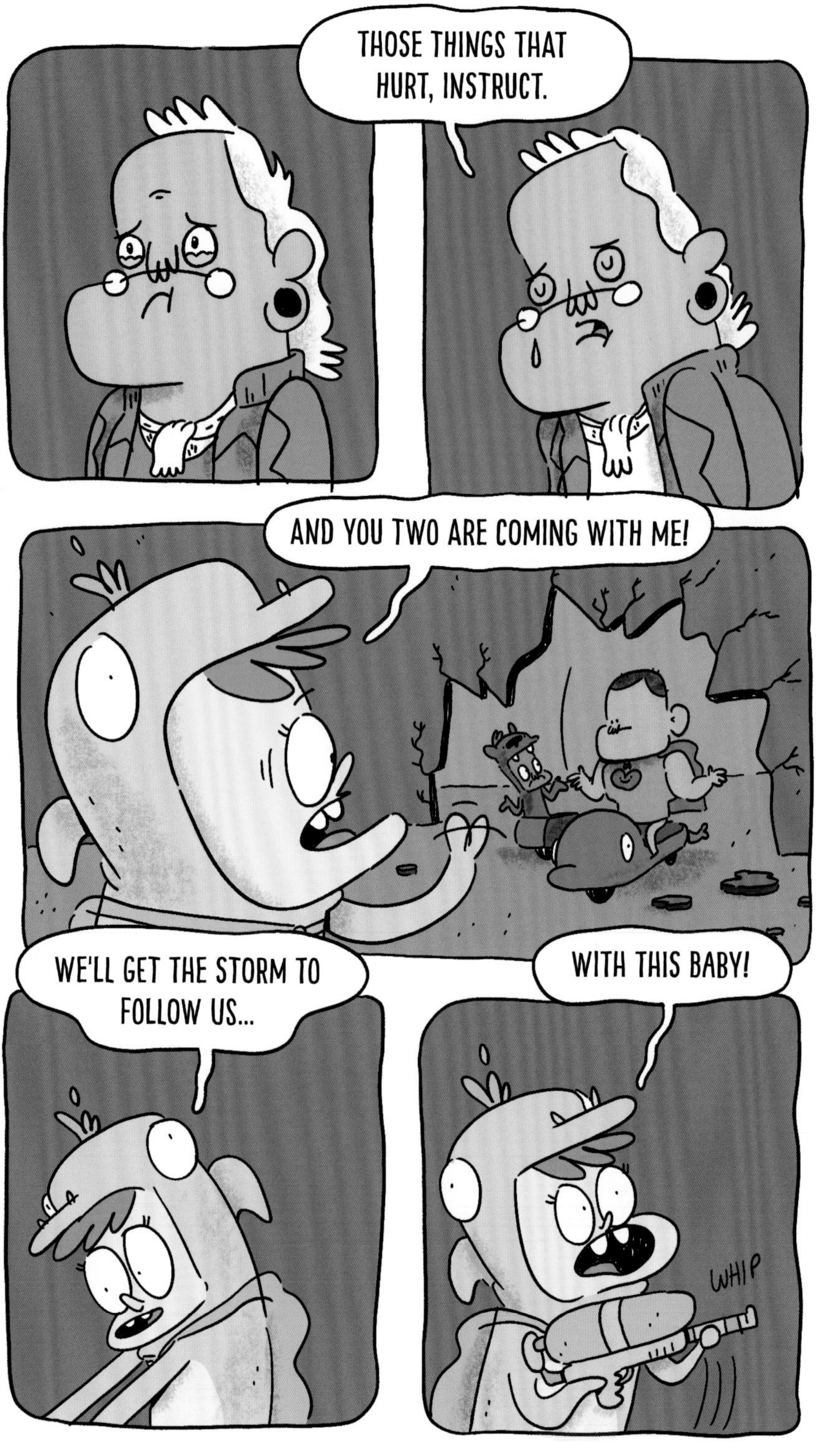
THOSE THINGS THAT HURT, INSTRUCT.
AND YOU TWO ARE COMING WITH ME!
WE'LL GET THE STORM TO FOLLOW US...
WITH THIS BABY!
WHIP

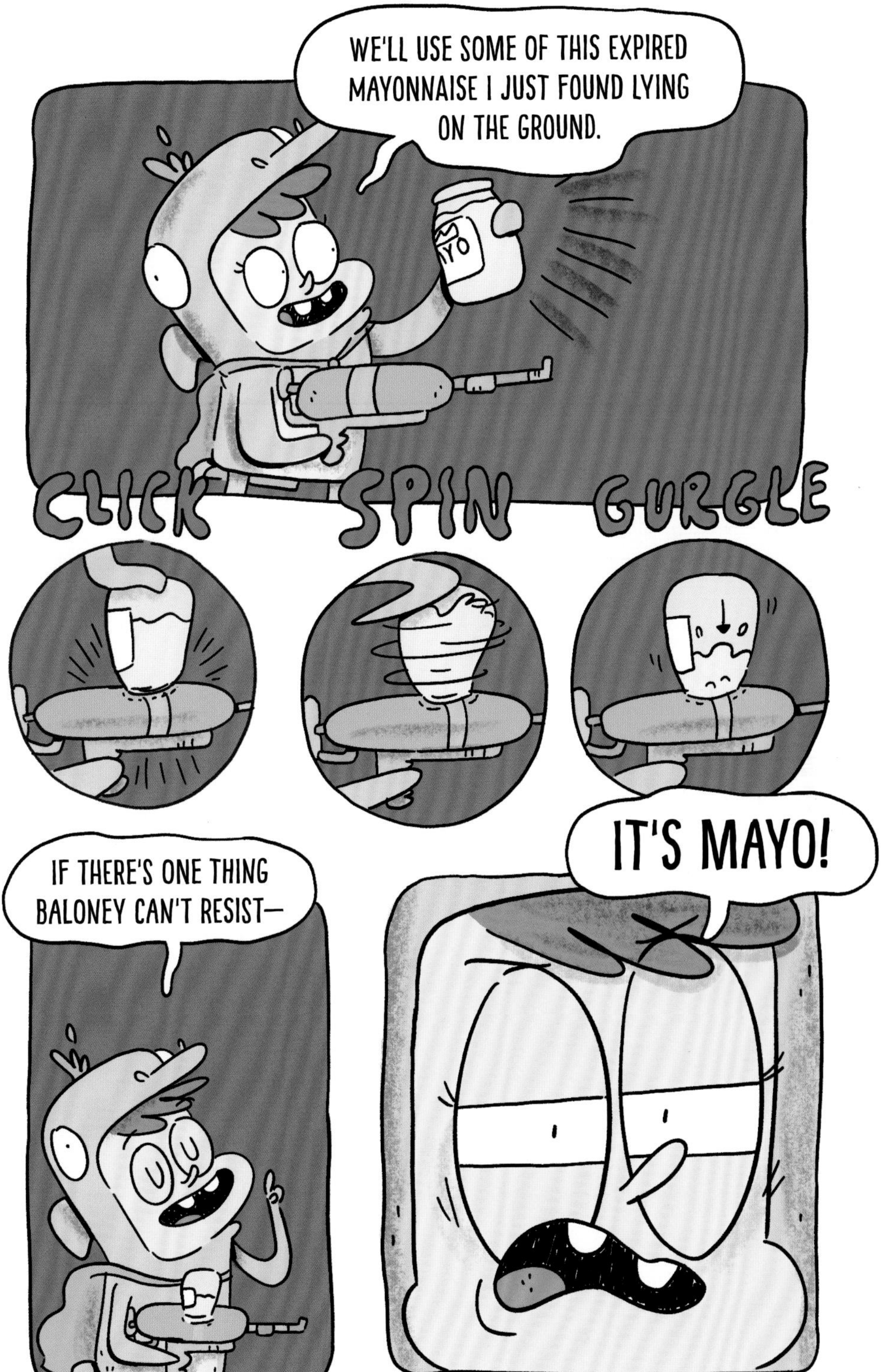
WE'LL USE SOME OF THIS EXPIRED MAYONNAISE I JUST FOUND LYING ON THE GROUND.
MAYO
CLICK
SPIN
GURGLE
IF THERE'S ONE THING BALONEY CAN'T RESIST—
IT'S MAYO!

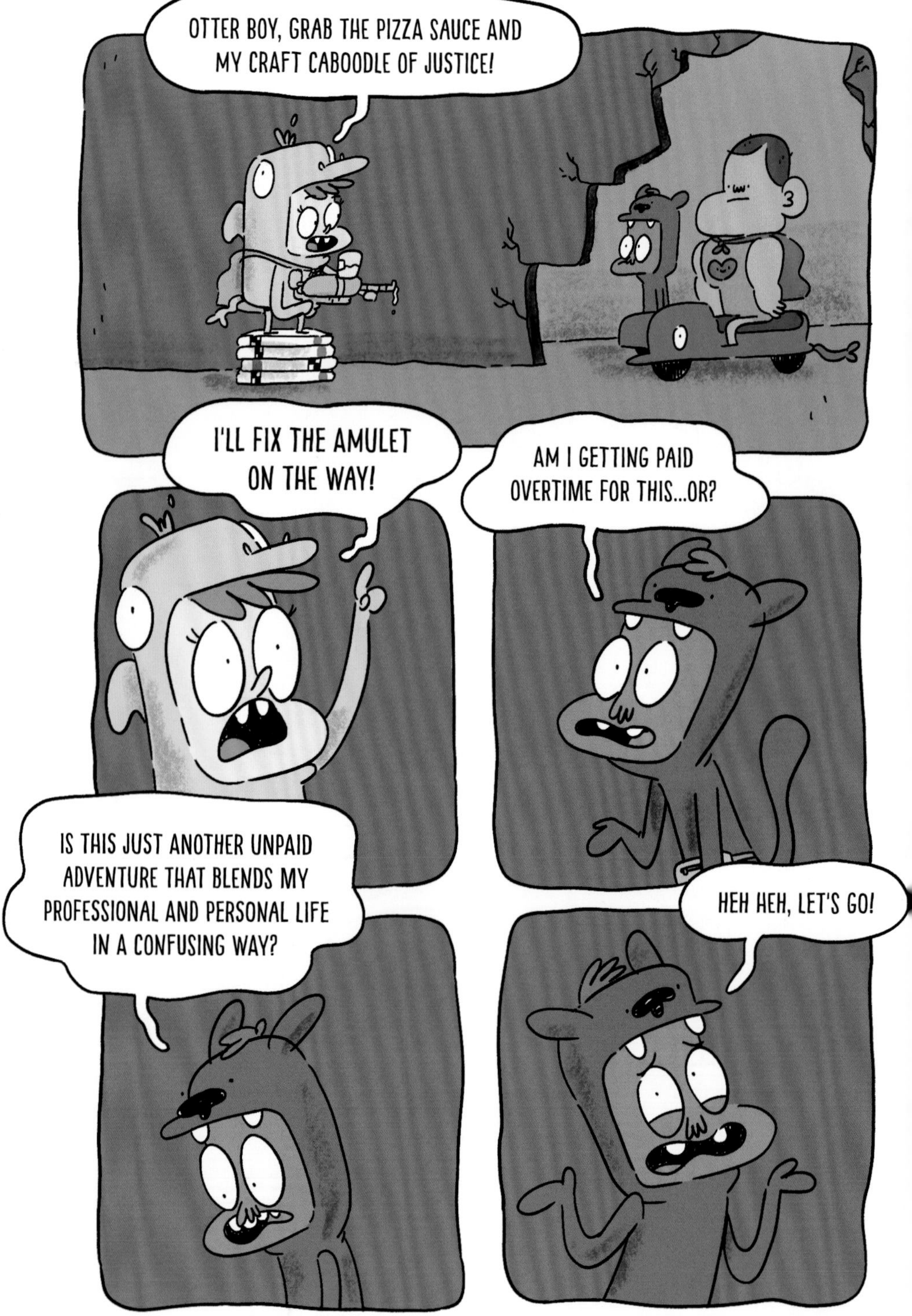
OTTER BOY, GRAB THE PIZZA SAUCE AND MY CRAFT CABOODLE OF JUSTICE!
I'LL FIX THE AMULET ON THE WAY!
AM I GETTING PAID OVERTIME FOR THIS...OR?
IS THIS JUST ANOTHER UNPAID ADVENTURE THAT BLENDS MY PROFESSIONAL AND PERSONAL LIFE IN A CONFUSING WAY?
HEH HEH, LET'S GO!

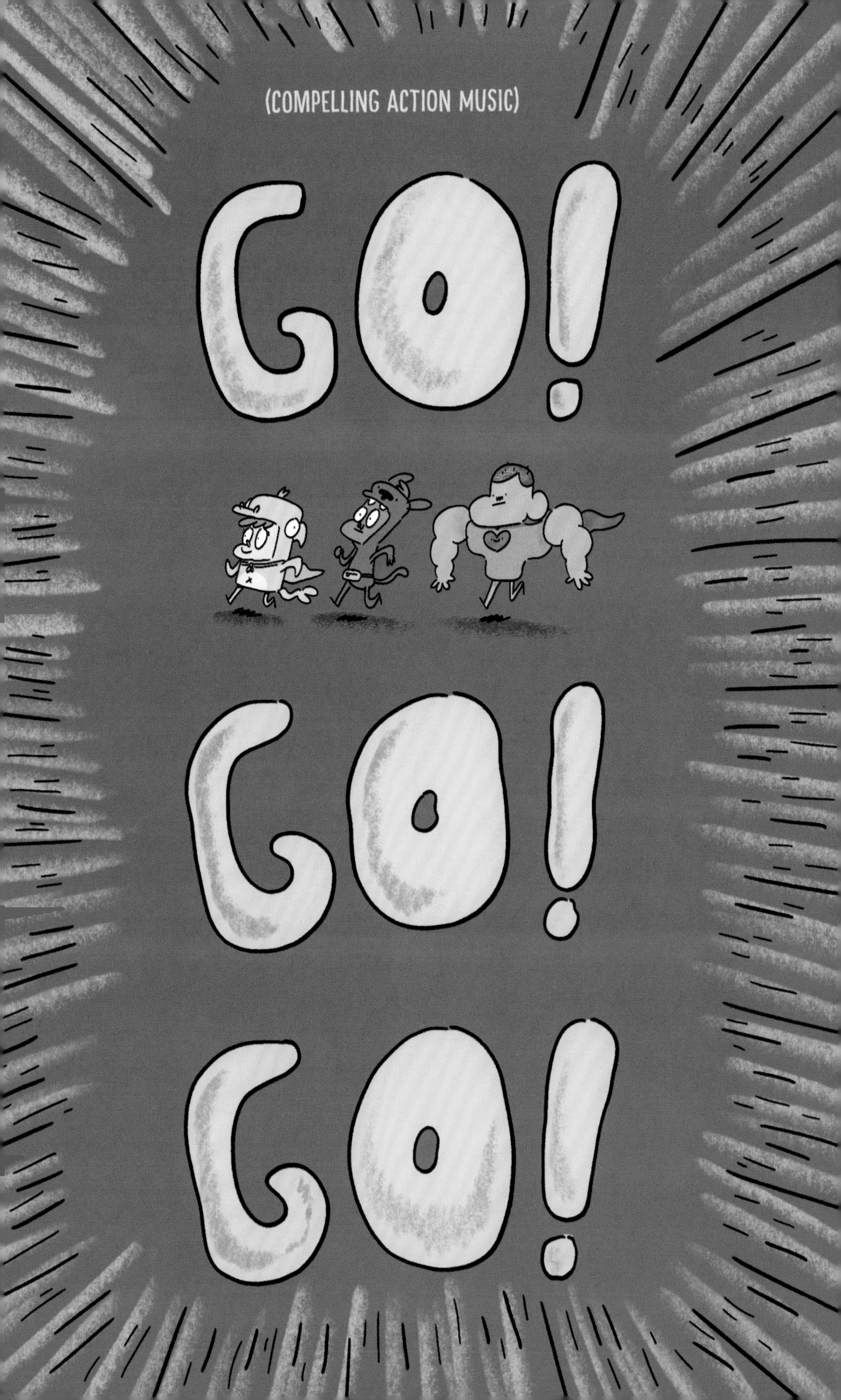

(COMPELLING ACTION MUSIC)
GO!
GO!
GO!

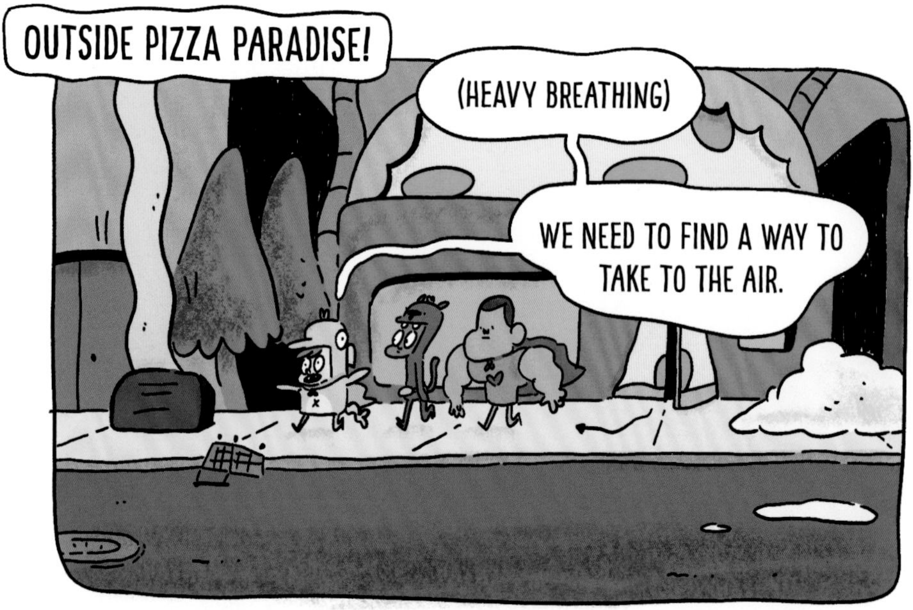
OUTSIDE PIZZA PARADISE!
(HEAVY BREATHING)
WE NEED TO FIND A WAY TO TAKE TO THE AIR.

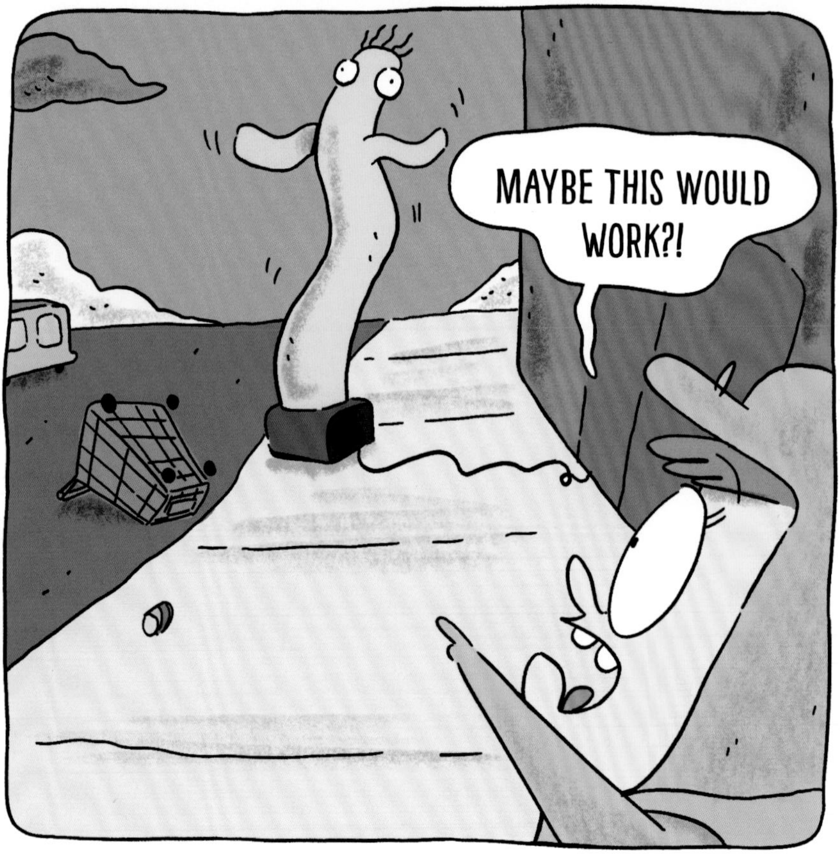
MAYBE THIS WOULD WORK?!

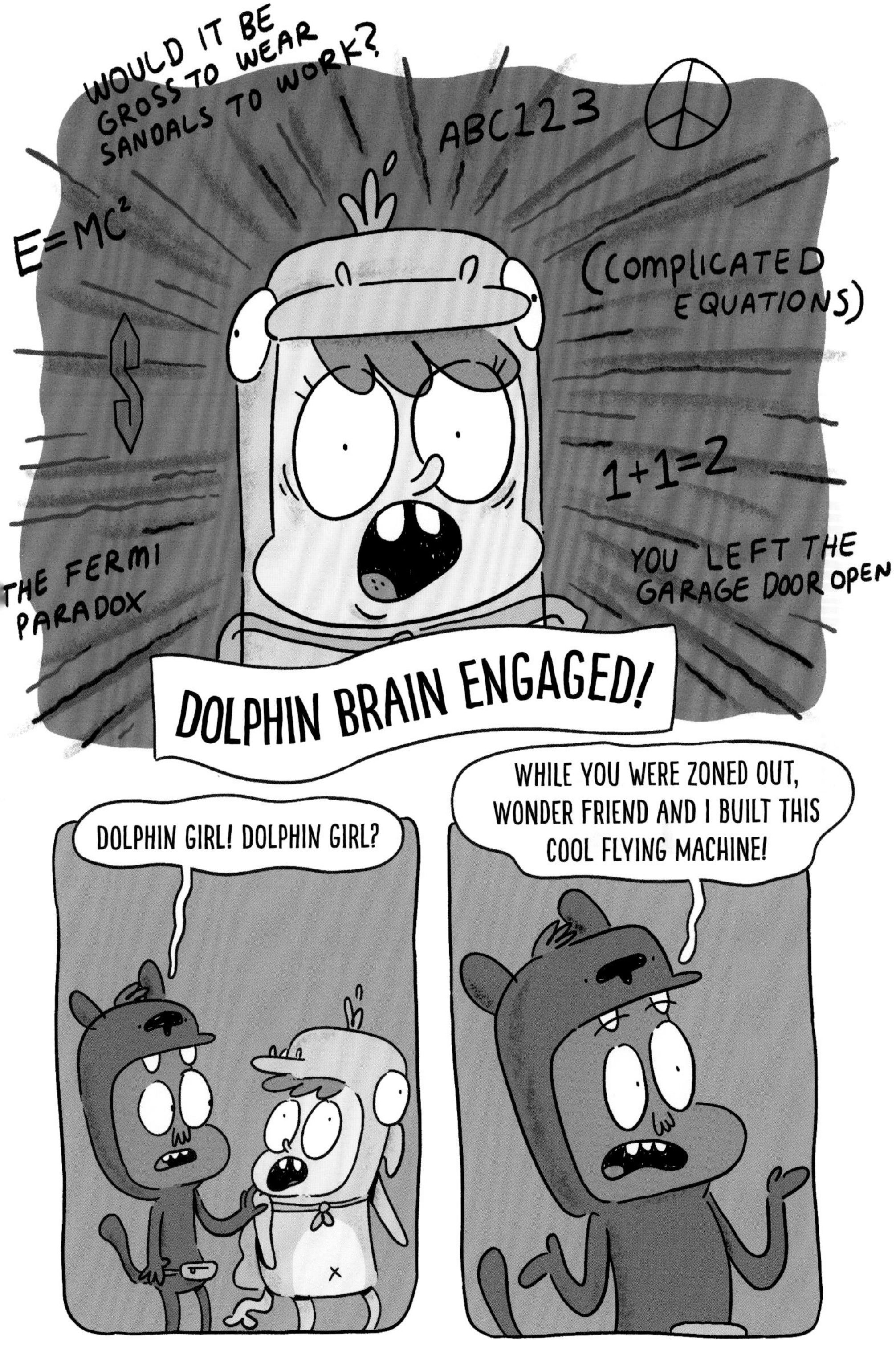
WOULD IT BE GROSS TO WEAR SANDALS TO WORK?
ABC123
E=MC²
(COMPLICATED EQUATIONS)
1+1=2
THE FERMI PARADOX
YOU LEFT THE GARAGE DOOR OPEN
DOLPHIN BRAIN ENGAGED!
DOLPHIN GIRL! DOLPHIN GIRL?
WHILE YOU WERE ZONED OUT, WONDER FRIEND AND I BUILT THIS COOL FLYING MACHINE!

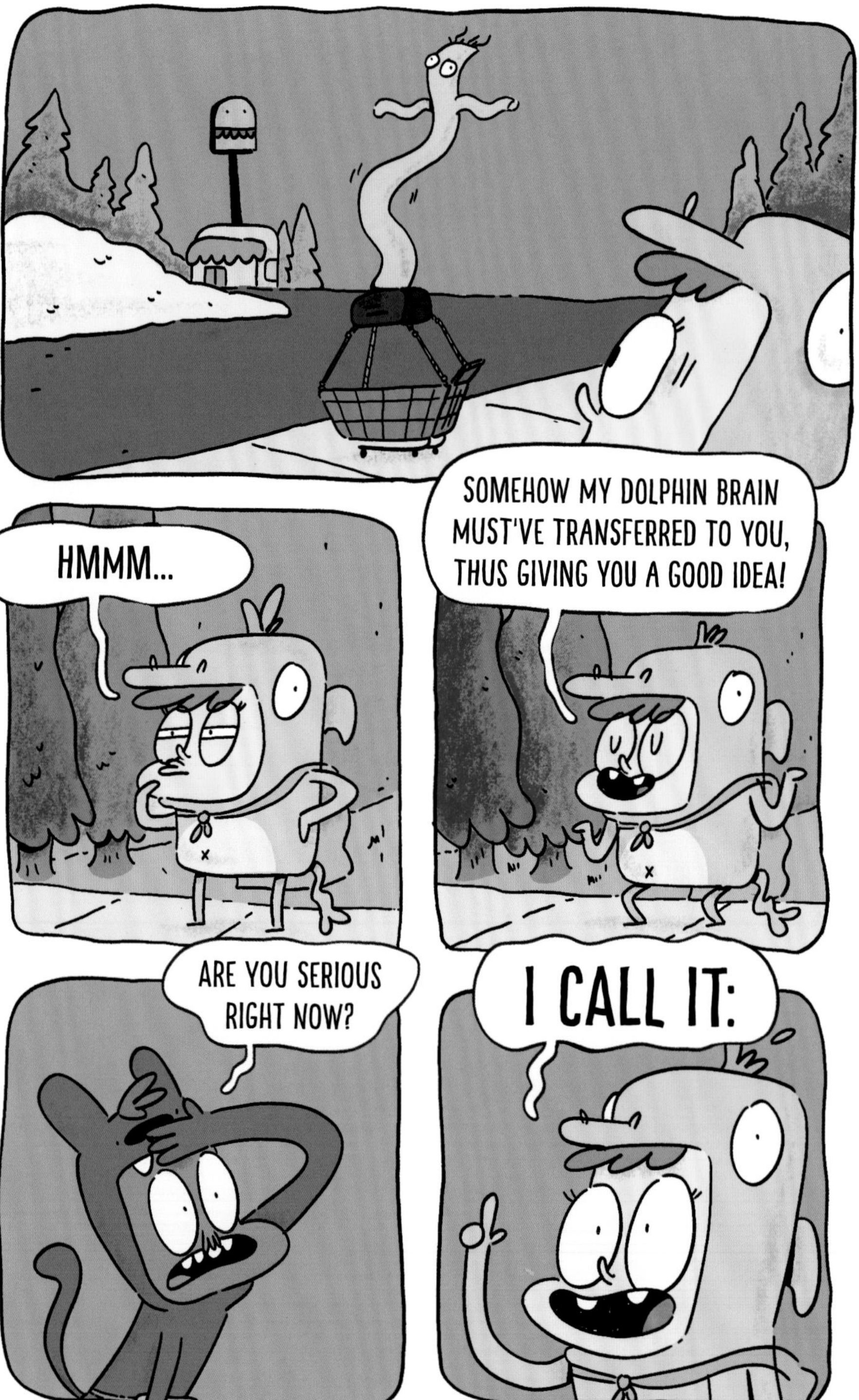
HMMM...
SOMEHOW MY DOLPHIN BRAIN MUST'VE TRANSFERRED TO YOU, THUS GIVING YOU A GOOD IDEA!
ARE YOU SERIOUS RIGHT NOW?
I CALL IT:

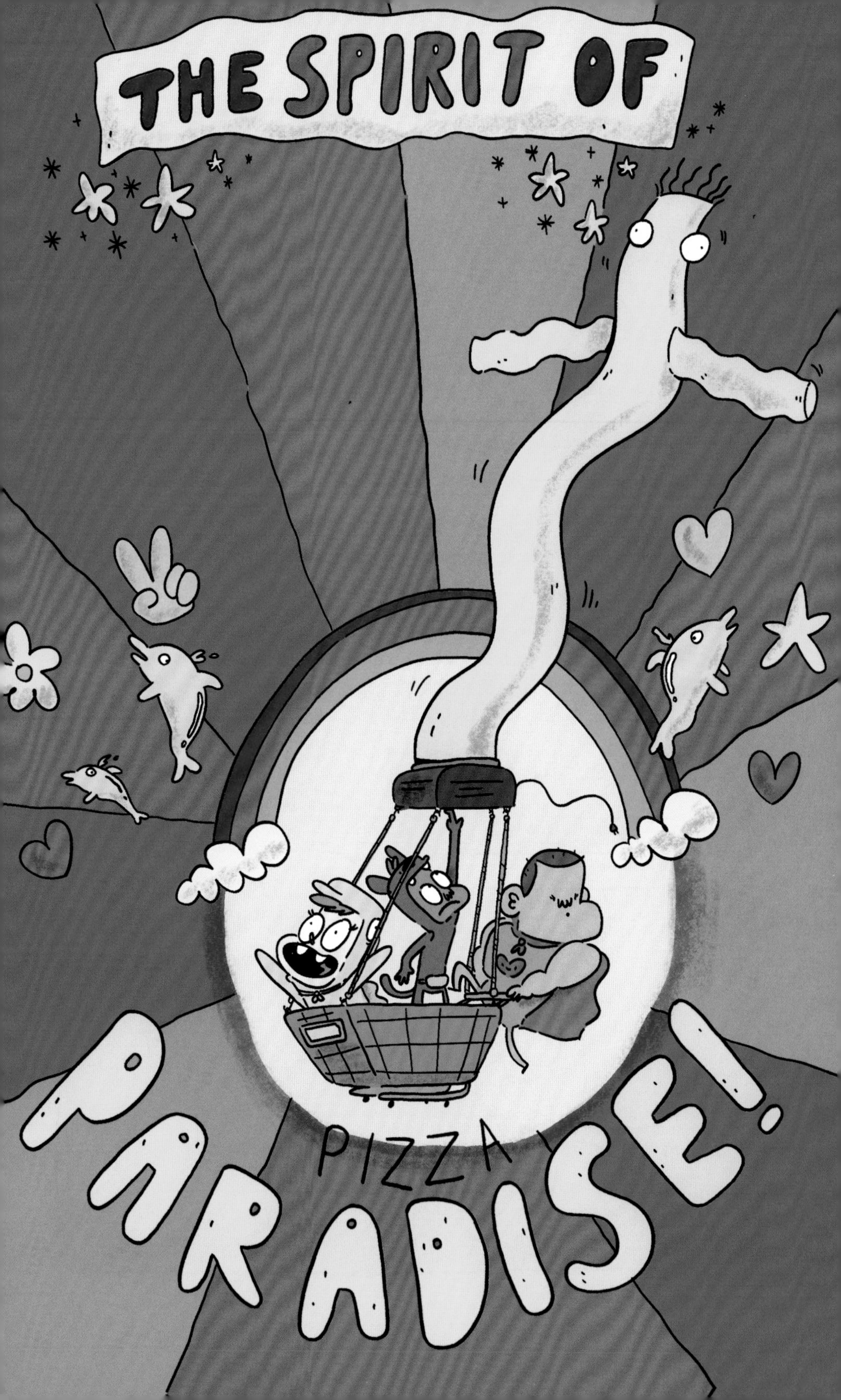
THE SPIRIT OF
PIZZA
PARADISE!

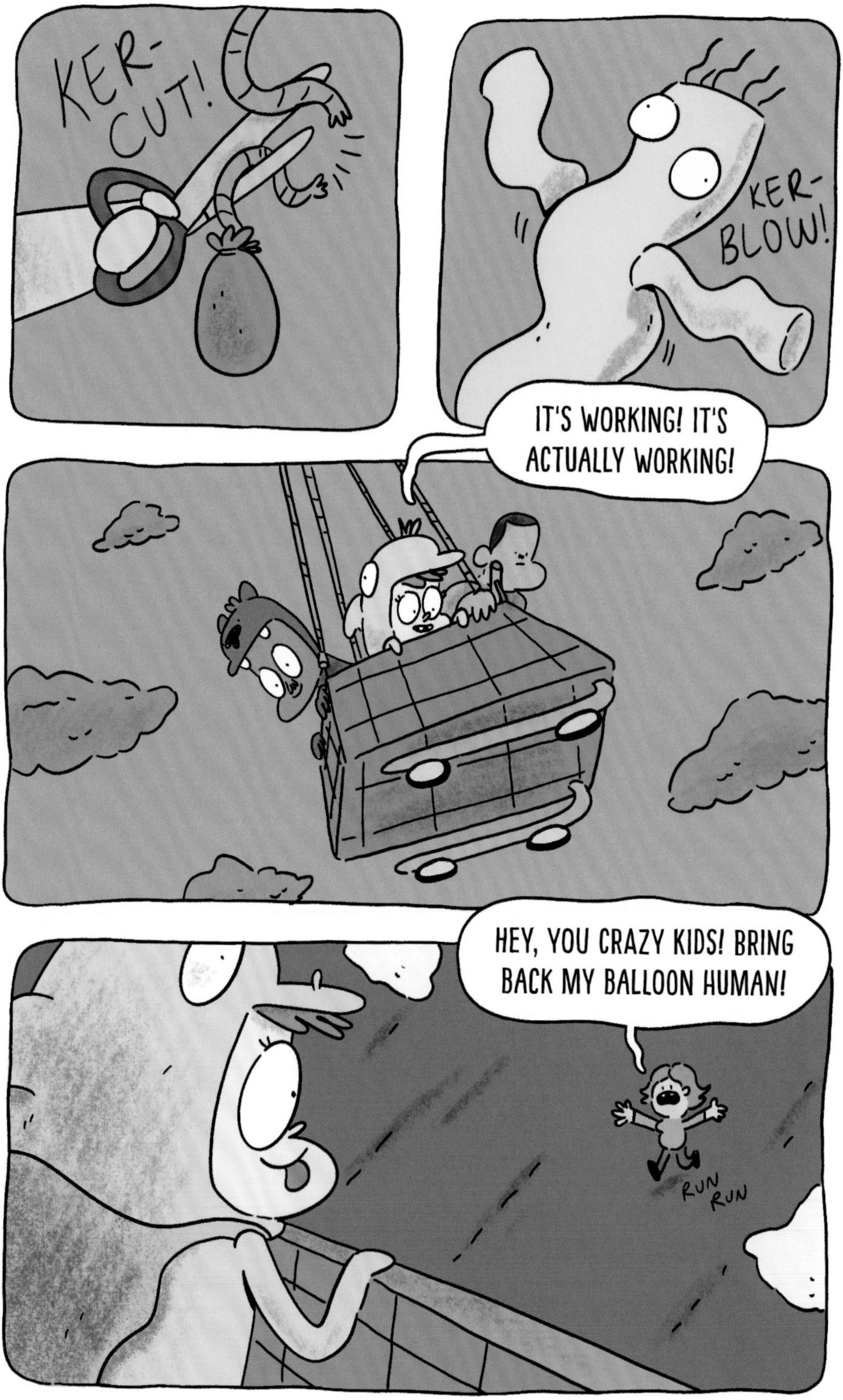
KER-CUT!
KER-BLOW!
IT'S WORKING! IT'S ACTUALLY WORKING!
HEY, YOU CRAZY KIDS! BRING BACK MY BALLOON HUMAN!
RUN RUN

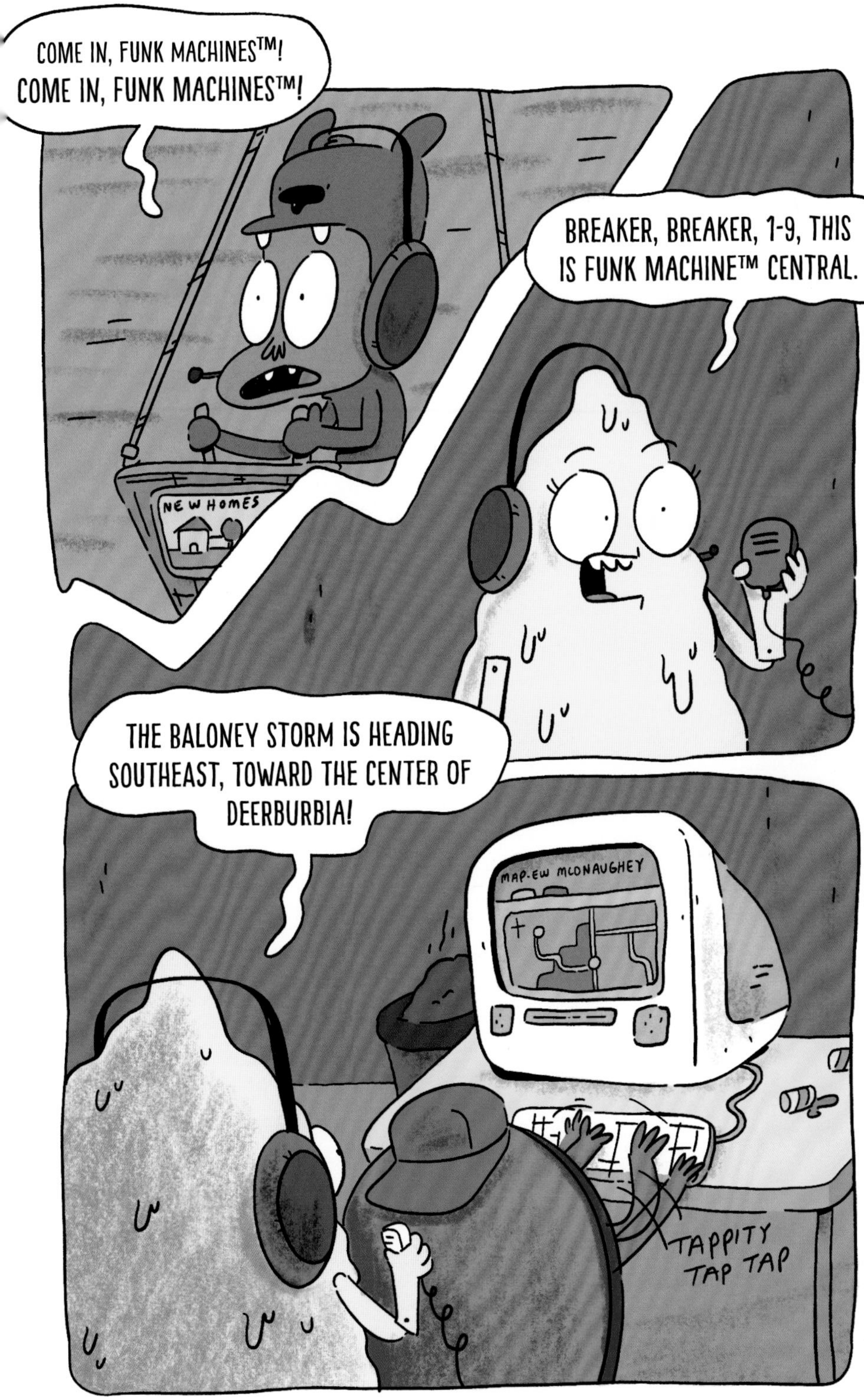
COME IN, FUNK MACHINES™! COME IN, FUNK MACHINES™!
BREAKER, BREAKER, 1-9, THIS IS FUNK MACHINE™ CENTRAL.
NEW HOMES
THE BALONEY STORM IS HEADING SOUTHEAST, TOWARD THE CENTER OF DEERBURBIA!
MAP-EW MCDONAUGHEY
TAPPITY TAP TAP

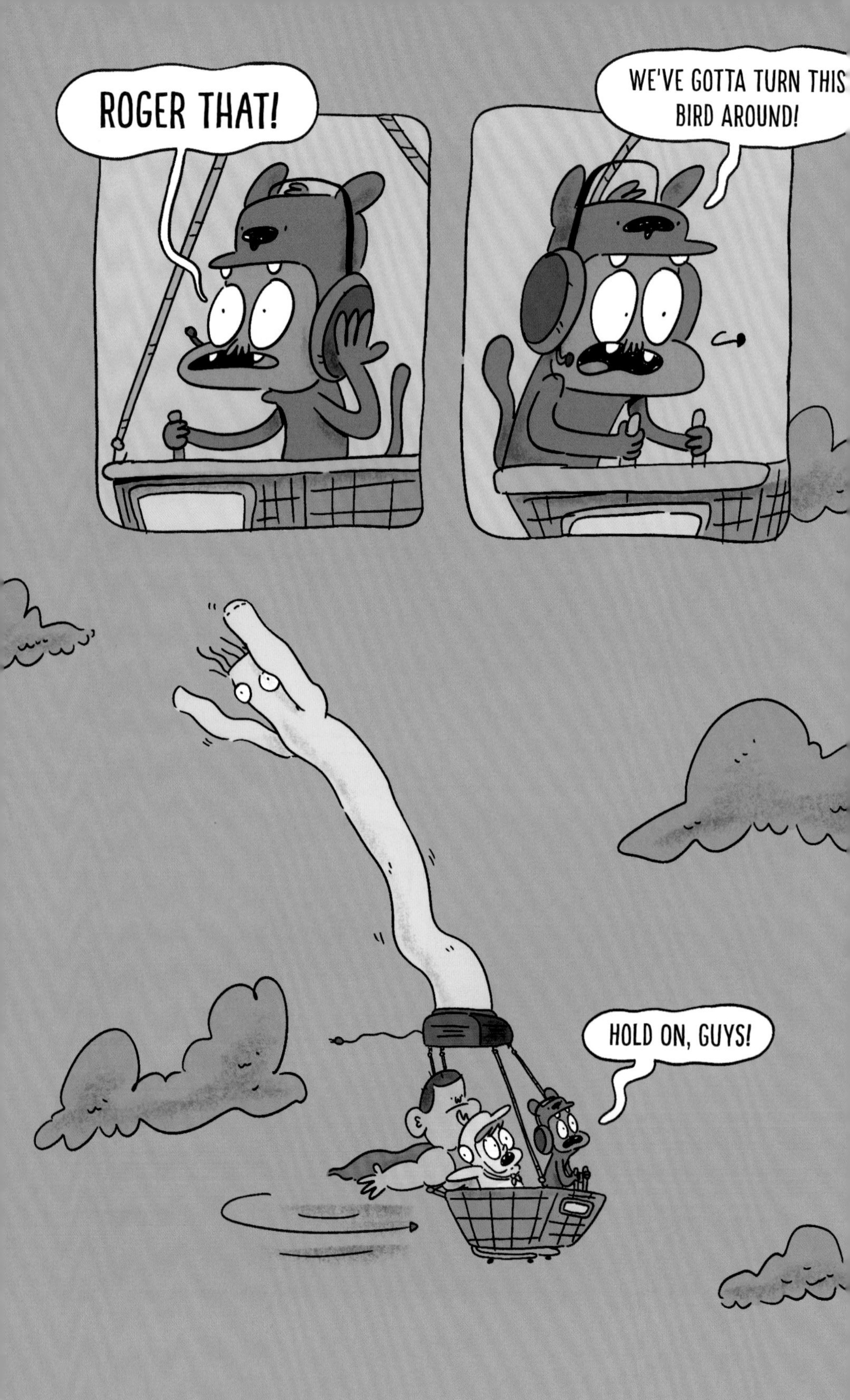
ROGER THAT!
WE'VE GOTTA TURN THIS BIRD AROUND!
HOLD ON, GUYS!

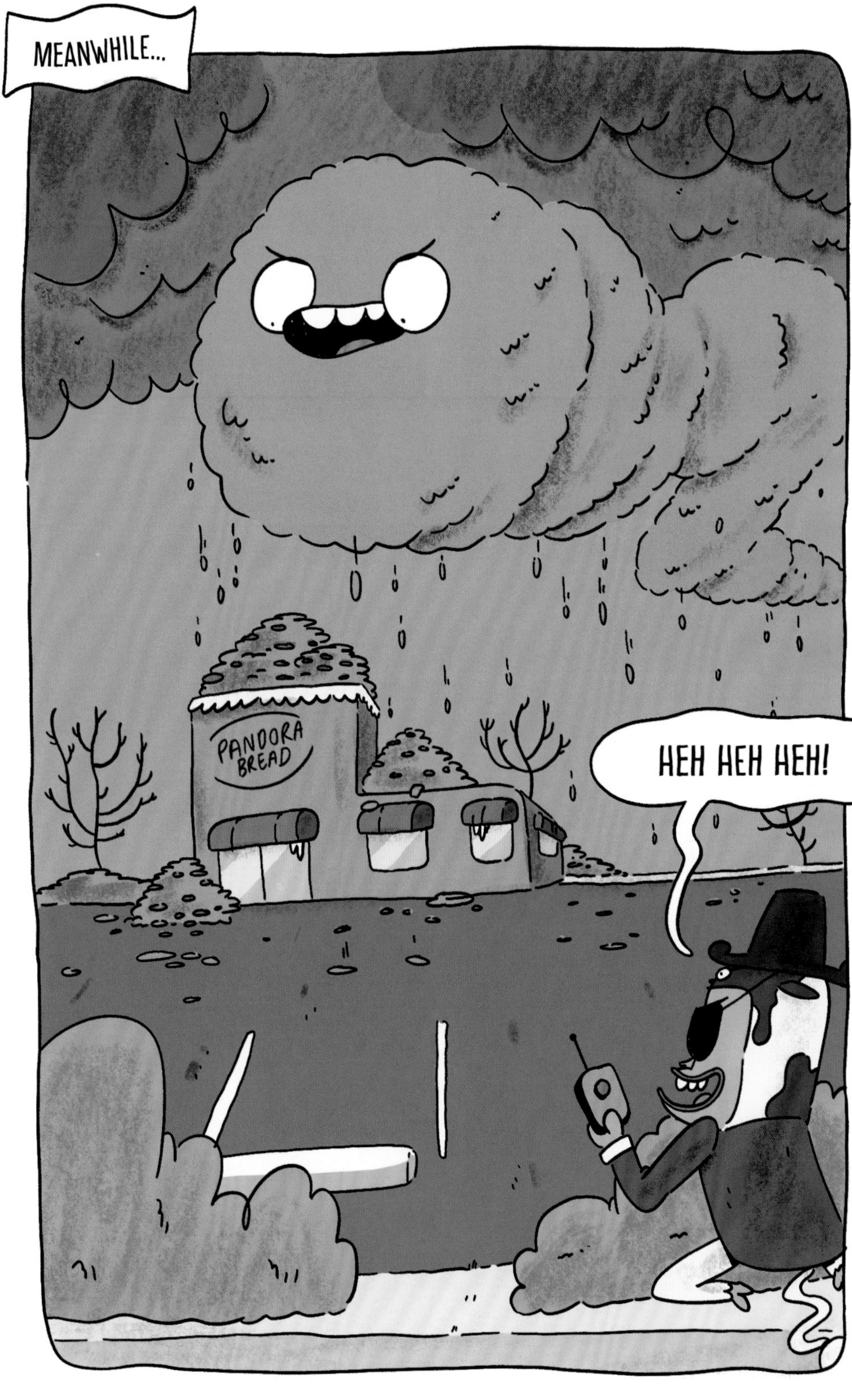
MEANWHILE...
PANDORA BREAD
HEH HEH HEH!

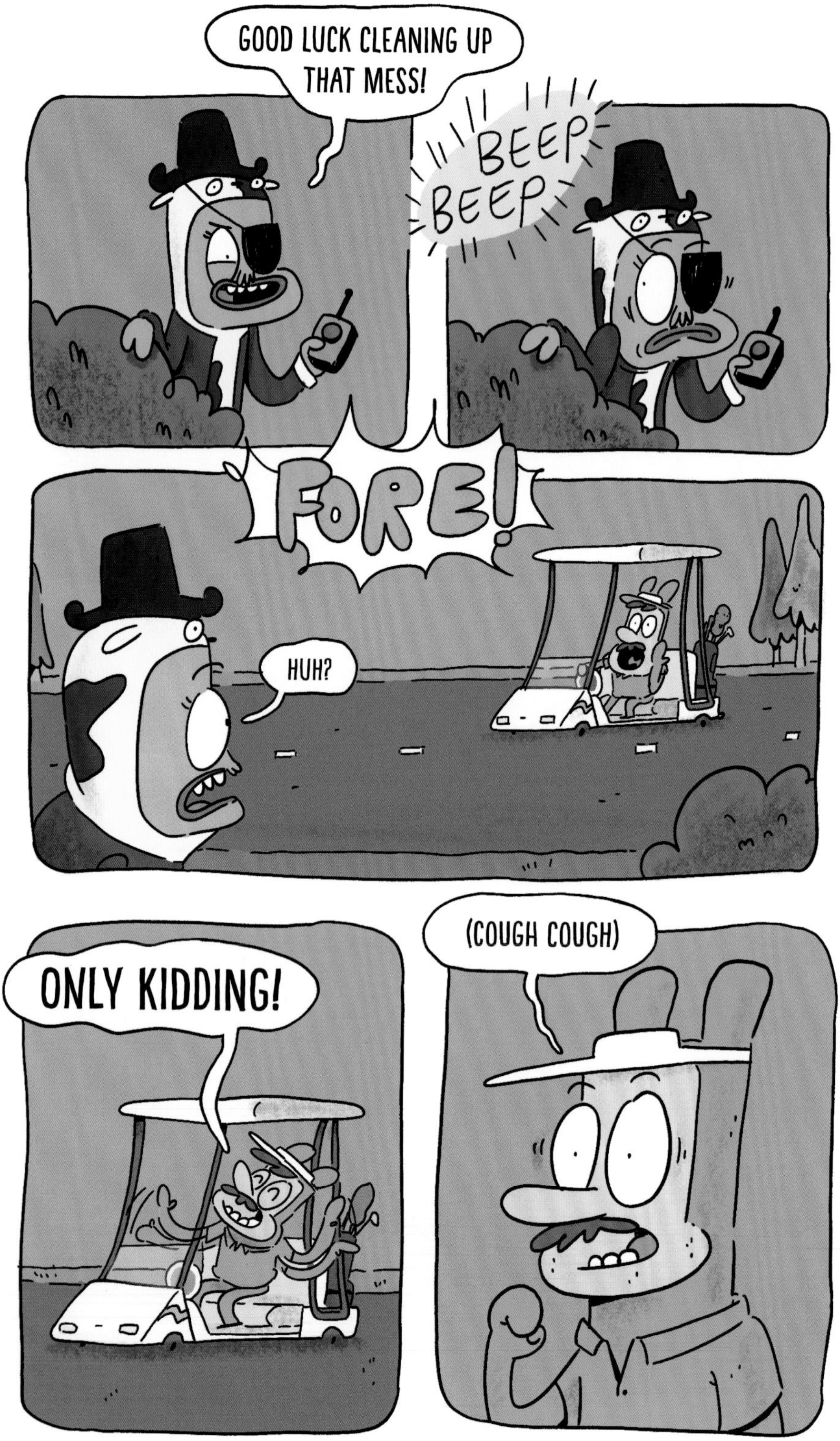
GOOD LUCK CLEANING UP THAT MESS!
BEEP BEEP
FORE!
HUH?
ONLY KIDDING!
(COUGH COUGH)

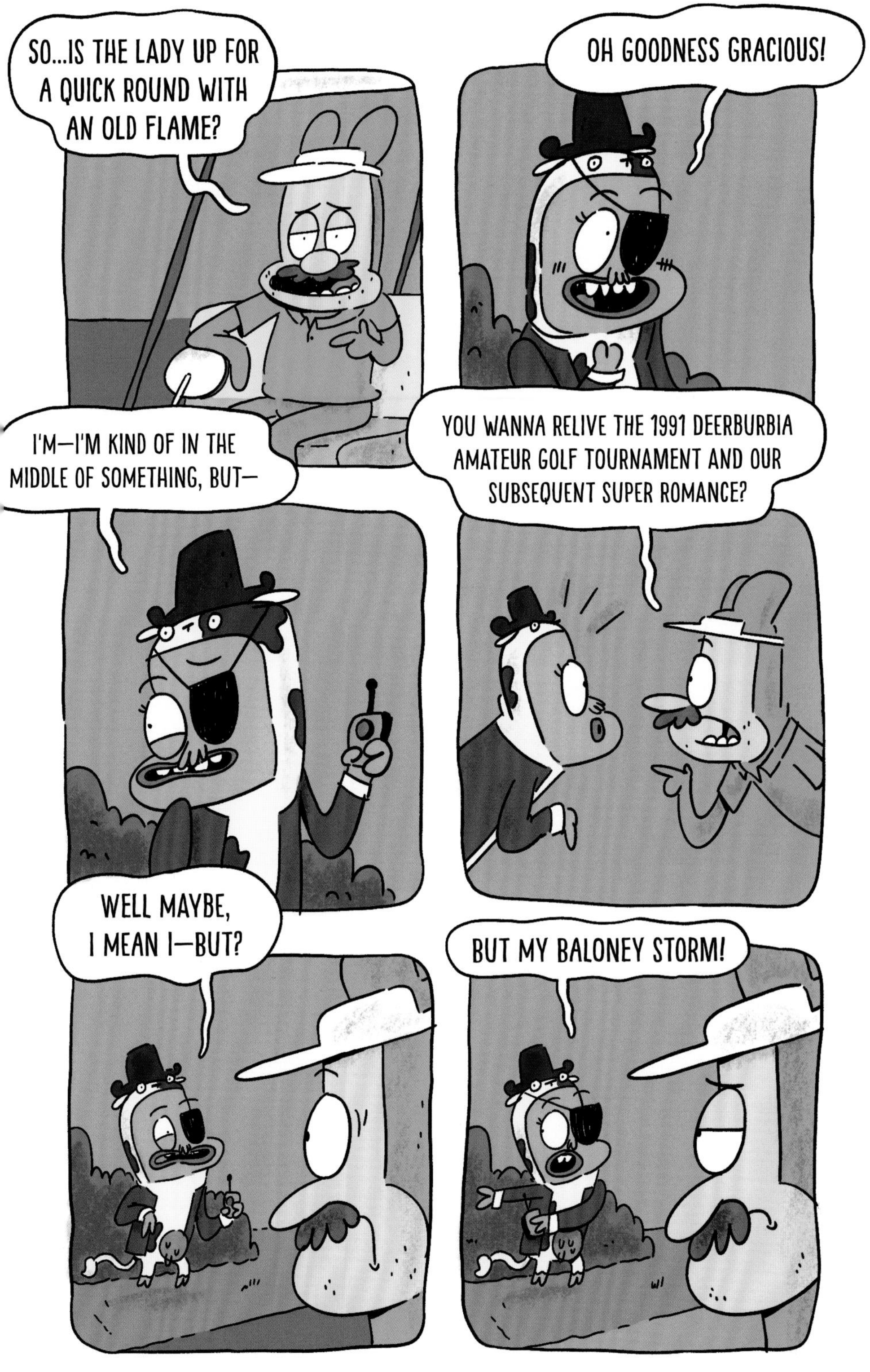
SO...IS THE LADY UP FOR A QUICK ROUND WITH AN OLD FLAME?
OH GOODNESS GRACIOUS!
I'M—I'M KIND OF IN THE MIDDLE OF SOMETHING, BUT—
YOU WANNA RELIVE THE 1991 DEERBURBIA AMATEUR GOLF TOURNAMENT AND OUR SUBSEQUENT SUPER ROMANCE?
WELL MAYBE, I MEAN I—BUT?
BUT MY BALONEY STORM!

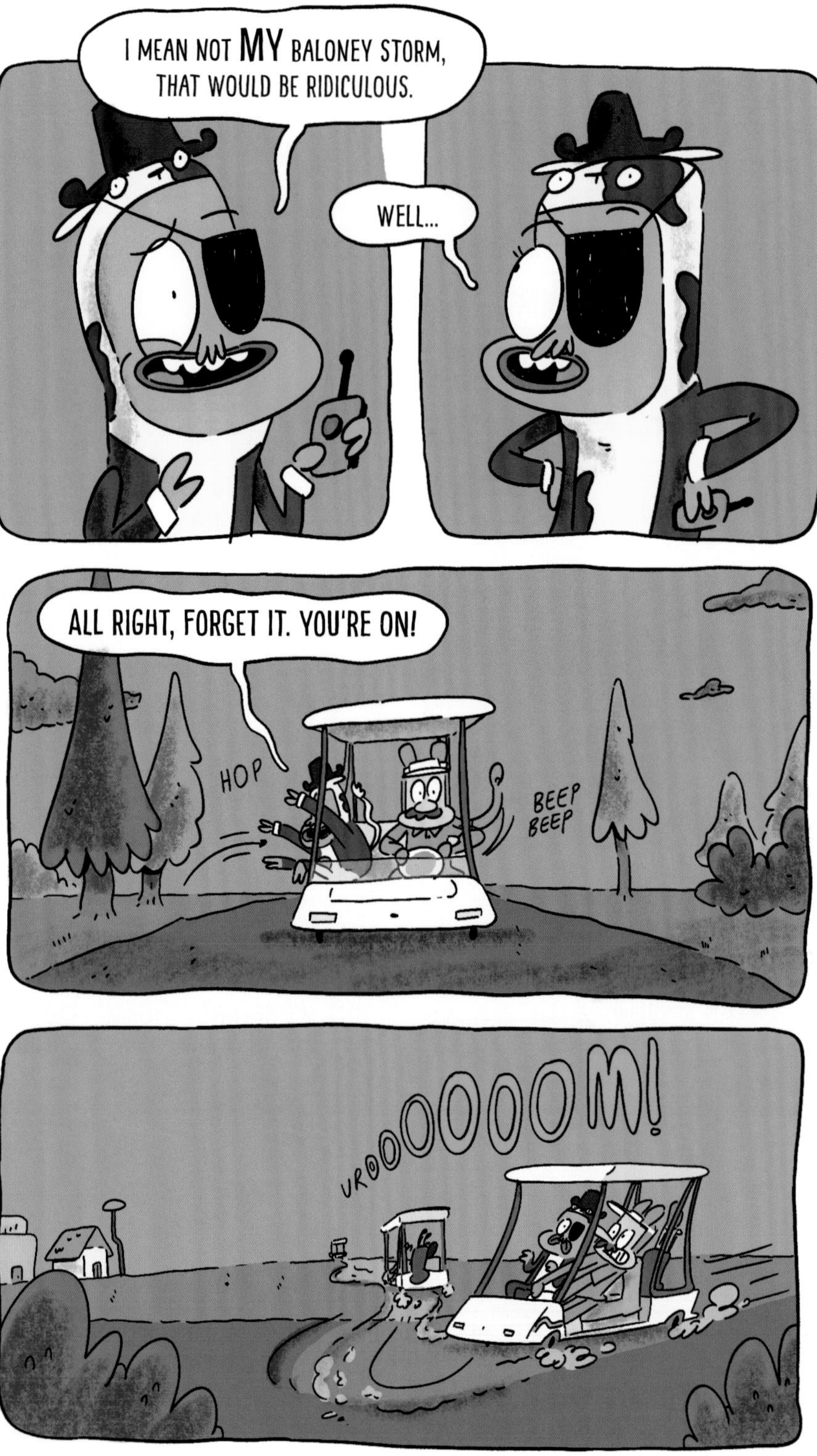
I MEAN NOT MY BALONEY STORM, THAT WOULD BE RIDICULOUS.
WELL...
ALL RIGHT, FORGET IT. YOU'RE ON!
HOP
BEEP BEEP
VROOOOOOOOM!

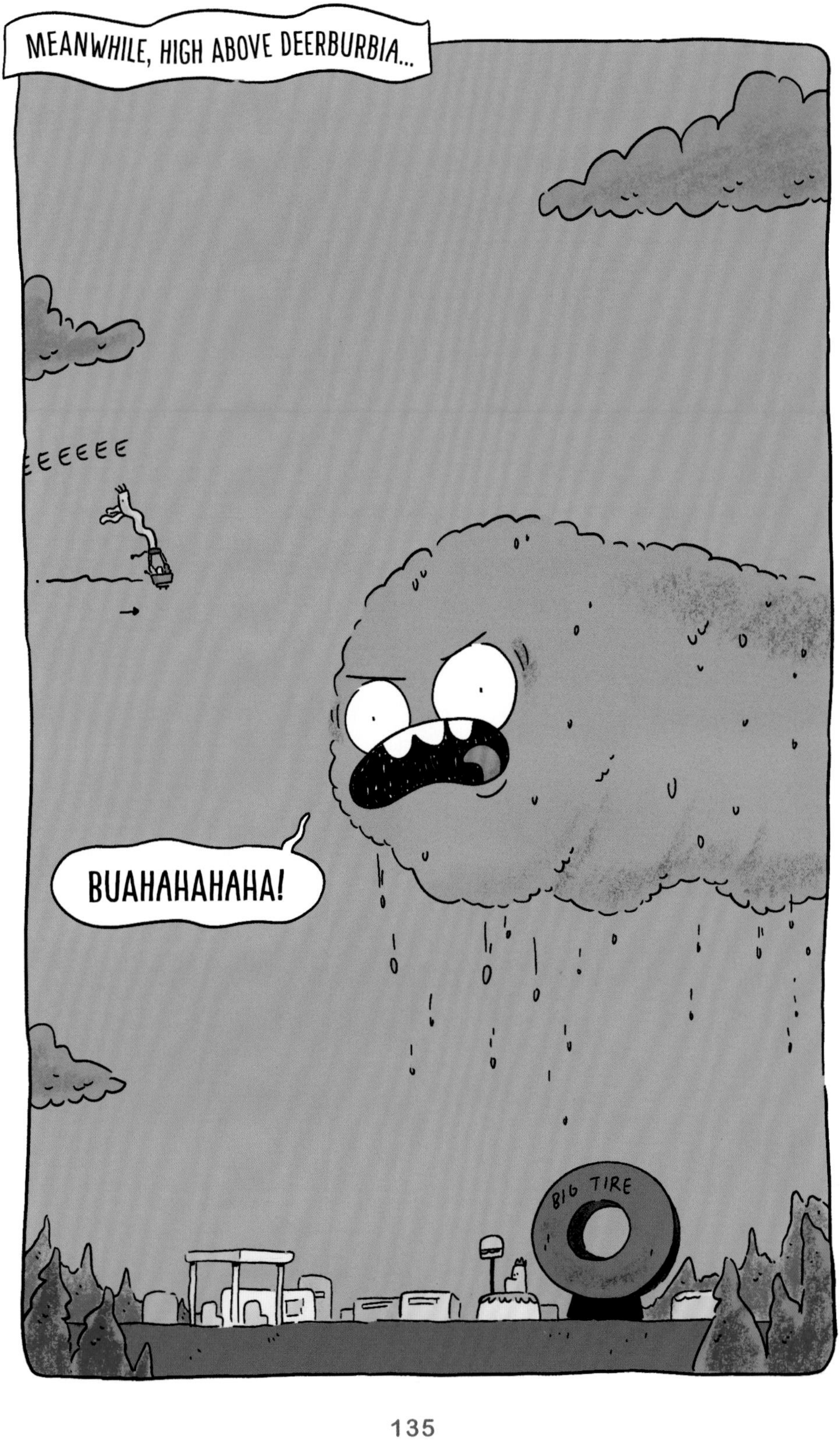
MEANWHILE, HIGH ABOVE DEERBURBIA...
EEEEEE
BUAHAHAHAHA!
BIG TIRE

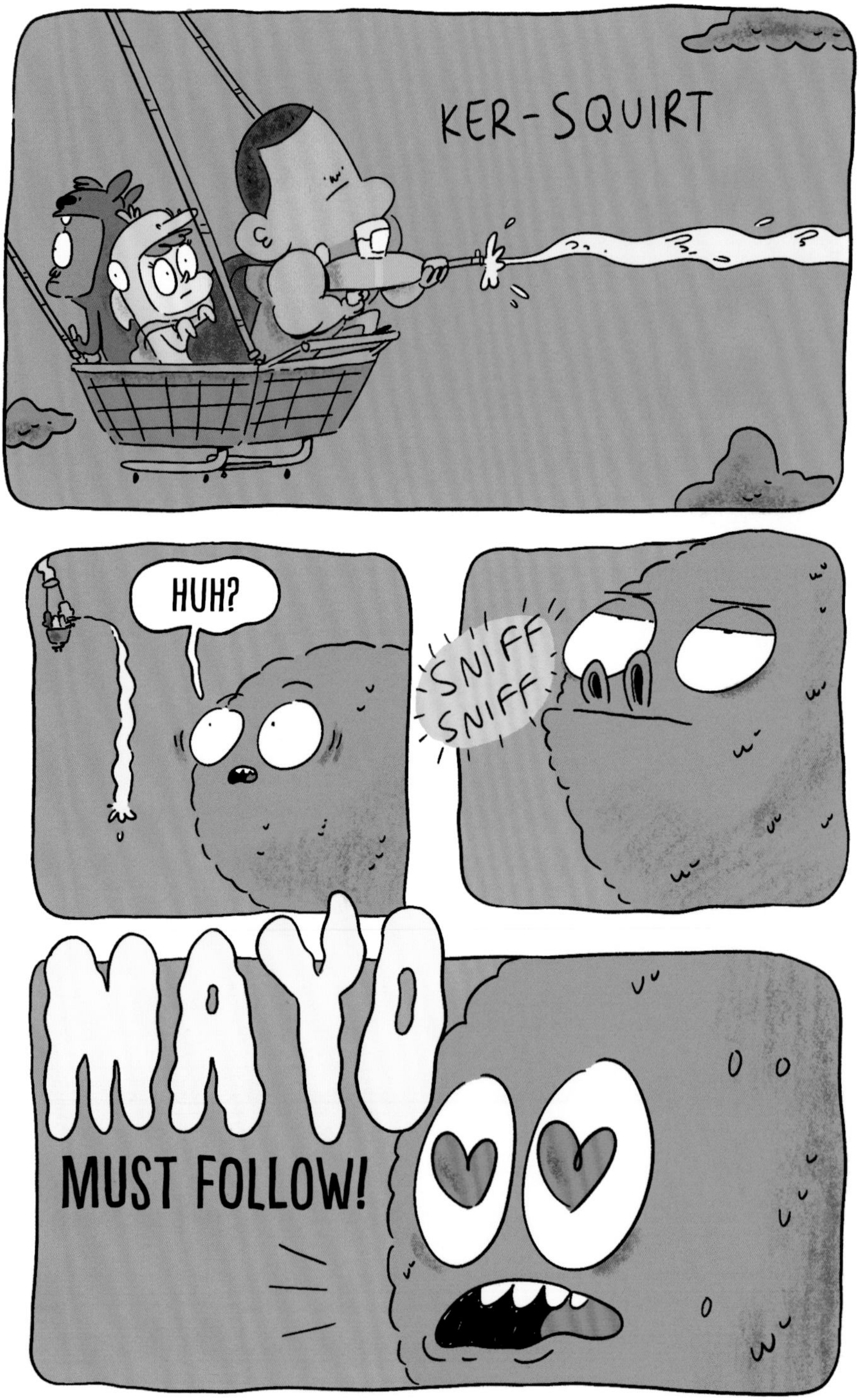
KER-SQUIRT
HUH?
SNIFF SNIFF
MAYO
MUST FOLLOW!

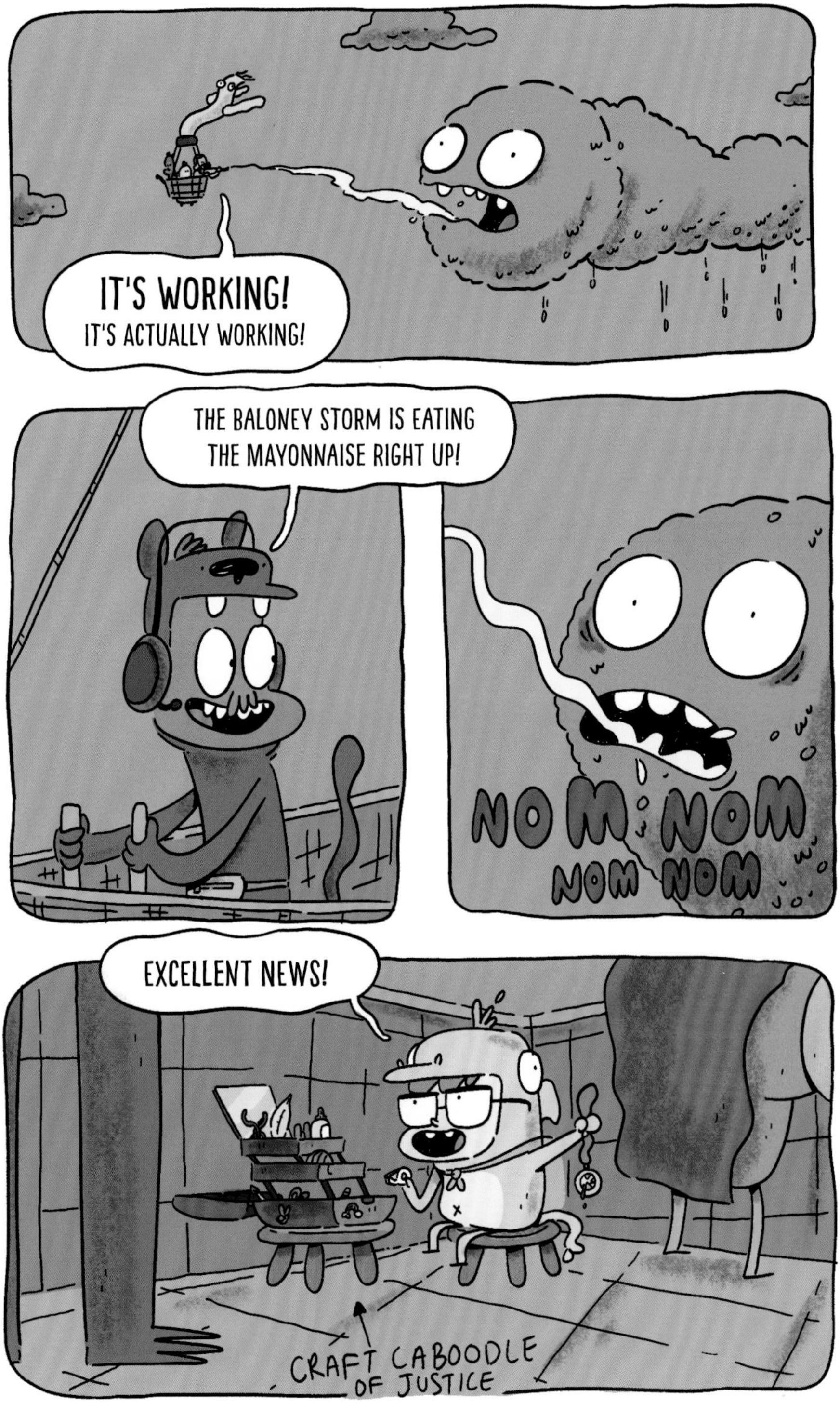
IT'S WORKING!
IT'S ACTUALLY WORKING!
THE BALONEY STORM IS EATING THE MAYONNAISE RIGHT UP!
NOM NOM
NOM NOM
EXCELLENT NEWS!
CRAFT CABOODLE OF JUSTICE

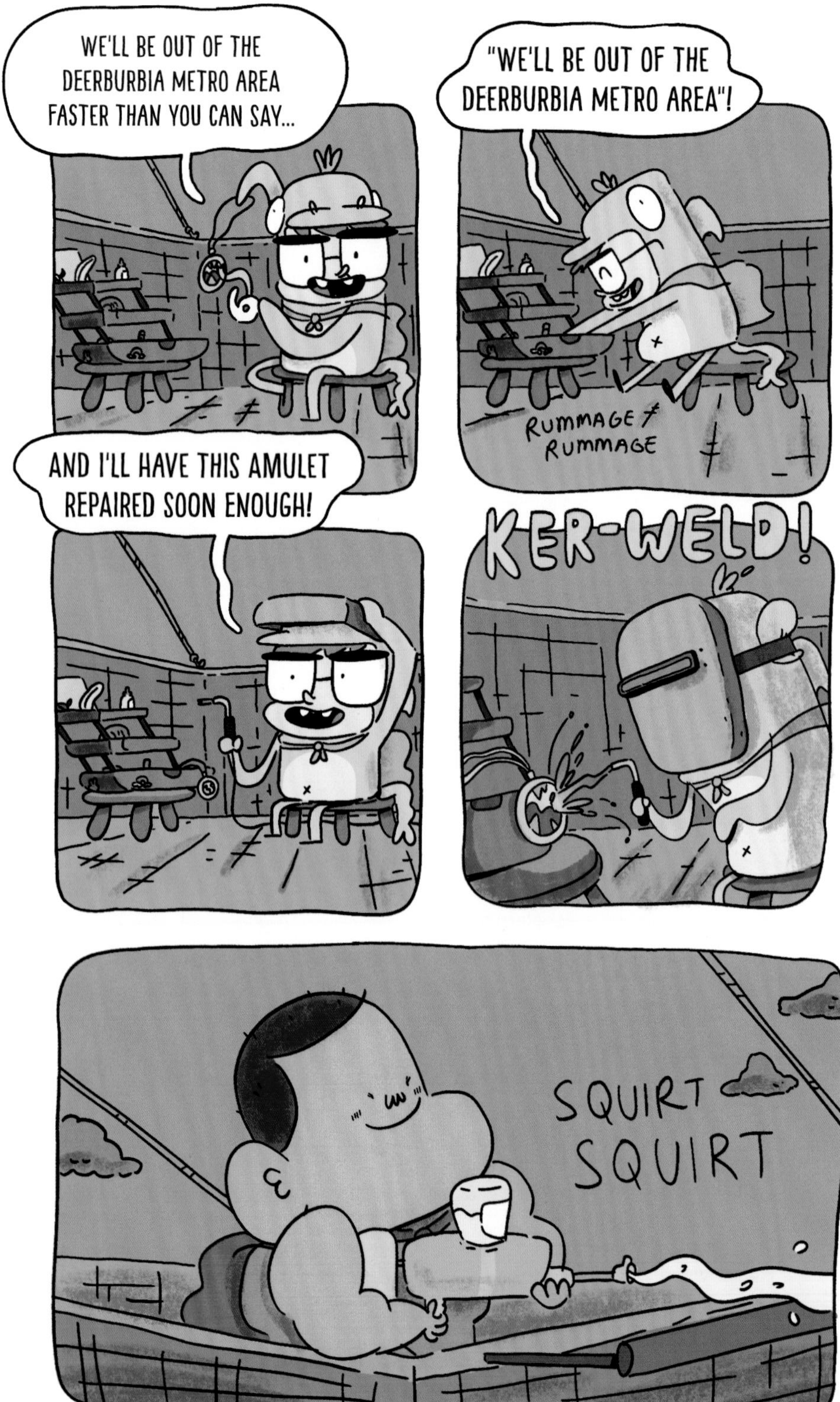
WE'LL BE OUT OF THE DEERBURBIA METRO AREA FASTER THAN YOU CAN SAY...
"WE'LL BE OUT OF THE DEERBURBIA METRO AREA"!
RUMMAGE RUMMAGE
AND I'LL HAVE THIS AMULET REPAIRED SOON ENOUGH!
KER-WELD!
SQUIRT SQUIRT

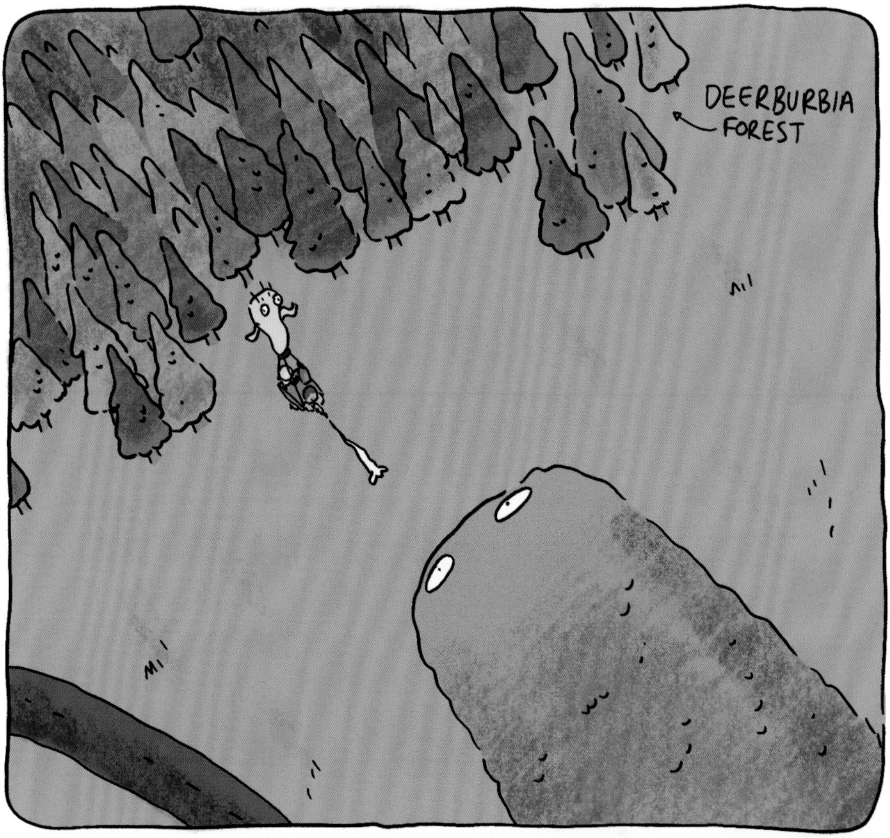
DEERBURBIA
FOREST

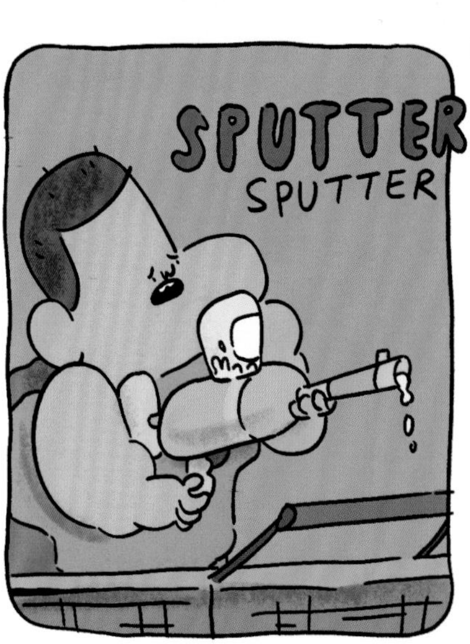
SPUTTER
SPUTTER

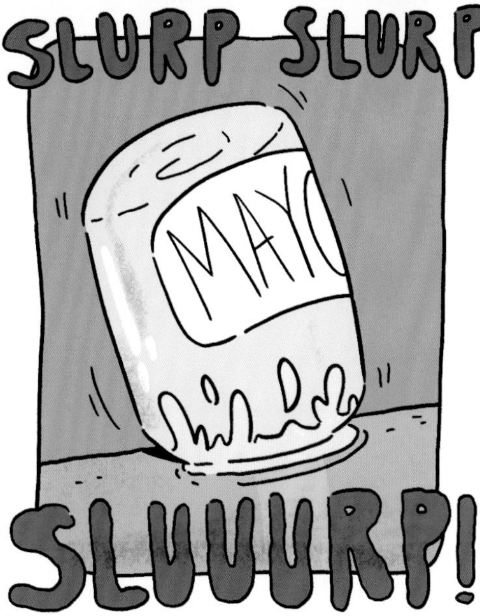
SLURP SLURP
MAYO
SLUUURP!

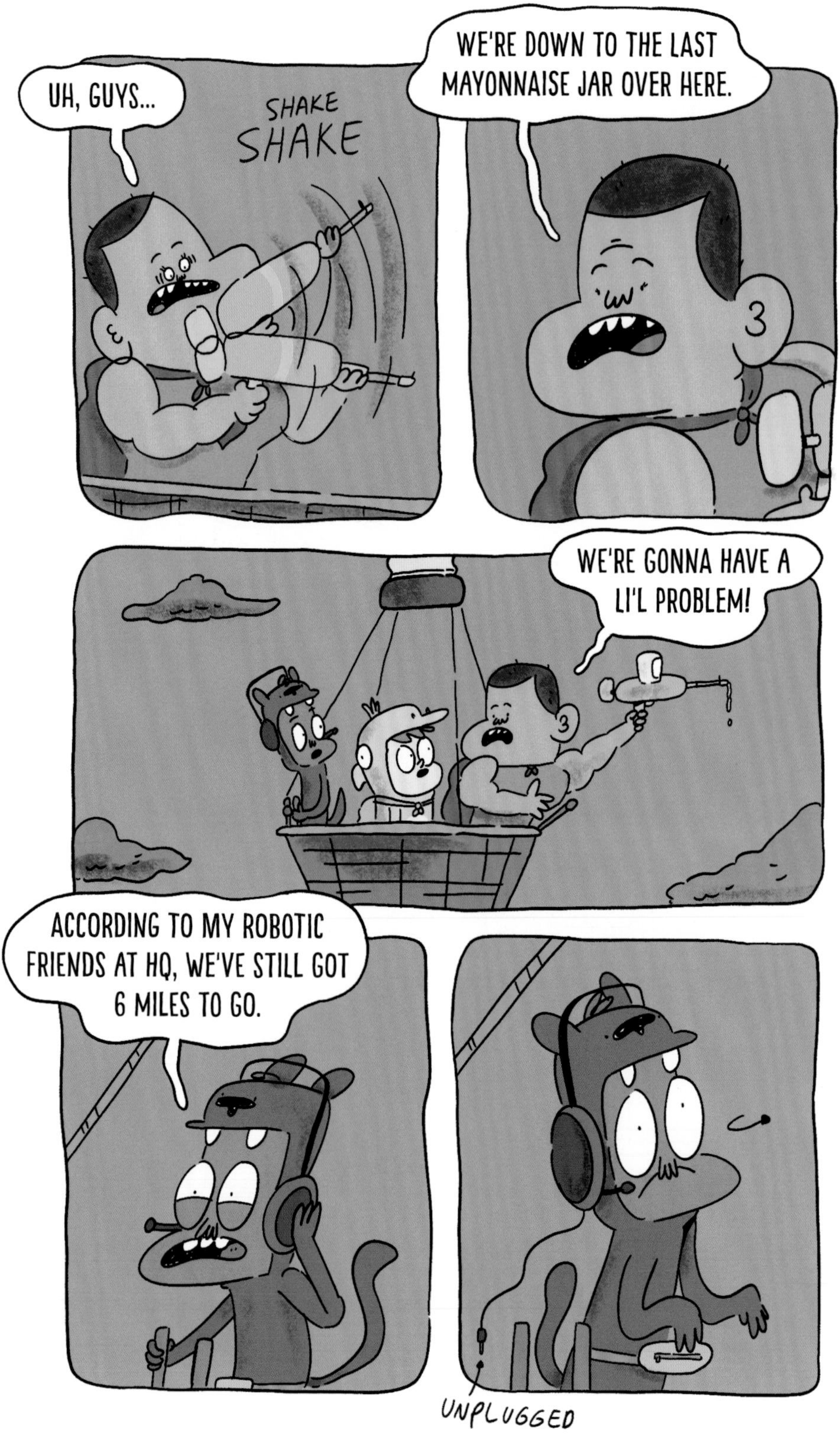
UH, GUYS...
SHAKE
SHAKE
WE'RE DOWN TO THE LAST MAYONNAISE JAR OVER HERE.
WE'RE GONNA HAVE A LI'L PROBLEM!
ACCORDING TO MY ROBOTIC FRIENDS AT HQ, WE'VE STILL GOT 6 MILES TO GO.
UNPLUGGED

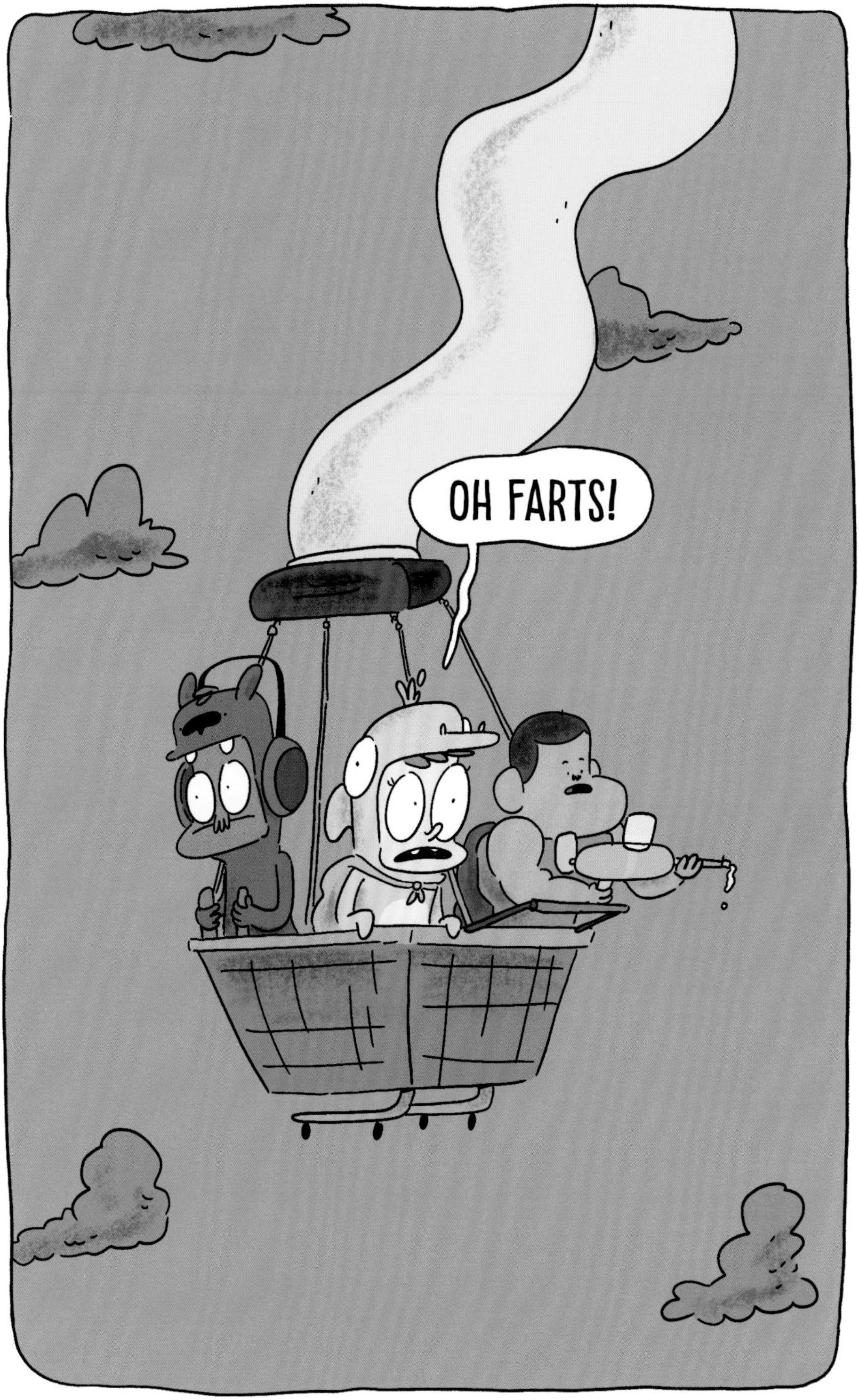
OH FARTS!

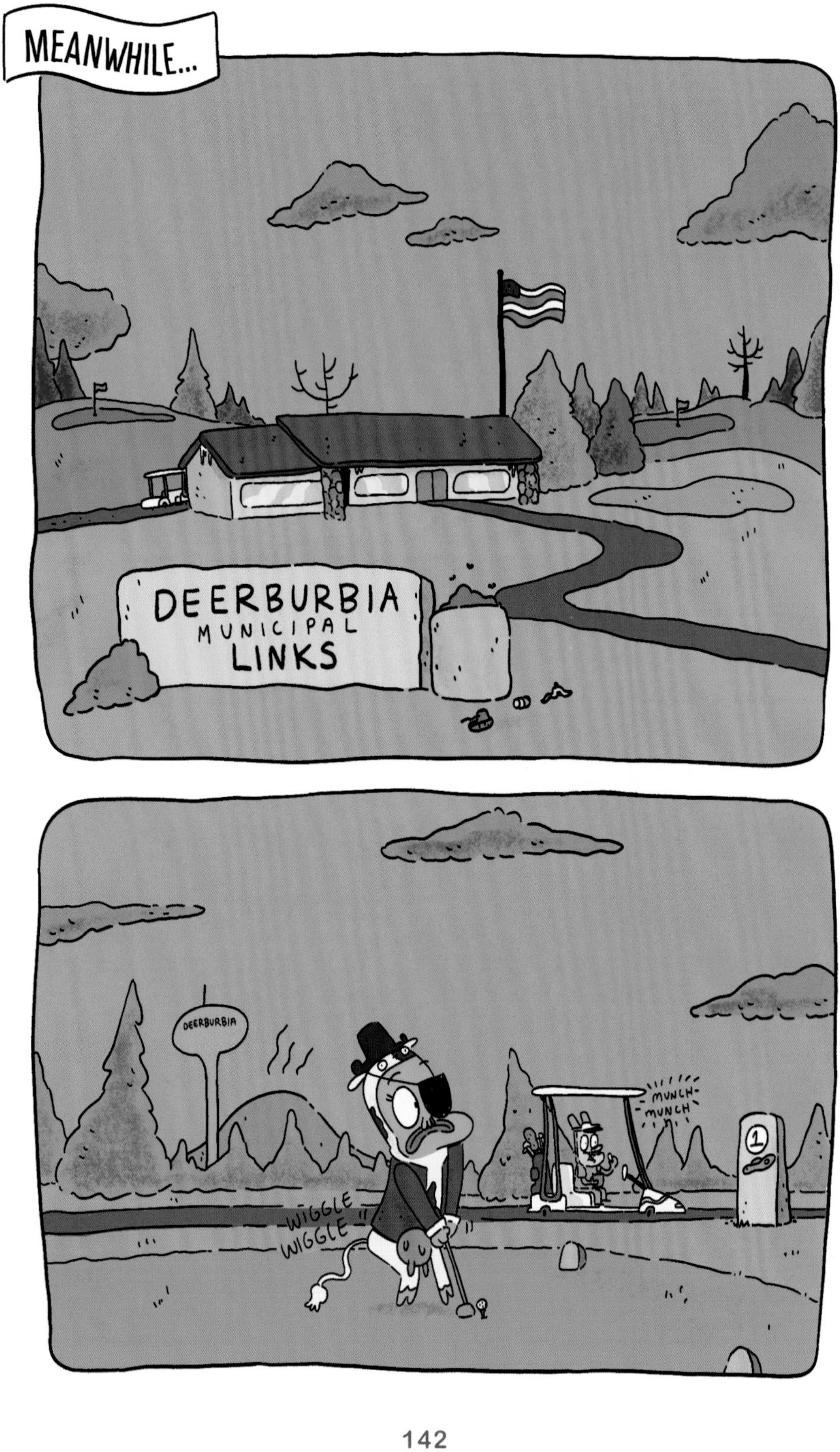
MEANWHILE...
DEERBURBIA MUNICIPAL LINKS
DEERBURBIA
MUNCH MUNCH
WIGGLE WIGGLE

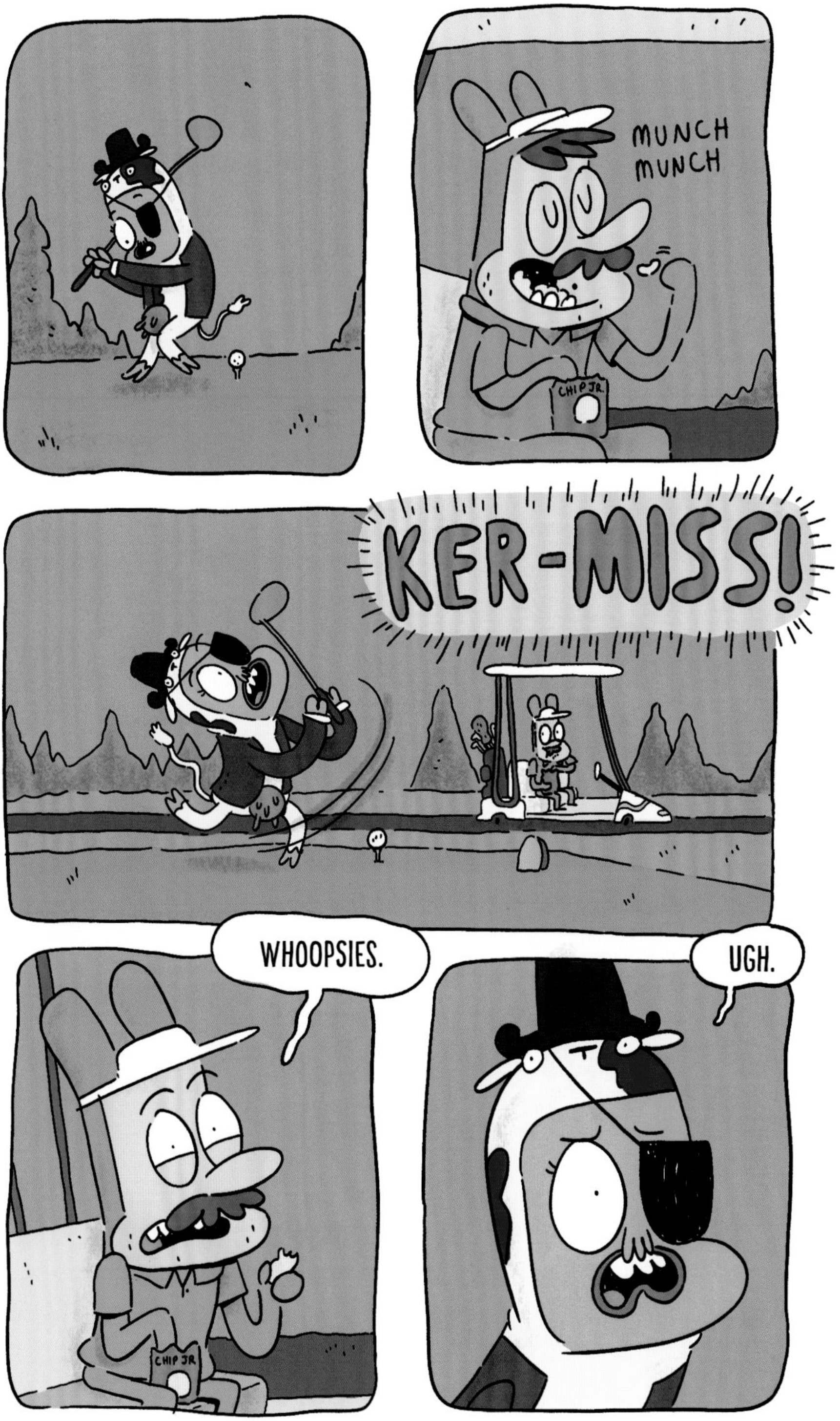
MUNCH
MUNCH
CHIP JR.
KER-MISS!
WHOOPSIES.
UGH.
CHIP JR

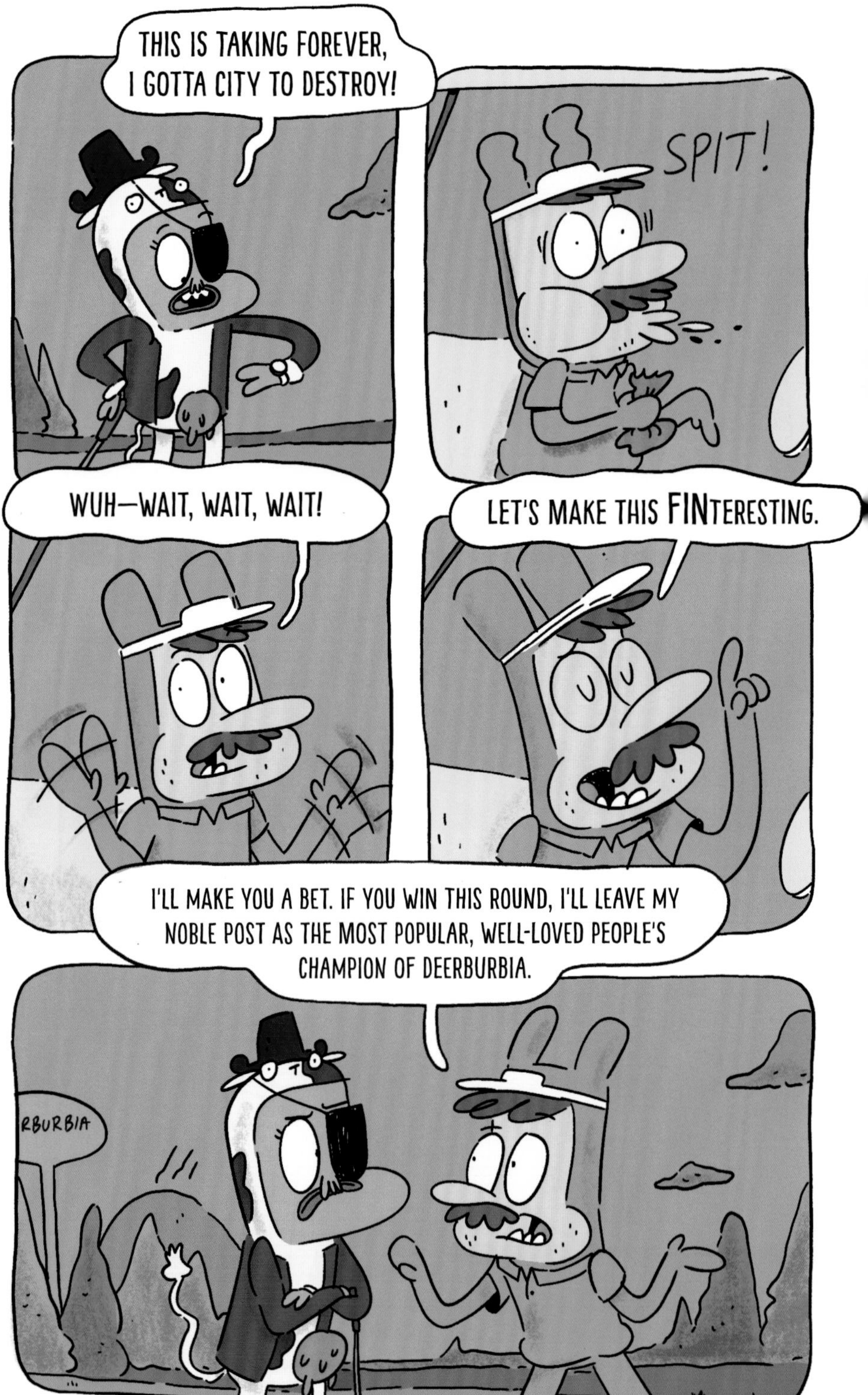
THIS IS TAKING FOREVER, I GOTTA CITY TO DESTROY!
SPIT!
WUH—WAIT, WAIT, WAIT!
LET'S MAKE THIS FINTERESTING.
I'LL MAKE YOU A BET. IF YOU WIN THIS ROUND, I'LL LEAVE MY NOBLE POST AS THE MOST POPULAR, WELL-LOVED PEOPLE'S CHAMPION OF DEERBURBIA.
RBURBIA

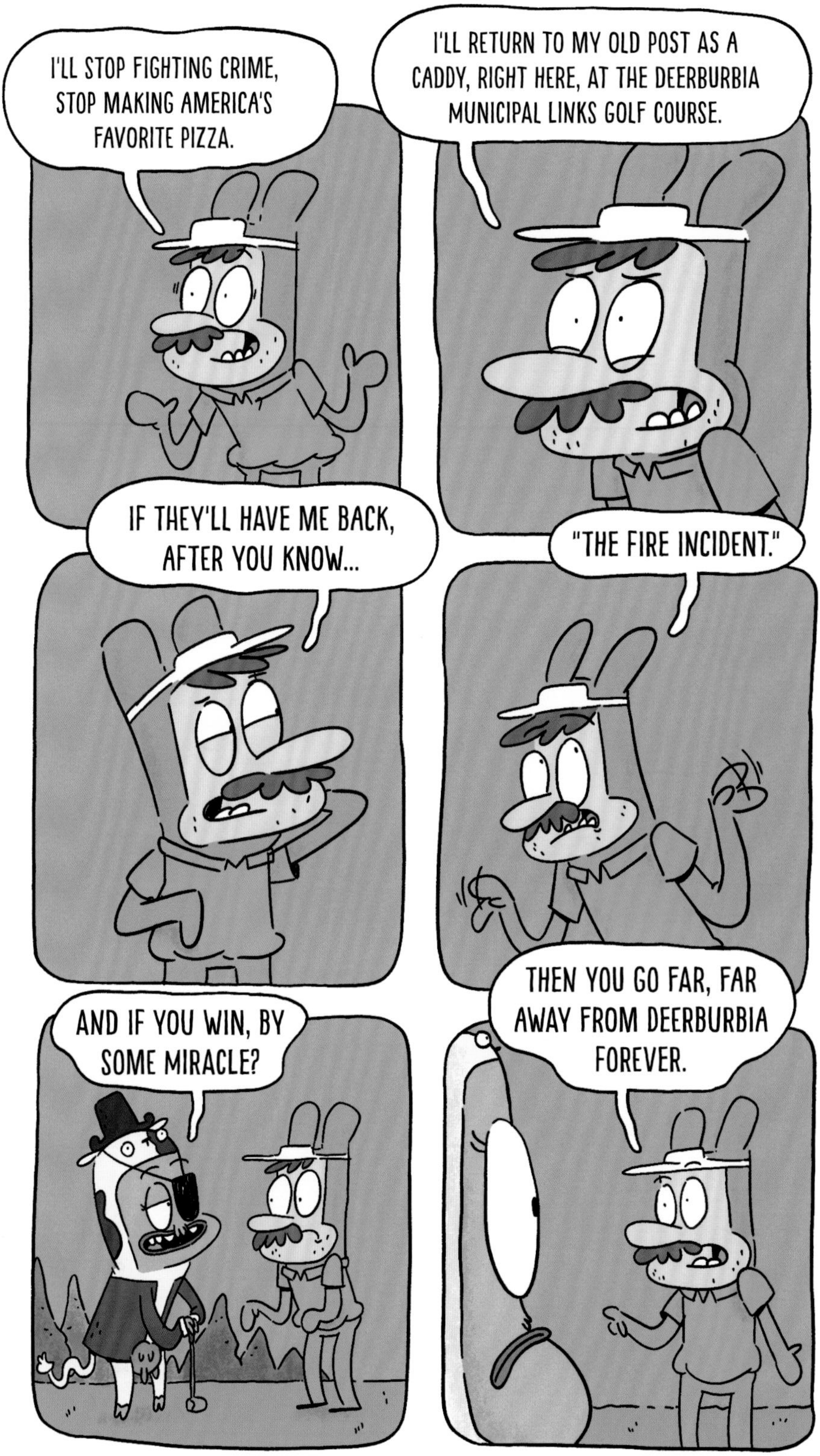
I'LL STOP FIGHTING CRIME, STOP MAKING AMERICA'S FAVORITE PIZZA.
I'LL RETURN TO MY OLD POST AS A CADDY, RIGHT HERE, AT THE DEERBURBIA MUNICIPAL LINKS GOLF COURSE.
IF THEY'LL HAVE ME BACK, AFTER YOU KNOW...
"THE FIRE INCIDENT."
AND IF YOU WIN, BY SOME MIRACLE?
THEN YOU GO FAR, FAR AWAY FROM DEERBURBIA FOREVER.

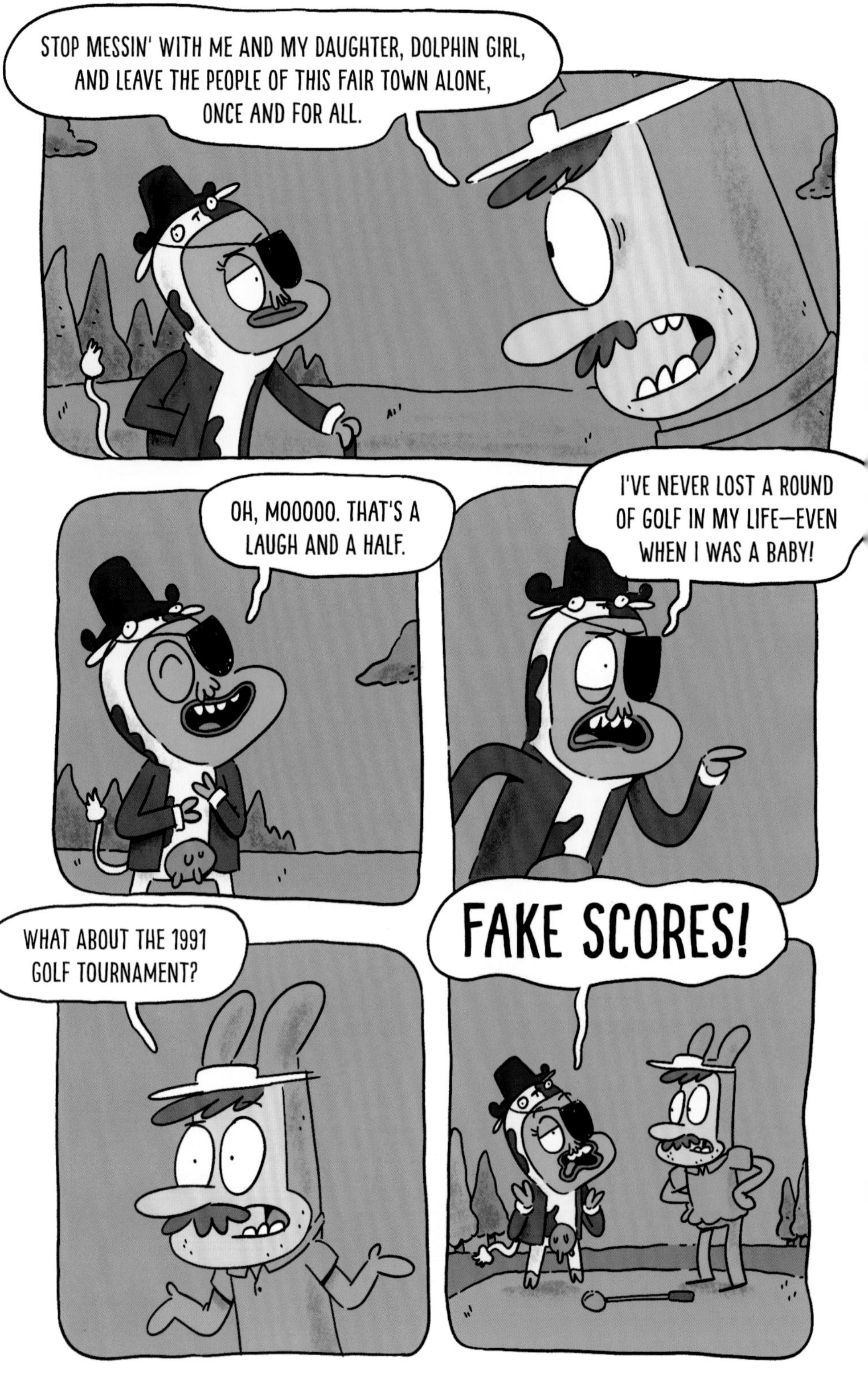
STOP MESSIN' WITH ME AND MY DAUGHTER, DOLPHIN GIRL, AND LEAVE THE PEOPLE OF THIS FAIR TOWN ALONE, ONCE AND FOR ALL.
OH, MOOOOO. THAT'S A LAUGH AND A HALF.
I'VE NEVER LOST A ROUND OF GOLF IN MY LIFE—EVEN WHEN I WAS A BABY!
WHAT ABOUT THE 1991 GOLF TOURNAMENT?
FAKE SCORES!

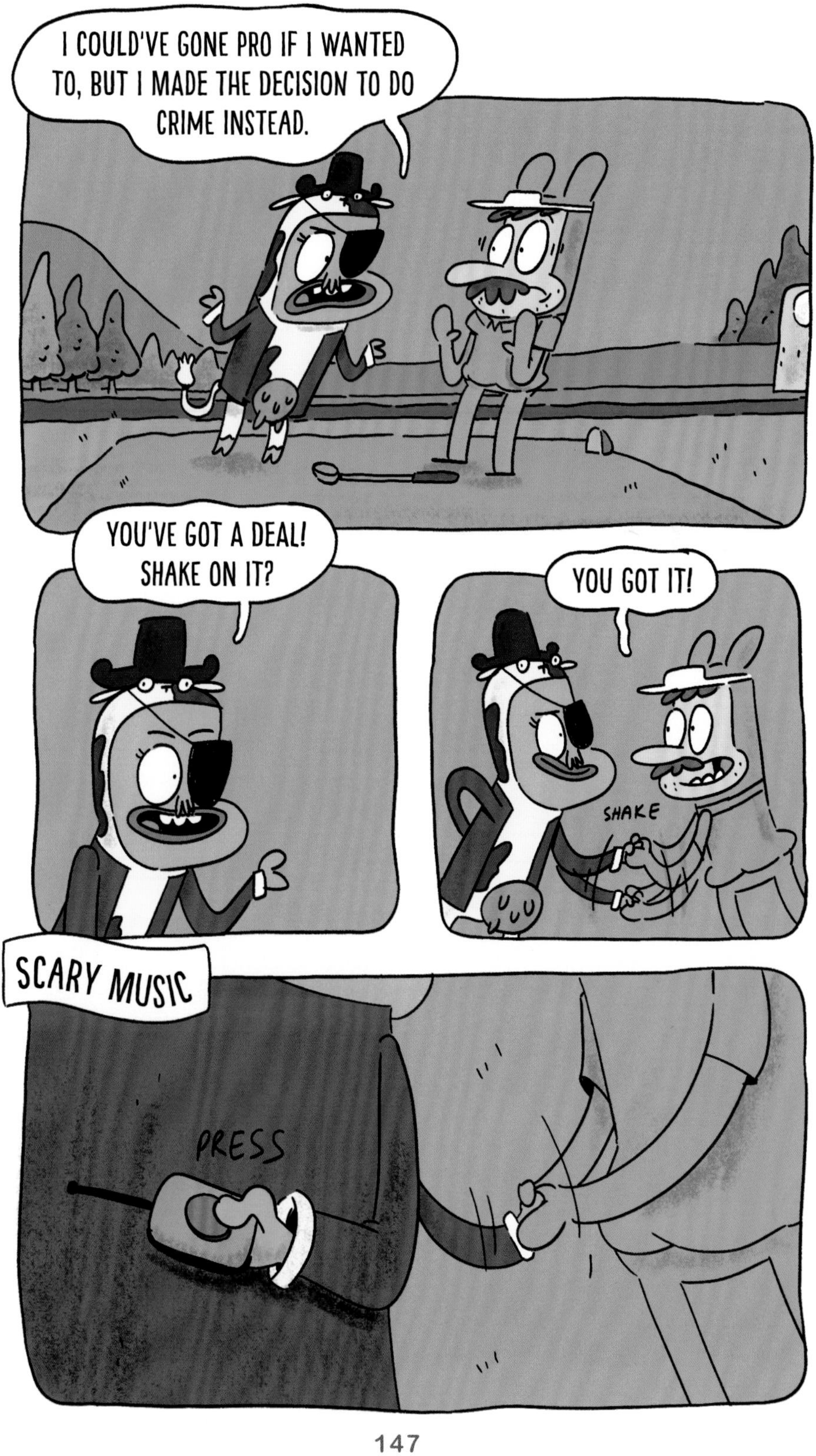
I COULD'VE GONE PRO IF I WANTED TO, BUT I MADE THE DECISION TO DO CRIME INSTEAD.
YOU'VE GOT A DEAL! SHAKE ON IT?
YOU GOT IT!
SHAKE
SCARY MUSIC
PRESS

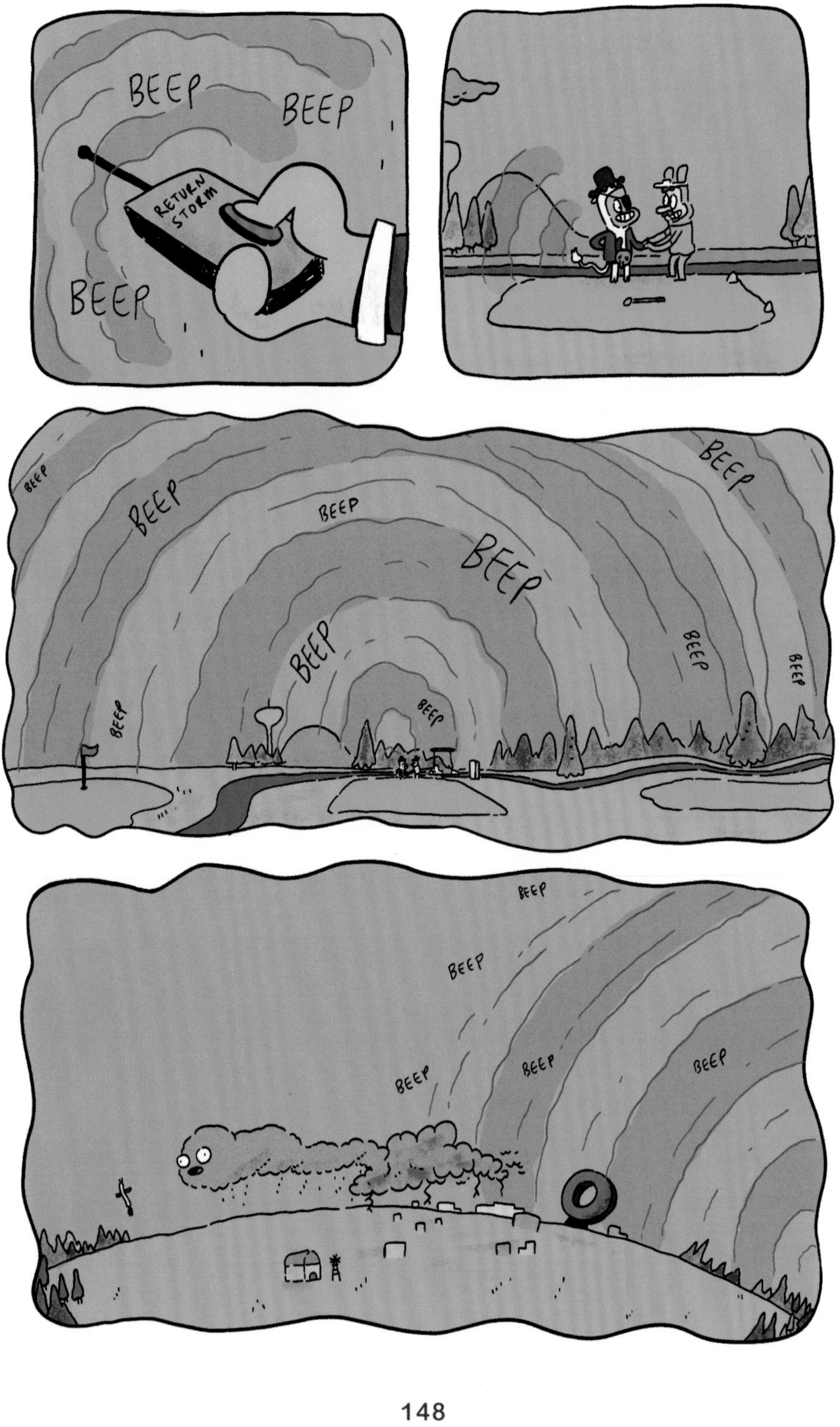
BEEP
BEEP
RETURN STORM
BEEP
BEEP
BEEP
BEEP
BEEP
BEEP
BEEP
BEEP
BEEP
BEEP
BEEP
BEEP
BEEP
BEEP
BEEP
BEEP

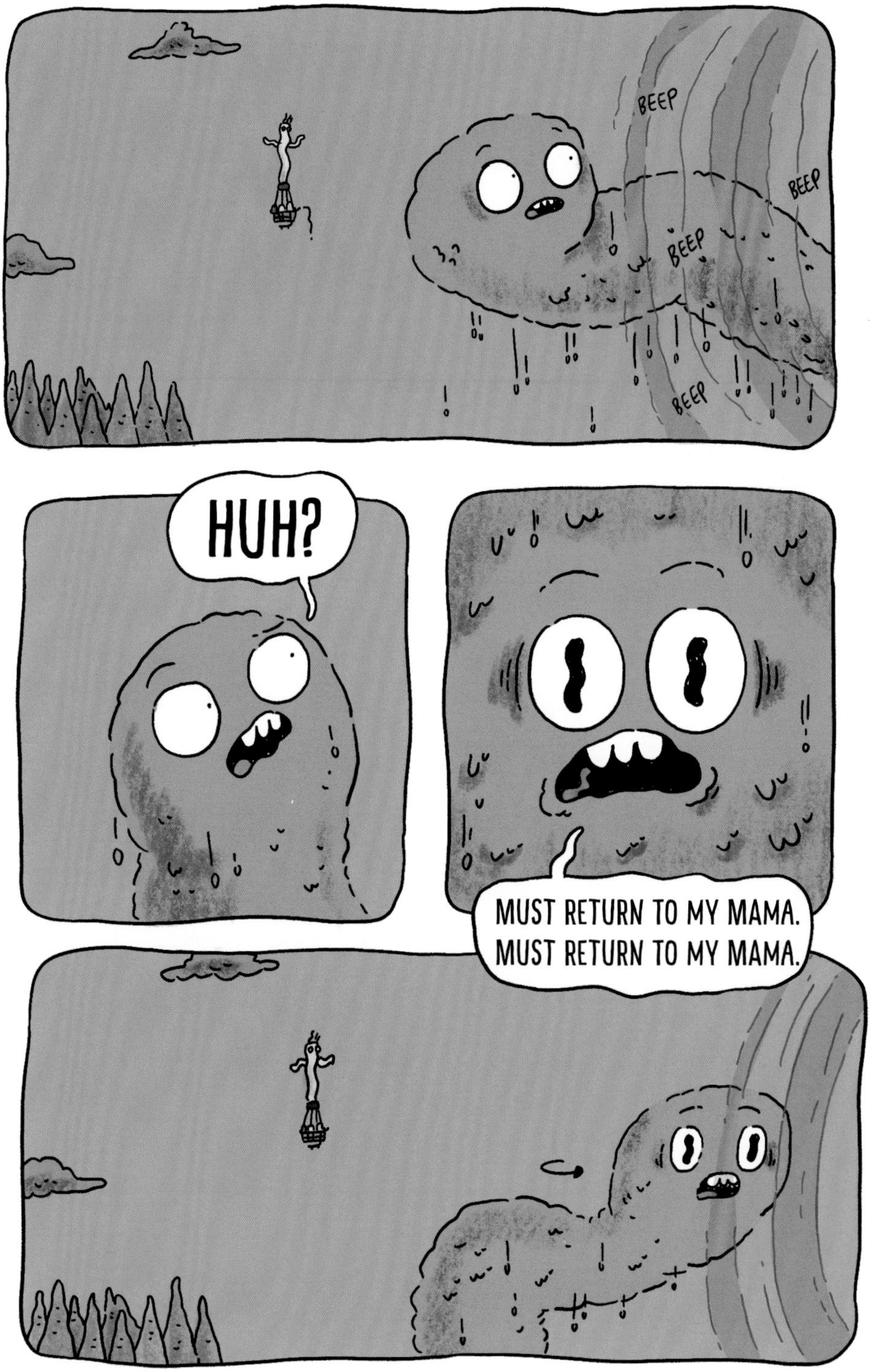
BEEP
BEEP
BEEP
BEEP
HUH?
MUST RETURN TO MY MAMA.
MUST RETURN TO MY MAMA.

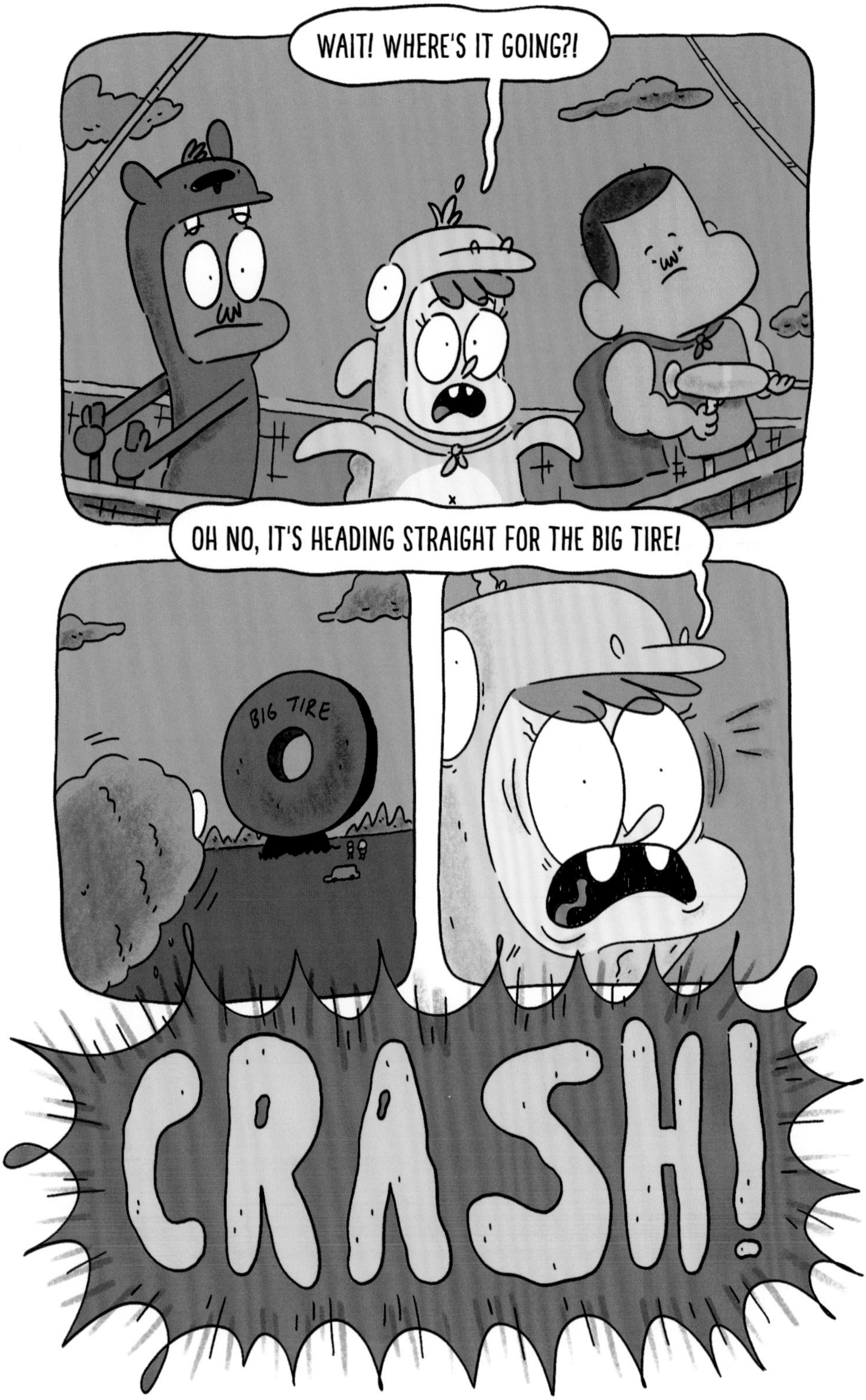
WAIT! WHERE'S IT GOING?!
OH NO, IT'S HEADING STRAIGHT FOR THE BIG TIRE!
BIG TIRE
CRASH!

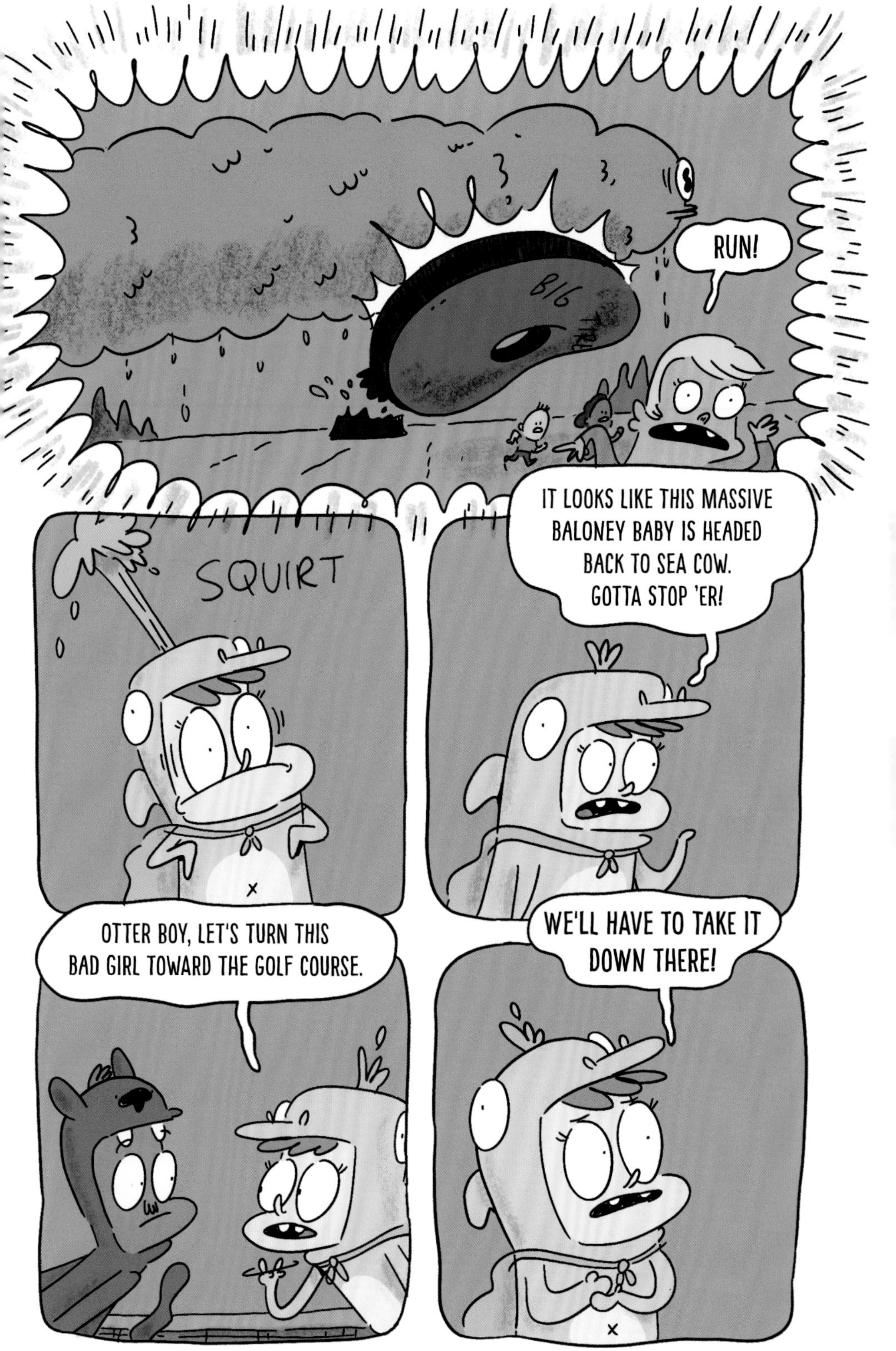
RUN!
B16
SQUIRT
IT LOOKS LIKE THIS MASSIVE BALONEY BABY IS HEADED BACK TO SEA COW. GOTTA STOP 'ER!
OTTER BOY, LET'S TURN THIS BAD GIRL TOWARD THE GOLF COURSE.
WE'LL HAVE TO TAKE IT DOWN THERE!

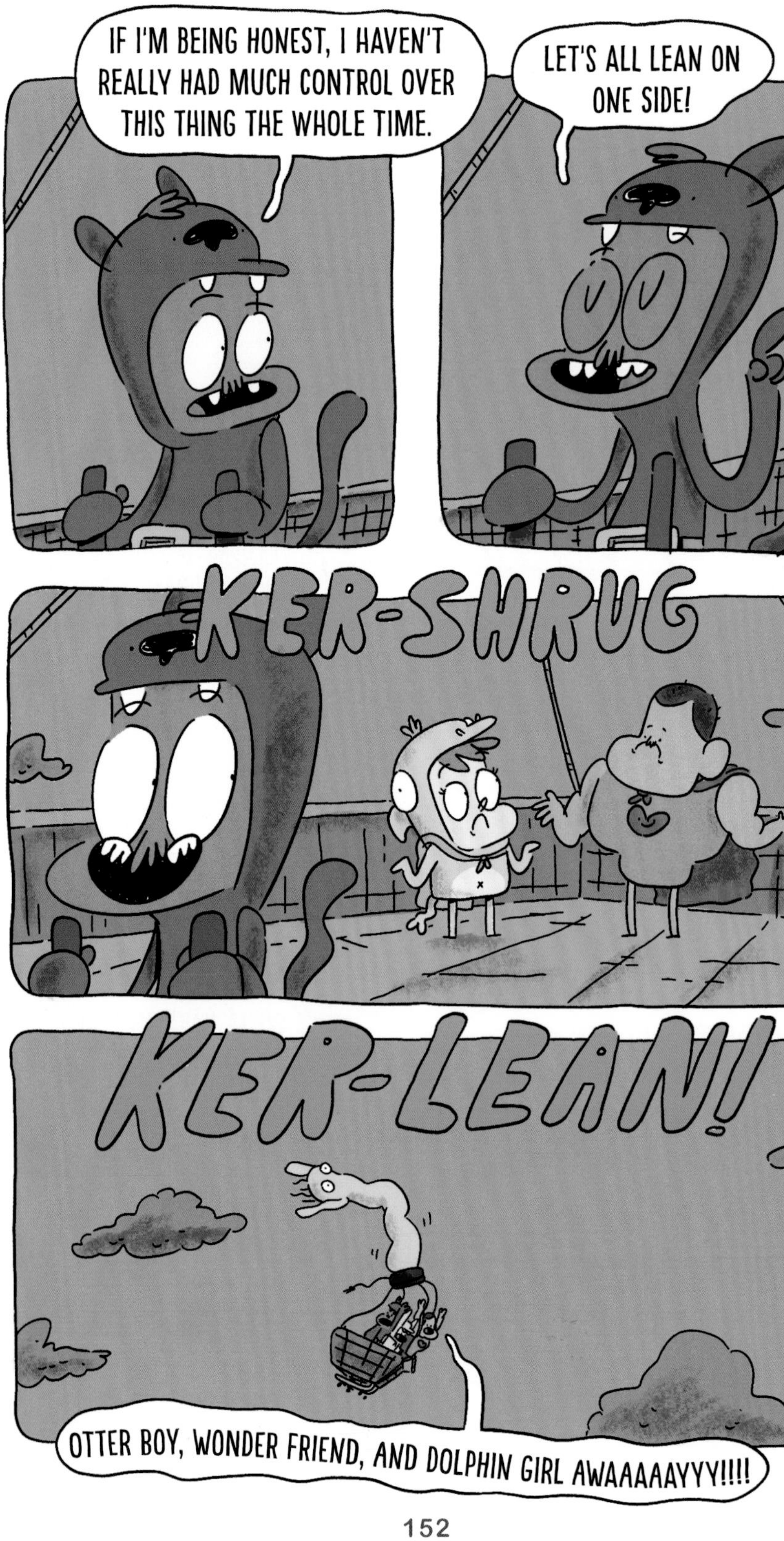
IF I'M BEING HONEST, I HAVEN'T REALLY HAD MUCH CONTROL OVER THIS THING THE WHOLE TIME.
LET'S ALL LEAN ON ONE SIDE!
KER-SHRUG
KER-LEAN!
OTTER BOY, WONDER FRIEND, AND DOLPHIN GIRL AWAAAAAYYY!!!!

PART THREE

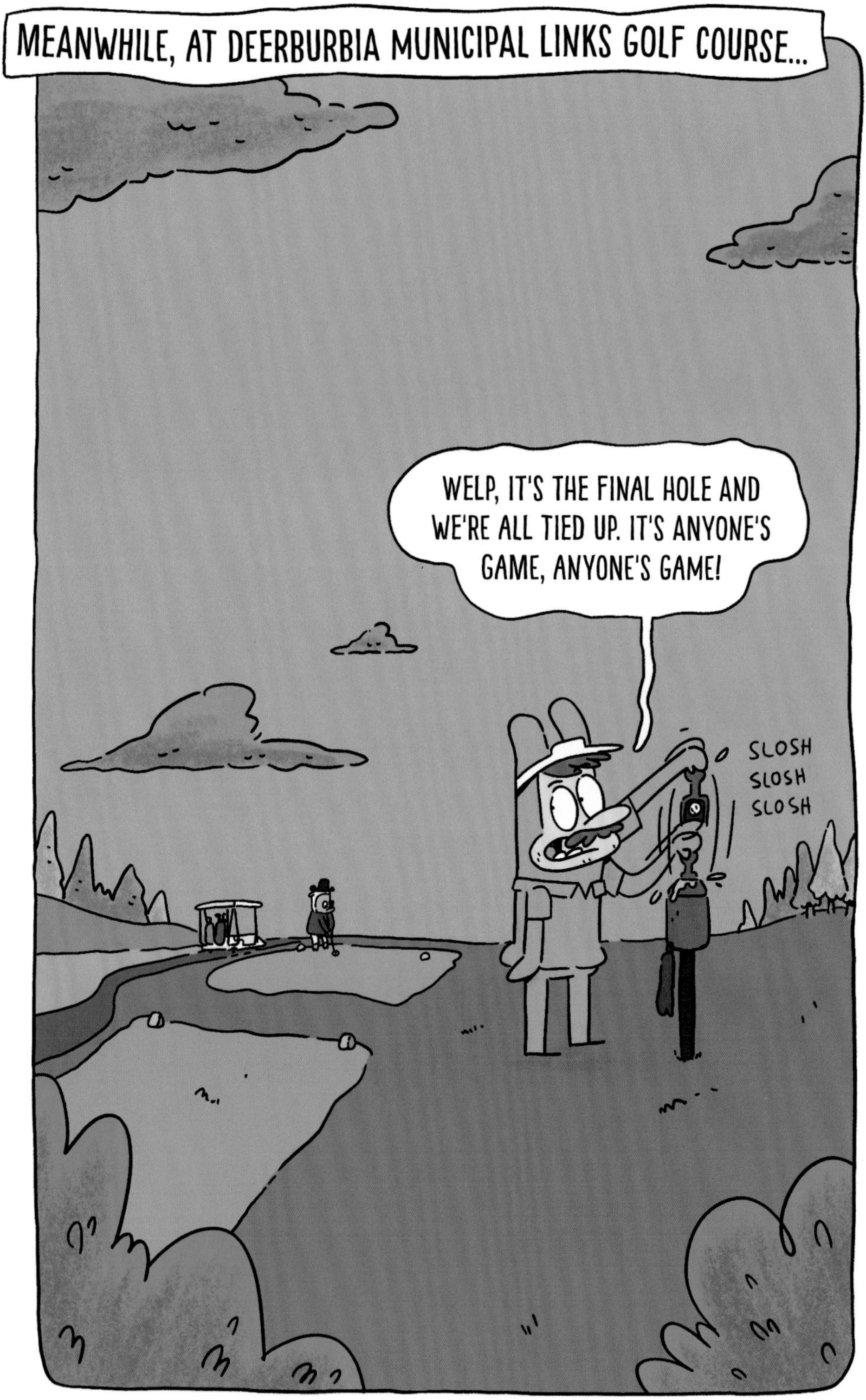
MEANWHILE, AT DEERBURBIA MUNICIPAL LINKS GOLF COURSE...
WELP, IT'S THE FINAL HOLE AND WE'RE ALL TIED UP. IT'S ANYONE'S GAME, ANYONE'S GAME!
SLOSH SLOSH SLOSH

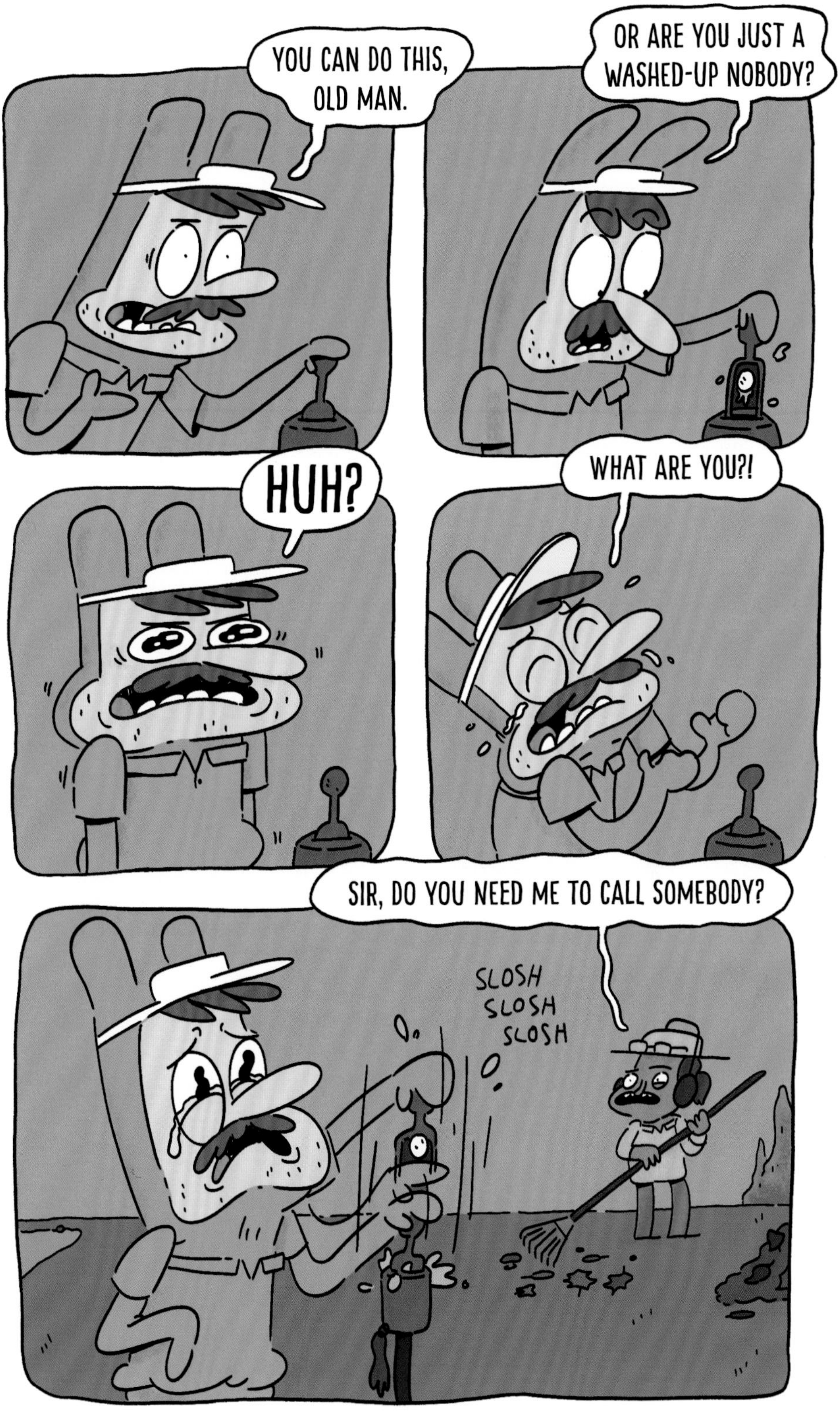
YOU CAN DO THIS, OLD MAN.
OR ARE YOU JUST A WASHED-UP NOBODY?
HUH?
WHAT ARE YOU?!
SIR, DO YOU NEED ME TO CALL SOMEBODY?
SLOSH
SLOSH
SLOSH

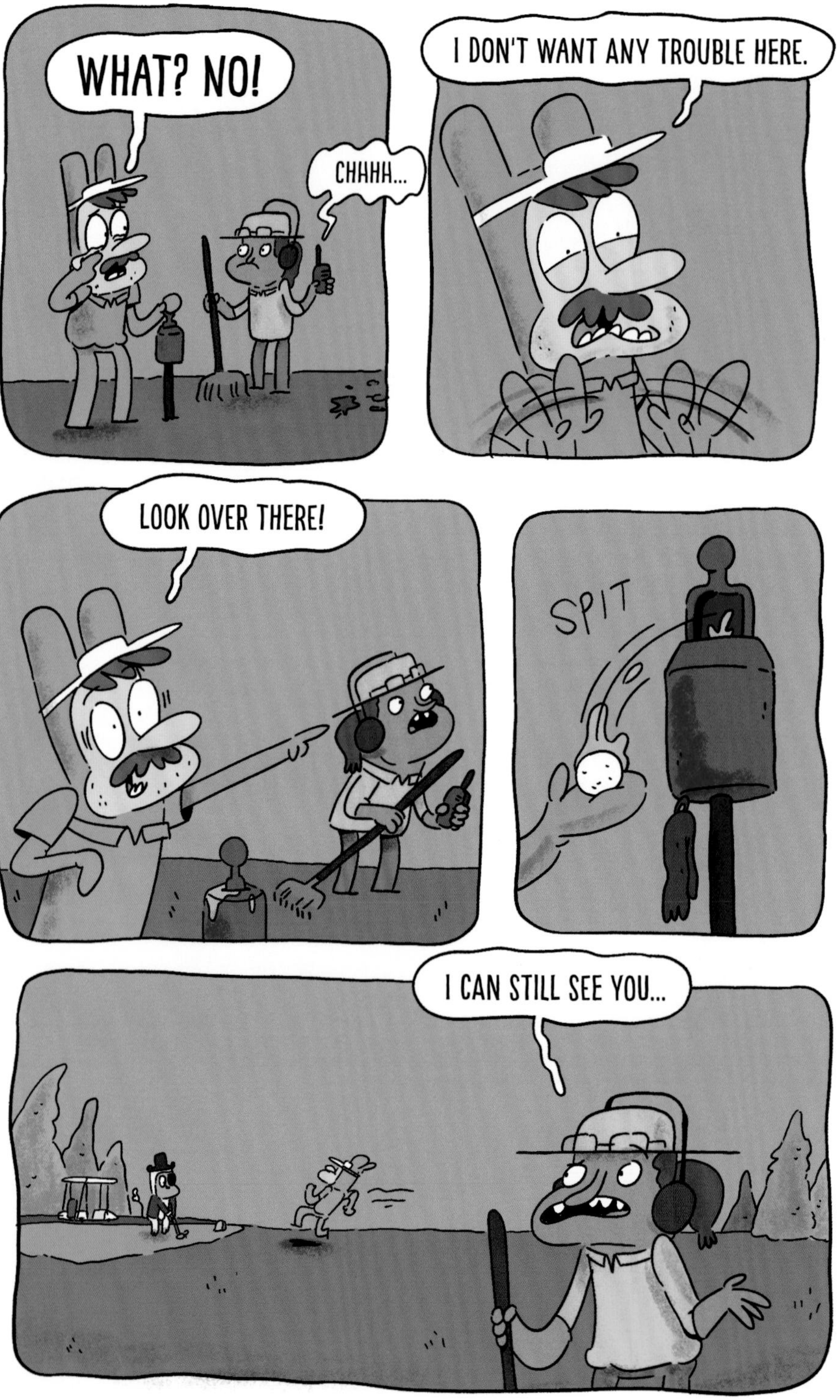
WHAT? NO!
CHHHH...
I DON'T WANT ANY TROUBLE HERE.
LOOK OVER THERE!
SPIT
I CAN STILL SEE YOU...

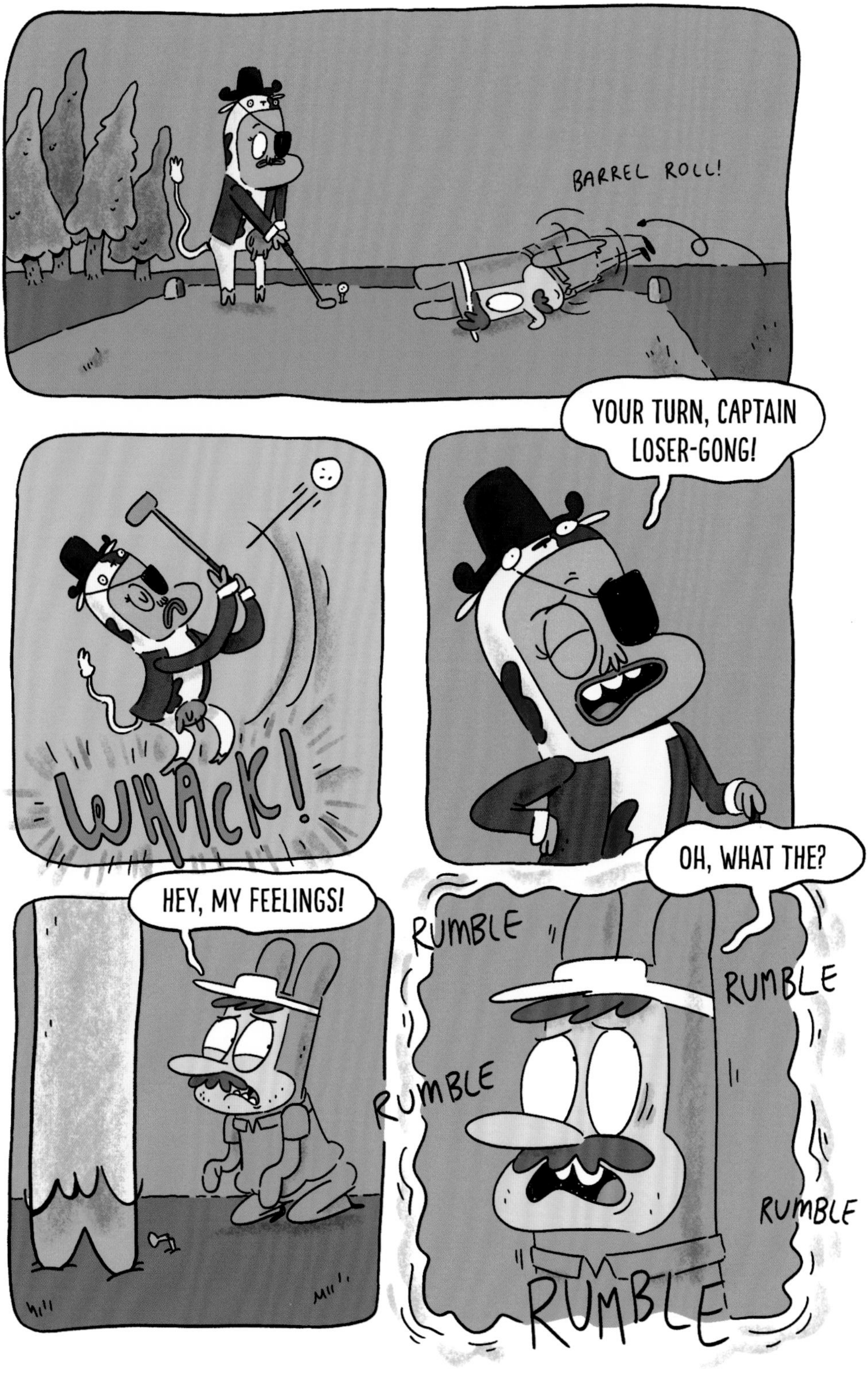

BARREL ROLL!
WHACK!
YOUR TURN, CAPTAIN LOSER-GONG!
HEY, MY FEELINGS!
OH, WHAT THE?
RUMBLE
RUMBLE
RUMBLE
RUMBLE
RUMBLE

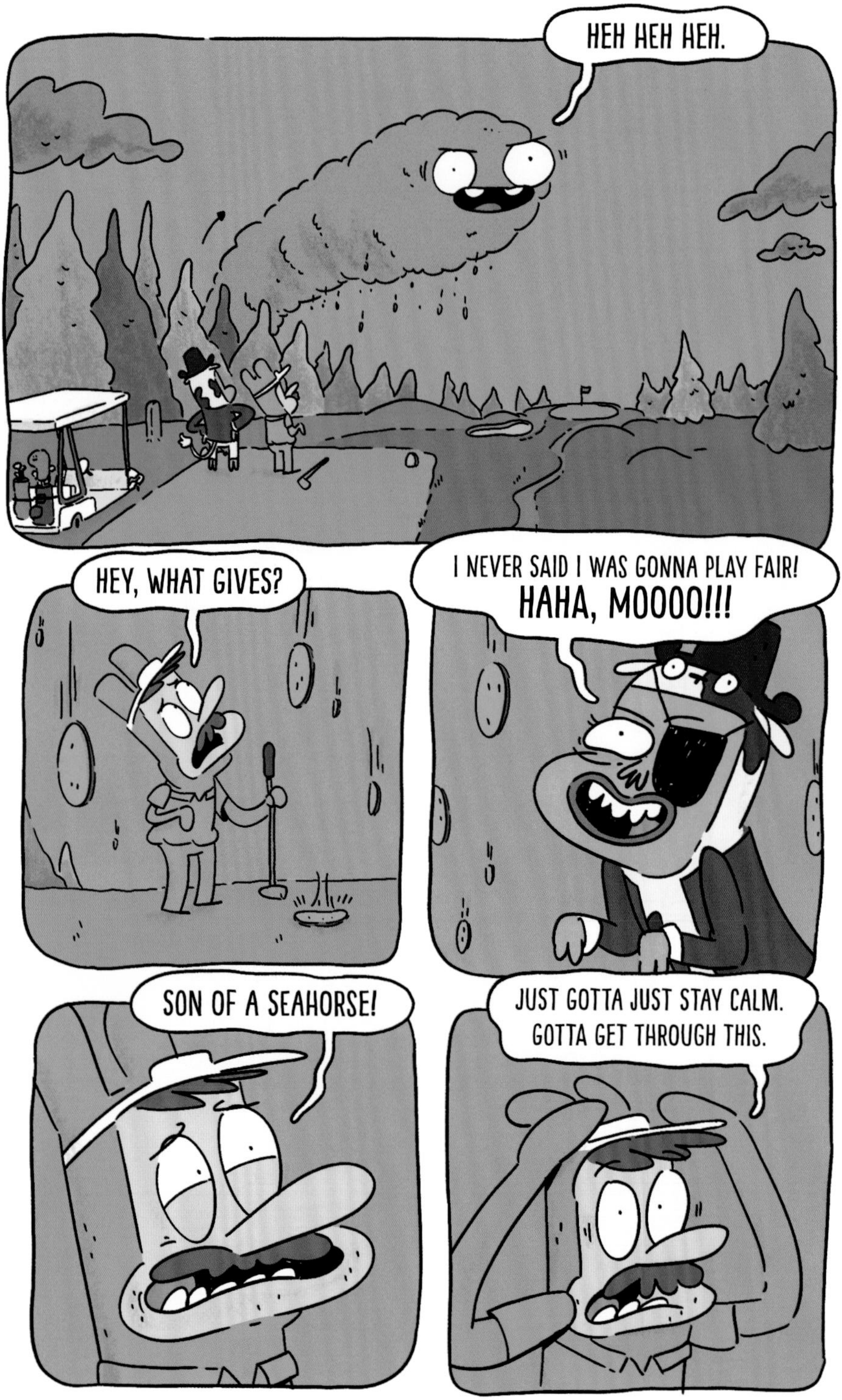
HEH HEH HEH.
HEY, WHAT GIVES?
I NEVER SAID I WAS GONNA PLAY FAIR! HAHA, MOOOO!!!
SON OF A SEAHORSE!
JUST GOTTA JUST STAY CALM. GOTTA GET THROUGH THIS.

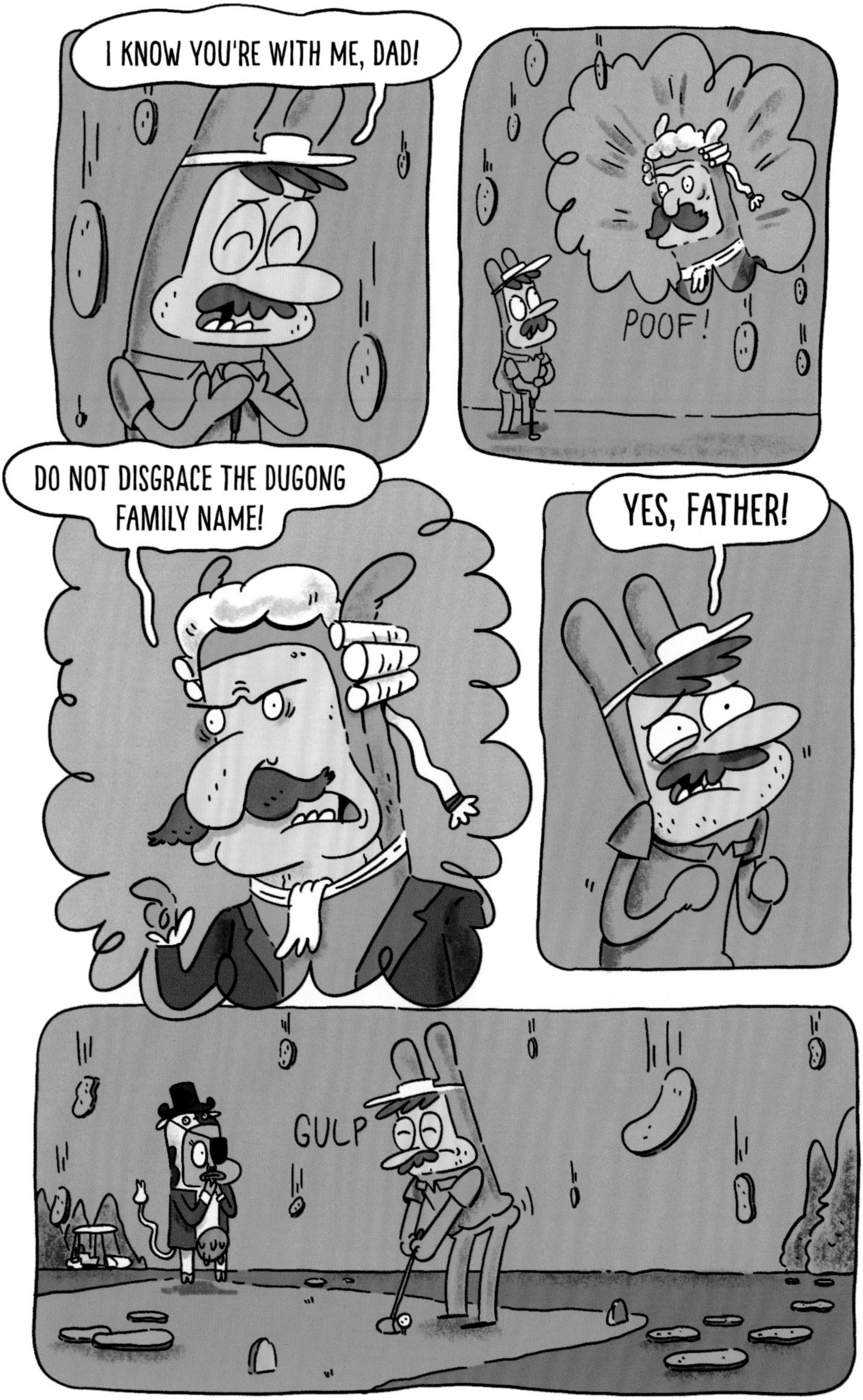
I KNOW YOU'RE WITH ME, DAD!
POOF!
DO NOT DISGRACE THE DUGONG FAMILY NAME!
YES, FATHER!
GULP

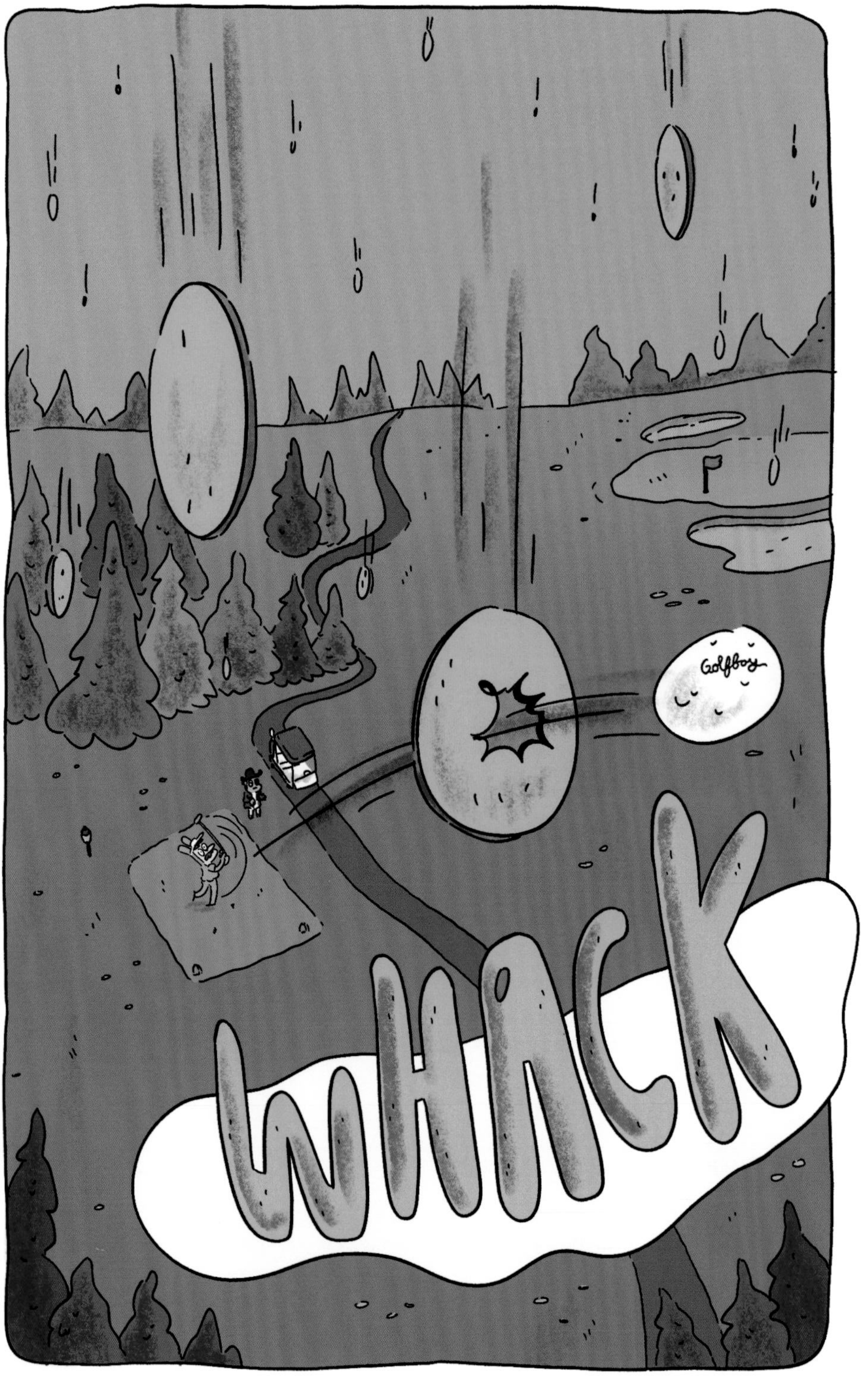
Golfboy
WHACK

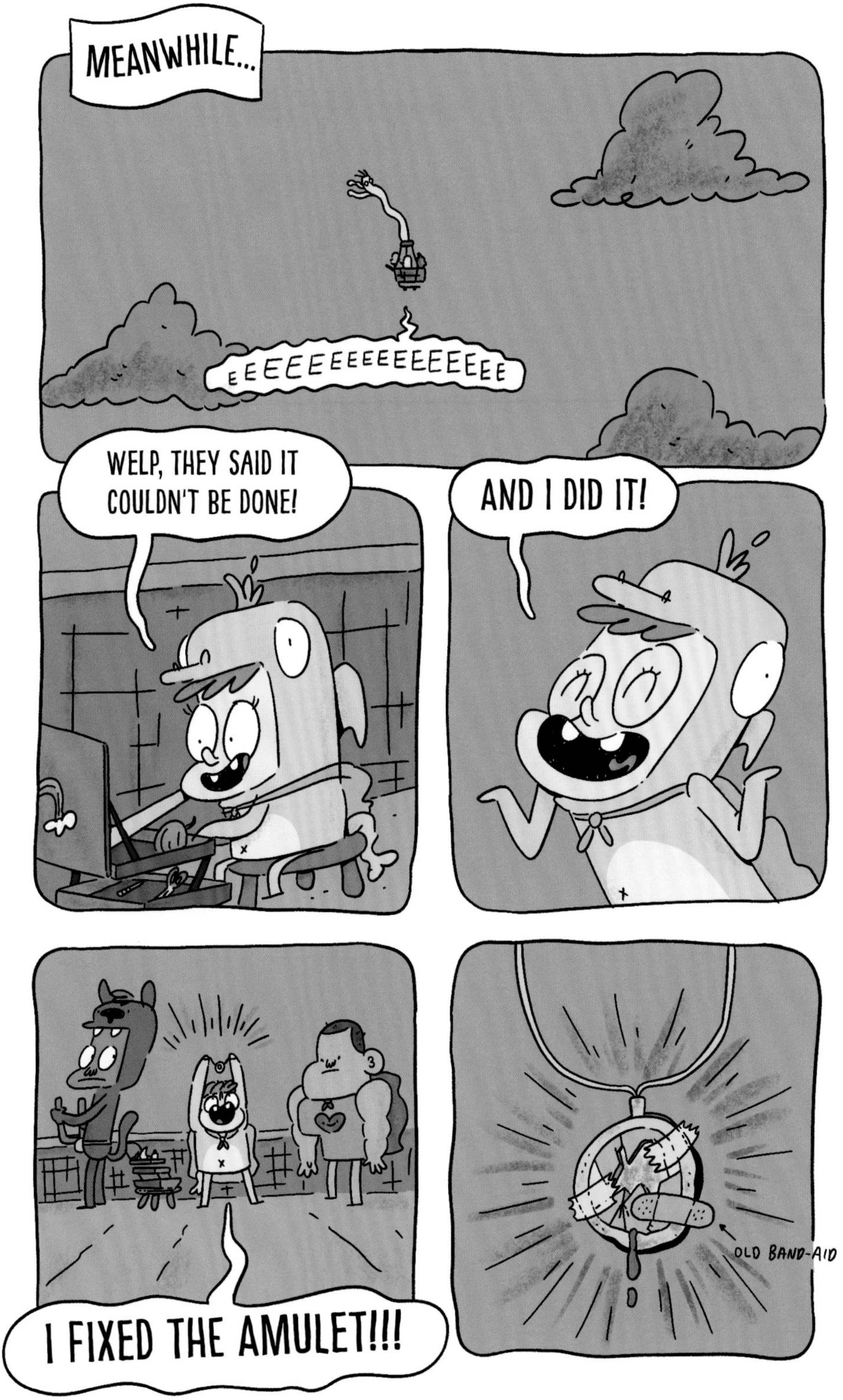
MEANWHILE...
EEEEEEEEEEEEEEEEEE
WELP, THEY SAID IT COULDN'T BE DONE!
AND I DID IT!
I FIXED THE AMULET!!!
OLD BAND-AID

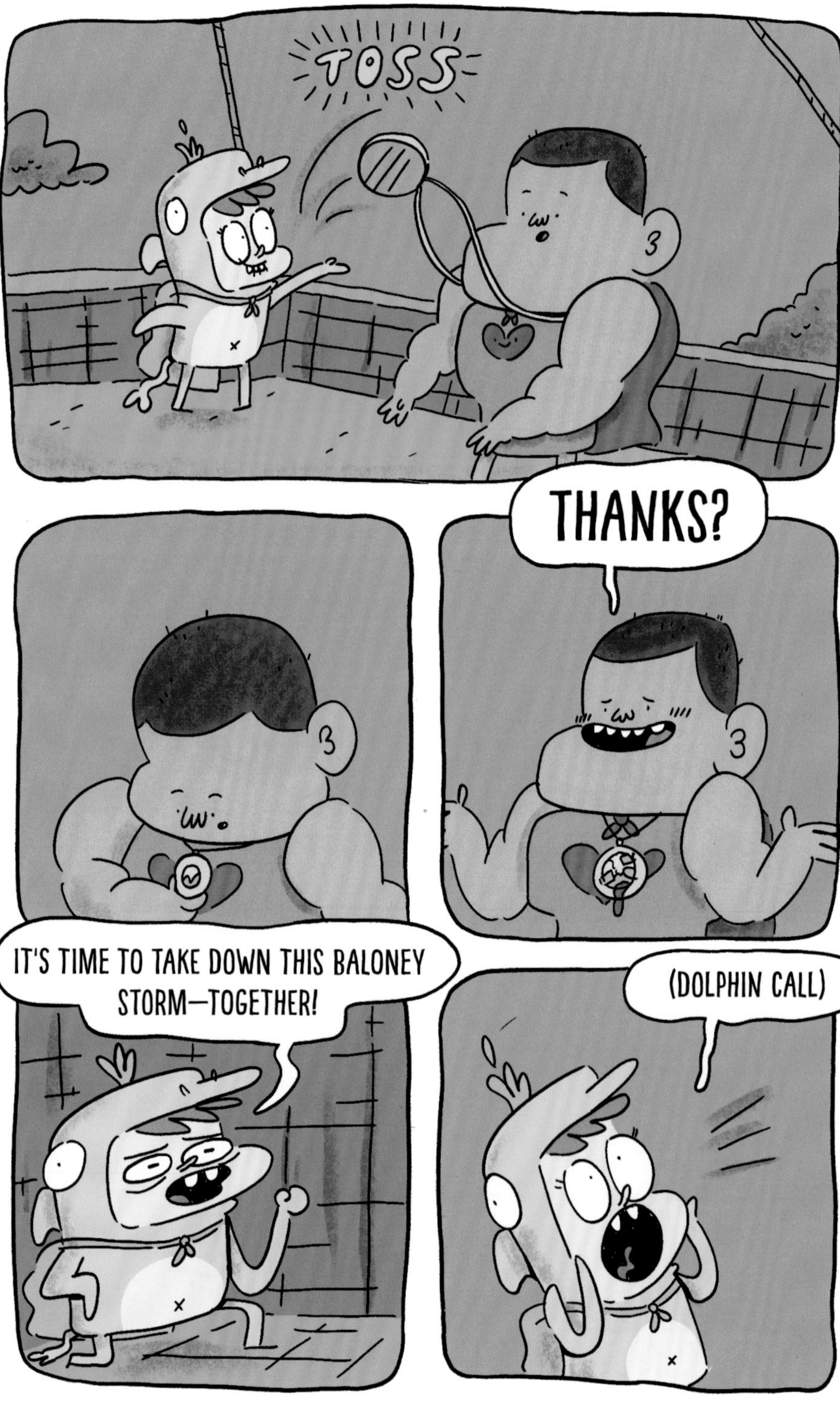
TOSS
THANKS?
IT'S TIME TO TAKE DOWN THIS BALONEY STORM—TOGETHER!
(DOLPHIN CALL)

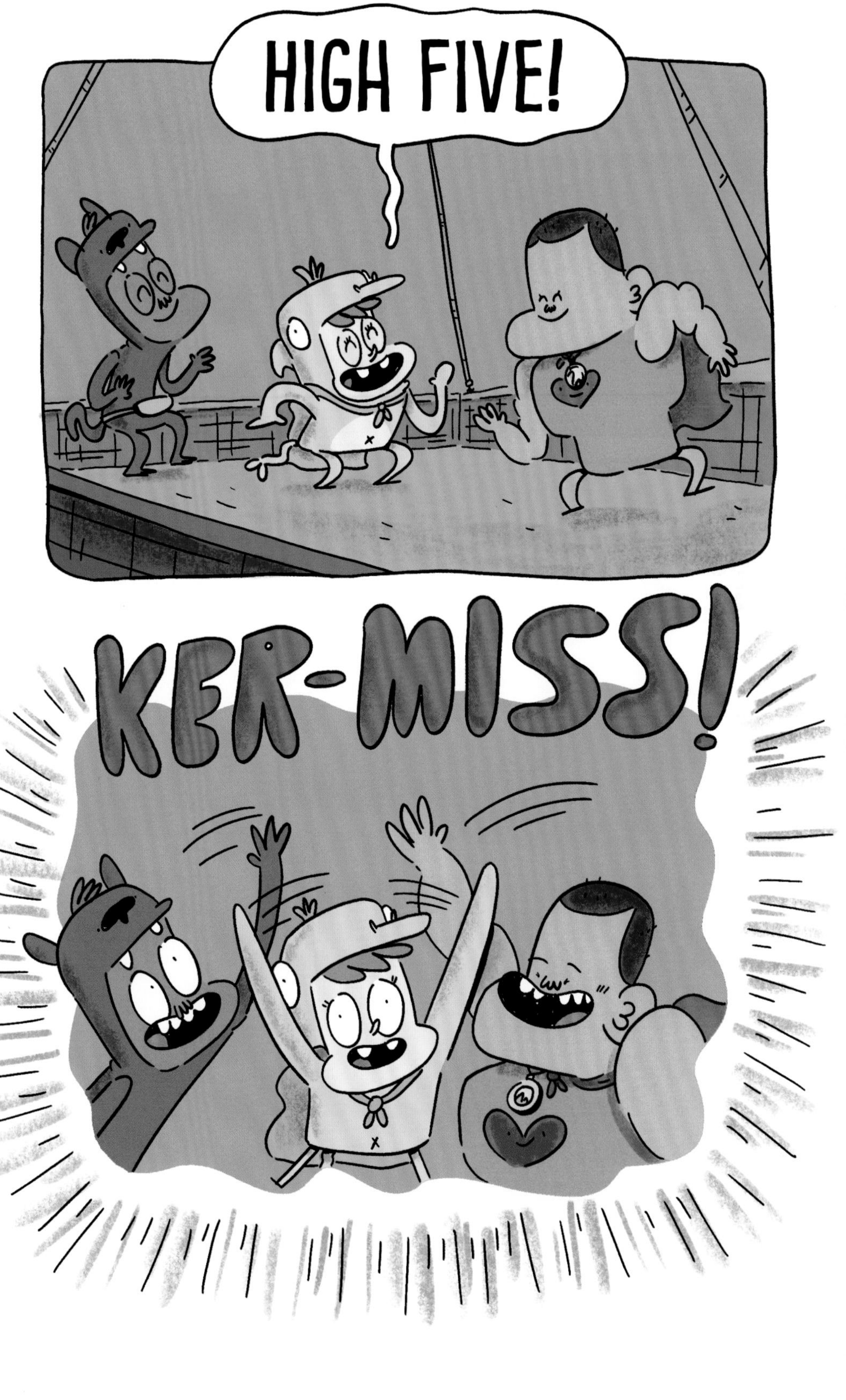
HIGH FIVE!
KER-MISS!

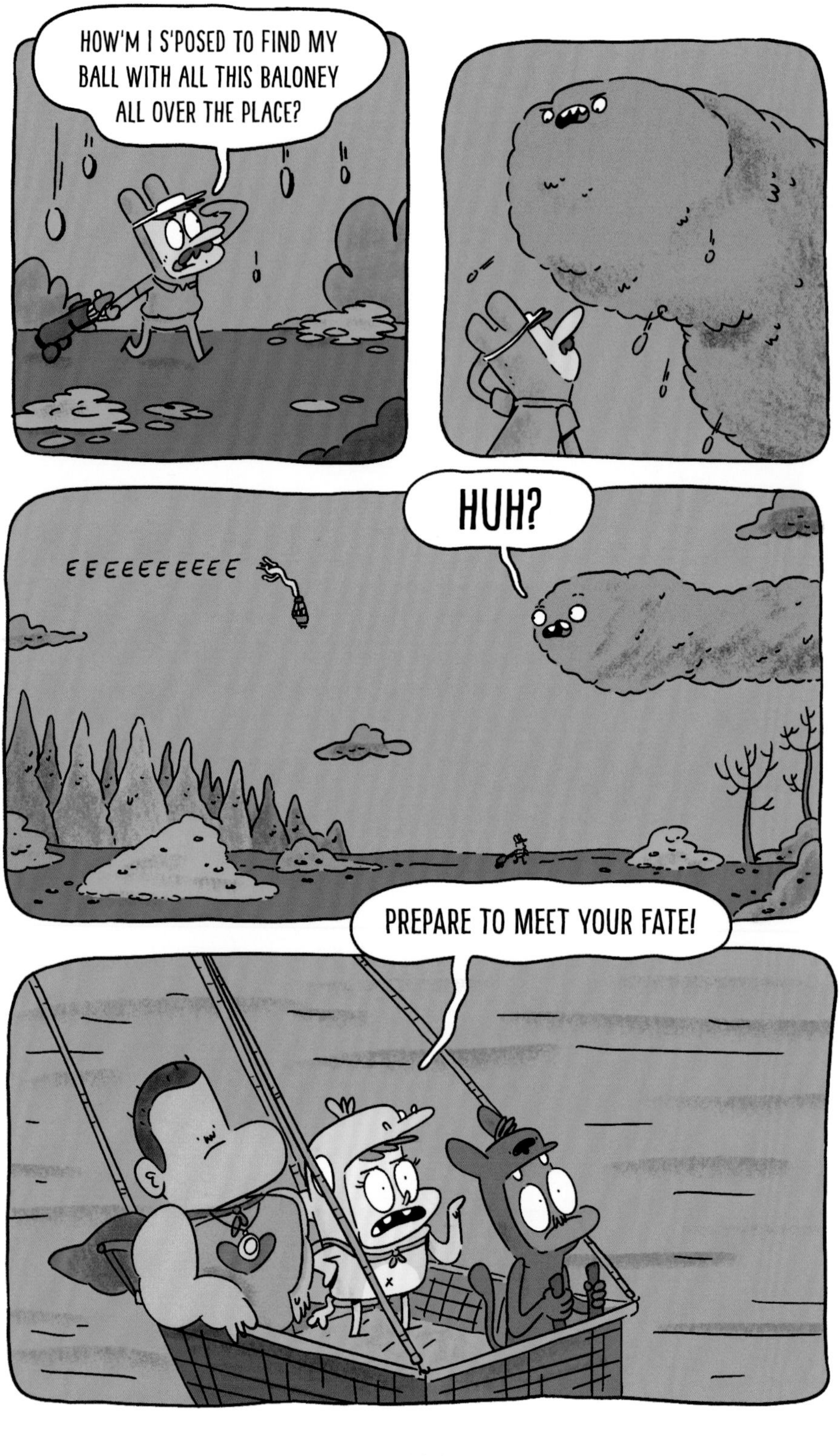
HOW'M I S'POSED TO FIND MY BALL WITH ALL THIS BALONEY ALL OVER THE PLACE?
HUH?
EEEEEEEEEE
PREPARE TO MEET YOUR FATE!

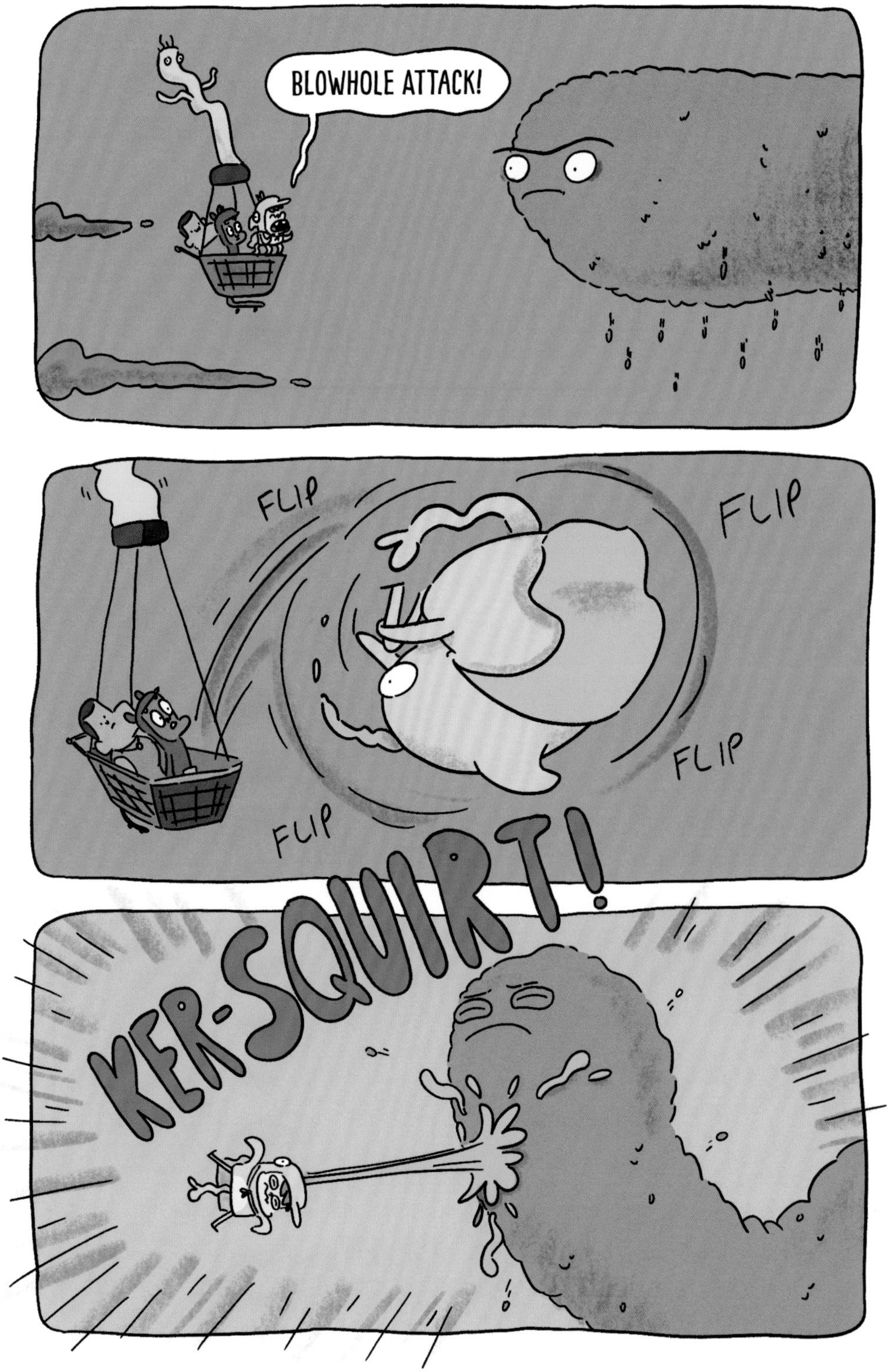
BLOWHOLE ATTACK!
FLIP
FLIP
FLIP
FLIP
KER-SQUIRT!

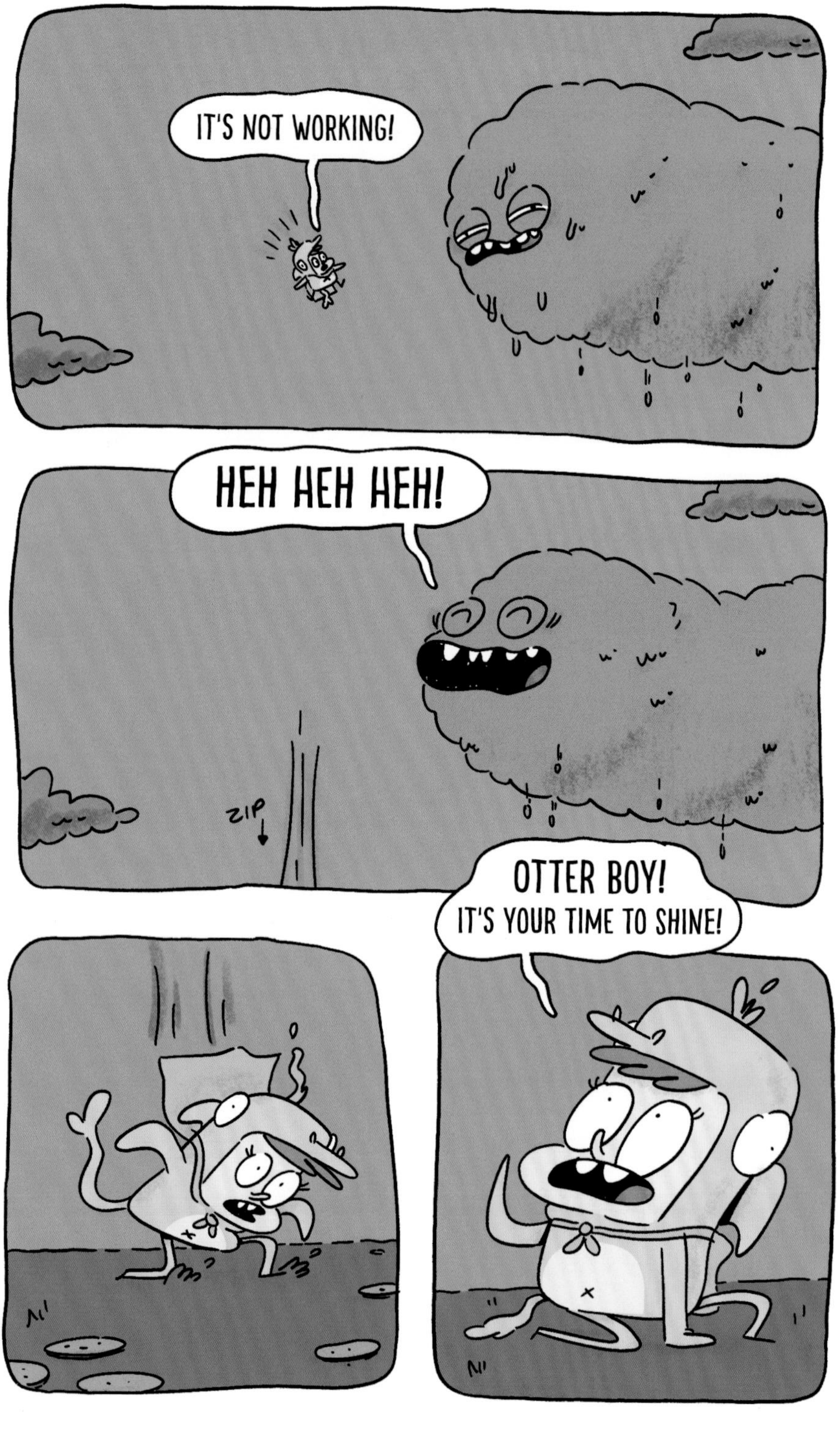
IT'S NOT WORKING!
HEH HEH HEH!
ZIP
OTTER BOY!
IT'S YOUR TIME TO SHINE!

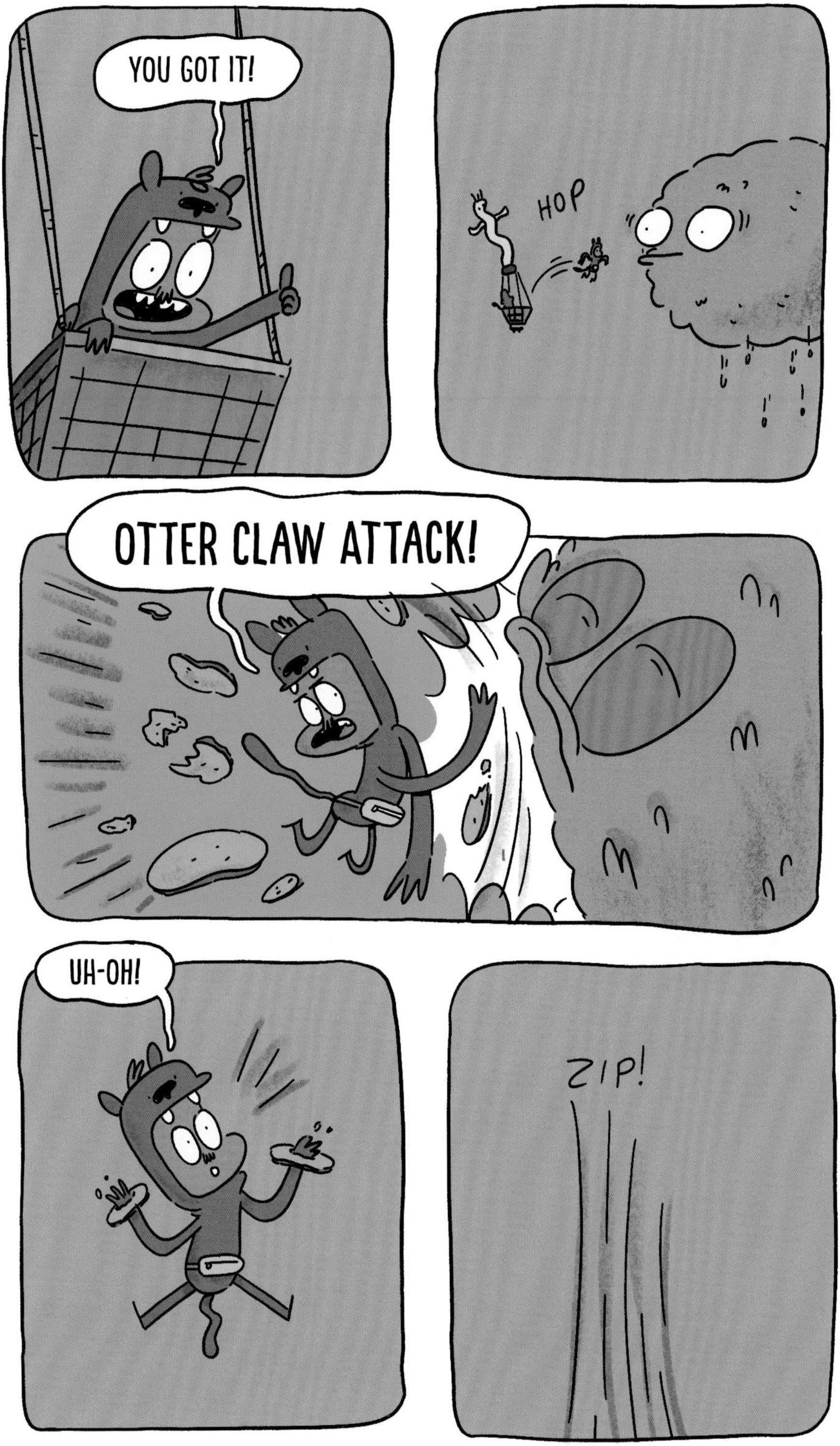
YOU GOT IT!
HOP
OTTER CLAW ATTACK!
UH-OH!
ZIP!

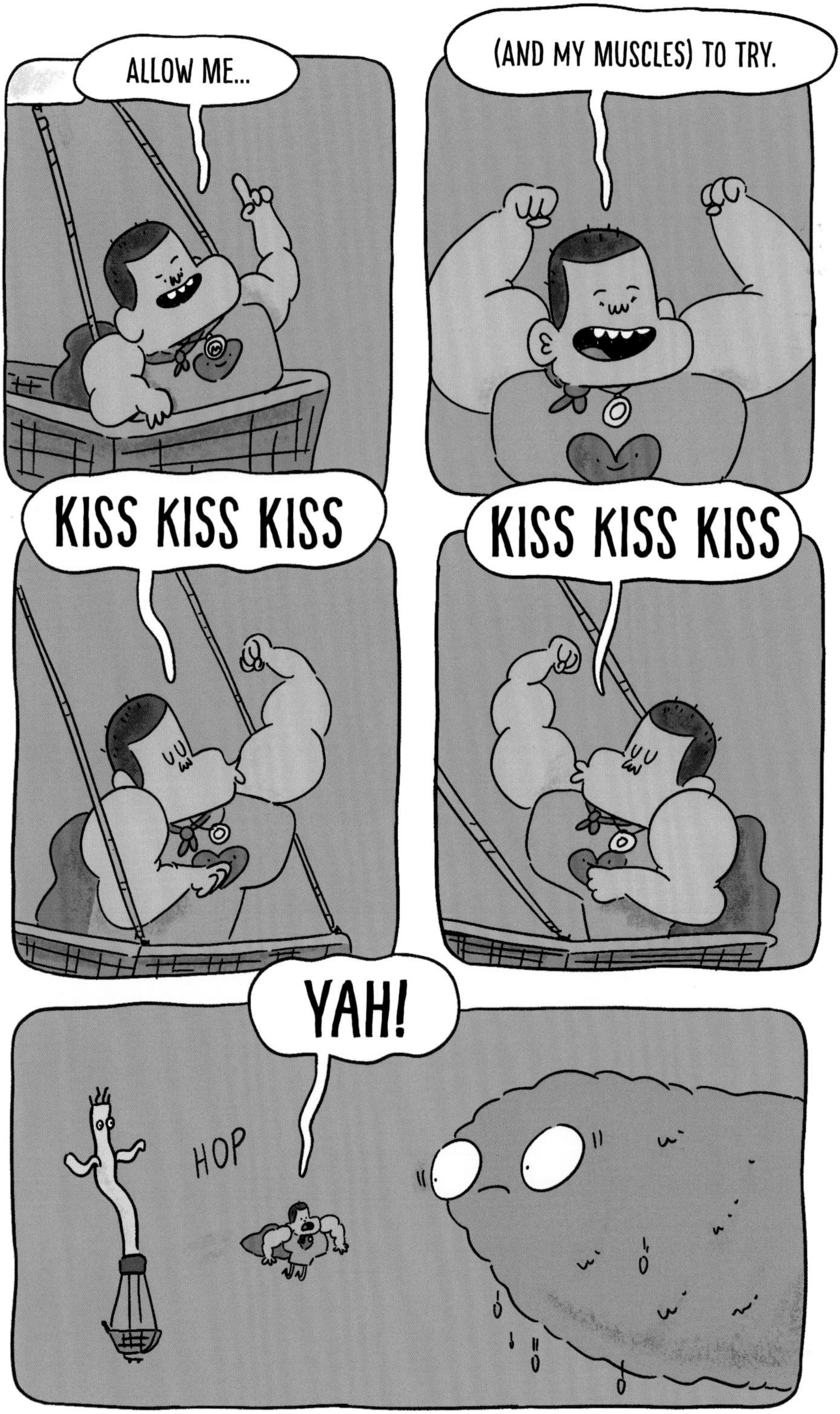
ALLOW ME...
(AND MY MUSCLES) TO TRY.
KISS KISS KISS
KISS KISS KISS
YAH!
HOP

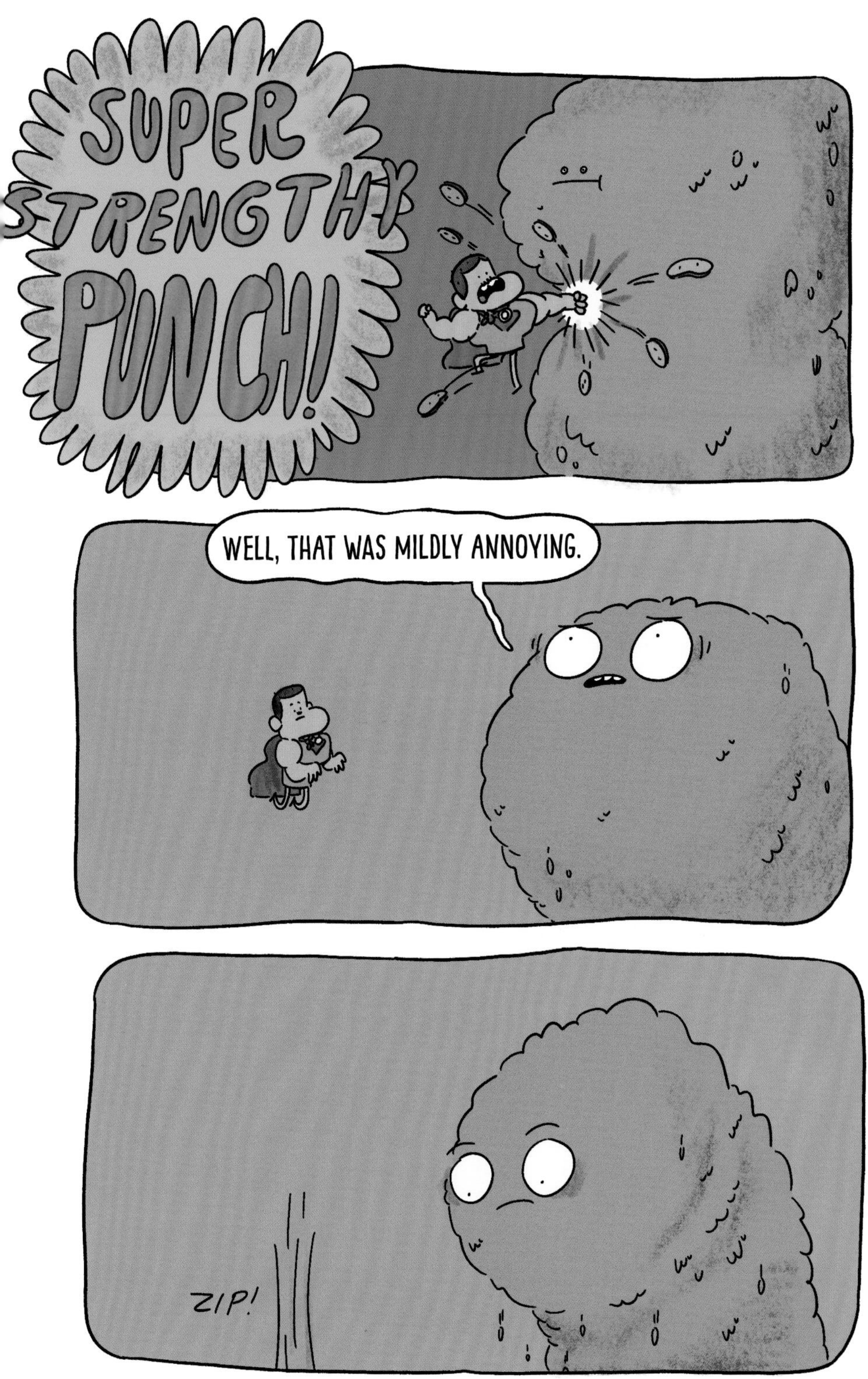
SUPER STRENGTHY PUNCH!
WELL, THAT WAS MILDLY ANNOYING.
ZIP!

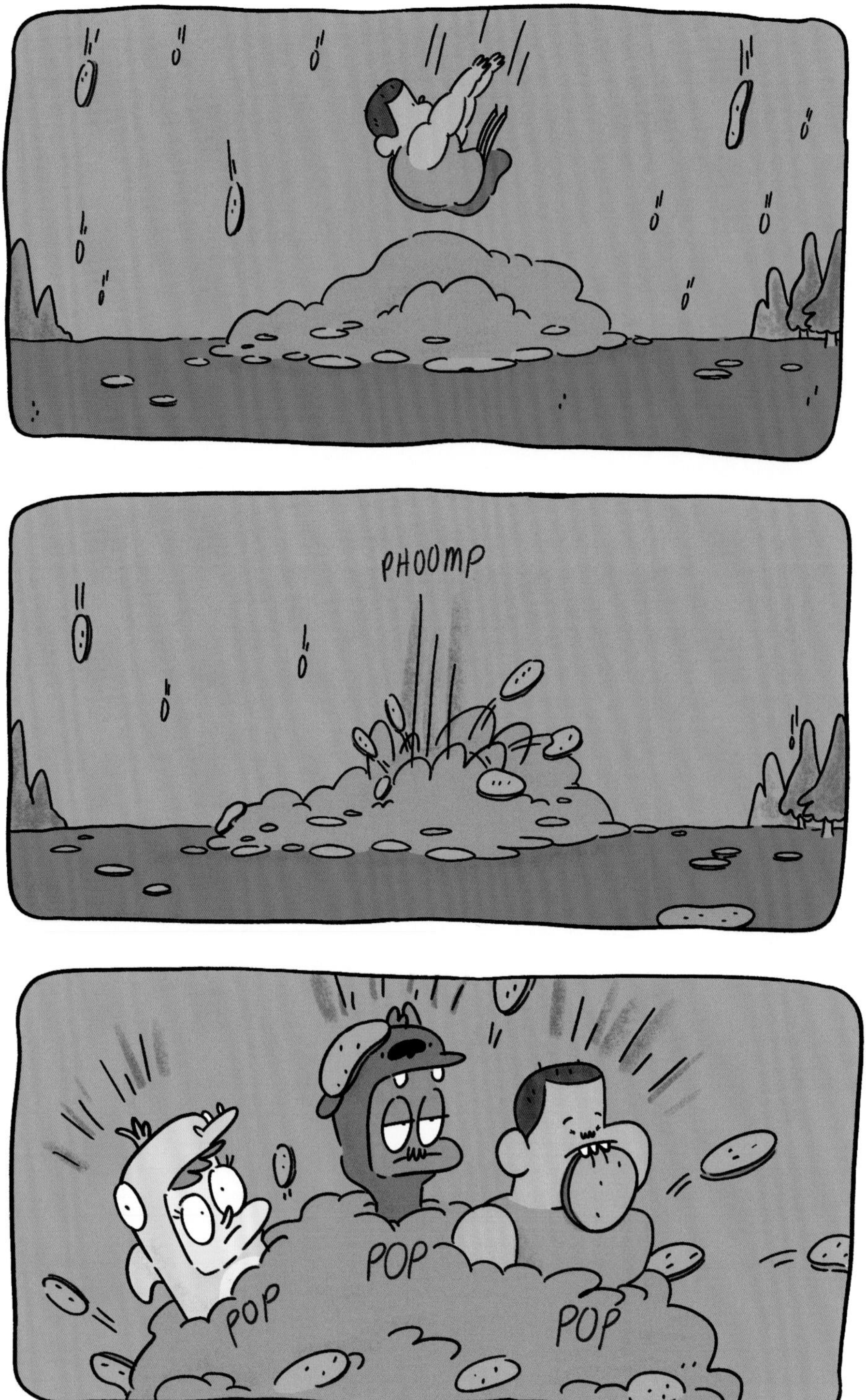
PHOOMP
POP
POP
POP

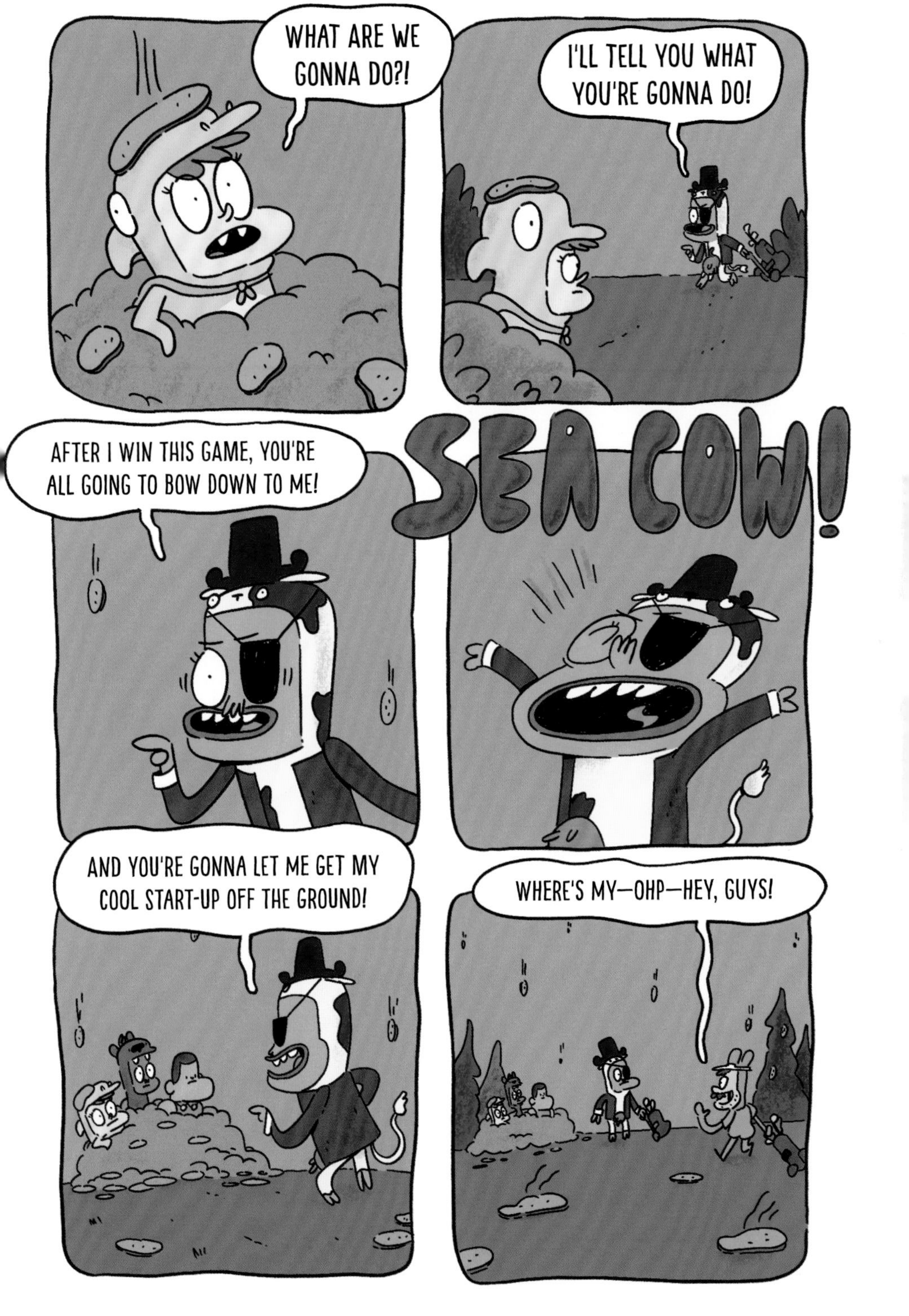
WHAT ARE WE GONNA DO?!
I'LL TELL YOU WHAT YOU'RE GONNA DO!
AFTER I WIN THIS GAME, YOU'RE ALL GOING TO BOW DOWN TO ME!
SEA COW!
AND YOU'RE GONNA LET ME GET MY COOL START-UP OFF THE GROUND!
WHERE'S MY—OHP—HEY, GUYS!

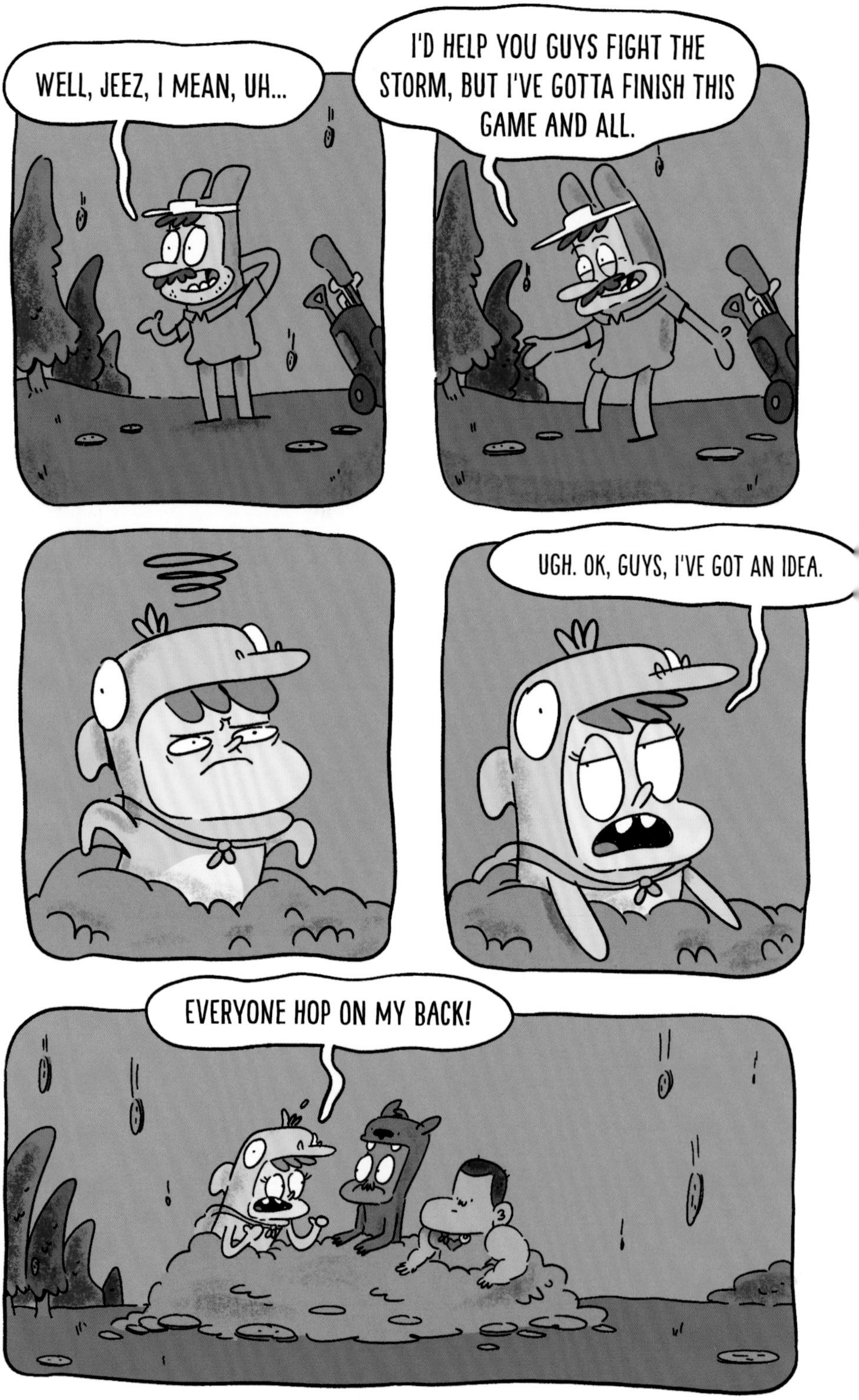
WELL, JEEZ, I MEAN, UH...
I'D HELP YOU GUYS FIGHT THE STORM, BUT I'VE GOTTA FINISH THIS GAME AND ALL.
UGH. OK, GUYS, I'VE GOT AN IDEA.
EVERYONE HOP ON MY BACK!

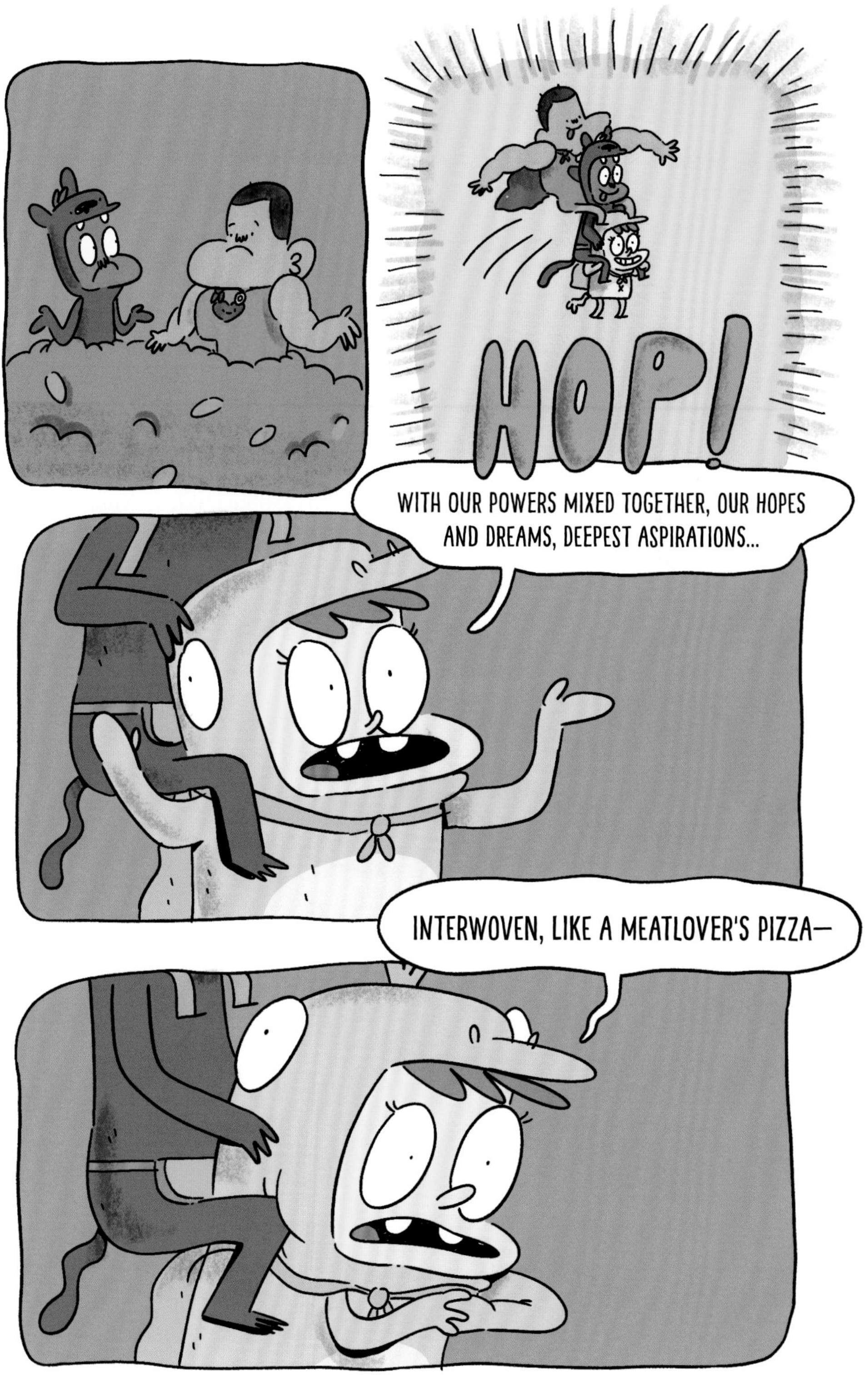
HOP!
WITH OUR POWERS MIXED TOGETHER, OUR HOPES AND DREAMS, DEEPEST ASPIRATIONS...
INTERWOVEN, LIKE A MEATLOVER'S PIZZA—

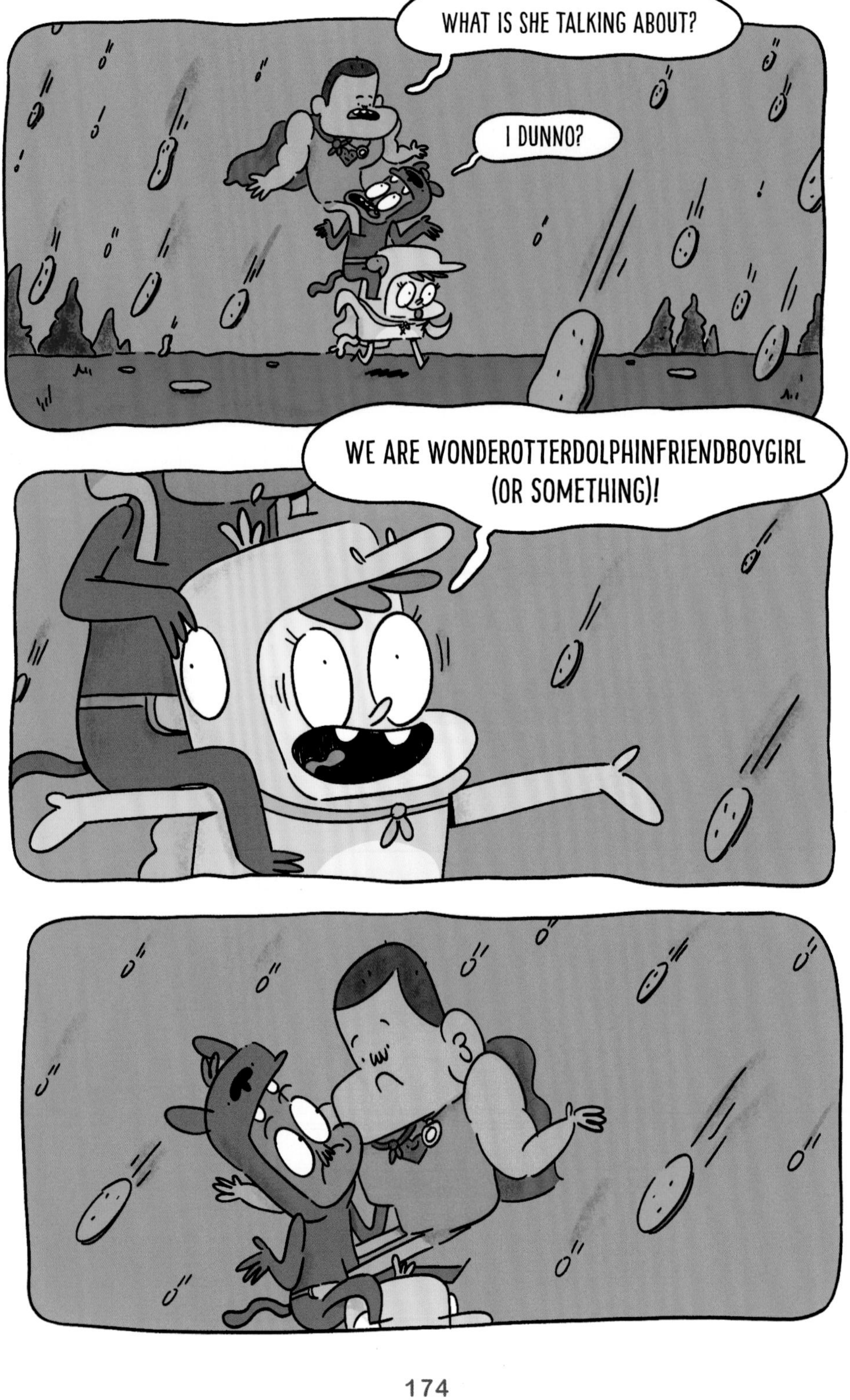
WHAT IS SHE TALKING ABOUT?
I DUNNO?
WE ARE WONDEROTTERDOLPHINFRIENDBOYGIRL (OR SOMETHING)!

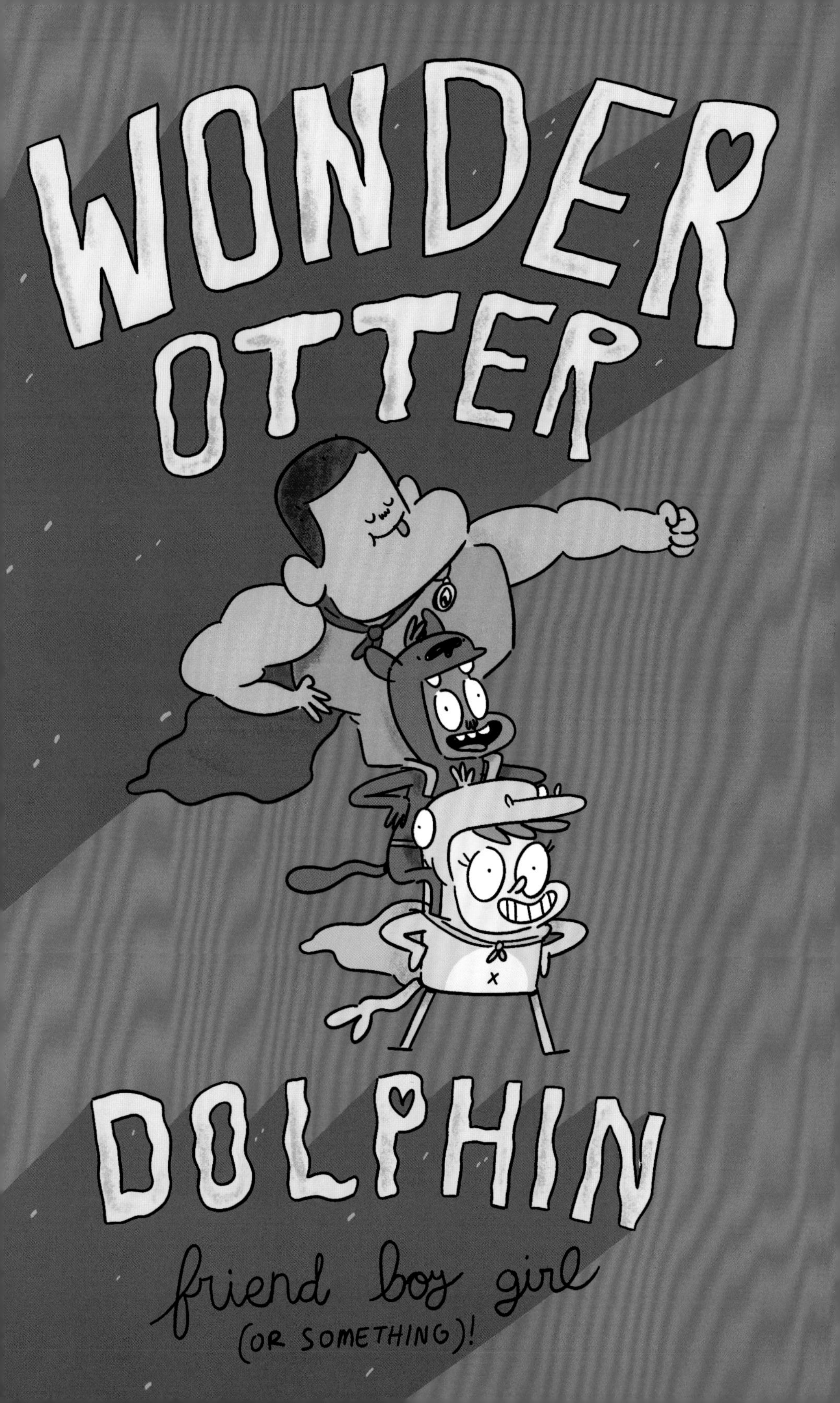
WONDER OTTER
DOLPHIN
friend boy girl
(OR SOMETHING)!

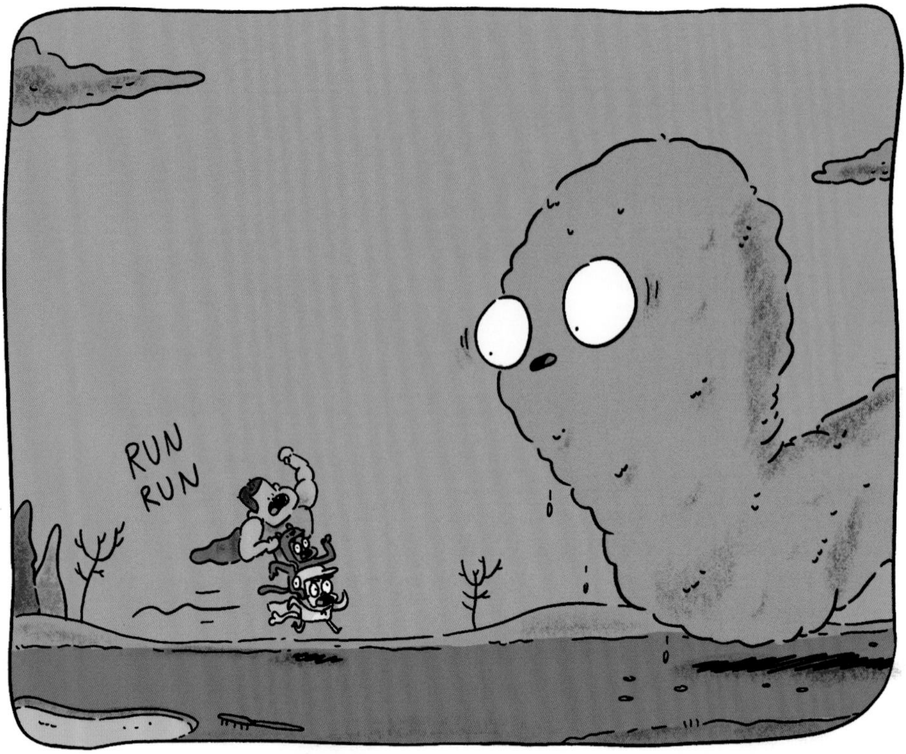
RUN
RUN

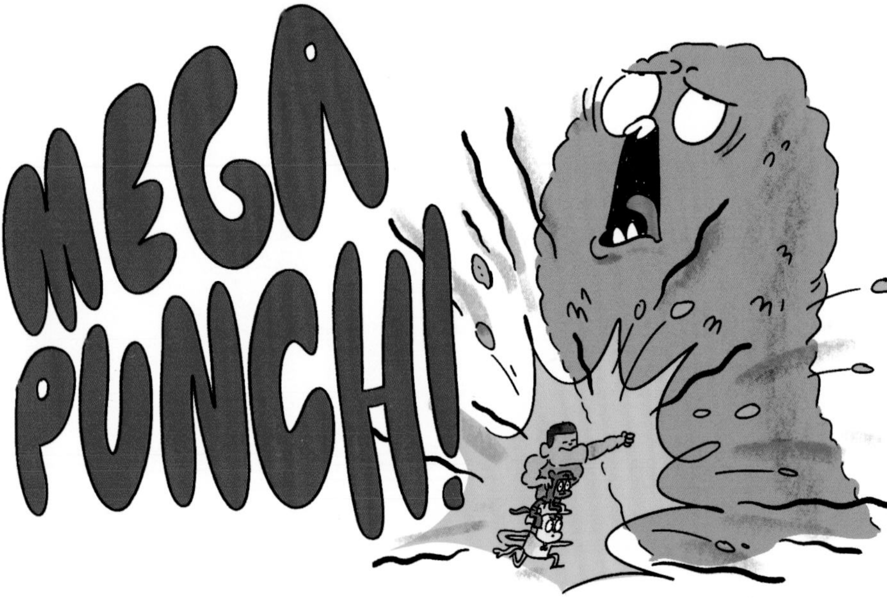
MEGA
PUNCH!

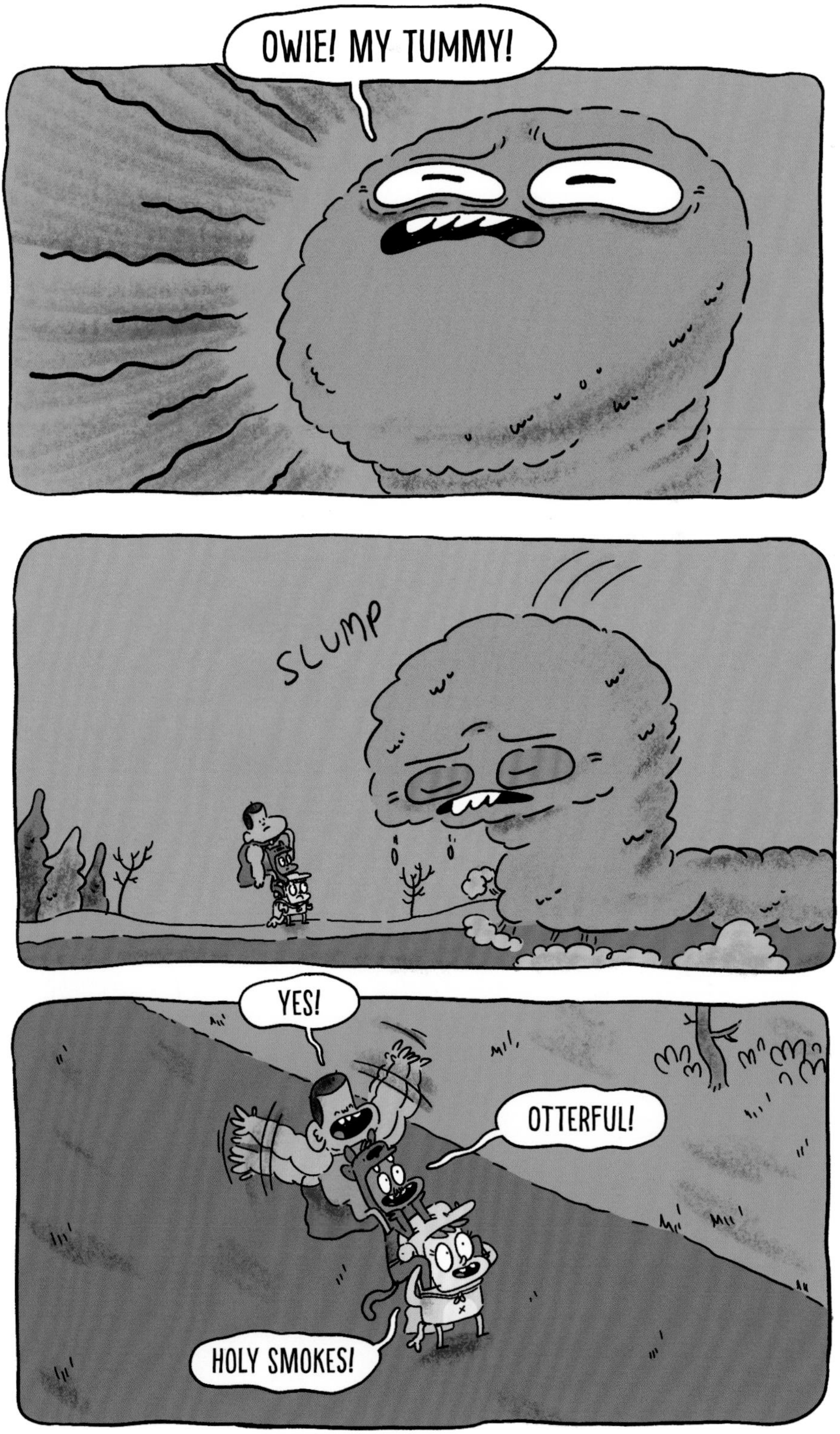
OWIE! MY TUMMY!
SLUMP
YES!
OTTERFUL!
HOLY SMOKES!

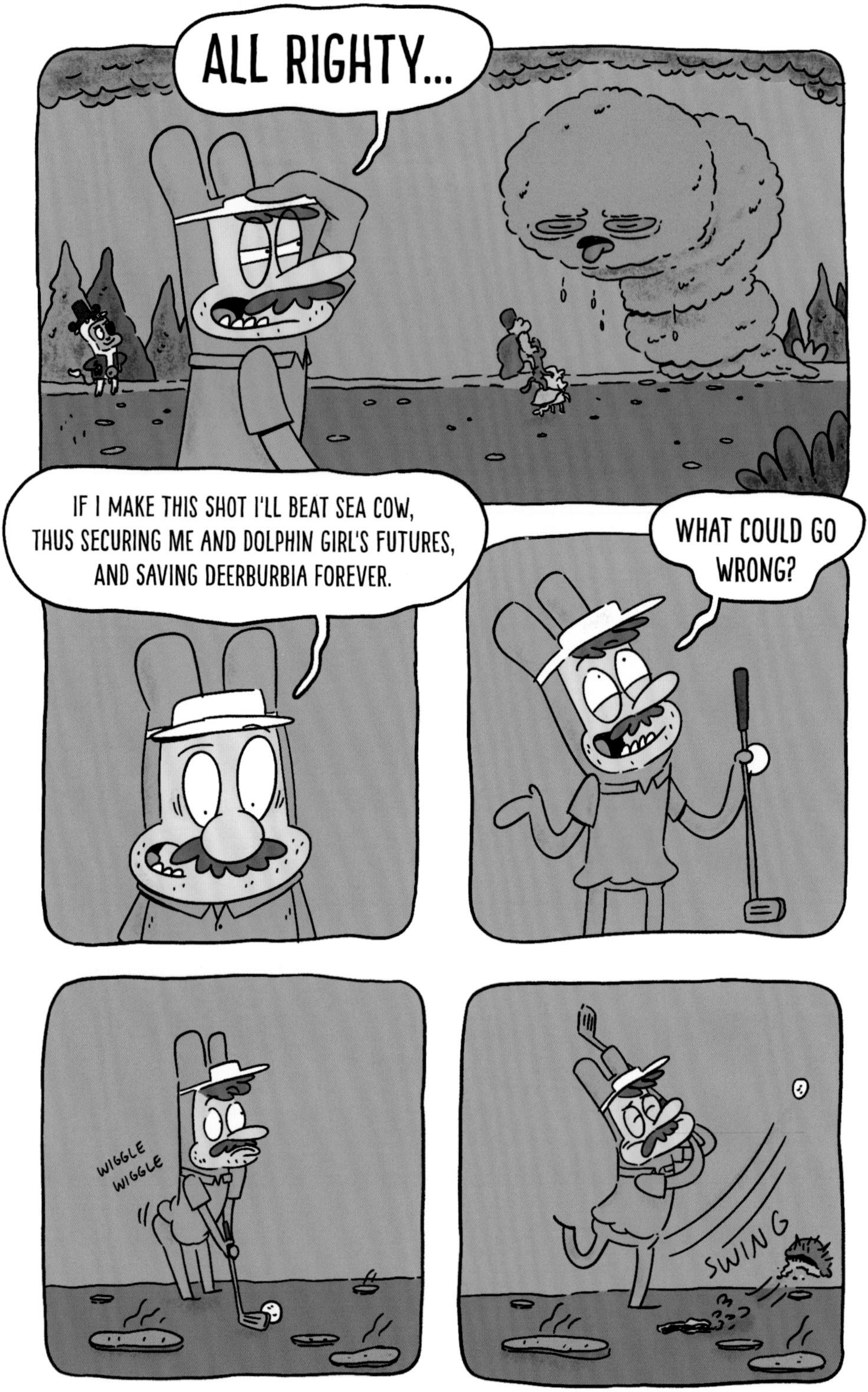
ALL RIGHTY...
IF I MAKE THIS SHOT I'LL BEAT SEA COW, THUS SECURING ME AND DOLPHIN GIRL'S FUTURES, AND SAVING DEERBURBIA FOREVER.
WHAT COULD GO WRONG?
WIGGLE WIGGLE
SWING

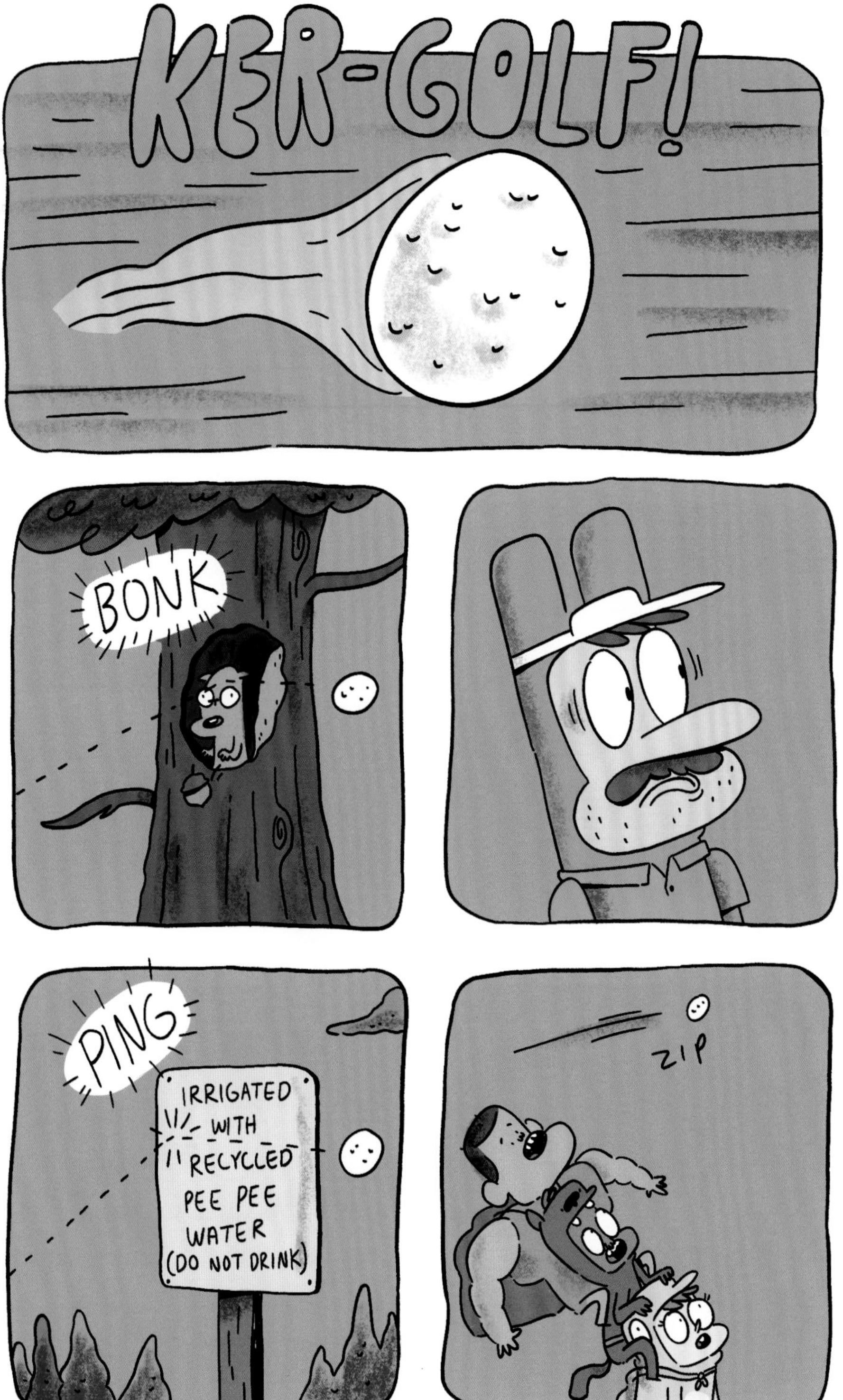
KER-GOLF!
BONK
PING
IRRIGATED WITH RECYCLED PEE PEE WATER (DO NOT DRINK)
ZIP

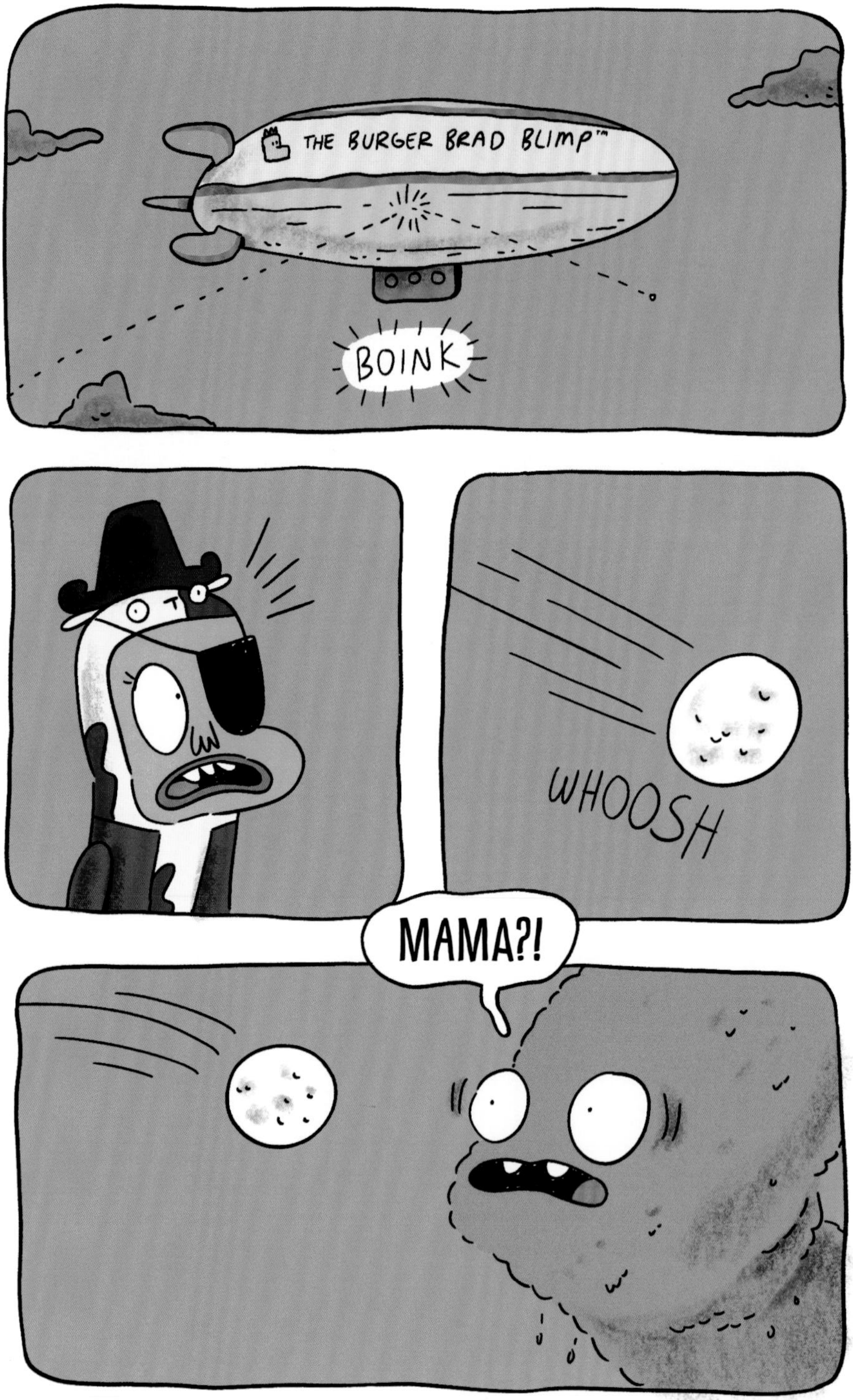
THE BURGER BRAD BLIMP™
BOINK
WHOOSH
MAMA?!

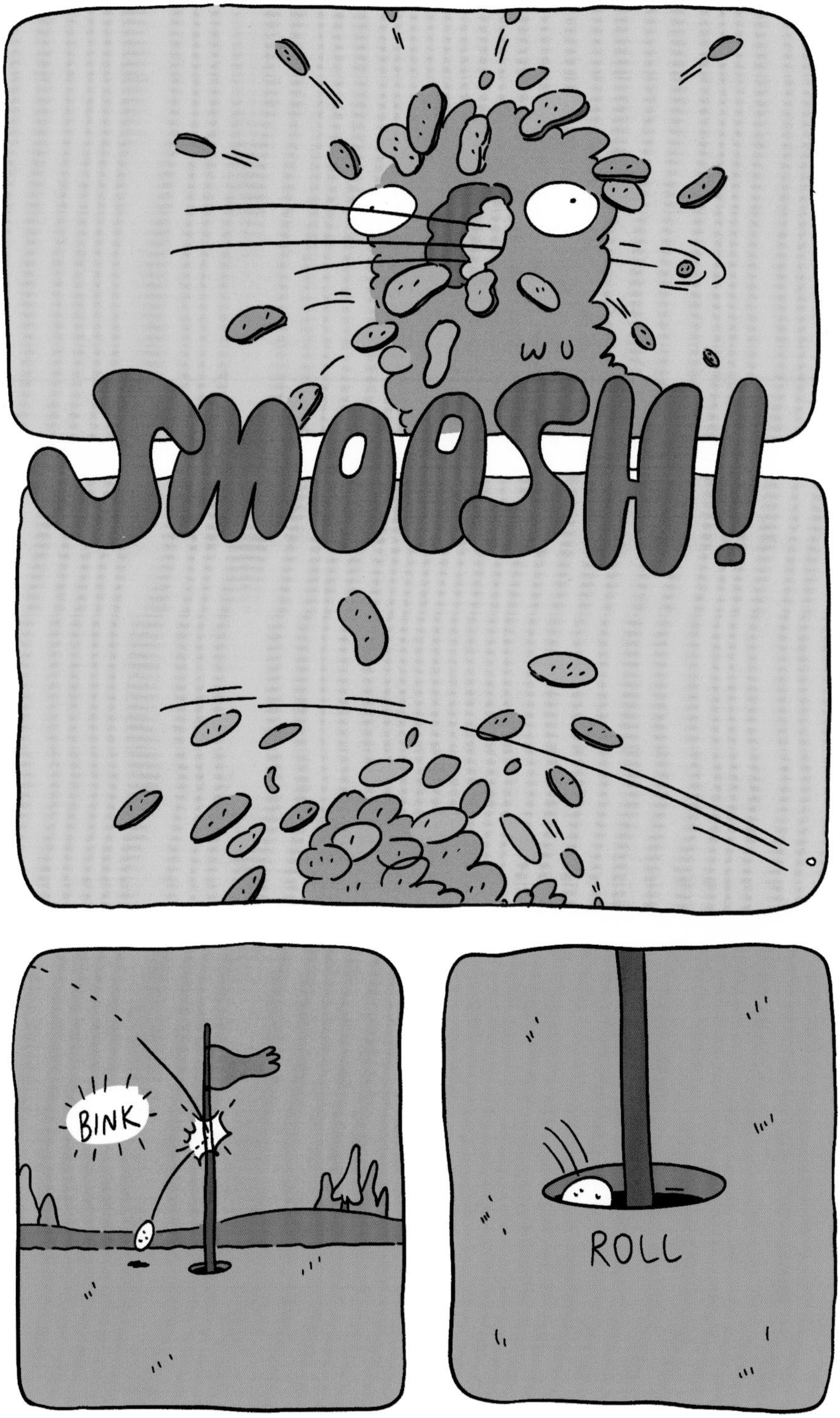
SMOOSH!
BINK
ROLL

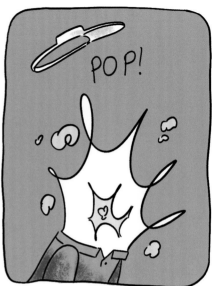

POP!

GURGLE
GURGLE

I DID IT!

YAY!

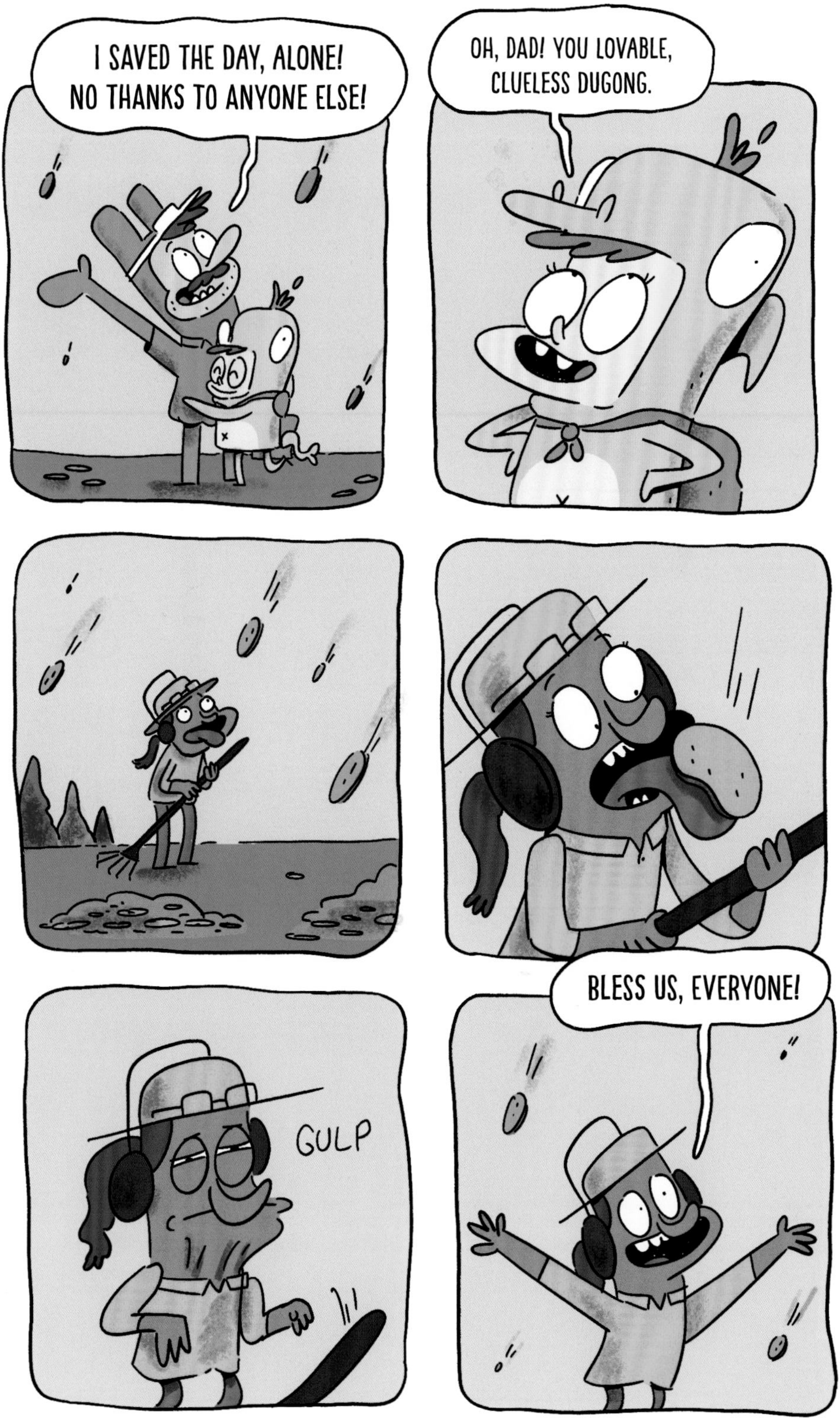
I SAVED THE DAY, ALONE! NO THANKS TO ANYONE ELSE!
OH, DAD! YOU LOVABLE, CLUELESS DUGONG.
GULP
BLESS US, EVERYONE!

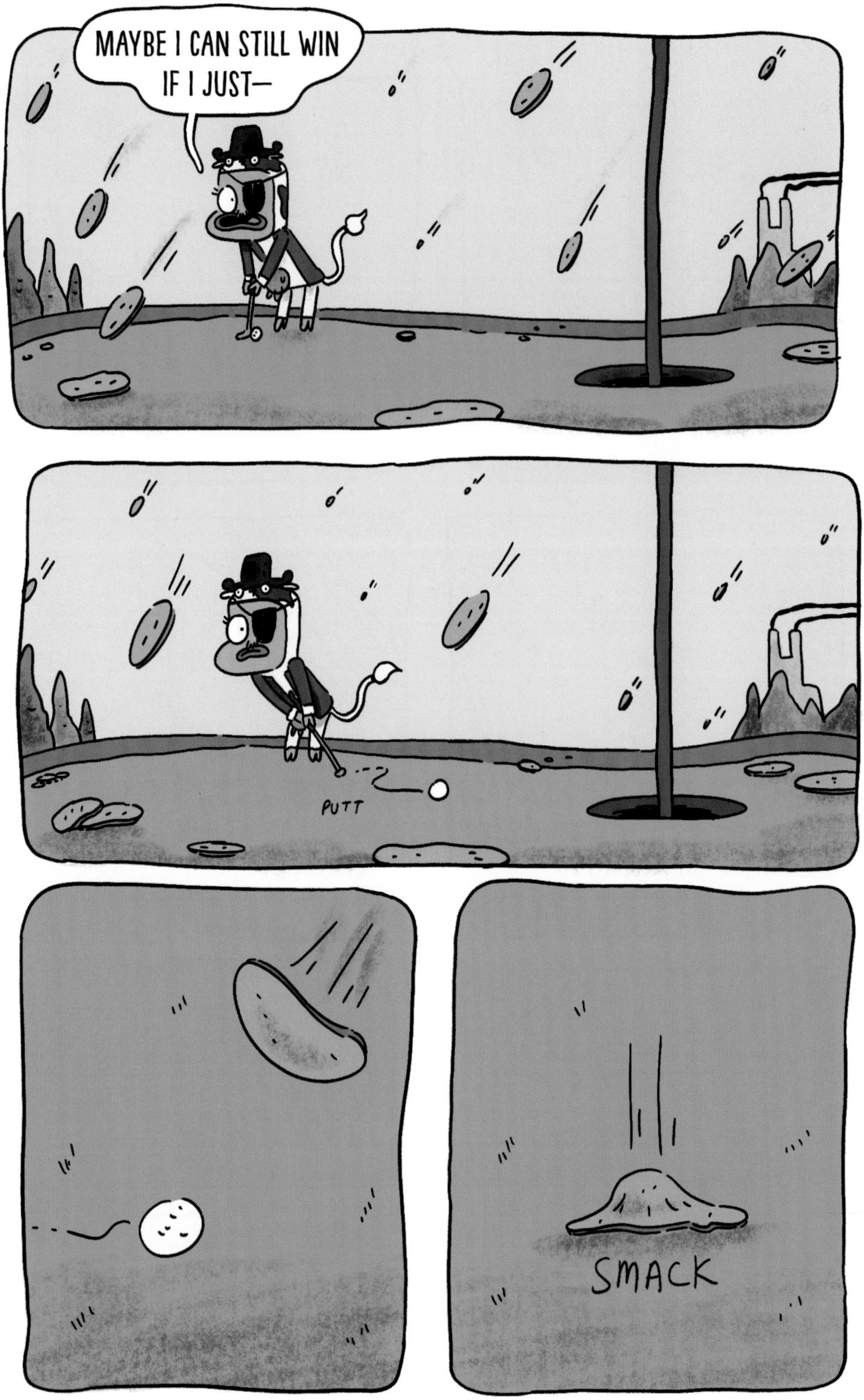
MAYBE I CAN STILL WIN IF I JUST—
PUTT
SMACK

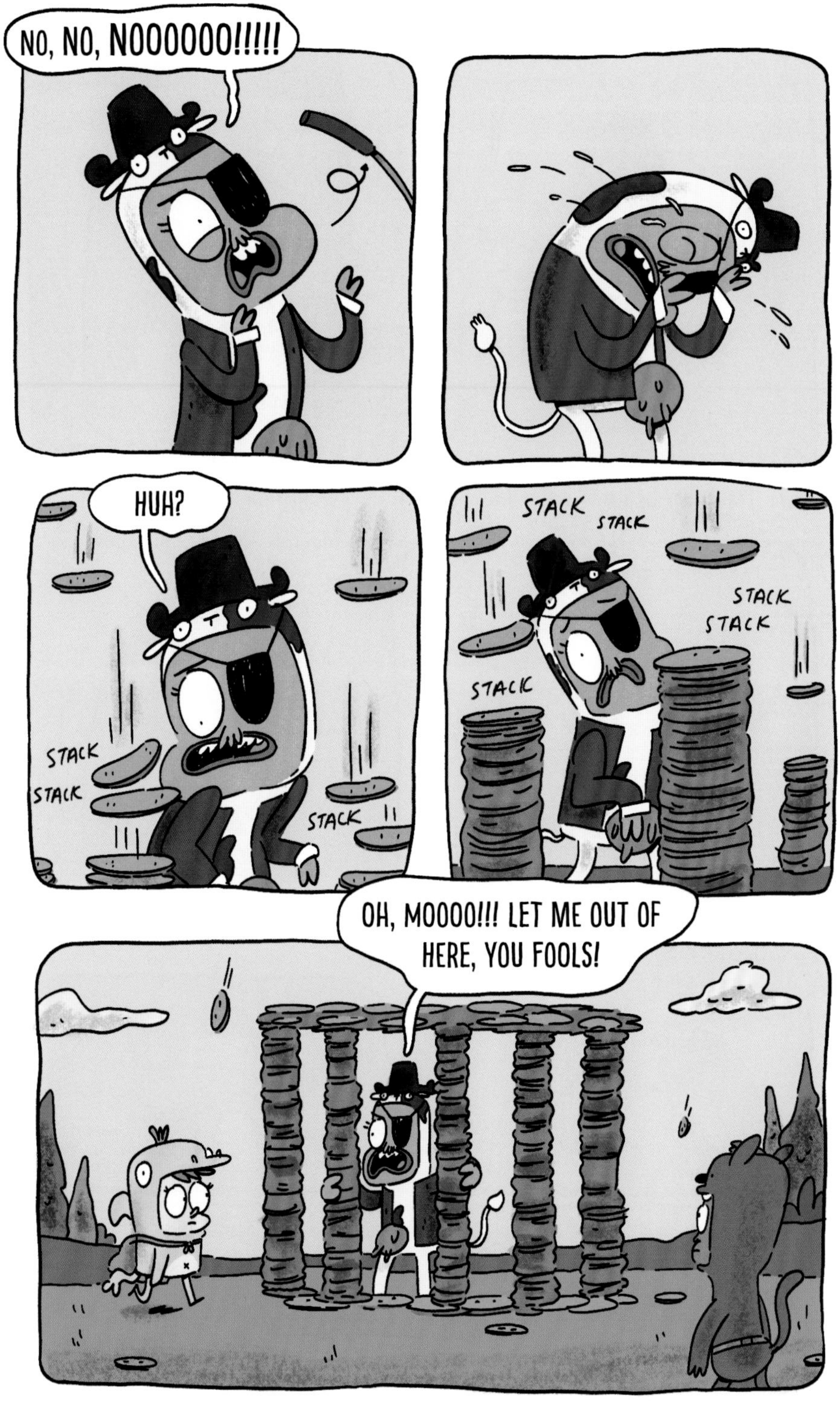

NO, NO, NOOOOOO!!!!!
HUH?
STACK
STACK
STACK
STACK
STACK
STACK
STACK
STACK
OH, MOOOO!!! LET ME OUT OF HERE, YOU FOOLS!

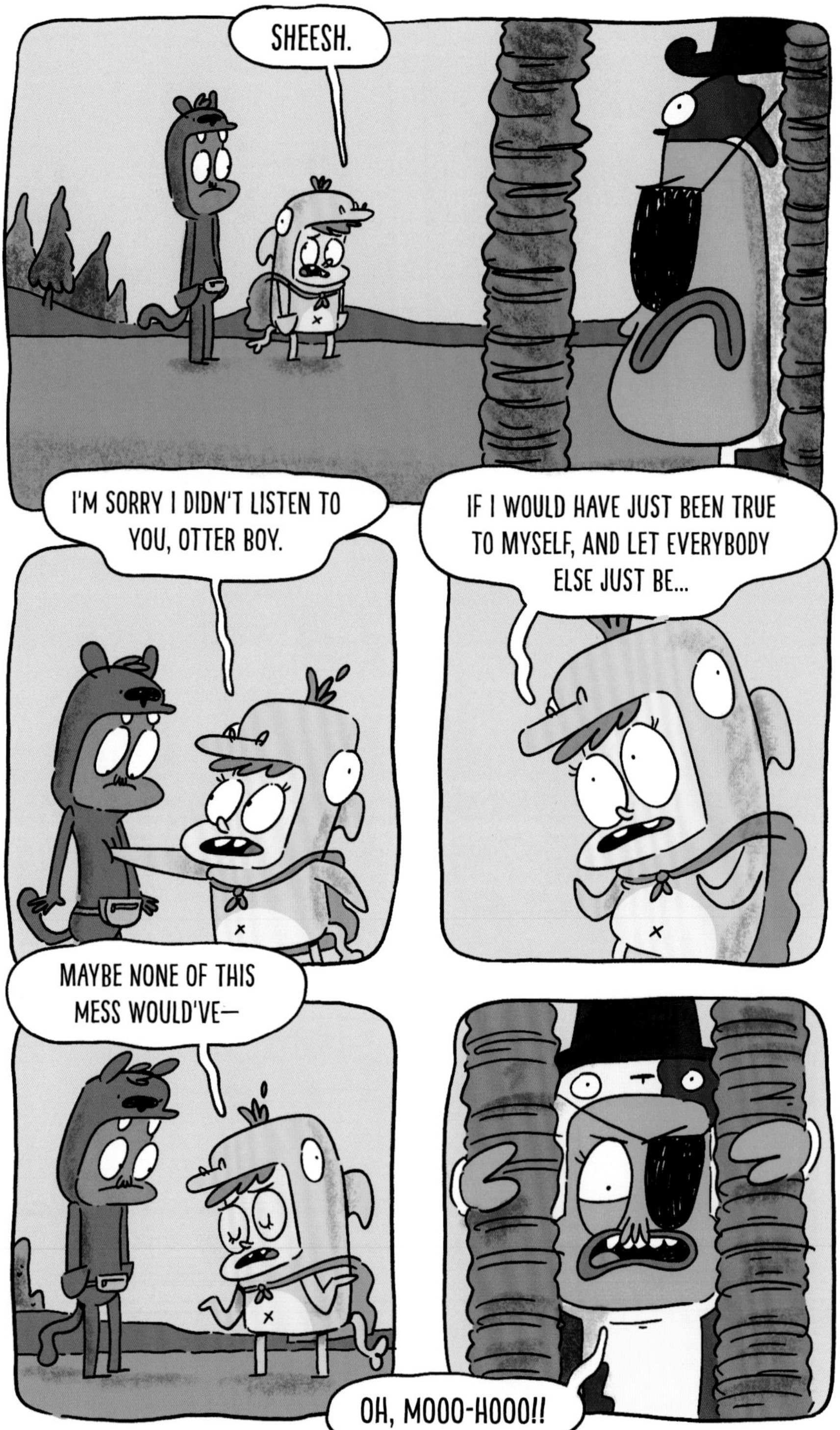
SHEESH.
I'M SORRY I DIDN'T LISTEN TO YOU, OTTER BOY.
IF I WOULD HAVE JUST BEEN TRUE TO MYSELF, AND LET EVERYBODY ELSE JUST BE...
MAYBE NONE OF THIS MESS WOULD'VE—
OH, MOOO-HOOO!!

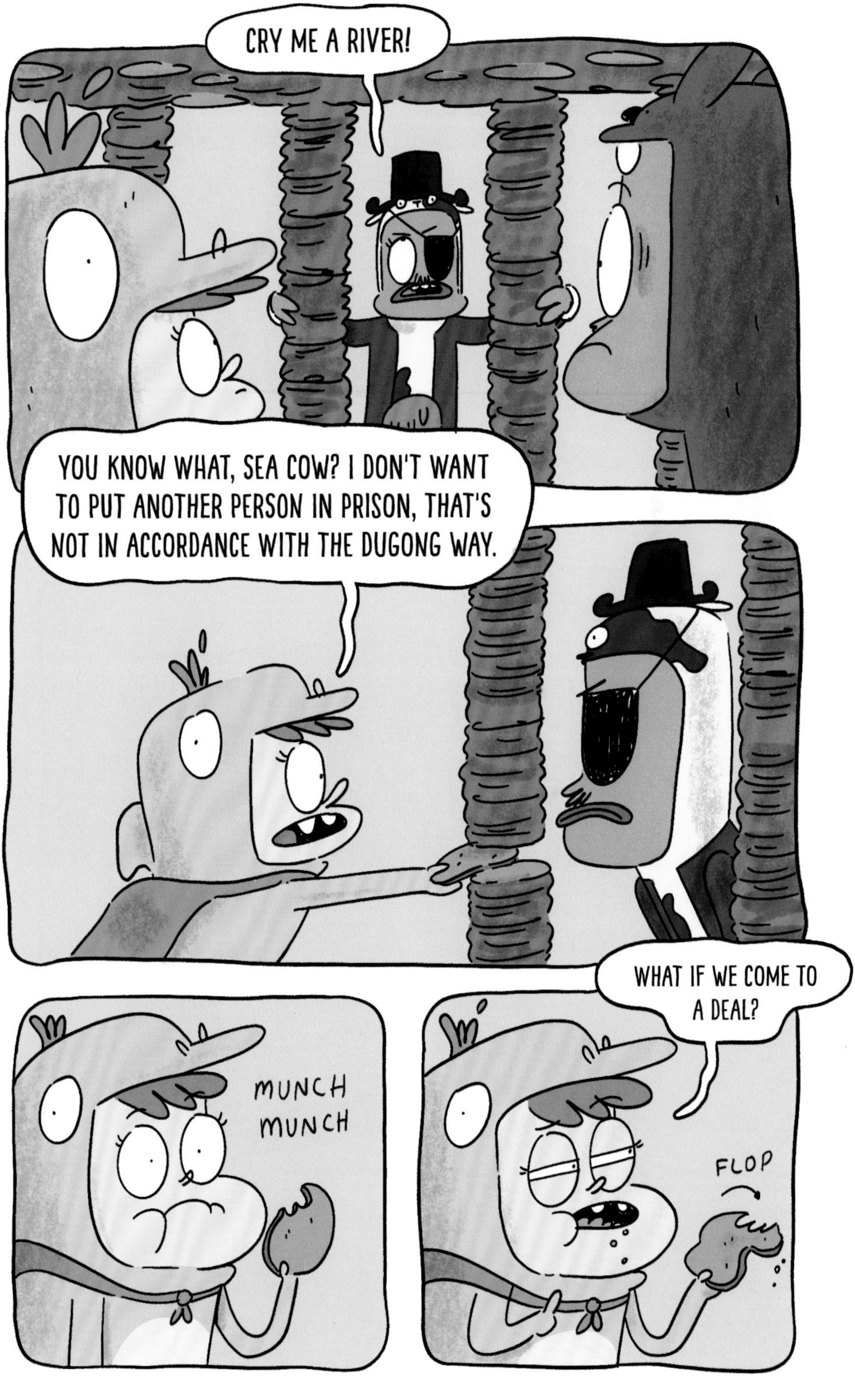
CRY ME A RIVER!
YOU KNOW WHAT, SEA COW? I DON'T WANT TO PUT ANOTHER PERSON IN PRISON, THAT'S NOT IN ACCORDANCE WITH THE DUGONG WAY.
MUNCH MUNCH
WHAT IF WE COME TO A DEAL?
FLOP

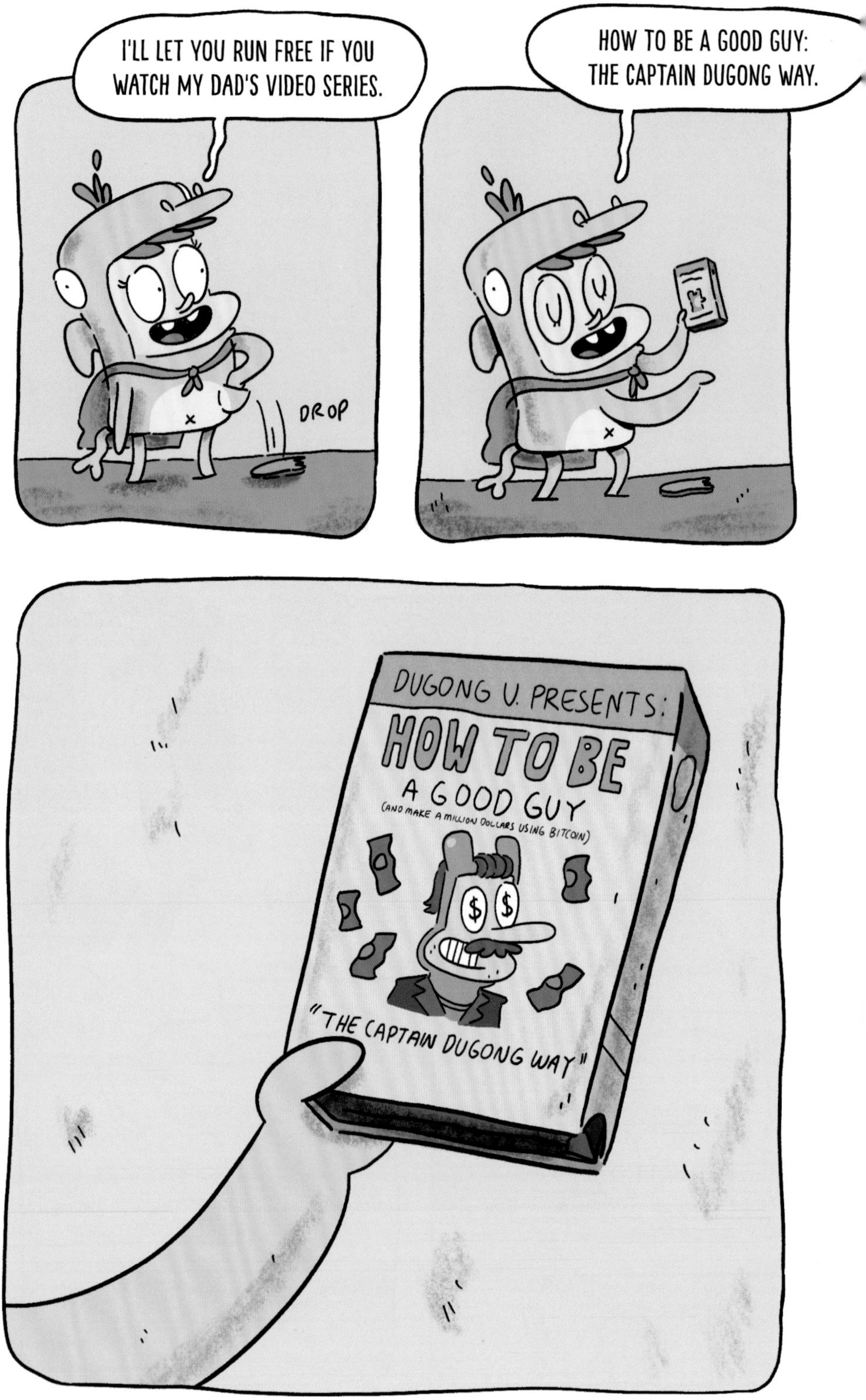
I'LL LET YOU RUN FREE IF YOU WATCH MY DAD'S VIDEO SERIES.
DROP
HOW TO BE A GOOD GUY: THE CAPTAIN DUGONG WAY.
DUGONG U. PRESENTS:
HOW TO BE
A GOOD GUY
(AND MAKE A MILLION DOLLARS USING BITCOIN)
"THE CAPTAIN DUGONG WAY"

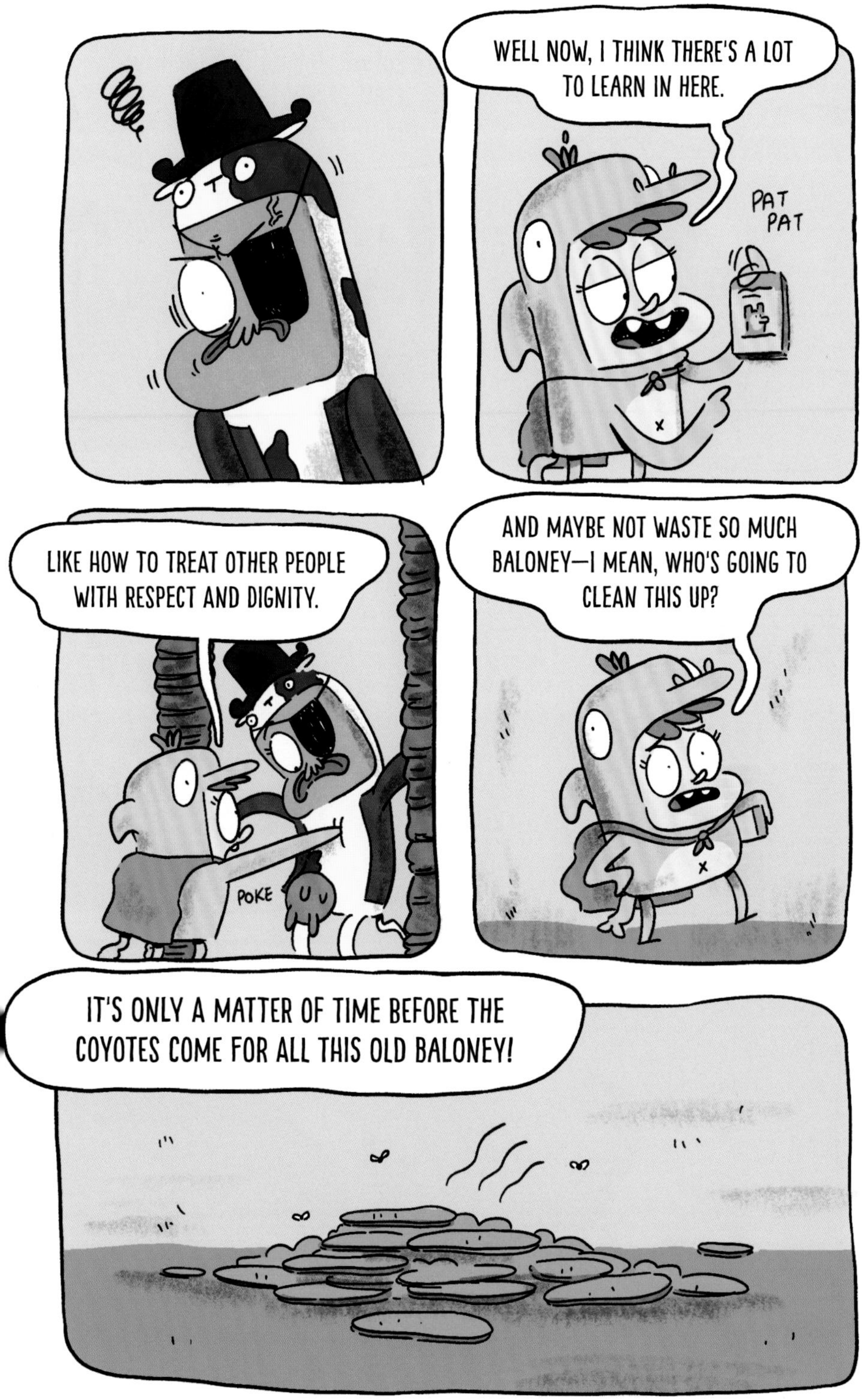
WELL NOW, I THINK THERE'S A LOT TO LEARN IN HERE.
PAT PAT
LIKE HOW TO TREAT OTHER PEOPLE WITH RESPECT AND DIGNITY.
POKE
AND MAYBE NOT WASTE SO MUCH BALONEY—I MEAN, WHO'S GOING TO CLEAN THIS UP?
IT'S ONLY A MATTER OF TIME BEFORE THE COYOTES COME FOR ALL THIS OLD BALONEY!

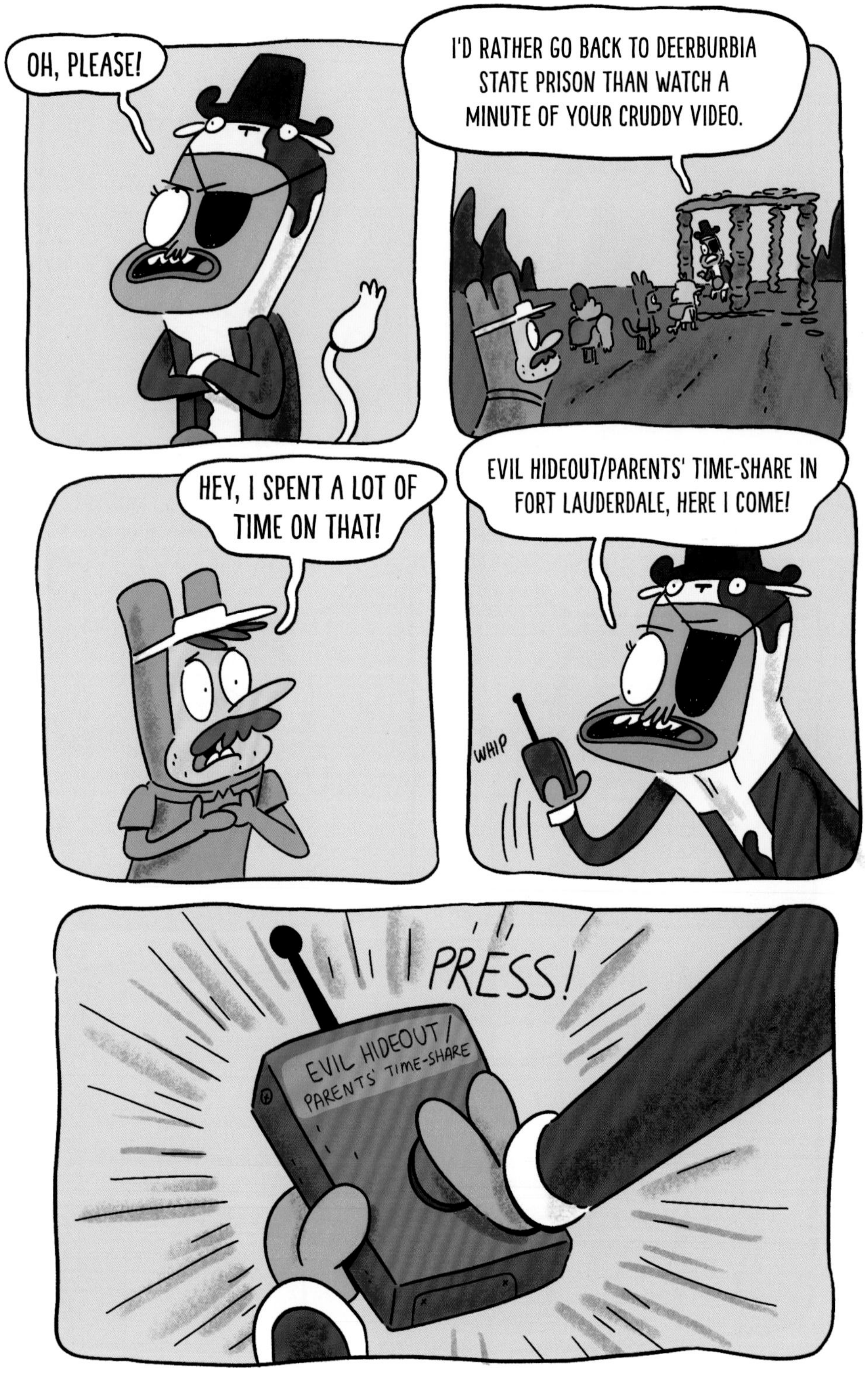
OH, PLEASE!
I'D RATHER GO BACK TO DEERBURBIA STATE PRISON THAN WATCH A MINUTE OF YOUR CRUDDY VIDEO.
HEY, I SPENT A LOT OF TIME ON THAT!
EVIL HIDEOUT/PARENTS' TIME-SHARE IN FORT LAUDERDALE, HERE I COME!
WHIP
PRESS!
EVIL HIDEOUT/
PARENTS' TIME-SHARE

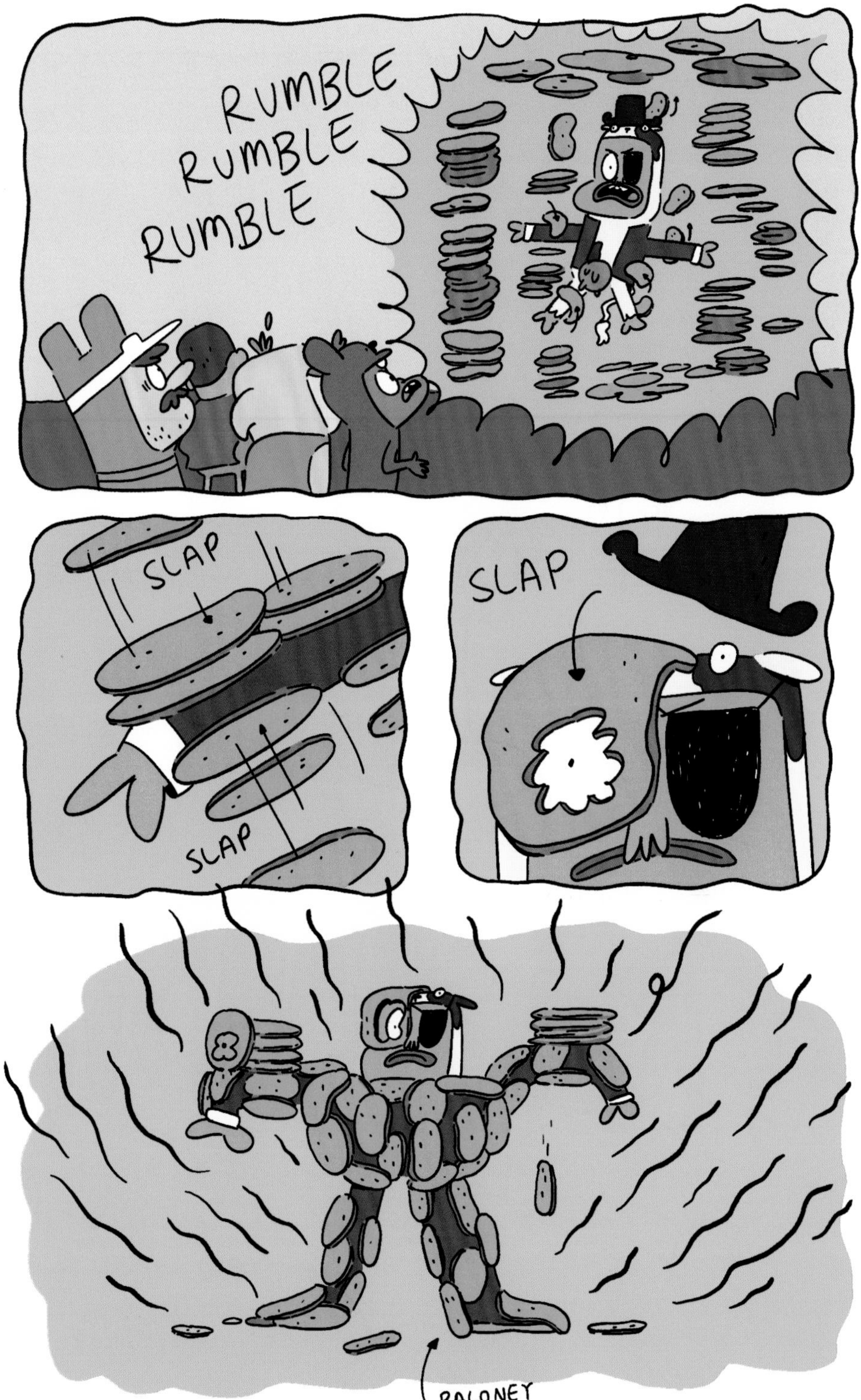
RUMBLE
RUMBLE
RUMBLE
SLAP
SLAP
SLAP
BALONEY
MECH SUIT

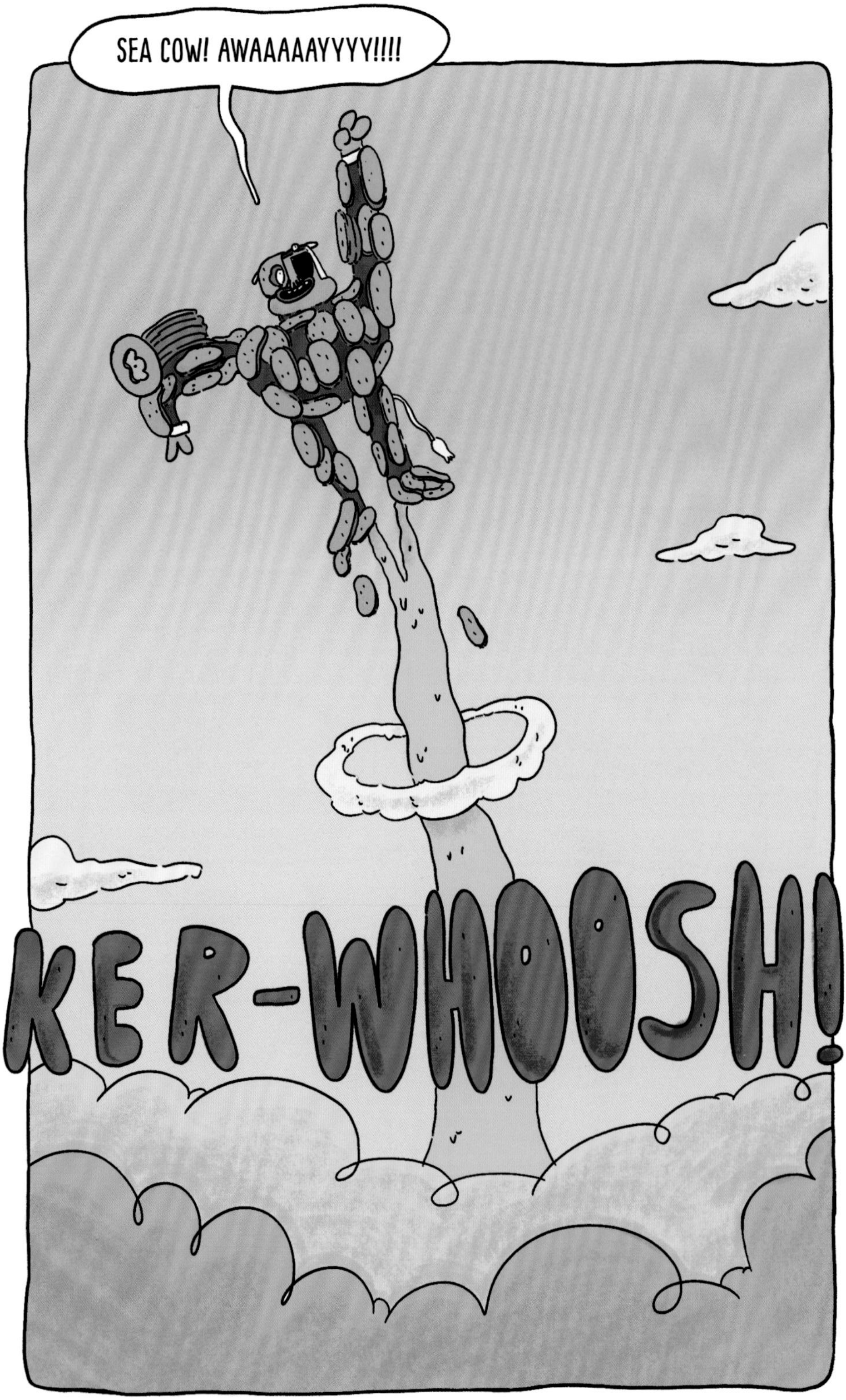
SEA COW! AWAAAAAYYYY!!!!
KER-WHOOSH!

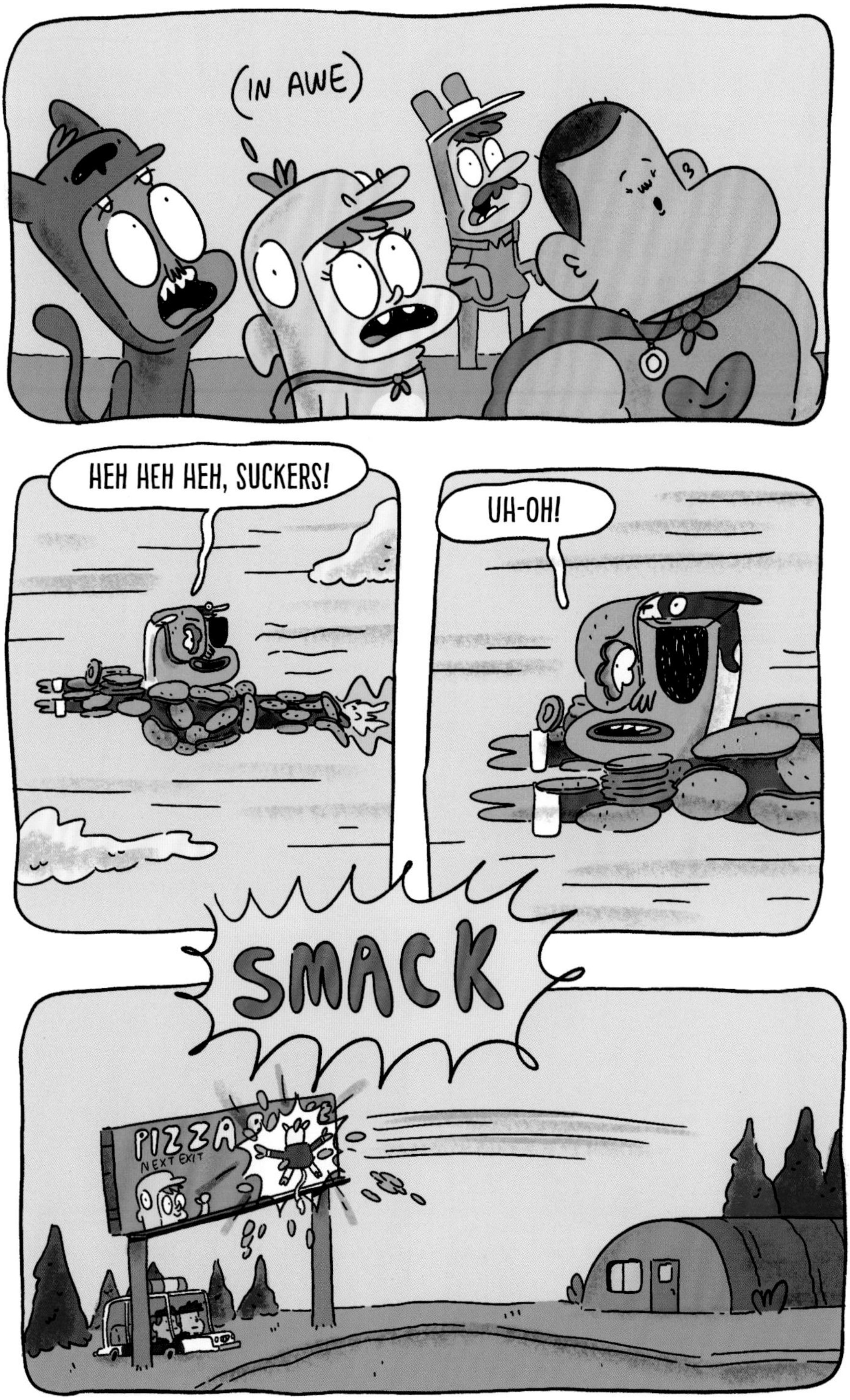
(IN AWE)
HEH HEH HEH, SUCKERS!
UH-OH!
SMACK
PIZZA
NEXT EXIT

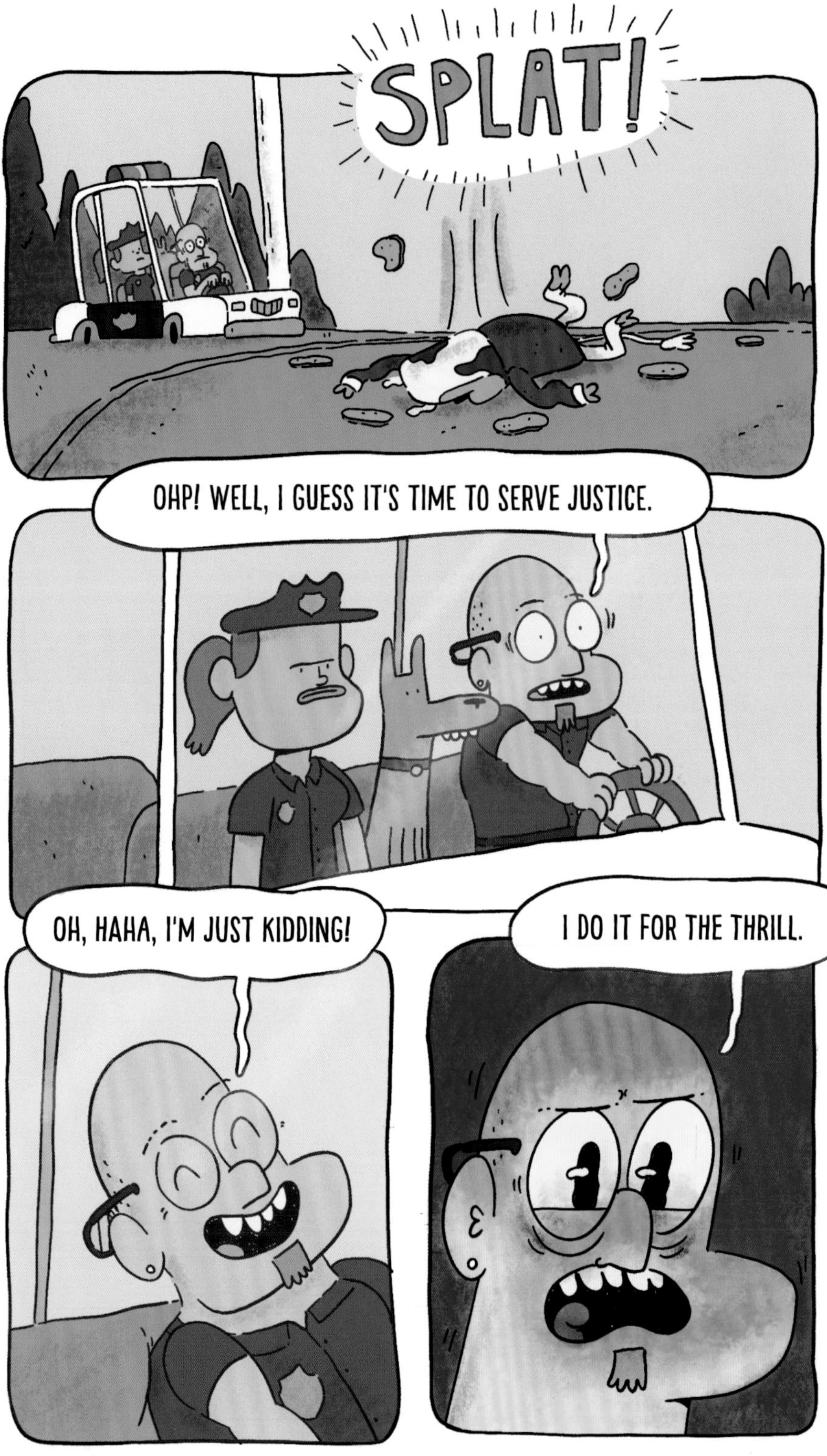
SPLAT!
OHP! WELL, I GUESS IT'S TIME TO SERVE JUSTICE.
OH, HAHA, I'M JUST KIDDING!
I DO IT FOR THE THRILL.

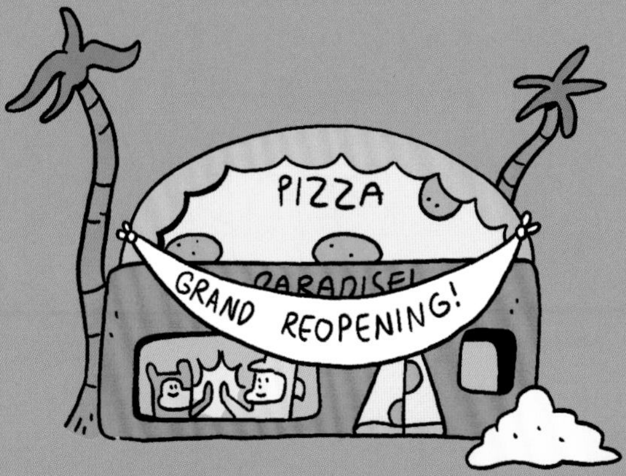
PIZZA
PARADISE!
GRAND REOPENING!

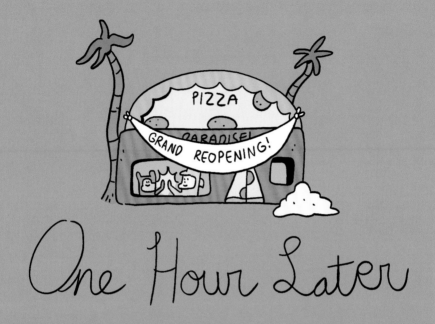

One Hour Later

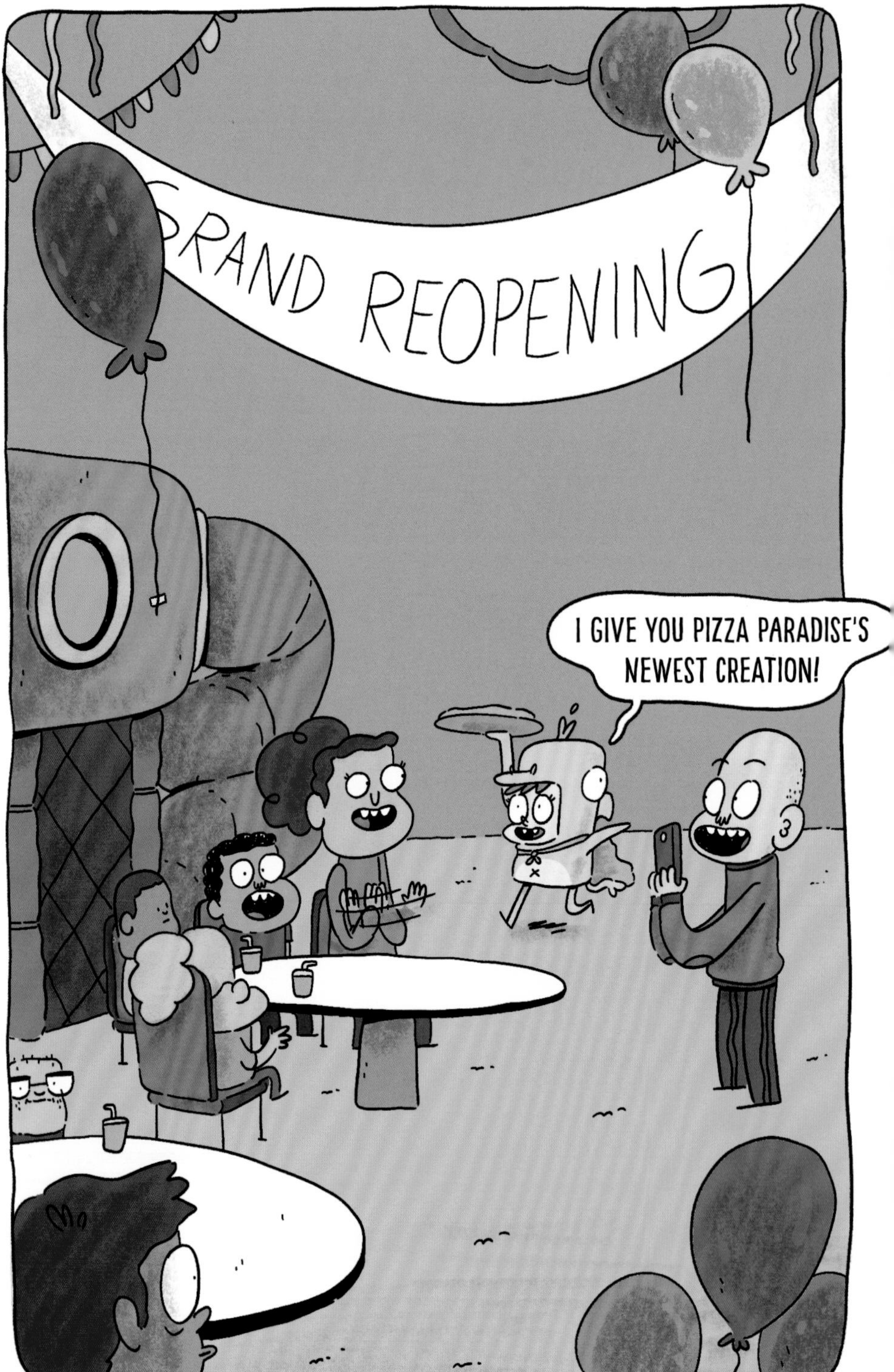
GRAND REOPENING
I GIVE YOU PIZZA PARADISE'S NEWEST CREATION!

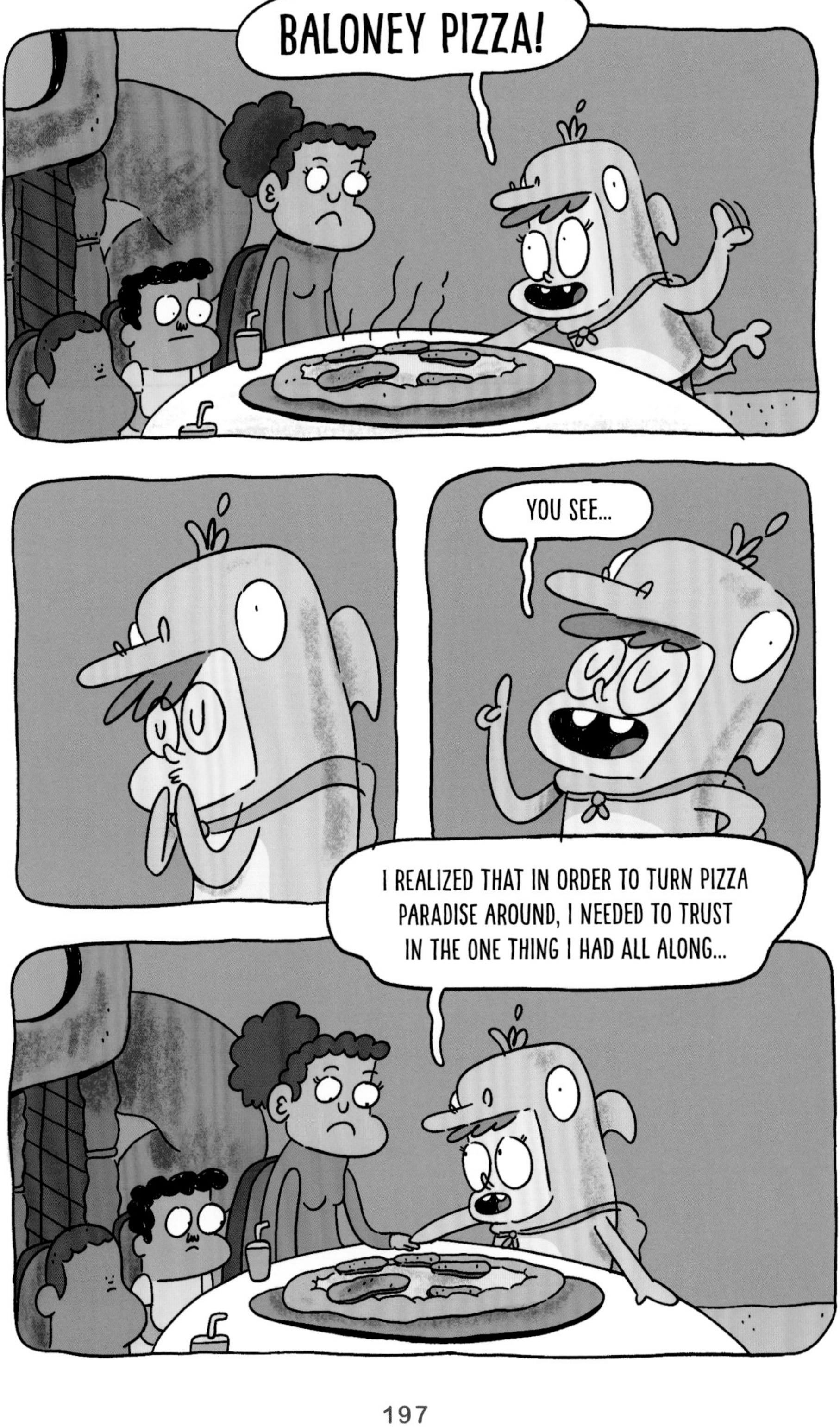
BALONEY PIZZA!
YOU SEE...
I REALIZED THAT IN ORDER TO TURN PIZZA PARADISE AROUND, I NEEDED TO TRUST IN THE ONE THING I HAD ALL ALONG...

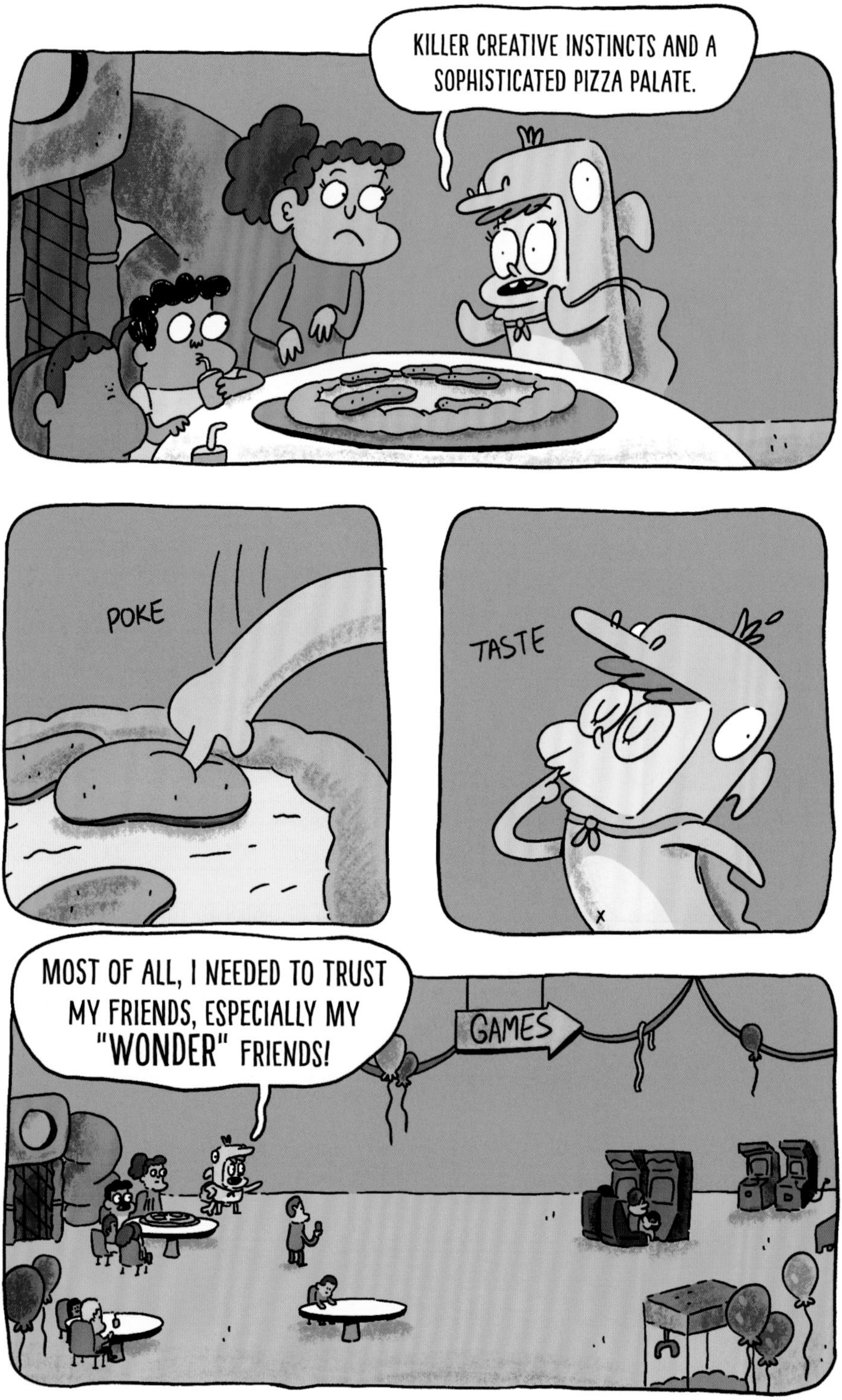

KILLER CREATIVE INSTINCTS AND A SOPHISTICATED PIZZA PALATE.
POKE
TASTE
MOST OF ALL, I NEEDED TO TRUST MY FRIENDS, ESPECIALLY MY "WONDER" FRIENDS!
GAMES

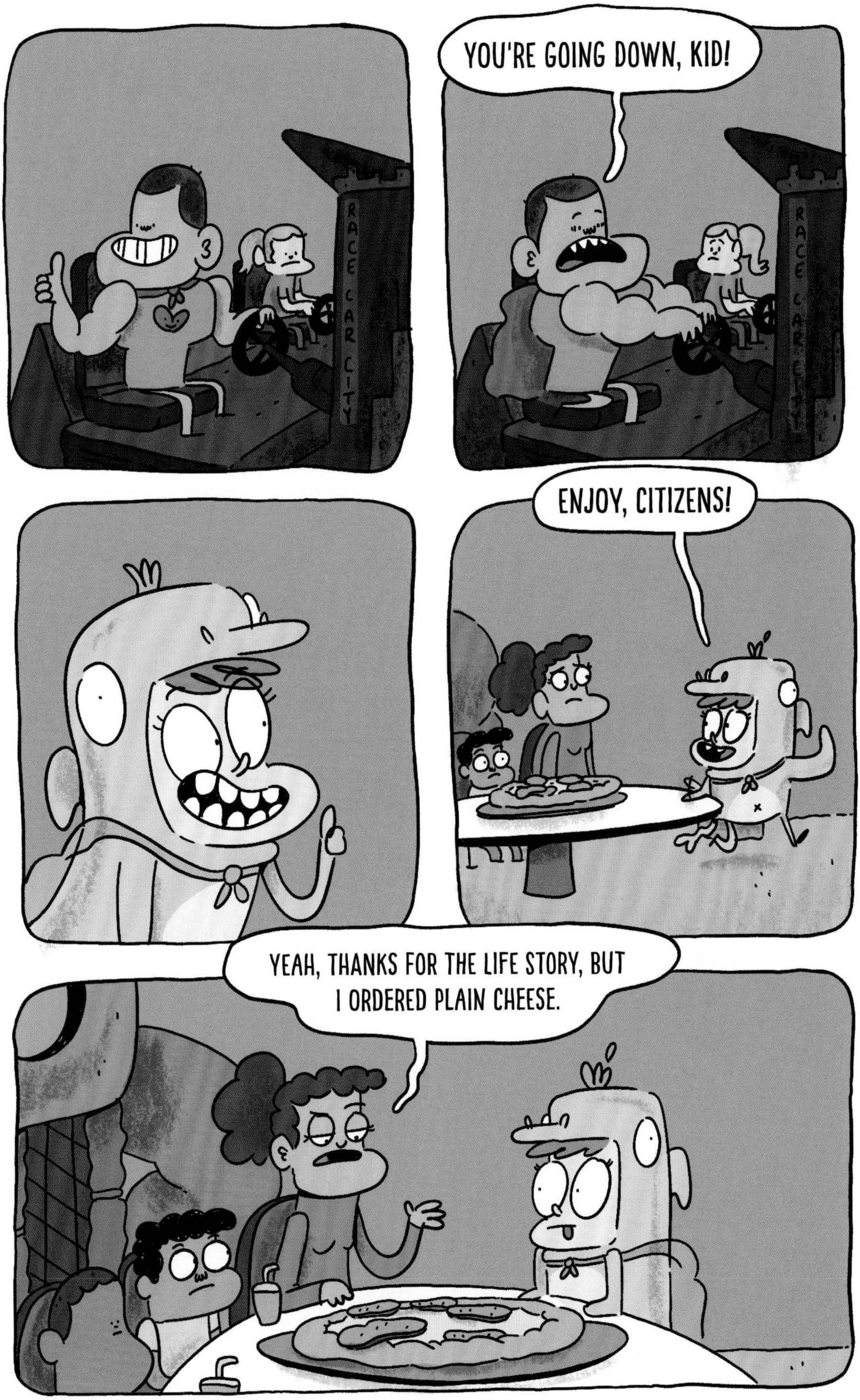
RACE CAR CITY
YOU'RE GOING DOWN, KID!
RACE CAR CITY
ENJOY, CITIZENS!
YEAH, THANKS FOR THE LIFE STORY, BUT I ORDERED PLAIN CHEESE.

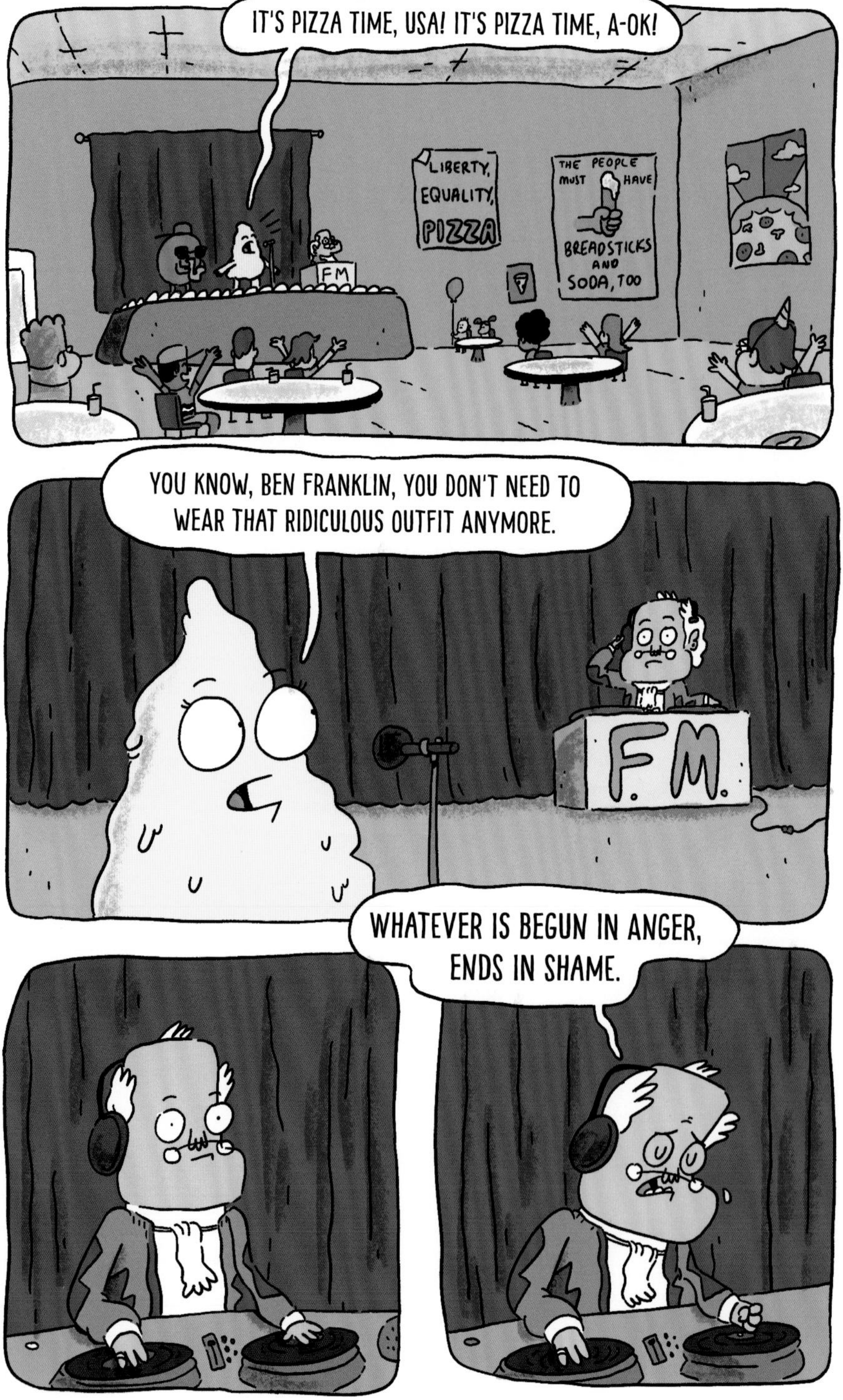
IT'S PIZZA TIME, USA! IT'S PIZZA TIME, A-OK!
LIBERTY, EQUALITY, PIZZA
THE PEOPLE MUST HAVE BREADSTICKS AND SODA, TOO
FM
YOU KNOW, BEN FRANKLIN, YOU DON'T NEED TO WEAR THAT RIDICULOUS OUTFIT ANYMORE.
F.M.
WHATEVER IS BEGUN IN ANGER, ENDS IN SHAME.

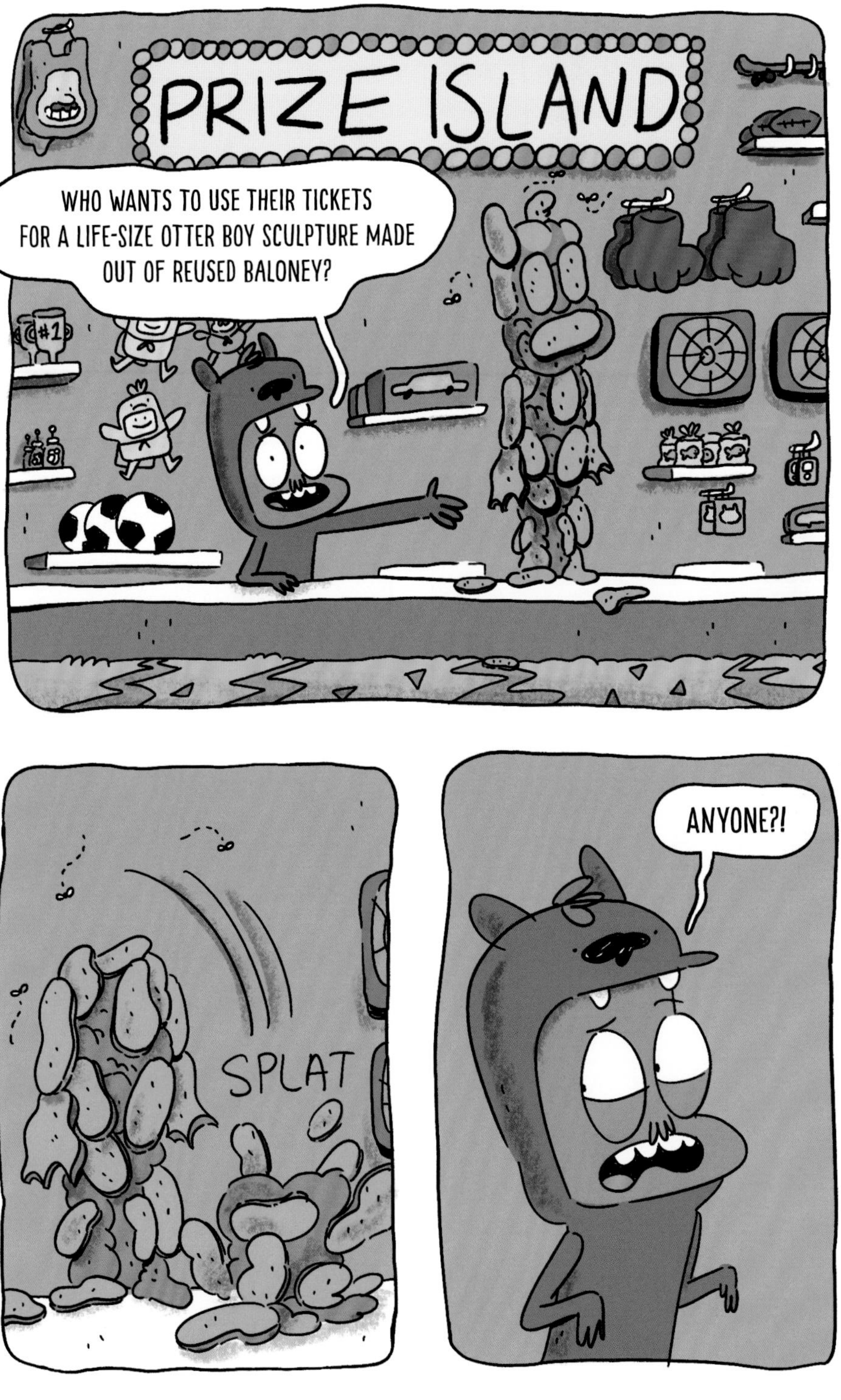
PRIZE ISLAND
WHO WANTS TO USE THEIR TICKETS FOR A LIFE-SIZE OTTER BOY SCULPTURE MADE OUT OF REUSED BALONEY?
#1
SPLAT
ANYONE?!

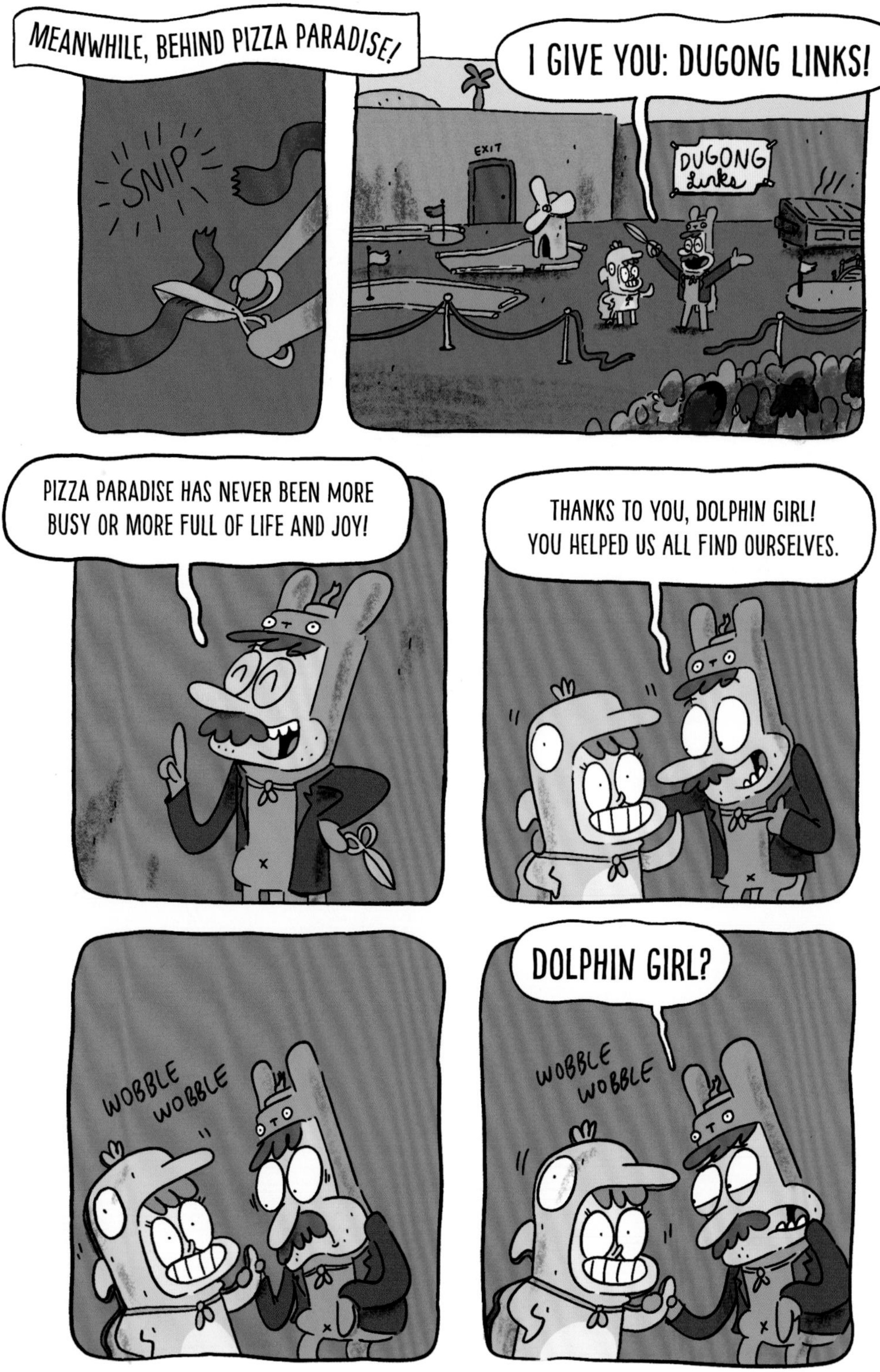
MEANWHILE, BEHIND PIZZA PARADISE!
SNIP
I GIVE YOU: DUGONG LINKS!
EXIT
DUGONG Links
PIZZA PARADISE HAS NEVER BEEN MORE BUSY OR MORE FULL OF LIFE AND JOY!
THANKS TO YOU, DOLPHIN GIRL! YOU HELPED US ALL FIND OURSELVES.
WOBBLE WOBBLE
DOLPHIN GIRL?
WOBBLE WOBBLE

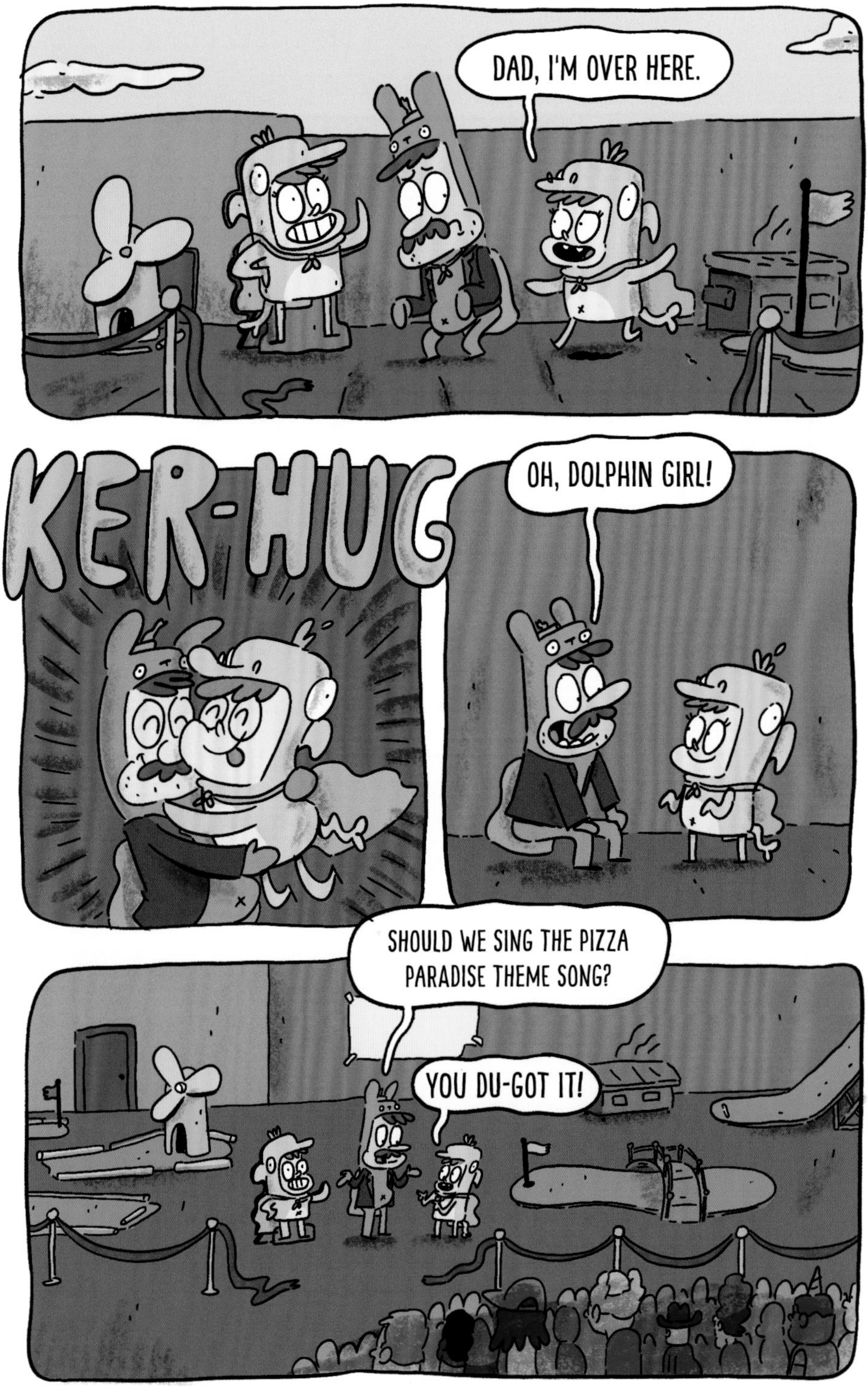
DAD, I'M OVER HERE.
KER-HUG
OH, DOLPHIN GIRL!
SHOULD WE SING THE PIZZA PARADISE THEME SONG?
YOU DU-GOT IT!

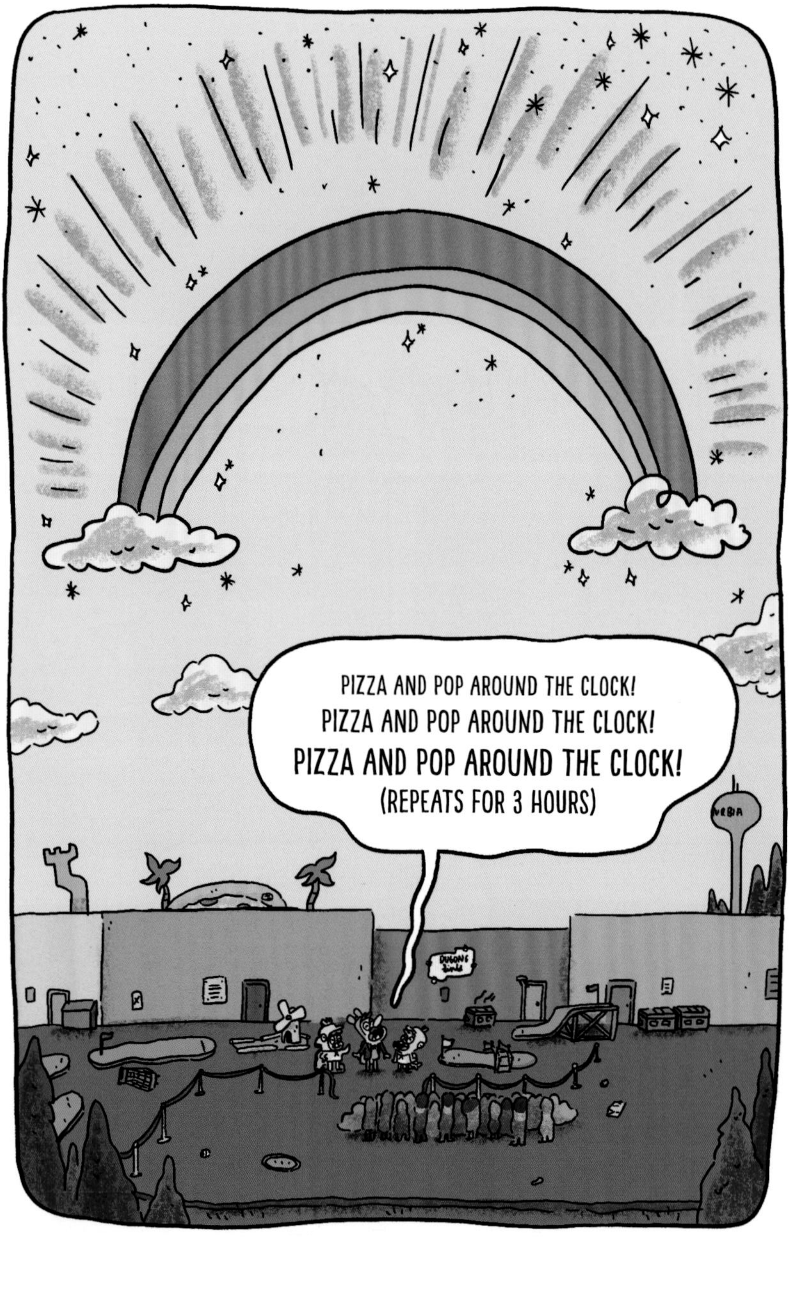
PIZZA AND POP AROUND THE CLOCK!
PIZZA AND POP AROUND THE CLOCK!
PIZZA AND POP AROUND THE CLOCK!
(REPEATS FOR 3 HOURS)

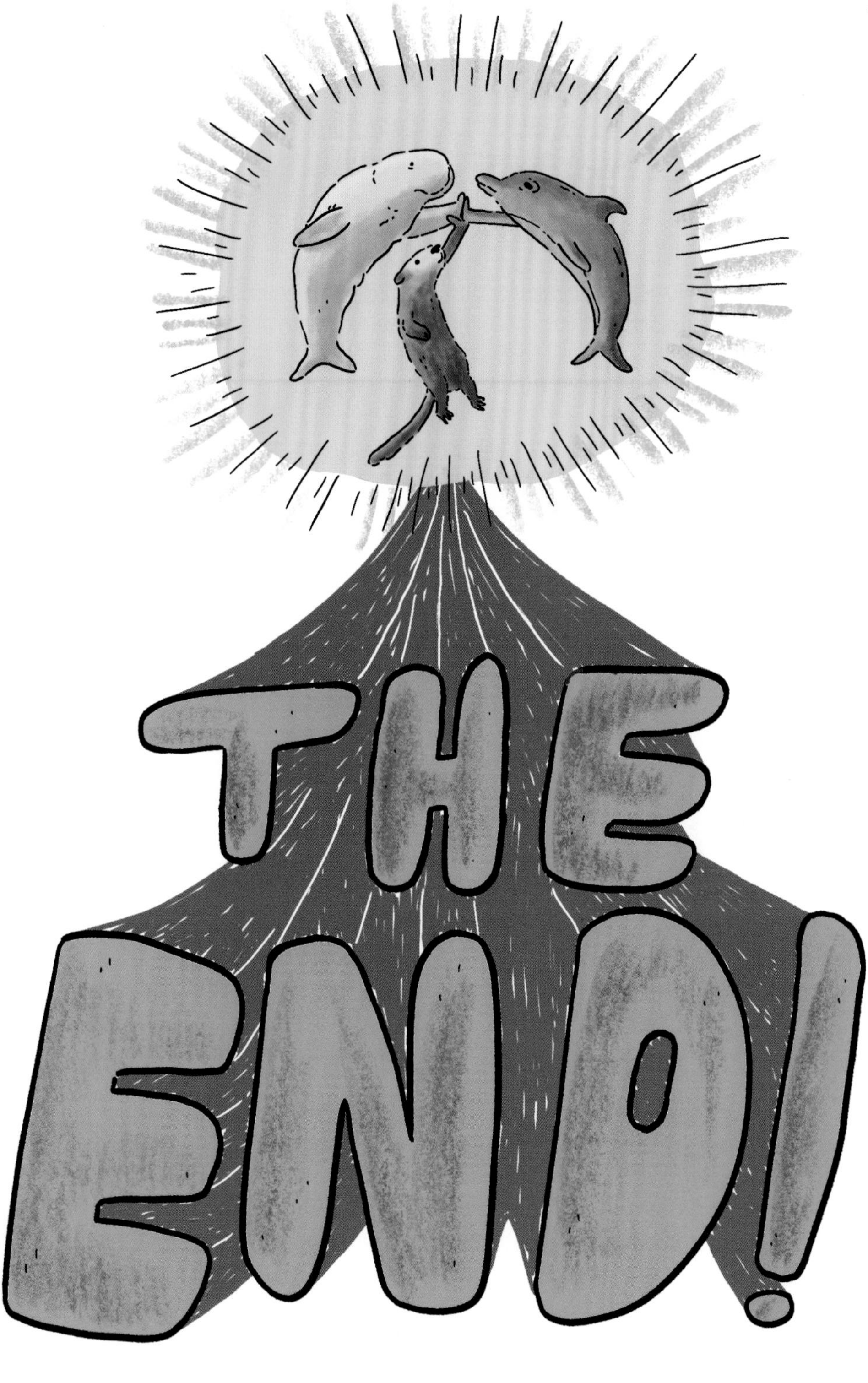
THE END!

ACKNOWLEDGMENTS

THANKS TO THE WONDERFUL AND PAINFULLY TALENTED LETICIA LACY FOR COLORING THIS BOOK AND ALL OF ITS BROKEN LINEWORK.

THANKS TO ALL THE FINE PEOPLE AT PIXEL+INK AND HOLIDAY HOUSE WHO MADE THIS BOOK POSSIBLE:

BETHANY BUCK, SARA DISALVO, MICHELLE MONTAGUE, TERRY BORZUMATO-GREENBERG, AND THE REST OF THE PUBLICITY AND MARKETING TEAM, WHITNEY MANGER FINE, KELSEY PROVO, ANDREA MILLER, RAINA PUTTER, LISA LEE, HANNAH FINNE, MIRIAM MILLER, JULIA GALLAGHER, MARY BRIGANTE, ALISON WEISS, AND DEREK STORDAHL.

AND THANKS TO THESE PEOPLE (WHO HELPED ME GET THROUGH WRITING A BOOK, DIRECTING A PRE-SCHOOL SHOW, DEVELOPING ANOTHER PRESCHOOL SHOW, LIVING WITH OCD, AND BEING A PARENT DURING A WORLDWIDE PANDEMIC IN THE YEAR 2020): MONIQUE, QUINN, AND ZADIE FOR LOVING ME, SUPPORT-ING ME, AND FILLING MY LIFE WITH LAUGHTER, VISCOUS PURE JOY, WONDER, AND '90S DANCE PARTIES. KYLE BOYD, FOR THE FRIENDSHIP. MY FUNNY FAMILY IN MICHIGAN: MOM, DAD, KRISTIN, KEVIN, LANDON, BENNET, JAKE, AND JESS, AND ALL THE SMITH, THOMPSON, AND COOLEY COUSINS THAT TAUGHT ME HOW TO BE FUNNY AS A KID. AMANDA BERKOWITZ—THERAPY WIZARD! THE LEYSENS BROS (NICK & GREG) FOR BEING AMAZINGLY HUMBLE AND FUNNY PEOPLE TO WORK WITH DURING THE DAY.

THANKS TO THE MUSICIANS THAT HELPED ME THROUGH THE WRITING PROCESS, ESPECIALLY:

JONI MITCHEL, DOLLY PARTON, ANGEL OLSEN, PHOEBE BRIDGERS, BOB DYLAN AND THE SWEET '70S SOUNDS OF THE LAUREL CANYON MUSIC SCENE, WHICH WAS OF GREAT COMFORT DURING A CRAZY YEAR.

AND THESE BOOKS (FOR HELPING ME OPEN MY EYES AND STEP OUTSIDE OF MY OWN HEAD FOR A BIT):

THE METAPHYSICAL CLUB BY LOUIS MENAND, *TURTLES ALL THE WAY DOWN* BY JOHN GREEN, *MAN'S SEARCH FOR HIMSELF* BY ROLLO MAY, *STATION ELEVEN* BY EMILY ST. JOHN MANDEL, AND *KEEP GOING* BY AUSTIN KLEON.

AND THANKS TO YOU, DEAR READER, FOR BUYING THIS BOOK (OR TRADING SOMETHING FOR IT ON THE SCHOOL BLACK MARKET). I AM SO GRATEFUL THAT SOMEONE ACTUALLY WANTS TO READ THIS!

SUPER YEARBOOK!

HEROES:

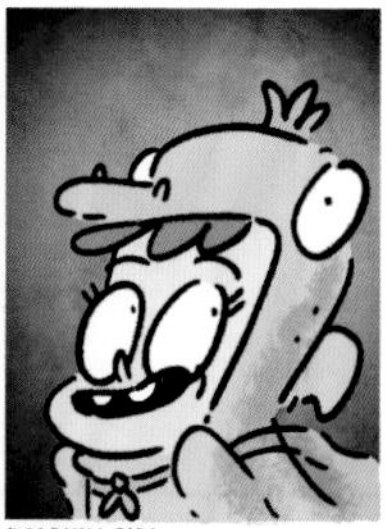

DOLPHIN GIRL

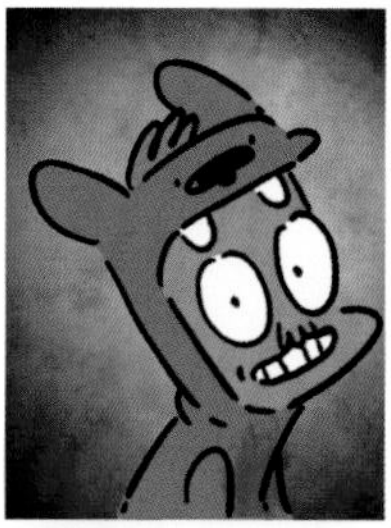

OTTER BOY

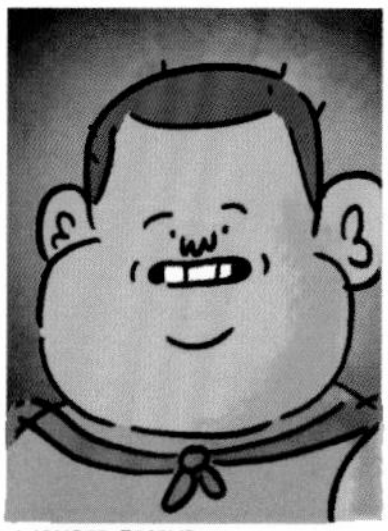

WONDER FRIEND

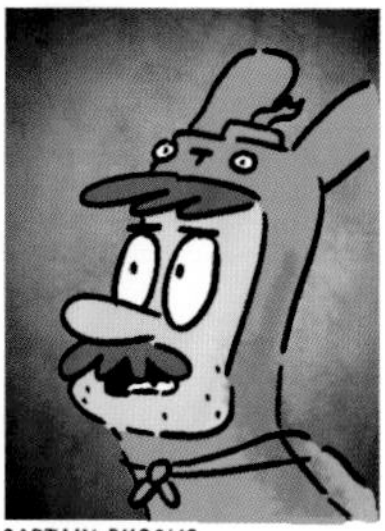

CAPTAIN DUGONG

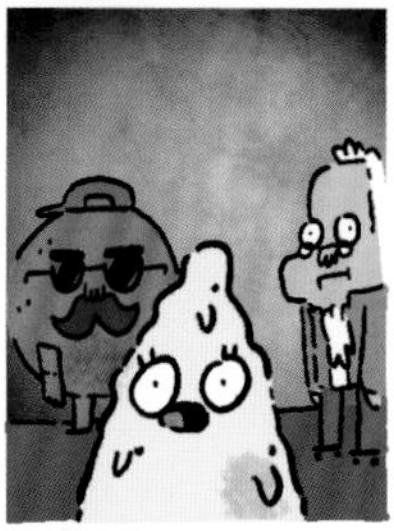

THE FUNK MACHINES

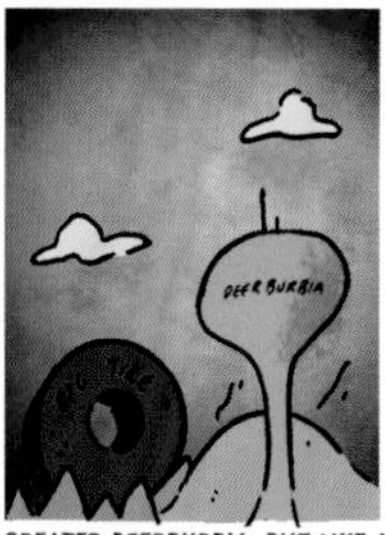

GREATER DEERBURBIA, BUT LIKE AS A CHARACTER ITSELF, YOU KNOW?

VILLAINS:

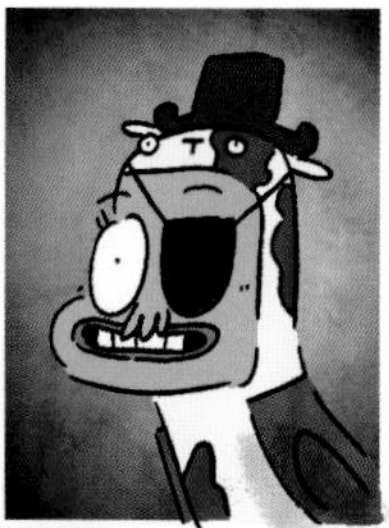

SEA COW

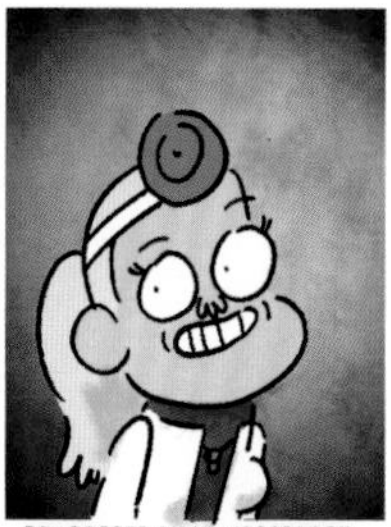

DR. SOCCER VON MOMCOACH

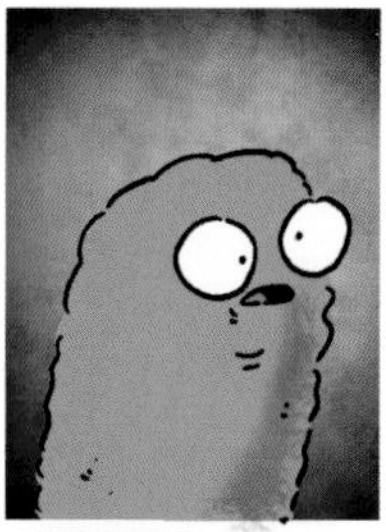

THE MEATLOAF

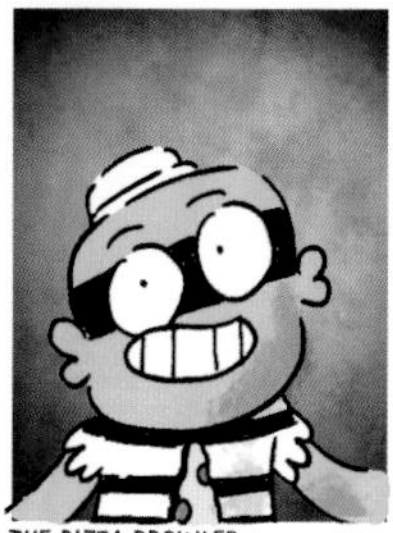

THE PIZZA PROWLER

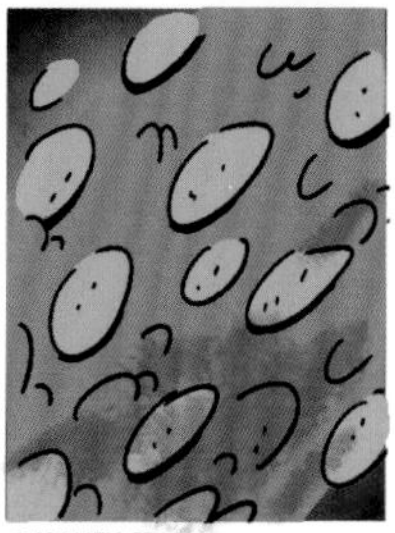

BALONEY STORM

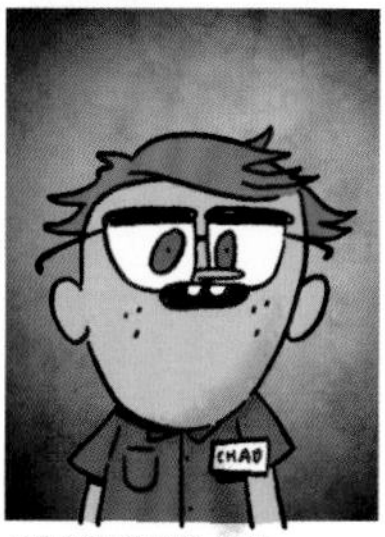
CHAD

AND SOMETIMES CHAD

VOTE :

BEST COUPLE: ____________

MOST LIKELY TO SUCCEED: ________

BEST ROBOT BAND: __________

CUTEST LAUGH: ______

MOST CREATIVE: _____

CLASS CLOWN: ________

MOST LIKELY TO BECOME A PART OF A PYRAMID SCHEME: ____________

ABOUT THE AUTHOR

ZACH SMITH IS A CARTOONIST, AUTHOR, ILLUSTRATOR, AND SHOW CREATOR. CURRENTLY, HE IS CREATING AN UPCOMING SHOW FOR NICK JR. AND WORKS AS A STORYBOARD ARTIST IN THE ANIMATION INDUSTRY. ZACH LIVES IN THE SUBURBS OF LOS ANGELES WITH HIS WIFE, TWO DAUGHTERS, AND TWO DOGS. BEFORE BECOMING A PROFESSIONAL ARTIST, HE DELIVERED PIZZA FOR A LIVING.

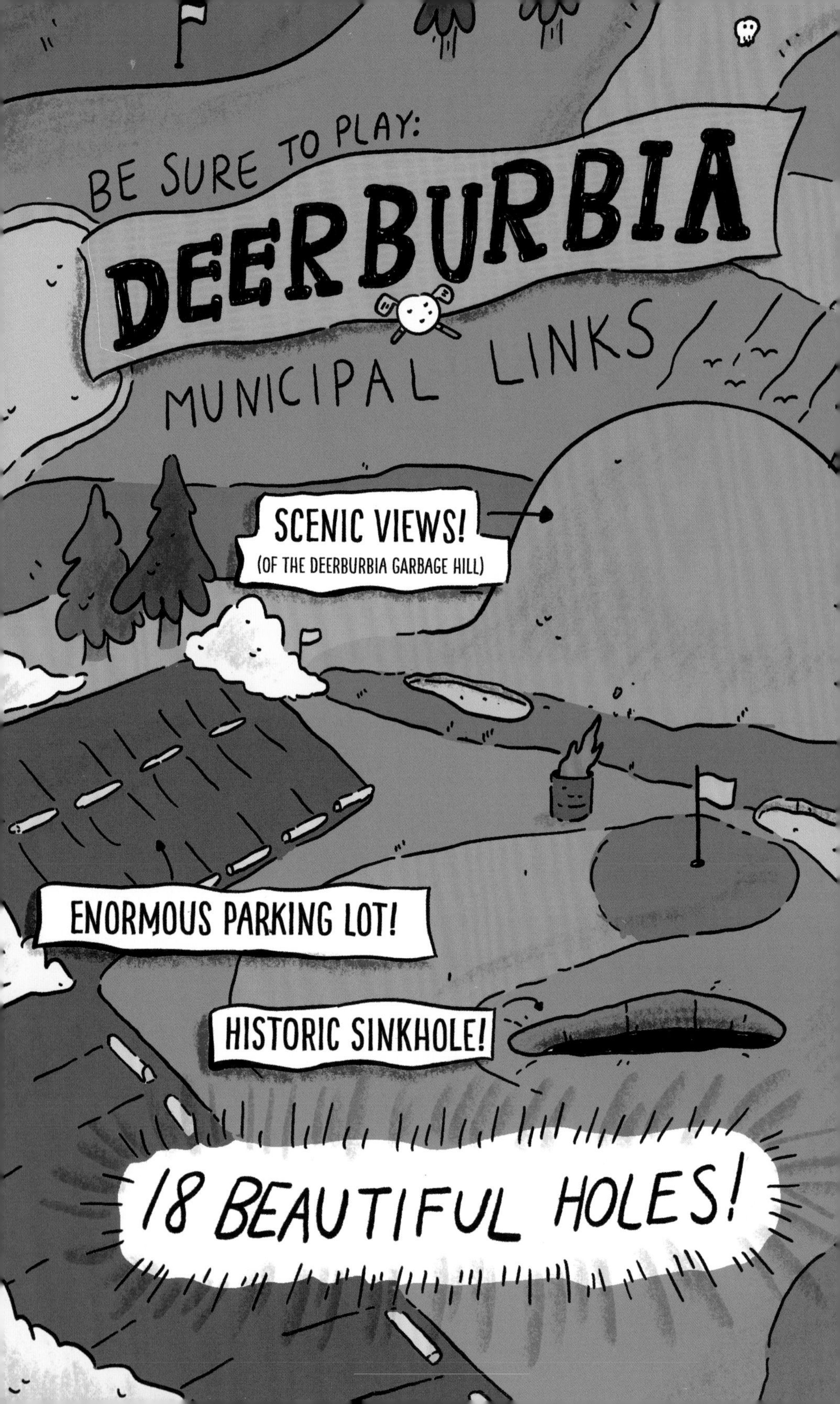

BE SURE TO PLAY:
DEERBURBIA
MUNICIPAL LINKS
SCENIC VIEWS!
(OF THE DEERBURBIA GARBAGE HILL)
ENORMOUS PARKING LOT!
HISTORIC SINKHOLE!
18 BEAUTIFUL HOLES!